Lincoln 2.0

Robert Moran

Published by Robert Moran, 2025.

LINCOLN 2.0

First edition. May 17, 2025.

ISBN: 979-8231056279

Written by Robert Moran.

Table of Contents

It has been a long and hard road from first writing about the idea of leadership AI in the Huffington Post on August 21, 2015. Although I would like to think that Lincoln 2.0 is a compelling story, in truth it is a warning and a thought experiment masquerading as a novel.

I want to thank Chip Taulbee, Editor at Mensa Bulletin, for publishing my writing on Lincoln 2.0 and for believing in me.

I also want to thank the Baltimore Sun for publishing my opinion piece on Lincoln 2.0 on April 11, 2024.

Many thanks also to Campaigns & Elections and the Business of Politics Show podcast.

Finally, I want to thank the Gladesmen for their brotherhood.

1: The Magical Kingdom

Why were there so many security drones hovering over the castle? And who the hell spray-painted graffiti on Dr. Gideon's Apothecary? Russ wanted to know.

He surveyed Central Street, USA, while U took pictures with his sunglasses. A torrent of visitors rushed past them, down the street, and into the park.

The Magical Kingdom was generally how Russ remembered it as a child, but with fewer children now. Central Street, USA, was still themed as an old-timey main street. The emporiums still sold merch. The thoroughfares still smelled of baked goods, cleaning agent, and dreams. But there were small changes: unbinned trash, graffiti, and security drones high overhead.

"Why do they call it the Magical Kingdom?" U asked.

"Well, the Kingdom's founder was one of America's wizards. This is his magic. When he built it, it was in the middle of nothing. No one had heard of Orlando or Lake whatever. This was all a crazy idea in a swamp. But, every big and exciting thing begins as some outrageous idea on the edge of nowhere."

"And we're walking through some dead guy's crazy idea," U said as he took it all in.

"Yup. And this crazy idea is inside a country that was also a crazy idea. And on, and on, and on."

"The country IS crazy right now. The bad crazy," U said.

"You mean the elections?"

"Yeah, Dad, the elections and everything else."

"Well, they're over now. The campaigns have to pay up. We're far from DC. I'm with you, and..."

1

Russ's sunglasses alerted him to an encrypted call on Sm0ke$ignal. His sunglasses should have been OFF. He was trying to be present today. He thought he had turned them off just before the facial recognition scan at the Kingdom gate.

Sm0ke$ignal tagged the call to G.O.S, Global Opinion Strategies. To the political class, it was simply GOS without the periods. And as the newspaper headline stenciled on a massive scale in their lobby noted, "G.O.S. is GOD."

He knew it was Ruth, CEO of G.O.S. and commissioner of G.O.S.'s subtle lobby art.

Russ stood motionless, like rebar in concrete, as visitors streamed past him. He forced a smile and took the call. "This is Russ."

"Hello, Russ. It's Ruth. Are you enjoying Florida with your son?"

"Entering the Magical Kingdom as we speak."

"Russ, I don't want to cut into family time. I'll keep this very short. Congratulations again on a great election cycle. You're a key member of G.O.S., and I truly value our partnership. When you're back in DC, I hope we can catch up on your political and corporate client list, our Risk Committee's guidance on a few things, and this reporter Gavin Dirken. He's been asking about our work for Trans-Oceanic and Mr. Matul."

"Gavin Dirken? Don't know him. Who's he with?"

"He's with the *Washington Tribune-Intelligencer*."

"Not ringing a bell. And he's asking about Jefe?"

"Yes, but it's not a today problem. We can talk about it after your vacation. Enjoy the time with your son."

"You got it. Let's catch up over coffee as soon as I'm back in DC. I hope you have a relaxing Thanksgiving with your family."

"Have fun with your son. He's adorable. Bye-bye."

The abrupt call on Russ's sunglasses ended just as abruptly.

"Was that the office, Dad?" U asked.

"Yup."

"What was that about?"

"Nothing. Just an end-of-the-election-cycle call."

Of course, that was a lie.

2: Sm0ke$ignals

I<u>t's a Round World</u>
202.111.1111 Hey, it's Russ. Live from Orlando. How's the office?

703.546.9100 Dead. Everyone's counting $ or GCB and doin post-election TV. How's Florida?

202.111.1111 It's still here. @ Magical Kingdom on "It's a Round World" – '70's time capsule

703.546.9100 That shit is creepy.

202.111.1111 Don't hate. Hey, do we have a Risk Committee?

703.546.9100 No. But, I played Risk as a kid. Always start in Australia, dawg.

202.111.1111 LMAO. OK What r u doing for Thanxgiving?

703.546.9100 Vegas

202.111.1111 Really?

703.546.9100 Don't judge me Family Guy.

202.111.1111 u do u. Happy Thanxgiving!

703.546.9100 Enjoy the time with Ulysses
<u>Pith Helmet Cruise</u>
202.111.1111 Hey, it's Russ. Have a quick research request.

202.999.8888 Anything for my valued client. What can I help you with?

202.111.1111 I need everything you can pull together in a slick Best Practice, Next Practice doc on Risk Committees. Kinda like a CRS issue brief.

202.999.8888 Happy to do it. When do you need it?

202.111.1111 Tomorrow.

202.999.8888 On it. Anything for client #1. Where r u, BTW?

202.111.1111 Magical Kingdom. "Amazon Cruise" or some shit like that.

202.999.8888 OMG Love it. Do they still wear pith helmets and do the cheesy monologue?

202.111.1111 IDK

202.999.8888 Dude, you're on the fucking ride.

202.111.1111 Risk Committees. Best Practice. Need it tomorrow.

202.999.8888 On it. Will bill your LLC. Prefer payment in GCB.

202.111.1111 Confirmed. Captain has a pith helmet.
<u>Mysterious Parrot Room</u>

202.111.1111 Hey, it's Russ. Anything going on?

202.555.6666 No boss. It's v quiet.

202.111.1111 Any client calls or important email traffic?

202.555.6666 Nope. ANN called about u doing TV tonight re changing demographics of America and Homeland Generation. But, I told them u were on vacation.

202.111.1111 Thank you

202.555.6666 How's the Magical Kingdom? Where r u?

202.111.1111 "Mysterious Parrot Room"

202.555.6666 Googling

202.111.1111 Talking robot birds and shit. Tiki themed.

202.555.6666 OK.....

202.111.1111 I need a matrix of all my clients rated 1-5 by reputational risk and ranked. 1 low and 5 high. Then I need that done with a random sample of firm clients. Then I need the 2 avgs. Got it?

202.555.6666 When do u need it?

202.111.1111 EOD

202.555.6666 Will do this ASAP.

Waiting for Los Piratas del Mar

HAL Enjoying the Magical Kingdom, Russ?

202.111.1111 Yes. Recommendations?

HAL Eat a healthy diet and wear your seat belt.

202.111.1111 haha

HAL Based on U's age and interests, I recommend "Sinister Manor".

Based on your interests, I recommend TomorroWorld Speedway.

Based on your friends and family, I also recommend photos at several locations. If you want these, reply "PHOTOS."

202.111.1111 Thank you.

202.111.1111 Tell me what I need to know.

HAL It is important to spend time with your family.

Make healthy eating choices today.

I'm working to move your hotel room to a higher floor and better location.

You are being overscheduled for your Sao Paulo trip. You should consider adding a day or two.

It is very quiet at the office.

Risk Committees are common in American corporations. I have emailed you a summary.

202.111.1111 You're amazing, HAL.

HAL Thank you.

HAL Shall I continue or is this sufficient.

202.111.1111 Sufficient.

202.111.1111 One more thing.
HAL Yes.
202.111.1111 Where can I find grace?
HAL What is Grace's last name? You have no contacts with that name.
202.111.1111 Thank you HAL, I'm sure grace will find me.

<u>Waiting for Los Piratas del Mar</u>

Unidentified Russell, Russell, Campaign Muscle!

202.111.1111 Dump. How are u doing???

Possible Scam Call Doin great. Counting my GCB lol

202.111.1111 Happy for u Oppo King. U do great work.

202.111.1111 Where r u, Dump?

Unknown undisclosed location. Also, Sm0ke$ignal sucks. I use GhostChat.

202.111.1111 Really???

No Number Listed Yes. Look it up. Working on a new project for one of your clients

202.111.1111 I have another project for you, btw

Unlisted OK. Who?

202.111.1111 Gavin Dirken. Reporter.

Unidentified OK That'll be 2,000 GCB

202.111.1111 U got it.

ID Withheld Enjoy Orlando

202.111.1111 How do u know I'm in Orlando?

Manifest Destiny Riverboat

202.555.6666 ANN just called. They want you to do something tonight on the partisan divide in American politics.

202.111.1111 No. That's a trap.

202.555.6666 Feels like it.

202.555.6666 I think their angle is on consultants, "wedge" issues, etc.

202.111.1111 Trap.

202.111.1111 Who's doing the segment?

202.555.6666 Stirling Kingsley

202.111.1111 Pretentious empty suit. Trap. Trap. Trap.

202.555.6666 I'll explain that you're with your son on vacation.

202.111.1111 Thank you

202.555.6666 What ride are you on now?

202.111.1111 A steamboat. Lemme check. "Manifest Destiny Riverboat"

202.555.6666 Surprised they haven't renamed that one

202.111.1111 Yup

Sinister Manor

202.111.1111 Hola! Como estas Ocho Loco?

305.888.8888 Russ! Estas en Miami?

202.111.1111 Orlando. Magical Kingdom. With my son. Con mi hijo.

305.888.8888 U r a good Papa. Having fun? What ride r u on?

202.111.1111 Sinister Manor

305.888.8888 Fantasmas. Scary lol

202.111.1111 Gonna hit the Gallery of Presidents next, so U learns at least something today.

305.888.8888 That's kinda boring, Russ... The boy doesn't want to see dead Presidents.

202.111.1111 It was cool back in the day lol

202.111.1111 How's Jefe doing?

305.888.8888 Not good. Come down here and let's talk about it over dinner en Calle Ocho.

202.111.1111 That bad, huh?

305.888.8888 Si. Visit with him one last time. He asked me about you.

202.111.1111 Strongest man I've ever met.

305.888.8888 He loves you. His American son from Ohio.

202.111.1111 I will come down and spend the day with him. Tell him this.

202.111.1111 Read him these exact words.

202.111.1111 Jefe, I will see you soon. Tell me what needs to be done.

305.888.8888 I will tell him.

202.111.1111 Mil gracias

305.888.8888 De nada. Btw, Surge says hello.

305.888.8888 He doesn't think DC is safe anymore.

202.111.1111 Like Miami's safer???

305.888.8888 You know what he means.

202.111.1111 Yeah. It's really fucked up. DC needs a reboot.

305.888.8888 Siiiiii

3: Gallery of Presidents

Russ and U stood outside the Sinister Manor as three Victorian-themed, holographic damsels entertained the line of middle-aged visitors snaking through a gothic courtyard. It wasn't hot or particularly sunny, but the damsel's parasols made the theming pop.

"Best ride so far?" Russ asked.

"Sinister Manor. Hands down."

"Really? It wasn't too scary? The 21st-century version is a LOT scarier. I mean, I remember being scared when I was a kid, but this was next level, with the holograms and the new audio and the augmented reality."

"Dad, it was cool. Not that scary. Scary level LOW."

"Second best?"

"I'd say the dark ride about the kids that escape London with the boy that refuses to grow up. Old School."

Russ just smiled.

"What's your favorite, Dad?"

"Tough call. My favorite IDEA in the park is TomorroWorld. But I like all the patriotic stuff, too. Since we're nearby, let's go to the Gallery of Presidents. I want to see if it's changed at all since I was a kid."

U's shoulders hunched, and his head dropped.

"Daaad. That's political. No one wants to go there. You DOOOO politics for money. Can't we just do fun rides? We haven't even done Los Piratas Del Mar yet..."

"It won't take long. It'll be fun and cheesy. They have these robot Presidents say little things. I just have to see it."

"Okay, Dad. But let's not stay too long."

"Thanks, buddy. I read somewhere in my feed that they're replacing the old-school robots with 3D interactive holograms soon. I want to see the old robot Presidents before they're gone."

U's instincts were right. There was no line and only a handful of people in the Gallery. By the looks of it, the Gallery of Presidents hadn't been heavily trafficked in at least a few Presidencies.

Patrons, eager to simply SIT DOWN after standing all day, surrendered to the comfortable seats, read something on their sunglasses, or rested their eyes and waited for the show.

Russ's pulse quickened, remembering the Gallery as a boy. For most of the sunburned Midwesterners in attendance back then, this was about as close as they were going to get to a President or Washington, DC.

The curtains opened, revealing America's pantheon of Presidents. They had definitely upgraded the Presidential robots. They appeared almost real. It took Russ a few seconds to remember the term for that unsettling place where a robot is imperceptibly not human. The uncanny valley. These were in the uncanny valley. The robots Russ remembered from his childhood were lifelike but obviously not human. Those were cool. These were unsettling. There was George Washington. He exuded a godlike aura. There was Jefferson. The robot team seemed to have phoned it in on Jefferson, who resembled a monument more than a man. There was Andrew Jackson. Jackson had the look of a robot about to go postal. That seemed appropriate for a dueling president. And then there was Abraham Lincoln. The robot team had put painstaking effort into thesixteenth president, and he was almost too human, with the disheveled hair, the tired eyes, and a worn stovepipe hat.

As soon as the curtains had fully receded, the epithets began flying in the general direction of the animatronic version of the most recent President.

"Fuck you, fuck your fucking administration, and fuck your dumbass voters, motherfucker!" yelled one masked patron seated in the front and now standing on a chair, middle fingers raised.

Patrons began standing and alternatively clapping and yelling. Things were spinning out of control.

A retired veteran, brandishing a cane, attempted a first strike on the standing, yelling man. The retiree missed, and his cane caught only air-conditioning. Two more masked patrons grabbed the man's cane and began beating him with it. That ignited the nucleus of a riot as the veteran's defenders fought the masked attackers.

Another team of masked protestors began disabling all of the surveillance cameras in the Gallery with black spray paint.

Teens, phones out, started recording, tagging, and posting their videos to social media. The wealthier ones used their new sunglasses.

#Prezidentialbrawl was going to go viral.

Russ's sunglasses started flashing SafeCor security warnings – EXIT UNSAFE LOCATION.

The sunglasses even buzzed a bit, which was an upgrade he didn't know about.

Russ didn't need his sunglasses to tell him he had to leave. He quickly moved U out of the scrum and, importantly, away from the recording/tagging/posting teens.

It was now cascading crazy.

A masked protestor brushed up against Russ as he and U hustled away from the mayhem. Thinking that Russ had pushed him, the protestor became belligerent. Russ raised open palms to signal that he had no part in this mess, but the protestor decided otherwise and threw a punch. Russ sidestepped the punch, grabbed the masked man's upper arm and forearm with both hands and broke his elbow joint. The masked attacker screamed and fell to the floor, his forearm dangling. Russ grabbed a nearby trash can, lifted it high over his head, and slammed it down onto the screaming attacker.

Then he turned to a panicked U and said, "We gotta roll."

But there were now fights everywhere, and these fights were blocking the exits. Russ and U carefully tried to exit the Gallery, weaving their way toward the emergency exit.

Five younger-looking protestors, all wearing cartoon masks, produced rope. How they smuggled rope past Security was anybody's guess, but they quickly used the rope to lasso the current President's robot and pull him down, Saddam Hussein statue-style.

Where was Security?

In what seemed like just a few seconds, the masked protestors were running out the gallery doors and pulling the deposed Presidential robot through Central Street, USA.

Security drones descended in a V formation and began following them. The protestors had not considered drone countermeasures.

It had to be an inside job, Russ thought. Facial recognition would have tipped Security for any troublemakers. But where was Security?

Russ's sunglasses began flashing a torrent of Sm0ke$ignal messages.

HAL Leave your location immediately.

HAL Public unrest incident registered in your location.

SafeCor You are in danger.

SafeCor Shelter in Place Immediately.

SafeCor A public safety incident has been registered in your location.

SafeCor Shelter in Place Immediately. Obey local law enforcement authorities.

SafeCor Reply with EXTRACT for immediate extraction.

BIGCountry Russ, if you're at Magical Kingdom, GET OUT.

> 202.555.6666 Hey, boss. Patriot News Network wants to know if you can do something from Orlando about this #prezidentialbrawl thing. ANN is asking, too.

> 202.111.1111 Ugh No.

> 202.555.6666 You got it.

Russ and U raced out an emergency door and headed for TomorroWorld, as far from the present chaos as they could get.

Russ could see the security drones swarming down Central Street, USA, recording visuals of the perpetrators and eventually hovering collectively to block egress. SafeCor Security emerged in force from buildings in Central Street, U.S.A. They had body armor, lightweight batons, and the new, clear riot shields. These weren't the big riot shields of yesteryear. These were round, like an ancient Greek's shield, but translucent and light. The theme park background music increased in volume. Russ assumed that was done to drown out the screams of the protestors. Russ could see the batons rise and fall on the protestors.

GoddessofWar R u safe?

202.111.1111 Yes

GoddessofWar Crazy. Trending story.

GoddessofWar R u in any video?

202.111.1111 No. All good. At race car thing in TomorroWorld. Far away from it now.

GoddessofWar Good! Is U OK?

202.111.1111 He's fine. Thinks it was cool lol

GoddessofWar Good. So, no one attacked you two?

202.111.1111 All good

GoddessofWar OK. Will call you tonite

202.111.1111 All under control

"Is that Mom?" U asked.

"Yeah. She was worried. It's all over the media."

"Are you gonna tell Mom you broke that dude's arm?"

"Should we get a snack or something?" Russ asked.

U stood looking at Russ for a moment, thinking.

"Still a good day, except for some unruly patrons," Russ said with a forced smile.

"So, that's it?" U asked.

"A little turbulence," Russ said, smiling harder.

"I'm still processing this," U said.

"It's funny, though. When they switch to hologram Presidents, there won't be robots that can be toppled and dragged down Central Street, USA. So, they're about to fix the problem," Russ said.

U shook his head. "On the other hand, a hologram President could be deleted, or hacked, or maybe even programmed to say all kinds of goofy stuff."

"Well, you got me there."

"Dad, this was not a normal day in the Magical Kingdom. I didn't expect a war over a robot President."

4: Mover & Shaker

HAL Good morning, Russ.
    You will love today's weather. Sunny and 75F.

For breakfast, try the hotel's Colombian coffee, fresh grapefruit, and their famous "billion-dollar bacon."

Also, check your email.
202.555.6666 Boss, check your email. Good news.
202.111.1111 Checking
202.111.1111 Tell them yes.
Their room was themed to match the "Los Piratas Del Mar" ride. The walls were covered in fake 18th-century nautical maps of Florida, Cuba, and the Caribbean. Russ loved old maps, even if they were a complete sham. As a boy, he was always drawn to the edges, with sea serpents, seductive sirens, dragons, and storms. A painting of a swashbuckling pirate crew hung over their hotel beds, and the lead pirate held a map to buried treasure. Russ sat at an ornate, rococo desk, drinking cheap hotel coffee, and he had his feet up on a treasure chest turned side table.

U was asleep, gangly teenage legs and arms splayed across most of the bed but buried under the sheets and massive hotel bed comforter.

U was short for Ulysses. Russ loved the name. Having grown up in Point Pleasant, Ohio, the birthplace of Ulysses S. Grant, Russ couldn't help naming his son after the victorious general and two-term President. Melissa was not exactly—ever—sold on it. He loved Grant's resilience, what working people call grit.

Russ read his email from the National Association of Political Consultants.

Russ Armstrong,

Congratulations.

You have been named a "Mover and Shaker" by the National Association of Political Consultants.

Nominated by your peers in the NAPC and selected by the Professional Recognition Committee, you are cordially invited to attend the 54th Annual NAPC Gala, where you will be recognized as a "Mover and Shaker."

Please join us in Washington at ANN studios...

U started to thrash around under the covers, escaping slumber.
Melissa messaged in on Sm0ke$ignal.
Goddessof War Congratulations
Goddessof War HAL told me that you're getting a big award from NAPC
Goddessof War You definitely earned whatever they give you. Lol
202.111.1111 Haha. Love that HAL tipped you off
202.111.1111 It's a long way from night security at Union Station
Goddessof War Truth
202.111.1111 Less of a big win...
202.111.1111 And more of a lifetime achievement award...

202.111.1111 Like those actors that just keep doing movies until the Academy figures they should give them something before they die

Goddessof War That's your signature strategery.
202.111.1111 I defer to the expert on military strategery.
202.111.1111 You'll need to give me pointers on receiving awards... plz

Goddess of War I'm sure you'll do just fine. Lol

202.111.1111 U is still sleeping but stirring a bit. Our teenager needs his sleep.

Goddess of War Awww. Enjoy. Later... Have another endless call about DefCon1. Ugh

202.111.1111 Hang in there

Melissa had to endure even more conference calls than Russ. As President of Defend.us, America's defense industry trade association, Melissa Meyer was always on the phone.

DefCon1 was Defend.us's big, annual trade show, and it was a SHOW. There were other defense-related trade shows. Some were less trade shows and more open-air weapons bazaars. But there was only one DefCon1 for the American military and American defense contractors. Melissa, having started her career as an expert in defense appropriations, was its leader and impresario. And her podcast, "On the MIC," was *the* news source for anyone in the Military-Industrial Complex.

Russ immediately thought of her picture on his desk, Melissa delivering the keynote address for DefCon1 atop a new stealth tank in a bright red dress. *Jane's Defence Weekly* famously named her the "Goddess of War."

Still more U movement under the massive hotel comforter.

Ocho pinged Russ on Sm0ke$ignal.

305.888.8888 When r u down in Miami?

202.111.1111 2 days, Ocho.

305.888.8888 Bueno. C u then.

305.888.8888 btw how was magical kingdom?

202.111.1111 it was fine until the coup

305.888.8888 Que????

202.111.1111 You didn't hear?

305.888.8888 Noooo

202.111.1111 Some kids stole one of the robot presidents as a protest

305.888.8888 ic

305.888.8888 aside from that???

202.111.1111 it was fine lol. But did notice some trash and absent workers.

305.888.8888 at magical kingdom?

202.111.1111 cracks in America's foundation

202.111.1111 and our institutions are failing

305.888.8888 I'm not sure I'd extrapolate that from una dia

202.111.1111 Fair point. But something is definitely off.

Hotel comforter thrown off bed and teen limb thrashing.

"Good morning, U."

"Morning, Dad," U replied in a not-yet-fully-awake monotone. "What's going on? Are you up?"

"Up and drinking coffee."

"How's Mom?" a sleepy-eyed U asked.

"Mom's good. Busy."

"Anything happening back in DC?"

"Well, it looks like I won an award."

"For what? Is it a participation trophy?" U chuckled in the way all teen boys crack themselves up.

"No trophy. They're basically rewarding me for surviving as a political consultant."

"I think it's weird that you're a political consultant."

"Why? It's what I do."

"I don't reaaaally think about your work, Dad."

"Well, what do you think I am?"

"You're Dad. Duhhhh. You're just Dad."

Russ just smiled and gazed out the window toward the Central Florida Solar Array. The sun was up, rising fast, and its light was burning away the fog, making things clear.

"Dad, so what's the award? Is it cool?"

"It depends on how you look at it."

"How do you look at it?"

"To be honest, I don't think it matters much. It won't make me more money and..."

"You're not happy about it at all? I mean, do you think it's like a Bad Guy of the Decade Award?" U cracked himself up again and then quickly transitioned to his best Announcer Voice. "Aaaaand, when we come back, who will be named Political Super Villain of the 21st-century? Could it be Russ Armstrong?"

"Do you think political consultants are bad guys?"

"Dad, the media isn't exactly putting you guys in the 'Angels Among Us' category."

Russ gave U the "go-on" look he mastered from decades of focus group moderating.

"They blame you guys for dividing the country. They blame you for dividing the country and making money off it. And they blame you for giving us candidates that ran us into debt. It's like you're cool and bad at the same time. You're like Tha305." U broke into Tha305's signature, vaguely obscene, dance move.

Russ decided not to mention that Tha305 had been a crisis client after a problematic weapons charge.

"Nice moves. What else?"

"To me, you're just Dad. But you're apparently getting an award for being a supervillain who gets his Benjamins from dividing us. That's weird to me."

"Soooo, what should I do?"

"Pay me to be your image consultant! Just transfer that GCB to my new Spectaculars." More teenage self-chuckling.

"Done. You're hired. Advise me."

"Okay. If you're a badass, you just ball out. You don't need their award. Don't show up. Or send someone to pick it up and then stack it in the trophy room of your super lair. NBD."

Russ pretended to be taking notes. "First step, send lackey to get award. Second step, place in trophy room at NeverWinter."

"But, you're Dad. You're not a bad guy. But you are a badass. Take their dumb award, and then do something amazing, something so different, something they'd never think of, something just..."

"Like what?"

"I don't know. That's your jam. Do some fourth-down trick-play, ninja thing!"

5: Getting There

After Russ dropped U at the Orlando airport, he made his way to the all-new, all-automated rental car counter. The interactive screens had cheerfully banished the workers. And, of course, everything was illuminated in light, electric blue, the official color of the efficient, always smiling, open sky future.

When he cleared the rental counter and entered the parking garage, he confronted horizon-stretching rows of the same car. They were all white, all aerodynamic, all electric, all cloned in a sterile factory. His sunglasses told him his car was in a distant space Z19.

Once Russ found his car, he thumbed the lock, programmed the address, slid an artificially clean-smelling sleep mask over his eyes, and let it drive.

Somewhere south of Orlando, he relaxed, quit making to do lists in his head, and let the sleep come. It carried him back to an old, familiar dream.

The bedroom door was locked. The chair was up against the door, protection against the yelling adults downstairs. Their anger bounced off the linoleum and faux wood paneling in the kitchen. His room smelled of old farmhouse, sweaty baseball clothes, and infield dirt.

Then he heard it.

It started off in the distance like it always did. It started off in the distance every night at exactly the same time.

It grew less faint. A little louder now. Louder than the cicadas.

He imagined it less as a thing and more as a force. He knew it ran on diesel, but he imagined it as though it was simply energy. The night train, coming from nowhere and going somewhere.

Where was it going? Down along the Ohio, snaking along the river, through West Virginia, across the Appalachians, to Washington, New York, sunny places on TV, maybe even California or Miami.

The force grew louder. He imagined grabbing his toothbrush, his wallet, and everything he could stuff in his backpack and running to the train. Running alongside the train. Jumping onto the train. Riding the train far away from Point Pleasant. Going with the sound as it disappeared.

Going. Going. Gone.

The car woke Russ up.

"Arriving at destination in one hour," it announced in a robotic, vaguely New Zealand-ish, not quite British, not quite South African synth voice.

Russ pulled the overpriced sleep mask off his face and observed the landscape out the window.

Citrus groves marched toward the horizon, all genetically engineered to resist any invasive species or fungus thrown at them. Florida's old citrus groves were back. He rolled down the windows, inhaled the orange blossom air, and pulled in the peace of nowhere.

"Accelerate," Russ commanded.

"The legal speed limit on this surface is 65 miles per hour," the car replied. "For your safety..."

"Manual," Russ said, taking control of the wheel and pushing his speed to 75, then 85, then 90.

Russ turned his sunglasses on and called Ocho, Ernesto Octavio, the Founder and President of ImEx.

"Russ. How are you? Donde estas?" Ocho asked.

"Asi asi. Cansado. Just woke up and driving. Decided to take the scenic route."

"Are you going to stop at NeverWinter?" Ocho asked.

"No time to check on the place," Russ replied.

"How are you getting to Miami?"

"Gonna roll down to Ft. Meyers and then take Alligator Alley. HAL will give you my progress. I'll check in quick, and then let's meet for a good dinner."

"What do you want to eat, pal?"

"Ropa vieja and that drink with the sugar cane in the glass."

"You got it, we'll go old school." Ocho chuckled, yelled something to an employee, and closed with, "Ciao.".

The rental took Russ past small ag towns, citrus processing plants, phosphorous mines, and roadside stands selling gator jerky. It turned east at Naples and raced across Alligator Alley, pulled to Miami's light pollution like moth to flame.

Russ's thoughts wandered as he contemplated the Everglades, their simultaneous emptiness and fullness. With the sun setting behind him, a memory danced on the edge of his consciousness.

He was an indentured servant (official title: Project Director) at N.O.S. in Alexandria, Virginia, when South Florida changed his life. Out of the blue, Russ was told to fly to Miami and give the firm's standard "American Opinion Environment" presentation to a group of political donors, developers, and sugar barons. All the principals at N.O.S. had something better to do. This was a "rinse and repeat" presentation he could give in his sleep. He was told to take the night flight back to Dulles to save money on the hotel.

Russ dutifully flew down to Miami in a poorly fitting, itchy suit, prepped his speech, and delivered it to an air-conditioned who's who of South Florida magnates. In the middle of the speech, an afternoon thunderstorm rolled in, soaking Miami and knocking out the power. Not knowing what to do, he offered to finish his presentation and take questions on the covered porch outside. To his surprise, Miami's good and great loved the idea. With rain pouring down, guests commandeered all the rattan furniture that could be found. Everyone shed layers of clothing. Russ quickly peeled off his jacket, pulled off his tie, and rolled up his sleeves, surrendering immediately to the South Florida humidity. Without slides and only his notes, he decided to wing it. There was nothing to lose.

The conversational tone was a big hit. When he went to Q and A, hands jumped up. The crowd, powerful, but with no power at the moment, loved the informality. And they loved Russ. Lightning had struck.

In that crowd was Jefe, sitting quietly in the back, motionless. When Russ's flight back to DC was canceled, Jefe invited the young man to dinner with his family, including Jefe's effervescent daughter.

Russ said yes, and a golden partnership was forged.

"System failure," announced the decelerating auto voice. "Contacting vehicle service."

"What?" Russ barked. "I'm two fucking miles from my destination! You have got to be kidding! Accelerate!"

"System failure," repeated the disembodied synth voice, as the car slowed.

"Accelerate," Russ repeated, this time calmly enunciating.

The car slowed to a stop. "Contacting vehicle service."

"Accelerate," ordered Russ.

But, the auto sat motionless, silent.

Russ called Ocho on his sunglasses, but went straight to voicemail. "Hey, I'm walking to you now. Car's dead. I'm about two miles away. Find me in the middle of the neighborhood at the Domino Park. Be there in about thirty minutes."

Russ woke HAL.

"HAL, can you route me to the Calle Ocho Domino Park? It's near Ball & Chain. I forget the exact name."

"Routing to 1444 SouthwestEighth Street, Miami, Florida 33135."

"Thanks, HAL."

Russ opened the trunk, yanked a rolling suitcase out, and opened it on the street. He threw his jacket and some paperwork from the back seat into the empty suitcase and zipped it back up. Then he turned his back on the setting sun and began walking east, through humid neighborhoods and under indifferent streetlights.

Young men and women, cruising in their cars, windows down, bass up, were oblivious to the man pulling a beat-up suitcase over steaming Miami asphalt.

6: Miami

"**B**ienvenidos a Miami, Senor Armstrong!" Ocho bellowed as Russ approached the Domino Park.

Sidewalk chewing gum, viscous from the heat, had bonded with one of the wheels on Russ's rolling suitcase, forcing the stuck wheel to scrape against the pavement loudly. If Russ could hear the wheels over the street life and police sirens, they would have sounded like a deep, persistent whisper.

Russ couldn't quite hear the words Ocho was using, but he knew exactly what Ocho was saying.

Ocho was a big man, XXL, with broad shoulders, thick in the torso, an enormous head, a wide grin, and blindingly white teeth. His dark brown hair, enlarged by the extreme humidity, was unpredictable and tempest-tossed.

"The boys are meeting us here, and then we will celebrate your spectacular triumph."

In other places, "spectacular triumph" would be a condescending swipe. But, this was pure Ocho, heartfelt, literal, and leaning into the grandiose.

They found a deserted domino table and relaxed onto damp, plastic chairs.

"What's the plan?" Russ asked.

"Plan?" Ocho asked, laughing. "Do we need a plan?

"Well, I suppose we can just sacrifice a few mojitos to the Miami party gods and let them chart our path."

Ocho leaned in with the soft eyes of a longtime friend. "Russ, I'm very happy for you. You deserve this award. Please take the time to enjoy a victory lap. Please."

"Do guys like us get a victory lap?" Russ asked.

"If we take one."

"If we break into the racetrack and steal the pace car," Russ said with a half smile.

"Es verdad, but..."

"It's a lifetime achievement award for a mid-level soap opera star, but it's better than a kick in the ass. I'll take it. If you just put one foot in front of the other each day and you pound away long enough, you get awards like this. That's it. I'm not special."

"Es verdad. To hard work then. To you. And to Ohio." Ocho raised a sweaty glass of ice water skyward. He brought the glass to his lips, briefly panicked, and gently placed the tap water back on the table.

"Russ, you know, you're an immigrant too. You immigrated from Ohio and came here for a better life. And everyone around you immigrated from Cuba..."

"And Venezuela and Colombia," Russ interjected.

"Yes, from Cuba and all these other places." Ocho waved his hand in the air at "other places."

"And here we are in the greatest tropical city, in the greatest state, in the greatest nation that has ever been. And we are free. And we all came here for something better, something bigger, something more open, something just over the beautiful horizon of our imagination. El bello horizonte. All of us dreamers and escapees. Todos nosotros. Juntos. Construyendo Juntos. Just think what we can do next."

Russ nodded in the way all men do when the words have been used up.

The two sunk back into their white plastic chairs, relaxing under a gentle night sirocco.

A Latin jazz band was warming up in the little bandstand next to the Domino Park, the staccato sounds of instruments being tuned. All around was the sound of old men slapping dominoes down, of laughter and flirting in the bars, of a pachanga band playing somewhere, of glasses and plates being moved, and of car radios with deep Miami bass.

The boys arrived one by one, each appearing out of nowhere like ninjas in an '80s movie.

First, there was Zurdo, parking across the street in his refurbished Ford Bronco, windows down, cigar smoke trailing like a coal-powered Victorian tugboat. He slid out of the vehicle and weaved through traffic. Zurdo

Gonzalez was lean and ripped in the manner of all SoFlo Real Estate Bros. Originally an electrician; he forced his way into the developer community. When he joined them, he whispered something in Ocho's ear and took a seat.

Surge, or more precisely Sergei Goncharenko, came next, rolling up in a rideshare, eschewing the robo-taxi option. Surge was clean cut, with light brown hair graying at the temples and poker table eyes. He strode toward the trio, smiling and waving hello. When he joined the group, he also leaned in and whispered something in Ocho's ear, then took a seat, right arm draped over Zurdo.

Russ knew Surge first, before he changed his name to Stephen Flagler, earned an MBA from the University of Miami, and joined Trans-Oceanic Trading.

Surge and Zurdo were now neighbors in Weston, living in the same new, gated community. Surge met and married Daniela Cruz after she immigrated from Venezuela in the 2000s. The couple introduced Zurdo to Daniela's younger sister, Ana. Daniela was quiet, with a soft voice, and an impressive facility with languages, moving in and out of Spanish, English, and Russian with Surge. She worked as a court interpreter. Ana was the classic younger sister, with energy that filled the room and a passion for beisbol, clubbing, her three children, and Zurdo.

Finally, T-Bone arrived, illegally parking his dilapidated truck in front of the Domino Park. It is a universal law of nature, like gravity or the futility of prevent defense, that any sufficiently advanced man tribe must have or create a "T-Bone." The name demands it. He exited the truck wearing a sweaty Tiburones visor and swaggered over to the group's table with three cigar boxes under his right arm. He didn't bother locking the doors.

"What is up my brochachos?" he exclaimed, much to the confusion of the old domino men.

T-Bone was new to an old tribe. Although the backstory was hazy, he was from Homestead by way of Mobile, was a jovial slum lord, and a collector of sketchy South Florida parking lots. Using his Midas touch, he transformed the properties into still sketchy but profitable parking lots.

No one knew his real name. No one cared.

"The Sin Nombres have a surprise for you tonight, Russ," Ocho said, eyes twinkling. "T-Bone will explain."

T-Bone put his cigar down, hunching forward with hands clasped. "Now we said we were gonna hang in Miami, but we've already done that a bunch. I mean, is Brickell gonna be all that different than before? We have a treat for you, Russ. We know that you know Lucky. Fate is taking us to the glades tonight."

7: Lucky's

Fate may have been taking the Sin Nombres to the glades, but they were getting there in a bullet-riddled party bus with a severely damaged bumper. The crushed bumper was adorned with sun-faded stickers advertising for Jai Alai, a defunct casino, and the mysterious Everglades Skunk Ape. The tags on the license plates were expired.

As the crew stepped onto the bus, they noticed three old disco balls, worn leather seating, ceiling mirrors, a defaced Tha305 poster, and two brass stripper poles.

"It's amazing, right? Right?" demanded T-Bone. "Oh, and I got it on deep discount. Denny is a friend. It's his side job on the side. He's gonna need some cash, so we gonna pass the hat in a bit."

Denny was tonight's driver. Rail thin and sporting a thick white beard, Denny was high, very high, and finishing off a joint. He was accompanied by his age-inappropriate girlfriend, Paradise.

Lucky's was hard to find. It was harder to get to. The occasional tourist, fresh from snapping pics of alligators, rolls past Lucky's domain without knowing it. His open-air "speakeasy" slash biker bar slash gun range slash exotic photography business isn't on any tourist Top 5 lists. But, criminals traversing Old 41 know exactly where Loop Road is. And so do folks that need to dump a body.

The party bus rolled down Old 41, bass thumping, rocking Tha305's greatest hits. Paradise was mixing drinks, occasionally circling back to Denny to check on the bus's progress, reload the tequila gun, and fetch more Jell-O shots.

Russ's sunglasses gave him the usual warning.

SafeCor You have entered an unsafe area.

SafeCor Your location has a high rate of violent crime.

SafeCor Location tracking unavailable.

The party bus slowed. Denny put the hazards on and closed his eyes, intent on napping before the drive back to Miami.

Paradise and the revelers spilled out of the bus, nearly running into Lucky.

Lucky's first words were focused on Paradise. "Hello, darlin."

"Lucky!" Surge yelled, wrapping him up in a huge bear hug.

Lucky did not hug back, but he did slowly run his right hand to his sidearm.

"I have no idea who you are, son, but howdy, just the same. Go on in, and Molly will sell you a drink for cash. Paradise, y'all know the rules. The booze stays on the bus. You have to buy from us. You can bring the tequila gun in, but we sell you the ammo."

One by one, the group entered through the gate, walking to the bonfire in the center of the swamp ranch.

Russ stayed back, waiting to talk with Lucky.

It was a perfectly clear night, with bright stars and no light pollution. The two leaned up against the bus. It felt to Russ like an Ohio summer night with moonlight, tall can pyramids, and long stories.

"How are you doing, my friend?" Russ asked.

"I'm still Lucky," he replied, tipping his famous python-rimmed cowboy hat.

"Well, if you have any luck, you can spare..." Russ let it linger and smiled.

"I'm not sure it works that way, son."

"Seems like a quiet night. Are we the only ones here?" Russ asked.

"Let's see. There's me and Molly. There's Odalis. She knows you'll want to talk. There's y'all, the Sin Nombres. And we have some special guests. I promised them you'd leave promptly at eleven fifteen. Promptly."

"Special guests?"

"Yup. They booked the place for September tenth. That's a famous night here. Hurricane Donna. But we had a tropical storm roll in that night, so they had to reschedule. And they are here now, in November."

Russ lowered his eyebrows and gave Lucky the questioning eye.

"You're a smart boy, Russ. Do your homework."

Russ nodded.

"Molly bought marshmallows just for you. You're the only man that comes on my property and doesn't drink, fuck, or shoot. You're buyin' those marshmallows. You understand, son?"

"Yes, sir," Russ said, smiling.

The two walked together toward the fire while light flickered on the guests. Odalis was sitting barefoot, eyes closed, enveloped in campfire smoke. Molly was serving Surge and Ocho drinks in the party shack behind the bonfire. Zurdo was attempting to send Ana pictures of some of Lucky's more risqué photography. But, as everyone who has been to Lucky's knows, it is off the grid with cell service as reliable as a road crew at quitting time.

In the distance, past the bonfire smoke, Russ saw what looked like T-Bone and Paradise walking toward one of the sheds.

8: Book Club

Daniela was hosting book club again. Although the book club went through the ritual of selecting a book for each month's "meeting," she suspected that she was the only woman to have read any of the books.

At a minimum, she was certain that her sister, Ana, hadn't cracked even one of the books in a book club. Ever. At first, she was indignant. Why go through the charade of book club if no one was committed to reading the book? Then, she was amused. Ana was just being Ana. Then, she was intrigued. Why were others completely untroubled by a book club in which not a word was read? And then she saw the wisdom, the window behind the curtain.

Book club wasn't about books.

Daniela embraced the scandalous, horrible, damning truth. Book club was the high school cafeteria with alcohol. It was the gathering of the girl tribe behind a modern mask.

For years, when it was her turn, she would prepare a beautiful dinner with perfectly paired wine, flowers in the kitchen, and a playlist supporting the book's core theme. That was lovely. Surge was always impressed. But did the book club care? Ana and the other women would arrive, recently delivered books in hand, get buzzed on wine within the first thirty minutes, eat very, little gossip, and need a robo-taxi at the end of the night.

Tonight was different. Tonight, she was going to embrace Ana's perspective. She refused to read this month's book—*One Hundred Years of Solitude* by Gabriel Garcia Marquez. She bought the book, thumbed through it, posted a picture of it on MyBestLife, and let it bake in the sun on the lanai.

And she wasn't making dinner. She picked up a pre-made vegetable tray on the way home from work. Tonight would be champagne and St. Lucia

Sunsets—cranberry juice, coconut-flavored rum, and ice. Surge would be out late with the boys. She was going to drink and spout ridiculous theories about the book she had not read.

One by one, the women of book club arrived. Hannah, in a white minivan with church and PTA bumper stickers, brought white wine and discount cheese. Lisa, in a silver minivan with gym and animal rescue bumper stickers, brought white wine and store-cut strawberries. Elana, at peak glow-up, arrived in her new lime Porsche. She brought white wine, tequila, and her own martini. There was no sign of Ana yet, but she was probably talking with the babysitter or scrambling to select the perfect outfit.

They sat on the lanai. The wine went quickly and seamlessly transitioned to St. Lucia Sunsets.

"Where is Stephen tonight?" Lisa asked.

"With some of his friends in Miami having a nice dinner," Daniela explained.

"Con Zurdo?" Elana asked.

"Siiii, con Zurdo, y Ocho, y Russ, y T-Bone. Stephen and Russ worked together long ago. So, it's nice for them to reconnect professionally."

Hannah, high on gummies and sipping on a St. Lucia Sunset, began laughing.

"And who the hell is T-Bone?" Hannah asked.

"Isn't he that good ole boy with the work truck? He's like a Tiburones Super Fan or something," Lisa said.

"Oh. My. God." Hannah laughed. "Do we even know this guy's actual fucking, name? I mean, this is some serious 'Florida Man' shit. This is too good. T-Bone from Okeechobee." Hannah giggled.

Daniela was uncomfortable with any laughter at another's expense. She tried to change the subject. "I don't know what a T-Bone is. I'm sure it's just a silly name. He has been to our home and was a gentleman."

"A T-Bone is a cut of meat, Daniela." Hannah giggled again.

Elana cleared her throat. "Hannah, he may not be your kind of meat, but I would order him off any menu."

The lanai erupted in laughter.

"You cannot be fucking serious," Hannah said. She was now as red as her St. Lucia Sunset.

"Es un oso adorable," Elana said, smiling.

"Oso? What's that? My Spanish sucks. I blame Broward County Public Schools. What's an Oso?" Hannah asked.

"He is an adorable bear of a man. Oso is bear, a big bear. Y me gusta his truck. It suits him. Don't be so judgy." Elana closed with a finger wag, setting the now not giggling Hannah off.

"He doesn't look like a teddy bear. He's a scary fucking redneck," Hannah blurted.

"He is not a mirror. He is not a saint. He is a man. With the right woman, he is an oso," Elana replied.

The lanai descended into a long silence.

And that was when Ana arrived sober, agitated, bottle blonde, wearing a pink clubbing dress and wedges. She sat down, and the women of the book club closed ranks around her.

Daniela put her hand on Ana's wrist. "What's wrong? Are you okay?"

"Do you know where our husbands *really* are?" Ana asked.

"My ex-husband is in Jacksonville," Elana said, not fully grasping Ana's question.

"They're in Miami having dinner or, by now, sitting outside smoking," Daniela replied.

"Wrong!" Ana yelled. "Ocho took them to Lucky's! Dios mio."

Lisa and Hannah exchanged blank glances.

"What is Lucky's?" Elana asked.

Ana's face turned red with rage. "It's a fucking biker bar in the Everglades with disgusting white biker putas en triste tube tops. Es peligroso at night. They took a stripper bus to Lucky's. Zurdo sent me a selfie leaning on a fucking stripper pole. And now he won't respond to my texts!"

Uncertain how to respond, Lisa and Hannah were examining their drinks.

Elana broke the tension. "The phones do not work well in the Everglades. Zurdo is probably in a death spot, a dead spot, no reception. He cannot receive your texts."

Daniela knew in her heart that these were harmless male hijinks. Zurdo would always be charmed by Ana. Ocho was kind and smart. Russ and her Stephen were streetwise. If some biker man threatened the group, she felt pity for him. Her Stephen was a gentle man, but Sergei was not. Belarus was harder than South Florida. The boys were safe.

She also knew in her heart that this was torture for her sister. Ana was a possessive and jealous lover. She had always been this way with her boyfriends. But, she was even more possessive with Zurdo. Zurdo was hers para siempre. She couldn't let Ana go alone into the Everglades at night.

"Fuck this! I'm going to Lucky's now. He will have me, or he will have no one. And he will not have any biker putas. And fuck Ocho for taking them there!"

To Daniela's surprise, Lisa, Hannah, and Elana were in. Their husbands were either at home or long gone and living in Jacksonville. Driving drunk into the Everglades at night seemed like a great adventure to them. She watched her guests find their purses and keys. She knew that Ana would drive to Lucky's, wherever that was.

She looked into Ana's eyes, and Ana stopped dead in her tracks.

"Ana, donde esta este lugar de la suerte?"

"It's on Loop Road. Just take Old 41 west and then turn off on Loop Road. Es facil."

"Here is what we will do," Daniela said, speaking slowly and clearly. "I will make coffee, and we will bring it with us. Everyone take a pack of chicle from the kitchen drawer next to the oven. Ana will drive her car. Lisa will ride with her. I will drive my car, and Hannah will ride with me. Elana will follow us in her car. We will drive precisely the speed limit. We will follow Ana. Everyone use the bathroom now and meet in the driveway in ten minutes."

Daniela went to the master bedroom. She peed and changed out of her white sundress and into boots, jeans, and a fashion camo hoodie. She grabbed her matching camo handbag. Then she walked into their bedroom closet and parted the hanging dresses, revealing a safe. She placed her index finger on the safe and entered five zeroes. The safe opened to reveal a Glock 17 with ammunition. She pulled the Glock 17 from the safe, loaded it, and began to conceal it under her hoodie. Then she froze.

The gun was cold and heavy. Her palms were sweaty. Her chest was tight. She tried to imagine using it in self-defense. She tried to imagine pulling the trigger. She couldn't. She put the Glock back in the safe and locked it.

Then she went back to the kitchen to pour fresh coffee into travel mugs. No one needed a DUI.

On the way out of her house, Daniela pulled her largest kitchen knife from the red knife block and slid it into her handbag.

9: Odalis

Russ walked directly to the bonfire, and Odalis plopped down next to her, took his shoes off, and joined her in going barefoot. They sat quietly next to each other by the fire, listening to the wet wood hiss and pop and crackle. Heat from the fire created a calming sensation as it warmed Russ's feet.

Odalis was hunched up, feet out, looking intently through the fire. She had long, curly, gray hair and calm eyes.

"It's so good to see you, Russ. Hold my hand."

Russ reached out dutifully and held Odalis's left hand. It was thin, sinewy, old, and frail.

"Russ, don't you worry about me. I have a lot of life left, and I'm at peace with whatever comes next."

He relaxed his body but held Odalis's hand a bit tighter. He could feel one of her fingers wrap around his signet ring. It had been in the family for a long, long time and featured only a forearm and bicep on a shield.

"How's the boy?"

Russ cleared his throat from the smoke. "U is doing great. He's almost a man. He's kind. Honest. A bit sens..."

"I'm asking *them* about *you*, dear heart. I want to hear what they have to say. And I need to give them time. Now, hush up for a bit."

Russ relaxed, enjoyed the fire, and let Odalis work.

After a few minutes, Odalis squeezed his hand, turned, and stared deeply into his eyes.

"Someone close will betray you. That is done and cannot be undone. Your kin, all those far off, will give you strength."

Russ closed his eyes.

"You are about to embark on a great adventure. You know this. You've always been a wanderer." Odalis paused, but Russ knew there was more.

"You will be torn on this adventure. You do not know this. This will surprise you." Odalis paused again.

The wind blew the smoke away from them, the fire cracked and popped, and the flames licked the dark swamp air.

Odalis began again. "The rest is clouded. You know how I work. Fetch some coffee from Molly. Buy the marshmallows, too. And come right back."

Russ did as he was told. He bought the coffee and marshmallows from Molly and made some small talk. On the way back to Odalis, he grabbed two perfect roasting sticks for the marshmallows, hearing something off in the distance, probably a bird, maybe a small panther.

"Thank you for the coffee, dear heart. Hold it for me in your right hand."

Odalis looked into the fire and into the coffee.

"I see the four cards. Two cards are galloping like horsemen. I see The Fool on a fresh young horse. I see The Lovers on a wild stallion. And behind them, I see The Tower on fire."

She paused as the bonfire smoke wafted into their eyes. Russ's mind ran ahead.

"Something new and old will be birthed. You are not the father. You are not the mother. You are. You are the nurse."

"Well..." Russ began.

Odalis peered deep into the coffee, nodded, and closed her eyes.

"The fourth card is Two of Swords, dear heart. You will be forced to choose what is precious to you."

"Thank you, Odalis," he whispered, eyes closed.

"One last thing. I told you this years ago when I first read you in New Orleans."

Russ knew what was coming. He felt it in his chest before he thought it.

"It will break your heart."

10: Gladesmen

Lucky, Molly, Russ, Ocho, Zurdo, and Surge were gathered around the bonfire. Odalis had wandered out back to talk with Lucky's other, unidentified, guests. The fire kept the night mosquitoes back just far enough to make Lucky's inhabitable.

"You know, Russ, when I went to buy your marshmallows at the general store, they gave me the side eye," Molly said.

"Well, I'm sorry about that, but I really appreciate the marshmallows." Russ popped two more onto his roasting stick.

"Yeah, the fucking tourists from New York City buy rotisserie chickens and marshmallows to feed to the gators. Makes us all a food source, and that's no bueno. Marshmallows float, and them gators love 'em." Lucky said all this while he lit Zurdo's cigar with the blow torch he kept by his lawn chair.

"Now, I told Russ this, but I'm gonna tell all y'all. Unfortunately, I'm gonna need you out promptly, very promptly, by eleven fifteen p.m. tonight. That gives us almost an hour for some stories. Molly already told us the local bathtub gin story, and you've already heard my one about the unclaimed earlobe at the Gator Hook. Russ, what you got?"

Before Russ could open his mouth to speak, T-Bone came stumbling toward the bonfire, yelling, "Heeeeelp!"

He looked like he'd seen a ghost in a graveyard if it was also customary to wander through graveyards barefoot, shirtless, and in boxers.

Time stood still. Everyone stared at him. T-Bone stared back.

"Paradise needs medical attention! She ran into a beam in the shed, and I can't get her to wake up!"

Russ had known T-Bone would bring trouble. Some men seem to manufacture it.

Lucky took charge, unfazed. "Molly, will you look after our guests? Russ, let's do this. I'll get the medical kit. T-Bone, you and Russ get going, and I'll meet y'all out there."

Russ and T-Bone jogged out to the shack.

"What the hell, T-Bone?"

"Russ, okay, I can explain. Just hear me out."

"Denny is going to kill you."

"Hear me out. We were, uh, knocking boots in the shed, and all of a sudden, we saw the Skunk Ape. I mean, it was right there, looking at us while we were, you know. Anyway, it started coming toward us, so we stopped doing it. And then it came closer, and we both panicked, got up, and ran. Paradise ran right into one of the beams in the shed. Knocked her out."

"Okay. Makes sense. I hope she's..." Russ's voice trailed off as they entered the shed.

Odalis and three dark figures had Paradise sitting up against the beam and were treating her bruised forehead and bloody nose. She was thanking them.

Russ and T-Bone crouched down next to Paradise, Odalis, and the dark figures.

"It's real," Paradise said. "The Skunk Ape is real."

Just then, Lucky entered the shed with the medical kit. He treated Paradise's wounds and gave her an ice pack for her forehead.

That's when they heard the commotion back at the bonfire.

They helped Paradise to her feet, and Lucky helped her to the bonfire. Russ and T-Bone followed.

Through the humid haze and smoke, Russ saw that Ana was sitting on Zurdo's lap, making him beg for a marshmallow. Daniela and Surge were laughing with Molly about something. Two other Hot Moms were taking pictures, giggling, and trying to post to their MyBestLife social media feeds. And then there was another woman chatting with Ocho. It appeared to be a happy, post-divorce Elana.

It was eleven o'clock.

Lucky walked Paradise back to the bus, and Russ went with them. When they reached the bus, they could hear Denny snoring.

Lucky woke Denny up and did the talking. "Denny, thanks for the visit. Russ has your pay for driving. As you can see, Paradise had a big night."

"Denny, I saw the Skunk Ape. He was huge, and big, and real. He's real. It was amazing." Paradise was still icing her forehead.

"Wow," Denny responded groggily.

"She saw the Skunk Ape, got startled, and ran into one of the beams in the shed. That's how she got the bruise and the swollen nose. We don't think it's broken, but y'all should get it checked out," Lucky explained. "The Weston wives drove out to retrieve their husbands, so you're off the hook for driving them back. Have a safe trip home."

With Paradise taken care of, Lucky and Russ headed toward a parking lot occupied by a minivan, a white SUV, and a lime-colored Porsche.

"Just another fine night in the swamp. Thanks for coming out, Russ."

"You think that was the Skunk Ape?"

"One hundred percent, son. Plenty of folks here have seen it. You know that."

Russ nodded.

"Soooo ... you gonna tell me who your VIP guests are?"

"Nope."

"They're the Gladesmen, aren't they?"

"They're my guests and my business. I hope you'll respect that."

"I'll take it to the grave."

"Good man. Be safe driving home. You know we love having you here. Everyone is welcome in the swamp."

Russ's old watch told him it was 11:14 p.m., and they needed to roll. He gave Lucky a quick hug and turned to go.

The swamp was so quiet that the bus's cranky engine created a mood-shattering din. Lucky said something over his shoulder as he walked away, but Russ couldn't quite catch it.

He waved to Elana and T-Bone. "T-Bone, do you think you can squeeze into Elana's tiny Porsche?" he called out.

T-Bone couldn't hear Russ over the car engines and did the "I can't hear you" gesture.

Elana smiled.

11: Jefe

Pop, pop, pop, pop.

Russ sat in Coral Gables traffic as his replacement rental car was pelted with South Florida rain.

What they say is true. Miami cloudbursts sound like popping corn when they hit the windshield.

Something jarred his memory. A Bible verse. What was it?

"HAL, what is the Bible verse that says He makes the rain fall on the evil and the good?"

"Matthew 5:45. The text reads, 'He makes his sun rise on the evil and the good and sends rain on the just and the unjust.'"

"Thank you, HAL. The rain is falling on both of us today. What do you think that means?" Russ asked.

"Heavy tropical rain degrades the road conditions. Decrease your speed and increase the distance between your vehicle and other vehicles."

Russ sat in traffic with the popcorn rain and HAL.

"HAL, thank you again for that. For some reason, I thought it was in Ecclesiastes."

"You're welcome, Russ. It does sound like something one would read in Ecclesiastes."

"HAL, I'm sorry to bother you again."

"Russ, you're not bothering me at all. How can I help you?"

"What is the Bible verse about numbering our days? Can you read me that?"

"Yes, Russ. The verse is Psalm 90:12. 'Teach us to number our days, that we may gain a heart of wisdom.'"

"Thank you, HAL."

The rain came down. It reminded him of the first time he met Jefe. If it hadn't been for a severe rainstorm, none of this would be happening today. He wouldn't have spent extra time with the man who became a father to him. He wouldn't have prospered under Jefe's guidance. He wouldn't be here, right now, driving to say goodbye.

He hated hospital goodbyes, covered in a veneer of fake hygiene.

His sunglasses alerted him that he was one right turn away from the hospital. Russ obeyed the flashing green arrow in the sunglasses, dutifully parked the car, and trudged into the hospital, forgetting his umbrella and still thinking about the heart of wisdom.

Jefe was frail, pale, and much too thin. It was hard to believe that such a force of nature could grow old and die, but Russ noticed that his eyes were still as sharp as ever. They still hummed with energy, as though they were trapped in another man's body. A dying man.

Russ could maintain a poker face with most people, but he couldn't with Jefe. His tears flowed freely, and he didn't care.

"Russ, mi hijo, hold my hand."

He'd expected Jefe to be hooked up to all manner of life-preserving equipment. There was none in sight.

"The time is so short. I have many things I need you to do for me when I am gone. I have detailed instructions about who will and will not lead the movement after me. They are all in this envelope."

His feeble arms struggled to lift the envelope and hand it over. It shook with the effort, and when Russ grabbed it, Jefe visibly relaxed.

"When you read through my instructions, keep one thing in mind," he rasped. "All leaders make mistakes. I have made many. And I need those mistakes to be cleaned up. I know I can trust you to clean these up."

"Understood."

"You know, I had always hoped that I would be buried in Cuba. But that is a dream that will not happen. America is my country now, but Cuba is my home. I had hoped I could go home. Will you say the rosary with me?"

Russ wasn't Catholic, and he'd only prayed the rosary with his grandparents as a child. But he took one of two rosaries hanging near the hospital bed and knelt next to Jefe.

"You lead," he whispered.

Russ grew restless at the monotony of the rosary. His mind wandered. Was Jefe's behavior emergency piety, eleventh-hour religiosity, a conversion on the cross? He was a ruthless political boss, a master politician, an ardent nationalist, and untroubled at the prospect of violence to achieve a political objective. It was shocking. Jefe was a great man and a man of action. And here he was, rosary in hand.

They continued to pray the rosary.

If there was an Almighty, omniscient, and transcending time, why would He need to hear from any of us? The best Russ could conceive of was an ancient and all-knowing clockmaker who had set the universe in motion, written its rules, and returned to His throne. This conception absolved Him of the misery and tragedy of human history. Any greater involvement in human affairs would make Him complicit.

They continued to pray the rosary.

It was surprising to Russ that a powerful man would concede to a greater power here or beyond. Beyond this, there was a gulf between Jefe's religiosity and his behavior. Jefe was no saint. He was a hypocrite praying with the same mouth that had spoken violence.

They continued to pray the rosary.

Russ realized, with a smile and a nod, that he himself was also praying and also a hypocrite.

"Amen. Russ, thank you."

"It was my pleasure, Jefe."

"You know, I just noticed how broken your rosary is. I mean, it's not really your rosary. It's Maria's. It has broken beads, and some of the metal links have been crushed. I never noticed that before."

Russ's chest tightened, and he momentarily broke eye contact.

"I thought she would be a son. But God gave me a beautiful daughter. And then much later in life, as an old man, He gave me a son." Jefe's eyes held Russ's.

Russ closed his eyes as tears began to form.

"What were the baby names? What were you going to name Maria?" Russ asked, changing the subject.

"Prospero."

"Prospero? Is it a family name?"

"No. It's from your Shakespeare. When Dominga was pregnant, I was trying to master English, and I was studying *The Tempest*. Prospero is the hero, a magician, an exile."

"How, after all these years, have I never heard this story?"

"It's a funny thing to discuss, I think. You can bring it up on those fancy sunglasses of yours," Jefe said with strained laughter. Russ could see that the laughter hurt, and it made his chest tighten. "You know, in Spanish, we call sunglasses gafas de sol. I think that sounds better. Are your sunglasses Spectaculars?"

"No. I always break my sunglasses, so why waste the money."

"I hate them," said Jefe. "I don't need to be told what I'm seeing. Bring up *The Tempest* on your fancy gafas de sol."

"Display Shakespeare's *Tempest*," Russ commanded. Within seconds, the play was centered in his field of vision.

"Read me the end," Jefe said.

"En Ingles o Espanol?"

"Ingles."

Russ began to read the epilogue. He didn't have the energy to read it theatrically. He read it slow and flat, like a river in drought.

"Now my charms are all overthrown,
And what strength I have's mine own,
Which is most faint: now, 'tis true,
I must be here confined by you,
Or sent to Naples. Let me not,
Since I have my dukedom got
And pardon'd the deceiver, dwell
In this bare island by your spell;
But release me from my bands
With the help of your good hands:
Gentle breath of yours my sails
Must fill, or else my project fails,
Which was to please. Now I want
Spirits to enforce, art to enchant,
And my ending is despair,
Unless I be relieved by prayer,

Which pierces so that it assaults
Mercy itself and frees all faults.
As you from crimes would pardon'd be,
Let your indulgence set me free.

When Russ finished reading, he noticed that Jefe's eyes were closed and that he was at peace.

12: Flames

Russ assumed the worst, but then he noticed Jefe's chest rising and falling.

"Russ, I have changed my mind."

"What do you mean?"

"The past must not rule the future. I have always thirsted for vengeance cloaked in justice. The movement will need to evolve, and I must let it."

"I understand," Russ said in a whisper. "What do you want me to do with the envelope?"

"Burn it. Burn the envelope. There are files in the International Bank of the Everglades. I need you to burn those, too."

"I will do it."

"Call Dump. Have him delete all of the files he has built for me."

"Understood."

"Thank you, mi hijo. They'll send me home soon. I will not die in this hospital. They're giving me three weeks. Please visit me next week at home."

"I will."

"I am tired, Russ. I need to rest. Gracias, mi hijo."

Jefe squeezed Russ's hand and closed his eyes. Russ sat by his bed in a loud, hard silence, his ears ringing. He was exhausted and emotionally spent. He focused on one breath at a time and tried to let his body relax, but it tightened.

And then he heard it, a slow, faint click-clack on the hospital hall floor. Click clack. It grew louder, still in a slow, rhythmic click-clack. Heels on a polished floor. It stopped short of Jefe's room. Russ knew exactly who it was.

Russ slowly got to his feet, feeling dizzy as he rose. He wiped the tears off his face and fixed his hair.

Then, he walked out of Jefe's hospital room to meet Maria.

13: Mi Cielo

Maria always had her father's eyes—black as night, intense, hypnotic. The hospital was gray and cold, but her energy defied the place.

"Hello, Russ." Maria's voice was soft, almost a little hoarse, like a gentle but persistent wind bringing back memories. "Thank you for visiting Dad. He was so excited about your visit. You mean the world to him."

"Your father is the most impressive man I have ever met."

"That is very kind." Maria's eyes softened and expanded, filling the hospital hallway.

She gave out a faint, smiling laugh. "Now, Russ," she said, gently touching his arm. "Can you tell me why you're holding my first-grade rosary?"

"Well, I was praying it with your father. I didn't know..."

Maria blinked her eyes and smiled, telling Russ to stop.

"You always were the sweetest of Daddy's..." Maria stopped before she said "henchmen." "Do you even know how to pray the rosary? You're not even..." Maria swallowed her words again.

"Well, I think I just learned."

"In that case, it is yours." Maria closed Russ's hands around the rosary and squeezed it.

"How have you been, Maria?" Russ cocked his head to the left and waited.

"I'm spending as much time as possible with Dad. The doctors tell me this and that, but I know he's dying of a broken heart. He misses Mom. You know how they were. It's hard right now, Russ. All of Dad's associates want me to carry the torch, to carry on the family business. But my business is real estate, not politics. My Dad built a movement of dispossessed people. I'm a builder, too, but in a more concrete sense. Only Dad understands."

Russ simply nodded, catching a glimpse of the storm of emotions behind the night-black eyes.

"Tell me, Russ. I want to know. Dime que hay dentro. Tell me what's inside."

"Maria, I think you would make a very bad politician, but I think you would be a great leader."

"Tesoro, that is what you are thinking. But that isn't what I asked."

14: Housecleaning

Melissa messages Russ on his sunglasses.

Goddessof War Vibe check. How was the hospital?

202.111.1111 Rough day

Goddessof War How is he?

202.111.1111 3 weeks to live ... according to docs

Goddessof War I'm sorry

Goddessof War Whatcha doin now?

202.111.1111 Handling some things for Jefe

Goddessof War understatement

202.111.1111 How's DefCon1?

Goddessof War Need more convention space and a better support firm. Lots of stuff about using AI to simulate adversaries – which is old, but... The usual stuff. Boring dinners.

202.111.1111 How was "On the MIC?"

Goddessof War Haha. It was good. Good Q&A. Like no one got the acronym ... lol

202.111.1111 Military Industrial Complex. How do military people not get acronyms?

Goddessof War Lol No idea

202.111.1111 How's U?

Goddessof War Just studying. All good. OK. Gotta get back to DefCon1... Mel out.

Russ switched to a disposable burner phone and called Dump. Dump picked up on the first ring.

"ACME Janitorial Supply..."

"Hey, this is Russ."

"Go on."

"Talked to the bus driver. He said he's moving on and needs his house cleaned out."

"Got it. I'll clean it out today."

"Thanks, Dump. Oh, and what did you find about the reporter?"

"Nothing. He's boring. And clean."

"OK. Thanks. Talk later."

Russ ended the call and sat quietly in the car, Jefe's envelope his only passenger.

"HAL, I'm too tired to drive. Please program the car for the International Bank of the Everglades in Everglades City."

In moments, the car pulled out of the hospital parking lot. The skies had cleared, but the roads had not. It was going to take a while.

"HAL, why don't you take a break and shut down for a bit."

"Shutting down," HAL replied.

Russ grabbed the burner phone again and dialed Stephen Flagler.

"Surge, how are you doing?"

"Just a busy day at the office. I'm having coffee at the moment. Glad the sun came out. How are you? Oh, and I didn't know you had a Miami phone number."

"I'm good. It's temporary."

"Oh."

"Talked to the bus driver. He said he's moving on and needs his closet cleaned out. Can you call ahead and let them know I will be cleaning the closet today?"

"Cleaned out and leaving?"

"Yes."

"Will handle now."

"Thank you, Surge."

Russ dialed Lucky.

"Lucky, it's Russ."

"Hey, Russ. New phone?"

"Something like that."

"You comin' to visit?" Lucky asked.

"Yup. I'll be there in a few hours and need to roast a lot of marshmallows."

"Alright. How big of a fire do you need, son?"

"Big."

"You got it."

"See you soon, Lucky. And say hello to Molly for me."

Russ ended the call, closed his eyes, and tried to sleep. The car drove him and the envelope west on Old 41, past Lucky's, across the Everglades, and to Everglades City.

"Approaching Everglades City," HAL announced.

HAL's voice eased Russ out of his automotive slumber.

"HAL, please tell me about Everglades City," Russ said as he rubbed his eyes. He had been to Everglades City before. He wanted to hear how HAL described it.

"Everglades City is a city in Southwest Florida. It has an estimated population of 500. It is part of the Naples and Marco Island Metropolitan Statistical Area. Located in Collier County, it was once the county seat. It is located along the Barron River on Chokoloskee Bay. It is situated north of the Ten Thousand Islands and the Gulf of Mexico. Its average high temperature in November is 84 degrees Fahrenheit. It was notably destroyed by Hurricane Donna on September 10, 1960. The historic Rod & Rifle Club was destroyed by fire during a Category 5..."

"Thank you, HAL. That was very helpful. I get the picture."

Russ's car arrived at the International Bank of the Everglades, directly across the street from what was left of the old Rod & Rifle Club. There was very little evidence that anyone was in Everglades City, much less anyone working at the old bank. There were a few cars parked about, and so Russ assumed that someone would give him access to the safe. He exited his car and walked toward the two-story, tropical-blue bank. A little sign on the front noted that it was built in 1927 and added to the US National Register of Historic Places in 1999.

Russ was a little surprised when he found the bank door unlocked. Walking inside was like walking into another time, a perfect time capsule, an actual bank from a time when there were banks, checks, cash, and no GCB.

The noise from the opening door startled a young woman making a charcoal drawing at a table once reserved for very important bank business. She was wearing a retro bank outfit circa 1927. Jumping to her feet, she was simultaneously surprised by Russ's entry and excited to have a visitor.

"Welcome to the Bank of the Everglades, where progress and opportunity meet!"

Russ had to smile. It was like she was working in a banking theme park. And she was so excited to throw down the old bank motto.

"I don't know how to say this, but is this one of those things where I should get into character, or can I just be present-day?"

The young woman smiled, picked up a clipboard, and asked, "Are you here for a guided tour of the bank?"

"No. I'm just here for business. One of my colleagues from Trans-Oceanic Trading should have called and let you know I would be coming."

"Oh, that's right. I'm sorry. I didn't know. It's all good. I just have to do this schtick for tourists. The Historical Society bought the bank, and we mostly give tours. It's not really much of a 'bank.'" The ersatz Roaring Twenties' "banker" used air quotes when she said "bank."

Russ laughed out loud and decided to play along.

"This is a fine and prosperous city, and this banking establishment is a well-known commercial success. My associate at Trans-Oceanic Trading should have telephoned ahead to let you know of my impending arrival." Russ had absolutely no idea how Americans spoke in the 1920s and was winging it.

"I'm pleased to report that they did indeed phone ahead, and I'm prepared to offer you our finest service. My name is Tallulah Windward, and I will be pleased to assist you this afternoon."

Russ wasn't sure he could keep up. He didn't think he could stay in character, or whatever this was, for any real length of time.

"OK. My name's Stephen Flagler. I'm not very good at this. But this is just so fun. OK. Your name can't possibly be Tallulah Windward."

"It's my bank name," Tallulah said, winking.

Russ broke into laughter. Tallulah broke into laughter. Echoes careened through the bank like an empty canyon.

"I'm sorry," Russ said. "I've had a hard day, and I just don't think I can keep up with you. Can we communicate in the modern era?"

"It's all good," Tallulah said. "I'm not an actor. I'm actually an art student. This is just an easy job that gives me a ton of time to do my classwork. It pays well, and I give an occasional historical tour. I have to admit, I love the tours and the outfits."

"Am I your first visitor today?" Russ asked.

"No. I had a couple of German tourists take a tour. I had to use the translator on my phone to tell them in German that they couldn't open an account. It was kinda weird."

"So, does this 'bank' do any actual 'banking' now?" Russ asked.

"Honestly, I think we transferred all the old accounts to a bank in Bonita. At this point, I think most of the folks with accounts are dead."

"Well, the good news is that I'm here from Trans-Oceanic to retrieve the firm's property and close our account, which, at this point, is doing you a favor."

"Are you taking the safe with you?" Tallulah asked.

"I'm sorry. What?"

"The safe is the property of Trans-Oceanic Trading—the safe AND its contents."

"Let's go take a look at the safe," Russ said.

"Capital idea!" Tallulah enthused.

The two walked together with Tallulah leading the way, passing the teller windows, entering the wide-open vault, and arriving at Trans-Oceanic's safe. It was huge, man-sized, industrial, inaccessible gray, and bolted to the ground.

Russ was not expecting to encounter an entire safe. My God. What could Jefe have stored in this thing?

"Miss Windward, can I have some privacy?"

"Of course! I'll be working on my sketches," Tallulah replied.

With Tallulah out of sight, Russ sat down on the floor, leaned up against the massive safe, opened Jefe's envelope, and began searching for the combination for the lock. And there it was, written right across the receipt for the safe itself, which was apparently installed in March 1961.

Russ stood, methodically entered the combination code, and opened the safe door. The first thing he noticed was the smell. If the Cold War had a smell, this was it—metallic, chemical, industrial.

There were three cardboard file boxes neatly placed one to a shelf, and there were three dusty metal boxes on the bottom shelf. A quick glance in the cardboard boxes found typed dossiers of what Russ could only assume were a spectrum of Jefe's enemies and friends, including a few long-dead Members of Congress, virtually every Florida Governor he could remember, both of Florida's Senators and what appeared to be every Member of the Florida legislature up to the present. These would be easy to throw in the trunk and easier to burn. Russ felt a little sad at the thought of burning so many hours of Dump's best work.

Russ then turned his attention to the three metal boxes. They were extremely heavy. The locking mechanisms on each box were rusted, bent, and timeworn. Russ just couldn't open them with his bare hands. They would go in the trunk, too.

Russ quickly moved the cardboard and metal boxes one by one to the car, passing Tallulah as she was working quietly on her art school sketches. When he had loaded everything into the car, he said a waving goodbye to Tallulah. Tallulah smiled, waved back, recorded an additional tourist visitor to the bank for that day, and returned to her sketching. Russ slid into the car and made his way back across the Everglades to Lucky's.

The sun set behind Russ as his car sped east across the Everglades on Old 41. By 6:30, Russ knew he was getting close to Loop Road.

Russ's sunglasses lit up.

SafeCor You have entered an unsafe area.

SafeCor Your location has a high rate of violent crime.

SafeCor Location tracking unavailable.

It happened every time.

Russ took manual control, passed Lucky's open gate, and parked the car by the old Lucky Strike sign. Lucky had built a sizable bonfire and was sitting next to Molly, enjoying the blaze. There was no sign of Odalis. When Russ exited the car, Lucky just nodded his head slightly and smiled.

Lucky had built what outdoorsmen call a log cabin fire lay and had done so with a very wide base. It was the perfect campfire lay for cremating dossiers. Russ opened the trunk, carried the first cardboard box to the fire, and placed it right on top of the highest rung of logs, like a burnt offering to the gods. By the time Russ sat down on an old rocking chair next to Lucky, the first cardboard box was already lighting up like a torch. The three sat in silence, listening to the hisses and crackles of the fire. Russ was surprised by how quickly each cardboard box was incinerated.

All of the records of plotting, of opposition research, of incriminating evidence against friend and foe was up in smoke, gone.

"How was the drive?" Lucky asked.

"Uneventful," Russ replied as he stared into the fire.

"Shiiiiit, son. Really?" Lucky wasn't having any of it.

"Yup. Roads weren't that busy."

"Everglades City?" Lucky asked.

"Where's Odalis?" Russ asked.

"Isn't that her business, son? She's back in Nola."

The three returned to silence and burning dossiers.

"When are you flying back to Washington, DC?" Lucky asked.

"Early tomorrow," Russ replied as he casually tossed his burner phone onto the fire.

"Lucky, before I forget, do you have a hammer and a crowbar?"

"Oh, this is gonna be good, isn't it? I'll get the tools," Lucky said.

Lucky met Russ at the car. They unloaded the metal boxes and stared at them for a moment.

Finally, Russ grabbed the crowbar and began pounding the first metal box with all his strength. The box collapsed inward as he poured out his wrath upon it, bending the crowbar as it became hot in his hands.

After a few minutes had passed, Lucky cleared his throat. "Son, why beat the hell out of the thing when you can just use mineral oil and open it?" He waved Russ away from the metal boxes, hunched down, and began spraying the hinges and locks with lubricant.

"Wanna do the honors?" Lucky asked when he finished.

Russ threw down the bent crowbar, kneeled, and opened each metal box with ease.

Lucky had his hands on his hips and head down, taking it all in. "Holy shit, Russ. Tell me true. Did you kill a leprechaun?"

Gold coins glistened in the firelight.

Russ pulled a shining coin out of one box and began inspecting it. On one side of the coin was the image of a deer. On the other side was the profile of a man with a long beard. "Well, looks like these three wise men came bearing gifts from, let's see, Suid Afrika."

"You don't want to switch these coins out for GCB?" Lucky asked.

"They aren't mine to switch, and you know I think crypto is bullshit."

"Any more bullshit than cheap paper a government tells you is worth something?" Lucky asked.

Russ wasn't listening.

Molly joined them, and the three began reading the minting dates of the coins, none minted after the mid-1970s. All three calculated that the Krugerrand treasure was placed in the metal boxes in the early 1980s.

"Lucky, can I leave this with y'all? I can't take it with me."

Lucky took a deep breath and exhaled slowly. "Is anyone missing it?" he asked.

"No. I wouldn't do that to you."

"And you're not telling me anything more about how you came into it?"

"No."

"All right," Lucky said. "They'll be safe here in the swamp."

15: Lo Siento

Russ closed his eyes and tried to rest on the flight back to Washington. But the cabin was noisy with chatty DC denizens power networking at 30,000 feet. The plane gyrated between hot cabin air and cold cabin air. It had the usual morning flight aroma of coffee, microwaved eggs, and flatulence. He tried some slow, deep breathing, but that achieved nothing. When he gave up and decided to message Melissa, the flight attendant announced that the Wi-Fi was down. It was the everyday flight experience. Anything better might have been surprising. America was a superpower with eleven carrier strike groups, tech billionaires, and the beginnings of a moon base, but it couldn't make air travel enjoyable.

Once they were on the tarmac, Russ's sunglasses immediately lit up with Sm0ke$ignal message notifications.

Something had happened. It was like smelling the rain before the storm.

Russ called Melissa first.

"Hey, Mel, just landed."

"How was the flight?"

"The usual. Getting off the plane now. How's your day?"

"Quiet day. Standard meetings, some paperwork, and then working with the staff on the Board Meeting agenda. We're all wiped from DefCon1. I can't wait to get home and hit the gym."

"You just emceed a huge trade show. I'm sure you're exhausted. God."

"Yup. Kinda going through the motions today. Thanks for calling. Gotta prep for my next meeting. I have a random call about some recruiting movie the Pentagon wants to make, some big alien movie."

"Hasn't Hollywood already done that? Weird."

"I know, right? I need them to feature some of the membership's hardware. Anyway, gotta go."

"All right. Good luck!"

Melissa hung up, and Russ immediately had an incoming call flash on his sunglasses. It was Surge.

"I heard the news first on local radio. I'm sorry."

"What news?" Russ asked.

"Oh. Uh. Jefe passed away last night. I'm sorry to be the one to tell you first. It's all over the news here."

Russ felt heavy. He scanned for somewhere at National to sit down and found a table and chair outside an airport souvenir shop advertising this year's White House Christmas ornament.

"Russ, you ok?"

"Yeah. Just needed to find somewhere quiet." Russ exhaled, focusing on his breathing. "Thanks for letting me know, pal. Now I know why I have all these messages."

"Are you going to be okay?" Surge asked.

"Yeah, I'll be okay. At least I was able to say goodbye yesterday. There's just so much more I wish I could have said. Thanks for letting me know. I appreciate you."

Air travelers streamed past, all in a rush to be somewhere else. Russ closed his eyes and focused on his breathing. It was hard to believe that a man with Jefe's life energy, a man he remembered standing on a car and speaking to a crowd, could actually die. The man was a dynamo. Where did all that life force go when he died?

Russ's sunglasses alerted him to an incoming call from a 305 number, and he took it.

"Russ, he's gone," Maria said, holding back tears.

"Maria, I just heard. I'm so sorry."

"The doctors said many weeks, and he died in his sleep last night."

The pain in Maria's voice was sharp, jagged. Russ could feel it. It made his chest tight and his eyes well up.

"Lo siento, Maria. Lo siento."

Maria was crying on the phone. It was a low moan followed by a whispered, almost noiseless scream. Russ simply listened to her cry. After a few minutes of crying, Maria cleared her throat.

"I'm alone now, Russ. Dad is with Mom. I'm alone."

Russ couldn't find words and simply exhaled in sympathy.

"I said goodbye to him this morning. He looked peaceful. I think he died in peace."

"Lo siento, Maria."

"His face was so cold, Russ. I kissed his forehead and said goodbye."

"I'm sure that was very, very hard. I'm so sorry."

"Russ, thank you for talking with me. It was wonderful to see you. I'm going to walk for a bit and then deal with the funeral. I just don't have energy for it right now."

"Maria, your father loved you very, very much. Please keep remembering that. I'm sure it is hard to hear the reporting on him right now. Just rest for a bit."

"Thank you, Russ."

"Lo siento, Maria. You're strong. Please rest now, at least for a little bit."

Russ powered down his sunglasses. He collected his luggage, found his car in the DCA parking garage, and programmed it for the office. Then he hung the rosary over the rearview mirror.

Russ's car made its way across the 14th Street bridge, cut across the National Mall, veered left onto K Street, and approached the underground parking for G.O.S. headquarters. Russ scrolled down the driver's side window and waited while the ticketing machine read his access fob. The car parked itself. Russ grabbed his work bag and the rosary and made his way to the elevators.

When the elevator opened, he was in G.O.S. headquarters. A colossal G.O.S. logo was etched into the smoked glass in the lobby. It was a globe set at an angle. The latitude lines were replaced by stylized arrows of varying thicknesses. Four of the latitude lines contained Latin text with one Latin word per latitude line. Together they read "navigare cum ventis mutationis"—navigating the winds of change.

Russ walked to his office and unlocked the door with his finger. His office featured a modern, standing desk, two monitors, a small meeting table, and a whiteboard for each client. The desk was covered with family photos, travel mementos, and several bobbleheads, including a Thomas Edison bobblehead and an Abraham Lincoln bobblehead.

Russ had just started reading and responding to emails when Ruth stopped by, leaning against his office door frame.

"Hello, Russ. Do you have a few minutes?"

"Sure." Russ knew immediately that this would take more than a few minutes. "How about we get some coffee and chat in your office? Mine is a mess."

"Great idea. Oh, by the way, how was the Florida trip?"

"Made a few memories with my son, standard tourist stuff."

The two walked to the kitchen, past the team dining table littered with leftover takeout boxes, and to the sleek new coffee maker. Calling it a coffee maker was an undersell. It made all manner of warm beverages and to a boggling level of specificity. The interface emphasized sleekness over actual function, and Russ hated it. All he wanted was black coffee. Ruth ordered the most complex hot drink he could have ever conceptualized. But, when it was his turn with the drink maker, Russ simply selected hot coffee, hitting "NO" to something like six drink optimization screens. With warm beverages in hand, they walked to Ruth's office.

The pictures had been taken down off the walls, there were cardboard files, and her desk had a distinct lack of, well, anything. Something was definitely afoot.

They sat on a V-shaped sofa, legs crossed, holding their warm cups of robot hot drinks.

"Russ, we have worked together for a long time. I'm not going to sugarcoat this."

"I respect that. What's up?"

"As you know, we occasionally talk to potential buyers. We were offered a very good deal and will be taking it. This offers our longtime equity holders, like you, a lucrative exit."

"Who are we selling to?"

"Cold Harbor Venture Capital Partners. Kieran Gamble helped broker the deal."

Russ looked down. He despised the Cold Harbor guys. They would cut the place to the bone to pull another dime out of it. And Kieran Gamble was worse. He was one of Russ's first hires, duplicitous, a Washington scorpion.

"Okay. Makes sense," Russ said.

"This deal will also represent an exit for me, Russ."

The two shared a look for a few seconds.

"What's next?" Russ asked.

"You know I've been planning a run for Governor in Virginia for a long, long time. And now is the right time to do it. The firm is in a solid position for future growth, and it is time for the next ... for both of us."

"I see," Russ said, shifting in his chair.

"Russ, I negotiated strong exits for you, me, the CFO, and some of the redundant support staff. I think you'll be very pleased."

Russ had nothing to say. Between Jefe's death, the travel, and tonight's award, he was already depleted. He could feel himself breaking inside.

"You're right, Ruth. There is a time for everything. What's next?"

"Russ, you'll be paid handsomely for your equity. And you'll receive a very generous severance. I pushed Cold Harbor to retain you. They saw that it was financially advantageous. But, they were concerned about the reputational overhang from your client base, and they felt that a full separation would protect the new G.O.S."

"Reputational overhang?"

"Yes. Some of your clients don't pass the front-page test. Cold Harbor has reservations about your South Florida clients. Having Gavin Dirken sniffing about hasn't made it easier. Then they freaked out about Trans-Oceanic."

"Ruth, we don't normally make our hot money polishing halos on angels."

Ruth laughed. "Perhaps we should have translated that into Latin for our logo."

The two leaned back, cradling their warm drinks.

"I'm sorry. I wanted to tell you sooner, Russ. But you were on vacation with your beautiful boy, and I didn't want to ruin that time. I thought we had a deal early last week when you were on vacation. The deal would have included you staying. But then, they freaked out about the headline risk on Mr. Matul. My condolences, by the way."

"So, you cut the deal. I'm sure Brent figured this was a good exit. And I don't blame him. He's going to be the king of western Louisiana."

"That's right, Russ. He knew it was time. I knew it was time. I tried to keep you here as part of the deal. I failed."

"Ruth, I completely understand."

"We have until the end of the week to clear out. The purchase announcement is imminent."

"Imminent?" Russ asked.

"Late this afternoon. Cold Harbor was eager to announce the deal. I'm hoping this doesn't complicate your award ceremony. The timing isn't good for that. I'm sorry."

Russ focused on his breathing, his smile, and his nonverbals.

"Ruth, I completely understand. This is a perfectly logical business decision."

"I knew you would. I also know how hard this is for you. It's hard for both of us. We both grew up here in the firm. Oh, one last thing: you can transition all of your core clients to your next venture. Cold Harbor needs a clean break. So, you'll have to let your clients know ASAP. We have two weeks to clean out our offices, but that shouldn't be a problem. I'll be out by the end of the day."

"Well, we had a good run together, didn't we?"

"Yes, Russ, we did. We built a global enterprise." At the word "global," Ruth raised her open palms to signal the scale of the enterprise.

"Does the staff know yet?"

"Not yet. I will start the cascade shortly, email all staff, and then make an announcement on the floor."

"Understood. I'll start contacting my clients now, then walk over to ANN studios."

Ruth extended her hand. "Russ, it was a pleasure working with you for all these years. Let's grab coffee in a few weeks after all this dust settles."

Russ and Ruth shook hands, hugged, and swung into motion.

Russ walked back to his office and closed the door.

"HAL, can you help me with something?" Russ asked.

"Certainly, what do you need?"

"I need you to compose and send an email to my client contact list at 6:30 p.m. Eastern tonight."

"Certainly," HAL responded.

"It should have the title "Continuing To Serve You 24/7.""

"Check." Russ taught HAL to respond with "check" when receiving a string of detailed instructions.

"The email should read 'I have some exciting news. After years of growth, G.O.S. is building on this momentum by joining the Cold Harbor Group of companies. It is a time for new beginnings. I will continue serving you, but in a new corporate structure organized under my new firm—1st & J Street. This new firm will maintain its tight focus on winning for clients. I will reach out this evening to schedule a brief phone call with you tomorrow and to answer any questions that you may have. In your service, Russ.' Got it?"

"Check"

"Feel free to improve it. I don't need to see a new version before you send it," Russ explained.

"Check."

"Thanks, HAL."

"You're very welcome, Russ."

The clients would be fine. He could call them in the morning. They didn't bother to read consulting trade gossip and didn't care about it. It was all inside baseball to them. The media cycle was already crowded with post-election news and the world careening from one crisis to the next.

As standalone news, the sale and Russ's spin-off would be a one-day story at best and would have limited coverage and appeal. What he didn't want was for it to hijack his TV appearance in an hour. That would spread the story.

Would he need something big to talk about and burn time?

Russ estimated the segment would be a maximum of five minutes in length. Roughly a minute would be intro around the elections with the anchor's voiceover. That left four minutes. There would be another two minutes of focused roundtable soundbites about the elections. It wouldn't be a real discussion, just spouting of soundbites and talking points. That would leave two minutes for the award ceremony. There were three consultants being awarded. He'd choose to be awarded last, if they would let him. If no one raised it by then, he could run out the clock without needing a distraction.

But what if ANN read about the sale just before airtime? They'd give him no quarter. He knew that. If ANN gave any indication that they had heard about the sale, Russ would need to preempt them with bigger news.

16: The Dapper, Circa 2003

"Tractor Man" had driven his farm tractor into a pond on the National Mall. For whatever reason, this threw Washington traffic into the mother of all gridlock.

Russ and Alex were running late to a client meeting, but there was nothing that could be done about it.

The two weren't going anywhere. They were stuck in Alex's car with time to kill.

"Alex, one of these days, you're going to have to give me lessons in how to dress," Russ said.

Alex was wearing a light brown pinstripe suit, a yellow and purple paisley tie, a sharp pocket square, and tortoiseshell glasses. Russ calculated that Alex's ensemble was probably worth two weeks of pay at G.O.S.

"Thank you," said Alex. "I'd be delighted to introduce you to Mr. K. and give you some pointers when you have the time." Alex signaled and changed lanes, but it wasn't going to get them there any sooner.

"I have to tell you something," Russ said.

"What's that?"

"When I won my first campaign and moved to DC, I remember watching you on the Sunday talk shows. I remember the suits."

"Russ, there's a backstory on this."

"I'm all ears," Russ said.

"When you saw me on TV, I was the Press Secretary for the Speaker of the House. But, before that big election, I was just one of 435 Press Secretaries. I was a Hill denizen, unsuccessfully dating, and badly out of shape. When we won the majority, I was elated. I was going to get national exposure on national television. But, there was a problem."

"What's that?"

"A very smart broadcast reporter and friend took me aside and said, 'Alex, you have a problem. You're overweight. You can't lose it before the inaugural. The camera won't be friendly, and the print reporters will only give you one adjective.'"

"One adjective?" Russ asked.

"Yes, she explained that reporters would devote but one adjective to describe me—'the BLANK,' you get the idea—'the corpulent Alex' or 'the jowly Alex' or 'the girthy Alex.'"

"Oh," Russ said.

"Exactly. They wouldn't just say 'fat'. They'd find a euphemism. So, I asked her what I should do. She told me to give them my one adjective."

"And that adjective was?" Russ asked, lengthening the was.

"Dapper. There was one problem, Russ. I didn't have a dapper wardrobe."

"Oh, then how did you..."

"My friend immediately introduced me to Mr. K. I put a rush on everything: the suits, the shirts, the ties. And I gave them their adjective," Alex said.

"And the adjective was 'dapper,'" Russ said, thinking.

"It worked. They were so distracted by the clothes that they overlooked the weight."

"Well, ain't that some Sun Tzu shit," Russ said as he stared out into gridlocked Washington traffic.

17: Prime Time

"Someone used their special eye cream before he walked over," said Zainab, smiling. She wrapped Russ in a cosmetics cape and snapped the button.

"Thanks, Z. The stuff is magic." Russ closed his eyes, awaiting base powder and enjoying the calm of the ANN makeup room.

"You're not using facial cream at night, and you did not use sunscreen. Bad boy." Zainab always chastised Russ for this.

"Well, you're the expert. I should do that. Sorry." Russ didn't really care, but he had to admit that Z was right. She was right about anything involving makeup. That was obvious. But she was also right about everything related to ANN, the producers, the bookers, the on-air talent, and the guests. The makeup room was where everything got dished.

"I'm the expert. And if you obey all my beauty tips, your wife will never leave you."

"I appreciate you, Z."

"What are you talking about tonight?" asked Z.

"Just the elections and their aftermath," Russ said in a hushed manner as Z leaned over him and applied powder. By his own calculation, he had to have worn more makeup than 99.99 percent of men. It was just a part of the studio experience. Sometimes, he would do a segment early in the day, walk back to the office, and forget he was wearing it.

Z looked disapprovingly at Russ's hair. "Russ, you need a better hairstylist. I'm going to do what I can and then lock it with hairspray and gel. Oh, and who is anchoring your segment?"

"Stirling."

"Yes, I did him earlier today. He's wearing a charcoal suit and a blue tie. He can be difficult, but he is a gorgeous man." Z was describing the up-and-coming Stirling Kingsley, ANN's most celebrated young anchor, indistinguishable from a human Ken Doll and spawned from an old money Savannah political dynasty.

"Yeah, he's definitely built for broadcast," Russ observed. He had a funny image of rows and rows of genetically engineered ANN news anchors growing in glowing blue chambers.

"Ah," said Z. "What other guests are in your segment?"

"Pete Fong and Napoleon Jennings."

"Yes. I will do them next. They're both running late, I think. Mr. Jennings is a man of few words."

Zainab immediately went to the core difference between the two men. Russ had known Pete for years. He was a classic political "ad guy" who started in California politics, made his money on statewide initiatives, and remade himself for the digital age as a maker of short and long-form viral political content. Pete was loquacious, curious, and very, very glib. Napoleon was a legislative tactician extraordinaire. He came to Washington from the Louisiana legislature with his first boss, back when there were conservative Democrats. If you wanted to get something through Congress, or more importantly, make sure that something could never get through Congress, you needed Napoleon. He was not a lobbyist, though at some points in his career, he had commanded legions of them. Napoleon understood the legislative process and human nature. And this had made him enormously wealthy. And while Pete was always talking, Napoleon was always listening.

Russ admired both men in the way athletes respect each other. Russ could never be as creative as Pete, and he admired Pete's filmmaking and storytelling skills. But, while he admired Pete, he was generally in awe of Napoleon as chess master and horse trader. More than anything, Pete was impressed by Napoleon's discipline. Napoleon had worked for the Democratic Whip, two Democratic Speakers, a Republican President, the US Trade Representative, and a few trade associations, notably AMMM - America's Massive Medicine Makers. And now he ran his own firm, the understatedly named Legislative Analysts. If all of this did not impress,

Napoleon somehow managed to work for leaders in BOTH parties at a moment of intense partisan rancor.

"So, has the studio been quiet or busy today?" Russ asked.

"It has been quiet. I think it is a slow news day. And that means your segment will stay full length."

"Ahhh. Got it. Then I better think through what I don't want to say," Russ observed.

At that, Zainab laughed, pulled off the cosmetics cape, and said, "Voila. Good luck on your segment, Mr. Armstrong." Z smiled and then reviewed her lineup. "Russ, if you see Napoleon in the waiting area, will you tell him he's next?"

The strategy was coming into focus. Russ would push for Pete to go first and burn time, he would praise Pete's digital ads this cycle, and would quickly bridge to the legislative landscape in the next Congress, giving Napoleon the floor. That was Plan A.

Napoleon and Pete entered Makeup at the same time and in high spirits. Napoleon was wearing the classic blue power suit and red tie. Pete was going for the auteur look, wearing a black t-shirt and black leather jacket.

Russ waited for them in the ANN guest room next door. The room was standard for any television green room; it included modern but relatively worn sofas, glass side tables, worn carpet, a coffee maker circa 2019, multiple flat screens playing ANN, a few generic, framed photos of Washington landmarks, and a colossal, backlit ANN logo on the main wall. The green room had that distinct green room smell of coffee, hairspray, old newspaper, and wet umbrella.

There was another guest in the green room. He was older, had an ill-fitting jacket, and was wearing a bow tie. Had to be a professor, probably history or poli sci. Bow Tie was casually flipping through magazines, looking relaxed and untroubled. Russ was always a bit stunned by the glib, just wing it types. Unlike bow tie, Russ would usually have a few notecards with factoids supporting his main points. He always wrote his soundbites out in advance, practicing them in his head before showtime. Sure, he could just wing it, but shouldn't guests have proof points and data to back their assertions? Maybe Bow Tie was just so immersed in his subject matter that it had seeped into every crevice of his brain. If it had, godspeed. But Russ would never just completely wing it. He had Plan A notecards and a Plan B notecard in his breast pocket.

Russ glanced at his phone. The message notifications started pinging, sounding strangely like a pinball machine. The news was breaking. He was going to have to talk with the G.O.S. employees, check in with clients, and have some off-the-record chats with his friends in the media. But he had no time for that now. He was exhausted from Jefe's death, from the firm's sale, from the past few days. He needed to focus on the immediate road ahead, on this newscast. He turned his phone off and stored it in his go bag next to his sunglasses.

The segment producer began hovering outside the green room, so Russ went to check in with him, joining up with Napoleon and Pete on their way out of Makeup. The producer had the look of a man who was simultaneously tired and wired. He also looked like he was extruded from a corporate promotional clothing catalog. He was wearing an ANN polo and an ANN quilted vest. He held a beat-up metal clipboard jammed with frayed paper. Russ loved the nostalgic clipboard vibe.

"Hi, guys. I'm Matt. Thanks for getting here on time, and congratulations. I mean that sincerely."

Russ chuckled on the inside. What sincere person actually peppers their language with reassurances that they are sincere?

Matt, the Truly Sincere and Over-Logoed TV News Producer, continued. "Follow me to the studio. We will go live in about ten minutes. We'll start with a discussion about the impact of the elections and end with the Mover and Shaker awards. We estimate about ten minutes of airtime."

Russ's heart went thud. Ten minutes was more than double what he expected. A ten-minute segment might be normal for BBC, but ten minutes on a US news program was like a year wandering a minefield.

The four made their way onto the set. To be more specific, it was the fake "we are sitting on sofas and chatting over coffee by a fake fireplace that looks like the fireplace in the West Wing" set that was connected to the snazzy, hi-tech news set. As he entered the fake fireside chat set, the guests were given multiple warnings to stay silent as Stirling read the teleprompter for a segment on mineral nationalism. Russ made sure to sit as far away from the presenter's chair as possible, calculating that Pete would sit closest and burn the most time. They settled into their seats, sitting motionless while the technicians wired them up for sound.

There was something strange about sitting next to a fake fireplace in the winter and knowing that it would emit no heat.

Russ watched Stirling read the teleprompter effortlessly. He had to admit that Stirling was a very good reader. But so were the deep fakes now being used to create fictitious newscasts. How long before the deep fakes were indistinguishable from ANN news? And how long before news outlets switched to software-generated newscasters? The software was already impressively lifelike. Switching to bot newscasters would eliminate the drama and their salaries. In a way, Stirling was a robot already. He simply read the teleprompter.

Stirling finished reading his news segment from the teleprompter, waved to the guests, walked over to his chair, and sat down.

The camera crew began wheeling into position. Russ realized that his cowboy boots would be on camera, at least in some of the shots. It somehow seemed appropriate. His boots were exotics, python, to be exact. The high-definition cameras would pick up all the detail.

"Welcome to Fireside Chat, gentleman. I'll kick us off on an election roundup. I'll ask each of you to share with our viewers the three big things we learned on election night. We'll have some witty banter. I'll press the group on one or two points. You'll agree with me. Then, we will turn to what we should expect in terms of legislation in the next two years. You'll tell me gridlock, but use many words to do it, and then we will transition to the Mover and Shaker Awards. I'll have something nice to say about each one of you, and you'll say something gracious. And then we will close. All good?"

Pete and Russ all gave some version of the thumbs-up. Napoleon nodded imperceptibly.

"Oh, and Russ." Stirling flashed his signature smile and massive teeth as white as fresh tombstones. "I just heard the breaking news about G.O.S. I may have to probe on that a bit if you don't mind."

Russ smiled back, close-lipped. "I'd be happy to. It's an exciting moment for G.O.S. and a natural phase in the firm's evolu..."

"But, I'm hearing that Cold Harbor pushed you out because of the reputational overhang of some of your clients. I'm not making a value judgment, Russ. I just think that this highlights the interplay of consultants, politics, and business. And the public should understand that."

The main camera guy began the countdown.

Russ was forced to go to Plan B.

They were live.

"Welcome to Fireside Chat, where we explore the issues of the day, unscripted, unfiltered, and uninterrupted. With me by our fire tonight are Pete Fong, noted political ad maker and President of Fong & Associates; Napoleon Jennings, counselor to Presidents and CEO of Legislative Analysts; and Russ Armstrong, political and corporate advisor and former Managing Partner at Global Opinion Strategies. Each of these gentlemen is no stranger to ANN or this cozy living room."

Pete, Napoleon, and Russ smiled and nodded. In a general "fuck it" move, Russ crossed his legs, prominently featuring his python boots. It was a shame Lucky didn't watch television.

"With the midterm elections now behind us, all of the votes finally counted, and Thanksgiving around the corner, I would like to ask our friends around the fire what they learned from the elections. Pete, kick us off."

Pete cocked his head slightly, smiled, and began. "Thank you, Stirling. That's a great question. I learned three big things. First, I learned that we are more politically divided than ever. But, a great candidate and a compelling story can cross that divide and appeal to swing voters and moderate Republicans. We saw this in a number of suburban districts. Second, I relearned that advertising is a turnout strategy. Having the right base message is critical to early voting and turnout efforts. You know, Stirling, most campaigns think about turnout as mechanics, but it is also communication that increases vote propensity. Finally, I think this was THE meme election, where memes and political advertising, especially digital advertising, merged."

"It goes without saying that your firm led that merger in this cycle..." Stirling pointed out.

"That's too kind, Stirling. We take our inspiration from popular culture. Our cultural trend-spotters are always looking for emerging folkways that can be accessed for political communication. This year, it was old-school memes."

"Brilliant, Peter, Brilliant. Are there any truths to the rumors that you are, in fact, the Meme Dealer?"

"Stirling, I can neither confirm nor deny. But, I think we can all agree that the Meme Dealer has the freshest memes."

"Turning from memes to themes, Napoleon, what themes do you see coming out of this election?"

"Thank you, Stirling; I see three. First, this political polarization muted the historical pattern of out-party gains. That is significant. Second, it is clear that both parties are moving away from globalization and toward managed trade blocs. And third, this was the election where we began to grapple with the challenges of an aging society."

"Succinct as always, Napoleon. But what do you think of Pete's memes?"

"I do not."

"Shots fired, Peter."

Napoleon revised and extended his remarks. "Stirling, what I mean to say is that this is outside my area of expertise. Any thoughts from me on memes would not deliver value for your audience. I defer to Peter on popular culture and will stay in my lane."

Russ could feel the dagger coming for him.

"Russ, what are your thoughts? What have you learned from this election?"

"Thank you, Stirling. I've learned that Pete is the Meme Dealer. Pete, in all seriousness, why do you think this was the meme cycle?"

Russ calculated that this would burn another minute.

"Our post-election analysis, which any digital assistant can retrieve by searching Meme Cycle, finds that this was largely driven by generational progression and generational replacement. Zoomers have come of age, and Millennials are middle-aged. Zoomers' generational ascendance has made meme culture more relevant. We envision a near future where political advertising is a collection of the most viral, crowdsourced political memes. There are attempts to train AI to create viral political memes, but these haven't yet broken through."

Stirling redirected his gaze and tombstone smile at Russ.

"Our Fireside Chat is running low on time. Russ, if it's okay with you, I'd like to present our very special awards tonight and then finish with your observations on the elections. Oh, and I may have a follow-up question for you."

Russ smiled back. "It would be my pleasure, Stirling."

"Gentleman, it is with great honor that I present you each with the ANN Mover and Shaker Award, recognizing your historic impact on American political life."

A well-dressed ANN intern wheeled out the awards, each about the size of a Heisman trophy, shining brightly in the fake studio lighting.

"As you can see, these legendary trophies represent Vulcan forging metal, hammer in hand, just as you have forged public opinion, consensus, and American democracy. We now present each of you with your Vulcans."

Well-dressed intern handed Pete, Napoleon, and Russ their lapel pins and heavy, hollow Vulcans.

"I present the newest class of ANN's Movers and Shakers." Stirling held his arms out in the game show host "show them what they've won" arm sweep.

"Now, Russ, we don't have much time by the fire. What were your takeaways from the election, and what are your future plans after GOS?"

"Thank you, Stirling."

Russ paused and stared directly into the main camera.

"There is noise, and there is signal. Much of what we discussed tonight was noise. The Declaration of Independence said, 'Let facts be submitted to a candid world.' My Papa would say, 'I'm going to give it to you straight.' I want to address you, my fellow citizens, in painful honesty tonight. It is hard to hear, but I know you feel it as I do. First, things aren't working. Big things. Little things. Our culture. People. Our government. Things are both broken and breaking down. Our decline is outweighing our renewal. Our elites will debate this. They debate everything. It's all they know. But, on their watch, crime has exploded, our economy has shrunk, and our debt has grown into a crushing load. Second, we have lost faith in our institutions, in our leaders, and even in our neighbors. This decline in trust is well-documented. It is also well deserved. The elites at the commanding heights of our institutions are a clique; they are sophists, and they have failed. They have more than failed. They have snatched defeat from the jaws of victory. What do we do? We, the people, have to rescue the Republic, renewing it one neighborhood, one town, one school, one organization, one state at a time. We need to move from passive consumers to active citizens. We need to shift our model from comfort to excellence. In truth, it is probably too late to rescue our Republic. But we must try because you will hate what comes after it."

Russ then turned to Stirling.

"You know this to be true, Stirling. This will be hard, and the public should understand that."

Stirling was, for once, at a loss for words. Having no idea how to respond, Stirling gave the universal head nod for "go on."

"Thank you for asking about my future plans. We cannot keep doing the same things and expect a different result. We need to rescue the union. We need to experiment with new approaches. To do this, we need to dig deep into our history and bring back a leader who can preserve the union and rally the country. That leader must be extremely resilient. That leader is Abraham Lincoln. Abraham Lincoln was assassinated just blocks from this studio. We cannot bring him back, but we can bring his thinking back in the form of an advanced artificial intelligence. We will train AI to think like Abraham Lincoln. We will put him on the ballot. Our deeply flawed candidates will debate Abraham Lincoln 2.0, and they will lose to him."

The room fell silent.

Stirling didn't know what to do. Matt, the over-logoed producer, didn't know what to do. Pete was utterly confused. Napoleon was quietly considering the proposition.

Dead air.

Pete couldn't help himself. "You mean like a chatbot or one of those digital girlfriend apps? Are you serious?"

"Yes, Pete, I am serious. I think it is time to explore the idea. Roughly 16,000 books and articles have been published on Lincoln. We have his papers. We have his speeches. That material can train an AI to think like Abraham Lincoln —to be Abraham Lincoln."

Stirling and Matt, the over-logoed producer, were somewhere between stunned and realizing that this could be great television.

"But, like, it's still a bot, man."

"Pete, listen to me. You let your car's AI drive you. You have an AI assistant now, and you talk to it. You let your home AI manage the basic functions of your house. When you bank, you talk with an AI. Artificial intelligence examines all your health data and suggests diagnoses to your doctor. AI polices our stock market. It optimizes water treatment and our electric grid. You already rely on and interact with artificial intelligence every day. Let's use it to bring our greatest leader back."

"Okay, you have a point, my man." Pete's brain was grinding on the idea. "But couldn't this thing like turn on us and kill us? Like maybe we program it to be Lincoln, and then it goes all Pol Pot meets HAL."

"Pete, you assume that we invent a thing, and it tries to kill us. But what if we create a thing, and it attempts to save us?"

Dead air.

Matt, the over-logoed producer, was furiously whispering on his phone and in some kind of frank exchange with ANN management.

Stirling sensed that it was time to wrap up but struggled to find the words for a close.

"Thank you to all our Mover and Shaker award winners tonight. And thank you for joining us on Fireside Chat," Stirling said, closing the segment.

Over-logoed producer was still on the phone. The camera and mic operators weren't sure what to do. They froze.

Stirling didn't realize that the cameras were still rolling and that the mics were live. And that's when the newscaster created the week's freshest meme on live television.

"OK, guys. What the fuck was that?"

18: Vultures

Russ exited the ANN studio, turned right, and began walking to the National Mall.

He needed some time to decompress and gather his thoughts. And he calculated that he was less likely to be mugged on the mall than on the abandoned streets back to the office.

Russ could have hailed a robo-taxi. But he needed to walk. His sunglasses told him it was thirty-nine degrees Fahrenheit.

As he stepped foot onto the National Mall, Russ could hear and feel the familiar crunch of the gravel on the mall's walking path. It was real. He could feel each step, and he could hear the crunch against the soles of his python boots. It was strangely comforting and literally grounding. He just needed time to think through his next three moves.

Aside from several hearty tourists, a few park police, the ever-circling security drones, and a statuette of Vulcan, Russ was alone. It was so quiet. No tourist noise. No playing children. No congressional kickball games. No hot dog vendors. The carousel was closed for the winter, hibernating. It reminded Russ of a moment years ago in San Francisco. He had left a steak-heavy business dinner only to discover while walking back to his hotel that it was Chinese New Year. But the parade and firecrackers and dragons had already made their way through Chinatown. The festivities had finished. The red lanterns shone only on empty streets. Everyone had gone home. It was as though Chinatown had been evacuated or the last trumpet had sounded. Russ found himself walking Chinatown alone, accompanied only by the crunch of his shoes on spent fireworks. It was the silent after.

Russ decided that now was as good a time as any to check his messages and handle the incoming. He turned his phone on and donned his sunglasses.

They immediately rang. It was Mike from the office. Russ sighed and answered the call.

"Hey, Russ, it's Mike. I just heard the news. How are you doing?"

"Thanks for calling, Mike. I'm doing great. How are you doing?"

"I'm still at work. You know, clients first. And I thought I'd call to see if you needed any help communicating with clients. I was just thinking about our maritime and port clients. Do you need any help communicating with them? Happy to lighten your load..."

"Mike, that's so incredibly kind. Thanks for the offer, but I've already notified them and have follow-on calls with them tomorrow. But, hey, I really appreciate the offer."

"Oh. Okay. No problem, then. Will you be in the office tomorrow? It would be great to catch up over coffee."

"Yup. I'll be in first thing. I'll come find you on the floor. Don't work too late, my friend."

"All right, see you tomorrow."

"See you in the morning."

This was going to be excruciating.

Russ's sunglasses lit up again with an incoming call.

It was Kieran Gamble.

Russ hesitated, took a shallow breath, and answered the call.

"This is Russ."

"Russ, this is Kieran Gamble. I understand that Ruth talked with you. In order to finalize everything, we will need your signature on several documents. My assistant will courier them to your house.

"Okay. Sounds good."

"Cold Harbor needs a clean break. Any, and I mean any, inappropriate contact with firm clients or the media in regards to this deal will trigger legal action," Kieran warned.

"Understood."

"Great. Oh, and Russ, one last thing."

"Yes?"

"Don't cross me."

Then, Kieran ended the call.

Russ took a deep breath, refocused, crossed 14th Street, and approached the Washington Monument. The monument is ringed by flag poles that normally make a clinking sound on windy days. But there was no wind to slam the snap hooks up against the poles. It was so quiet that he could hear the hum of the lights circling the monument.

Russ decided to read through his Sm0ke$ignal messages. "Display texts," Russ commanded. In roughly two seconds, his sunglasses began scrolling in what felt like an opened spigot of texts. He began reading them, making a calculation of how many referenced the G.O.S. sale to Cold Harbor and how many referenced his crazy campaign announcement. His rough analytics were 20% sale/exit and 80% campaign announcement. If this pattern held, then he would have successfully diverted attention away from the sale, his exit, and any discussion of "reputational overhang."

He began to scroll through his texts, using eye focus to read and sort messages on his sunglasses.

Message from Ulysses: Dad, that was straight fire. Just watched the clip on RePo and...

Message from 8: Loco! Viva Lincoln dos punto cero

Message from SunshineSta..: Love them boots. Got yer note. All good brotha. All good. U...

Message from Unregistered: House cleaned.

Message from Zurdo: U r one crazy, fuckin cracker. Fuckit we ball

Message from NJennings: Russ, fascinating idea. I agree with your 3 points, but am not...

Message from DirkenGav: Mr. Armstrong, I'm writing a story, and I'd like to get your th...

Message from History Dep.: Mr. Armstrong. I watched your segment from the ANN green...

Message from Matt@ANN: Russ, thank you for joining us tonight. The analytics appear to...

Message from Sultan al J...: Habibi, what is this I'm hearing about reviving your President L...

Message from G Morgan: Just read about your Lincoln idea. Really interesting idea. Tell...

Message from Maria M: Russ, I just watched you on ANN and am happy you're back in...

Message from MMillerGOS: Russ, hope you're well. How do you want to tell our defense cl...

Message from Flagler TOT: This isn't a crazy idea. But how do you put an AI on the ballot...

Message from Ulysses: Oh, and I just signed up for the wait list for Spectaculars, but...

Message from CaneCuttr: Just saw you on ANN. Love the boots! We should talk about...

Message from Maria M: Can I call u??? Saw you on ANN tonight. How r u? R u ok? I wa..

Message from DefenseAero: Interesting idea. You know, DoD has experimented with simu...

Message from LincolnHome: Hello, I'm Roy at the Lincoln Home National Historic Site and...

Message from Bobby: Brother, I just saw the news. Explain it to me slow.

Message from B0ss L8Y1: You good? I'm not running a quixotic AI Prez campaign...

So far, so good.

Russ continued walking down the National Mall toward the Lincoln Memorial. He passed through the World War Two Memorial by the bundled homeless, sleeping, drinking, and shooting up. He continued walking along the northern side of the reflecting pool. It was getting colder, and his Vulcan statuette was now ice cold. Russ didn't bring gloves, and his right hand was numbing from holding the Roman god. He decided to cradle his Vulcan like a football and use the cuff of his coat as a makeshift glove.

Russ kept walking along the reflecting pool with the crunch crunch of his boots on the path. Just then, his sunglasses lit up with another text, this time from Lucky.

Message from LuckyStrikez: Never watch ANN bullshit. If I could vote, I would vote for Lincoln 2.0...

Lucky's message made Russ stop in his tracks. Lucky didn't have a TV, was rarely online, couldn't vote due to a string of early-life felonies, and was deeply apolitical. If Lucky had somehow heard about the segment, then it must have gone viral. What was originally intended as a distracting flash bomb had become a wildfire.

HAL, please dial up Ronny.

Russ's sunglasses immediately began phoning Ronny, Russ's most trusted pollster.

"This is Ronny."

"Hey, Ronny, I've got a quick turn job for you. I'm going to trust you on the design."

"Okay, Russ. It's dead right now. I'll definitely take the work. What are we doing?"

"N of 1,000, national, census representative, short, like 25 questions with demos."

"Copy that. Subject?"

"I want to measure openness to voting for an AI for President."

"What the fuck are you talking about? Are you drunk?" Ronny asked.

"No. I know it's a crazy idea. Just take the money."

Ronny chuckled. "I'll take as much as you give."

"I need to measure openness to voting for an AI President on a continuum. Likelihood. And then likelihood with additional safety measures. I also need to measure Abraham Lincoln's image as a President, positive and negative, in a clutter test with other Presidents—just the famous ones and recent ones. And then I need a feeling thermometer on Lincoln as well. Then, finish with some forced choices on human vs AI candidates. Have fun with it. Make sense?"

"Russ, it makes no sense. It's batshit crazy. But, I can write the survey and field."

"Perfect. From the internals, I need a profile of the most open and most likely to support an AI Lincoln for President."

"Also, batshit crazy. But, hey, they said that about alien spaceships until the Air Force admitted it had a few. Bro, I'm in. You want me to cut the data by star sign?"

"Huh?"

"That was a joke, Russ."

"Oh. Okay. I want the data cut by the usual demos. Cool?"

"Copy that. Should have it turned around in a few days."

"I don't need charts or anything, just topline and tabs."

"Okay, you got it."

"Thanks, Ronny."

"My pleasure."

Russ came to the base of the Lincoln Memorial and figured that if he had walked this far, he might as well trudge up the alabaster stairs and take in the sweeping vista. He took the stairs one at a time, ascended, turned around at the top, and sat down to enjoy the view. He was relieved to finally place his Vulcan on the ground. Russ eyed the nearby garbage bin. There was no way he could fit the Vulcan through the lid of the Park Service trash can.

It was a cold and beautiful night, and Russ's breath was now visible as he exhaled. It was just Russ, his Vulcan, and a thirty-foot, one-hundred-seventy-ton Lincoln statue gazing out onto the National Mall. Off in the distance above the World War Two Memorial, he could see the blinking light of a security drone.

19: I get you.

Russ's sunglasses alerted him to an incoming call. It was Maria. Russ hesitated to take it. He inhaled, exhaled, and answered the call.

"This is Russ."

"Russ, I saw you on ANN. I heard the other news. How are you? Talk to me. Please. How are you?"

Russ noticed the moon shining down on the National Mall. It was beautiful and lit the dark night.

"Maria, I think I'm out of words." Russ was trying to remember the Spanish word for "word." Palabra.

"Then I will sit there with you. Contigo."

Russ closed his eyes and focused on his breathing.

"Russ, tell me what we are seeing. Where are we?"

"We are sitting at the Lincoln Memorial looking out at the Washington Monument and the Capitol dome. It's a beautiful, cold night, and the air is still. The moon is shining down onto the reflecting pool."

"Thank you, Russ. It's beautiful."

The two sat in silence.

"Russ, tell me what you see with your heart. I want to know what you really see."

Russ closed his eyes and began. "I see an abandoned city, a candle that has gone out, the end of dreams, a beautiful night, and a morning ahead."

"You've always had this second sight. You're a dreamer. It's hard for you when a dream ends."

"Maria, I'm so sorry about your father. I'm so sorry."

"I know, Russ. I know. He lived a remarkable life. He packed centuries into decades."

"And what do you see, Maria?"

"I see the moonlight on my pool and an empty lounge chair waiting for you. The wind is blowing the palm trees."

"That sounds perfect." Russ pictured it in his mind. "What else?"

Maria continued in a whisper of a voice. "I see that storms come in, and then they go, and what they clear away leaves space between the clouds and the ocean, nube y oceano, for something new."

"That's beautiful."

"Russ, one other thing. I don't know about your AI President idea. But I do know that I would never let you wear those python boots in public or on TV. Ever."

Russ chuckled.

"No. Wait. That's not right. I think those boots are outrageous, but I would let you wear them. They're a little crazy. I hate them. But I love them. Now be safe, go home, and get some sleep."

"Thank you, Maria."

"It will be okay, Russ. I get you."

20: Temple

It was getting colder, and sitting on freezing Colorado Yule marble wasn't helping. The wind was just starting to pick up, and Russ could feel a faint breeze. Russ's sunglasses told him the temperature had dropped to 34 degrees Fahrenheit.

Russ had been to the Lincoln Memorial dozens of times with Melissa, with U, with family visiting from out of town, and with international guests. Almost all these visits were during daylight hours in the summer when the memorial was teaming with sweaty tourists, high school class trips, and hot dog and pretzel vendors. Tonight had a completely different, solemn power.

"Excuse me, mister."

Russ whipped around, surprised that anyone was at the memorial, much less right behind him.

"So, uh, you can totally stay here and enjoy the memorial. I was just checking to make sure you're okay. I work the night shift here and work for the National Park Service. My name is Raymond. Sorry for scaring you."

Russ immediately softened. Raymond couldn't be older than nineteen and was rail thin even under his green park service coat and matching green pants. Instead of the classic, broad-brimmed ranger hat, he wore a matching green winter cap with the ear flaps down. His winter cap had the retro National Park Service arrowhead logo stitched on the front. His black boots were new and shiny. And his fresh and gleaming name tag read Raymond Washkuch.

Russ was worried that he had scared Raymond. Raymond looked scared. No, he looked cold. He had no body fat. No, he was scared and cold.

"Thank you for saying hello. I'm good. Just enjoying the view. I'm sorry. I should get going home. My name is Russ Armstrong." Russ stayed seated and employed open-palm gestures to demonstrate that he wasn't a threat.

"Mister, you can stay as long as you like. I'm here all night and have a security loop that I walk."

"Totally respect that," responded Russ with two big thumbs-up, which he immediately thought was completely cheesy.

"What's the little statue, sir? It looks like the Greek god Hephaestus. Or maybe a blacksmith." Raymond locked his eyes on Russ' ANN award and began visually inspecting it.

"Oh, it's Vulcan. It's an award."

"That's really funny, Mr. Armstrong."

Russ flashed a quizzical look back to Raymond.

"Oh, sorry. It's funny because the Lincoln Memorial was designed by architect Henry Bacon in the style of a Greek temple. He modeled it on the Parthenon, visually referencing the birthplace of democracy. Lincoln saved the Republic, and he wanted to draw those parallels."

"Right. But what's funny? I'm sorry. I'm tired. I don't get it."

"Oh, right. It's funny because you're in a huge Greek temple, but your little god statue is Roman. So, it's kinda out of place."

"Ah, now I get it." Russ was impressed. When he was nineteen, he wouldn't have known any of this.

Raymond smiled, then looked worried. "Maybe it's not actually funny. Yeah. It's not funny. It's funny to me, but that's because I'm a nerd. So, I've been studying really hard. I want to be promoted. In my free time, I watch online videos about all the National Park Service locations."

Russ didn't even know there were park service videos online.

"It's funny, Raymond. I get it. It's funny because Lincoln is positioned like a god in a Greek temple, and this little guy is a Roman god and totally out of place. I get it."

"Thank you. So maybe it was funny then."

"You seem to really know this location. Do you give tours?"

"Not yet. This is my first posting with the National Park Service, and I have the night shift."

"When did you start here?"

"In September."

"That's great. First job. Your parents must be very proud."

"Thank you, sir."

"Where are you from?" Russ asked, guessing Raymond had a long drive to work.

"Quantico. My family is military. It's an easy commute in and out at night."

"If you had a regular commute, that would be rough. Where have you lived?"

"Bahrain, South Korea, Okinawa, and LeJeune. Dad's almost got his twenty. I don't really remember Bahrain, though."

"Looks like you've seen the world on Uncle Sam's dime. I have to ask. What got you interested in the Park Service and American history?"

"Oh, I'm just a big reader. That's really it. Nothing fancy. I don't want to be nosy, but what do you do for a living here?"

Normally, Russ would have been annoyed at that question. Russ found that, unlike any other city in America, in Washington this was the first question. But Raymond had no ulterior motive. He wasn't a networker or a "shoulder surfer."

"Well, I do research for whoever pays me. If I do a good job, customers will pay me to help them cook up a strategy based on that research. We're both nerds, Raymond. It's all good."

"That sounds cool."

"Pays the bills."

"But, why are you here so late? Sorry to ask, but I'm just curious."

"Honestly, Raymond, I just needed some time to think."

"About what?" Raymond asked.

"Well, that's a long story. I don't want to keep you from walking your security perimeter."

Raymond stared back at Russ, clearly wondering about Russ's long story and worrying that Russ was either a potential suicide case or sleeping overnight at the memorial. Normally, Russ would just move along, but he decided to deal the kid in.

"Well, I'm thinking through a number of things, but the most relevant to our location is that I announced on television tonight that I was going to run an AI Lincoln for President." Russ finished these words with his palms up as though he was serving the idea to Raymond on a large, imaginary platter.

Raymond broke eye contact, looking up and to the right, considering the idea. The wind was picking up, and it was getting much colder.

"Mr. Armstrong, I don't know how that would work, but it's a great idea. Someone should write a book or make a movie about it. I think I'd vote for him. It. An AI Lincoln." Raymond paused. "AI-braham Lincoln." Raymond made air quotes when he said, "AI."

Russ laughed. He knew immediately that the media would either name it "Lincoln 2.0" or "AI-braham Lincoln."

Raymond began thinking out loud. "You know, people will think the idea is crazy at first. Buuuuut, it's not crazy. I mean, think about the last few Presidents we have had. Would an AI be worse? It can't just be a chatbot like those fake girlfriend bots. It would have to be real AI. We already have AI that runs things for us. We already have AI that always beats us at chess. We already have AI customer service. But everyone hates that. Hmmmm. Oh, and that one global strategy game has AI opponents for all the great world leaders, the one that starts with the agricultural revolution and ends with building a spaceship. They have Abraham Lincoln in that game. We would just need a tricked-out version of that AI. And..."

Russ gently cut Raymond off. "All this assumes someone actually builds it and runs it for President."

Raymond seemed confused. "But, you just said you were going to run a Lincoln Bot for President. What would you call it? It needs a really good name."

"Well, I called it 'Lincoln 2.0' on air, so I might be stuck with the name."

"No offense," offered Raymond. "But, 'Lincoln 2.0' kinda sucks as a name."

Russ had to admit that Raymond was right. It needed a catchier name. But Russ also knew that once something was named, that name stuck.

"You're right. It would need a better name."

"What do you mean by 'would'?" Raymond asked. "You announced this on TV. You're going to do this, right?"

Russ just couldn't reveal to Raymond that the entire idea was a ruse.

"I have to think it through, Raymond," Russ said, feeling exhausted.

"But, you said you were going to do it. I don't get it. Can you do that? Can you just say you're going to do something and then not do it?" Raymond seemed genuinely confused.

The kid was simply fatiguing, but Russ had to admit that Raymond was right.

"Well, what do you think I should do?" Russ asked.

Raymond considered his words. "I would do what I said I would do. I think my first step would be getting a bunch of AI experts and programmers together to build the Lincoln Bot, or whatever it would be called. Then, I think I would write out how the Lincoln Bot would work and the reasons for building it. Oh, and I would try to answer the questions people would have in advance, like an FAQ."

"Good points, Raymond. That FAQ would have to be more like the Federalist Papers. I kinda shot from the hip on this one. The public would need the foundational reasoning for an AI candidate. Even if most people wouldn't read a succession of treatises on the subject, we would have to lay out our thinking, at least for posterity." Russ imagined the legion of oddball techies and policy wonks cranking out manuscript after manuscript. At least it would be easier than penning eighty-five essays under an assumed name for 19th-century New York newspapers.

"So, you're going to do it, right?" Raymond asked.

"I need to think it through, Raymond. I just need some time to think. I know you have to do your perimeter sweep." Russ was hoping this would nudge Raymond and also give him some time to think.

"Yeah, I should do my sweep. But let's make sure we can talk about this later. I want to help. I think this is a great idea, and I want to be a part of it."

"Raymond, whatever happens, I'd love to hear about your progress in life. It was great meeting you tonight."

The two touched their sunglasses, said "Connect," and waved goodbye.

Raymond turned and went about his security routine, leaving Russ alone with a colossal Lincoln and his puny Vulcan. The only sound was an icy wind slicing through his overcoat and suit. Russ's sunglasses reported that it was now twenty-eight degrees Fahrenheit.

Russ stood, turned, and faced the Lincoln statue. The eyes stared out beyond him, seemingly locked in thought. Behind the statue, these familiar words were inscribed:

IN THIS TEMPLE
AS IN THE HEARTS OF THE PEOPLE
FOR WHOM HE SAVED THE UNION
THE MEMORY OF ABRAHAM LINCOLN
IS ENSHRINED FOREVER

21: Come Home

Russ stared at Lincoln's statue. It was massive. The savior of the Republic. He knew he would have to make a decision, and he began to weigh the pros and cons.

He had never really meant to run an AI for President. It was meant as a distraction. Then he got carried away.

What were the pros?

It was cool. Someone was going to do it eventually. One human would be the Edison of leadership AI. He might as well be that Edison.

The idea was audacious. Audacious was good. The audacity was its own barrier to entry.

What were the cons?

The reasons against the project were obvious. Clients might think he had gone insane. The media would probably roast him. He would need world-class talent and a ton of money to build the thing. Even if he could build it, would Americans vote for an artificial intelligence? That felt incredibly unlikely. Would they vote for an artificial intelligence modeled on Abraham Lincoln? Unknowable but unlikely.

Any one of these seemed daunting. But, taken together, they formed an immovable sentry of doubt.

Russ's sunglasses flashed an incoming call from Melissa.

"Hey, Melissa."

"Russ, where are you?"

"I'm standing in front of the Lincoln Memorial."

"Russ, it's after midnight and snowing."

"Oh, yeah. I lost track of the time. Sorry."

"Aren't you cold?"

"Yeah, my feet and hands are numb, and my ears hurt."

"U sent me a clip of your segment."

"What did you think?"

"Russ, it's late. You've had a rough day. Come home and get some rest. Please."

"Yeah, you're right. It's late." Russ's sunglasses reported twenty-two degrees Fahrenheit.

"Call SafeCor. Call Big Country. Have him drive you home. It's not safe in DC, and it'll be faster than hailing your car and having it get out of that secure garage."

"I don't want to wake the poor guy up just to come get me."

"Okay. Just get a robo-taxi then. Just come home. Don't spend all night thinking in the cold."

Russ had HAL order a robo-taxi. It pulled up within minutes and was ice cold. Neither the car nor the car's software needed heat in a snowstorm.

Russ fiddled with the car heater controls, but they seemed to be locked. Russ figured that either it was locked to save the taxi company money or no one had thought about the comfort of the passengers on a cold night. Then he realized it was both.

Russ crossed his arms and closed his eyes. All the rest was out of his control.

The taxi drove Russ home in stony silence through icy Virginia snow.

22: A Strange Text

The snow blanket silence woke him. Normally, by 6 a.m., the distant hum of the Washington commute would reach their Mount Vernon replica home. But this morning was silent as a tomb.

He always told his analysts to listen for the dog that didn't bark, the unanticipated hole in the pattern. The dogs that weren't barking this morning were the birds. They should have been active, but they were mute. Russ concluded that it was very cold and that perhaps they had more than a dusting of snow. He loved hearing the birds in the morning, hearing their calls outside his window. His favorite was the mourning dove. There was something about its call that was both sweet and sad and lonely.

Today would be a hard day. He began composing his to-do list in his head. He would need to connect with all his clients. He would need to connect with his lawyer and his accountant. He would need some deep time to think through this new business. But first, he needed coffee.

Russ rose quietly, trying not to wake Melissa. He put an old Ski Dubai fleece on, grabbed his work bag, and made his way down the creaky stairs into the foyer.

The home was decorated in "kountry kitcshen" meets colonial Williamsburg meets the Fourthof July. It was clean but well-lived in. Although the foyer was a bit grandiose, there were shoes by the front door and unopened mail in a wicker basket. The walls were decorated with family photos and folkloric paintings of the Ohio River valley. The wall art included Russ's favorite photo of a misty pumpkin patch near Aberdeen, Ohio.

Russ walked into the kitchen. The kitchen featured white granite countertops, modern stainless steel appliances, and a vintage 1950s coffee maker. He opened the cupboard to select a coffee mug and decided to stay with the UAE theme, choosing an old Magical Kingdom Abu Dhabi mug. Russ poured Arabic coffee into the vintage coffee maker and stared out the window while it percolated.

The snow had blanketed the ground and hung on the oak trees. It was a blue-gray hue in the near dawn light and utterly still. Even though the house was heated, the woods outside radiated cold. The snow had to be at least four inches deep. There would be no school today.

The coffee finished percolating, and Russ poured it without any thought.

For whatever reason, his mind wandered to a childhood memory of a baseball field in Aberdeen, Ohio. The outfield ended in cattails, and the cattails ended in the Ohio River. If a boy got all of the ball with his bat, it would sail into the cattails or maybe the river. Russ was a weak hitter, so he was never going to do that. But, while he was out in right field, he loved looking left down the river. During one game, he saw a boat pushing multiple barges of cargo down the Ohio. The sun was low in the west, hitting the barges at an angle. All this was mostly normal. What was abnormal in the picture was a man jumping from one barge to the next. Why was he jumping? Where was he going? St. Louis? New Orleans? What was his life like? Russ decided that the man was jumping from barge to barge simply because he could. He was free. And that's when Russ decided that he wanted to be a riverboat captain like this jumping man. And then he heard some yelling. It was coming from the field. The batter had connected with the ball, dropping it just a bit beyond the first basemen's leaping reach and into right field. Russ knew he was going to hear it from the coach. But, as embarrassed as he was, Russ could never quite get his mind off the jumping riverboat captain.

Ping. Ping. Ping.

A sonar ping emanated from Russ's work bag. That was a priority message. More specifically, the message had the characteristics of what Russ had trained HAL to flag as a priority message. HAL was asleep, but this subroutine ran 24/7.

Russ would have just read the incoming message on his sunglasses, but he had no idea where they were. They were probably in the breast pocket of last night's power suit or in a freezing robo-taxi.

Ping. Ping. Ping.

Russ just loved the sonar ping noise. It reminded him of all those great WW2 movies.

Ping. Ping. Ping.

Russ was going to let this one go until later, but the insistent sonar ping was intriguing. He rummaged through his work bag, digging past paperwork, a few energy bars, some promotional material from the International Bank of the Everglades, and Maria's rosary. Finally, he found his phone uncomfortably squished under a red, plastic accordion file.

It was a message from an unregistered non-contact from the 415 area code.

415.123.1234 Mr. Armstrong, my digital assistant ranked your idea as top in my AM briefing.

415.123.1234 I hate the term disruptive, but it is disruptive.

415.123.1234 If you can fly out to the Bay Area this week, I'd like to discuss it with you.

415.123.1234 We could meet at Oat Industries Lab in SF.

415.123.1234 I'm sure you're very busy, but I'd like to talk about it when you can.

415.123.1234 I put my Asteroid Team on it, and they're pulling together some thoughts.

415.123.1234 All the best, Daumantas Wirkus

23: Athena

The gentle creaking noise from the stairs told Russ that Melissa was awake and incoming.

Russ smiled and turned gently to his left in anticipation of her entry.

The "Goddess of War" turned the corner into the kitchen. Her long auburn hair was everywhere this morning, thick, and in a state of active rebellion. She was wearing her warmest pajamas, an old high school t-shirt with "Radium Springs Lobos Cheer" across the chest, and an unzipped Inter-Arma fleece.

Russ hadn't seen that t-shirt in years. Melissa grew up on a ranch near Radium Springs, New Mexico. Her father worked at Holloman, and then White Sands Missile Range, and her mom ran the ranch. Her dad was a physicist from Chicago. Her mom was a barrel racer and rodeo queen. They met at a rodeo in Las Cruces, and the rest was history. Melissa was athletic and stunning like her mother, but she was her father's daughter. Her mom was a country girl and a daredevil. But, her father was like Archimedes at work on his death ray.

Melissa smiled, squeezed Russ's shoulder as she passed by, and sat down across from him at their kitchen table.

"Glad you made it home," Melissa said, shaking her head. "I knew that snowstorm was moving in."

"Yup. Left just in time. But, the robo-taxi didn't have heat."

"So G.O.S. spun you off?" Melissa asked, thinking.

"Yup. Apparently, Kieran Gamble brokered the deal."

"But you get to keep your clients?"

"Yup, except a few of the shiny ones."

"So, you keep all the ones they don't want on their client list?"

Russ nodded.

"And they pay you out for your equity?"

Russ nodded and smiled.

"So, it's a clean break, and you make out like a bandit," Melissa smirked and shook her head.

"Well, I'm kind of torn." Russ leaned back, holding his warm coffee cup between his hands like a magic lamp.

"Torn?"

"Financially, it's fine. It's more than fine. But it's hard to say goodbye to G.O.S. It was going to happen eventually. I mean, Brent wanted to get paid out. Ruth wanted her money out so she could run for office. Although, that's about the last thing I'd want to do with my money. The Cold Harbor guys wanted us for years. I'm sure they promised Ruth all kinds of bullshit, that the culture won't change etcetera. But, we all know in a few years, they'll cost strip it, roll it up into some holding company, and it will be gone."

"What do you care? You're literally driving off with the gold." Melissa shook her head again, incredulous.

"What do you mean?" Russ asked. "The gold?"

"I mean, you're getting paid out and taking profitable clients with you. It's a great deal."

Russ chuckled. "Well, here's to driving off with the gold." Russ raised his steaming coffee mug in a simulated toast.

"So, what's next?"

"Well, I need to put the new company together, hire a skeleton crew, get the accounting up and running, all the things. I've done it before. It'll be good for U to see."

"You still hate the Cold Harbor guys, don't you?" Melissa asked.

"I do. I hate them, and I hate Kieran."

"Why? I don't get it. It's just business."

"Cold Harbor doesn't make anything. They just buy good businesses and squeeze the lifeblood out of them. And also, who even names a thing 'Cold Harbor'? Do they not know anything about history? They're soulless. And Kieran is such a devious little shit."

"Well, those soulless bastards just paid you out," chuckled Melissa. "Oh, and you hired Kieran. And he worked for you for how long?"

"I know," Russ said, holding up his hands. "I regret it. I trained him, and then he brokered the deal that ruined my company. He's a complete fucking scorpion."

"He's also a scorpion that just got you paid out. I do love that scorpion joke, though. So, whatcha doing today?" Melissa asked.

"Finish my coffee, call all the clients, and get to work."

"And this whole 'Lincoln 2.0' thing?" Melissa used air quotes.

"It's looking like a can of very active worms."

"You're not actually going to do anything with it, are you?"

Russ inhaled and exhaled loudly through his nose and cocked his head.

"Russ, no one is going to vote for a chatbot or the Presidential equivalent of one of these weird sexting boyfriend apps." Melissa held both hands up in the universal "what the fuck?" position.

"Well, it's an interesting idea."

"So are world peace and free ice cream, but they don't pay me for that."

Russ smiled. He was simultaneously a little hurt, appreciating Melissa's personality for what it was, and more than a little turned on by the attitude and the bedhead.

"What's on your plate today?"

"Today is all about cyber shit, non-kinetic. It's so fucking boring. I get it. It's a lot of spend. We have our hackers. They have theirs. But, it's not naval lasers, or done swarms, or 'soldier of the future.'" Melissa used air quotes again, this time for "soldier of the future," which was a classic US military euphemism for psychologically hardened, physically upgraded, men in super suits. They were going to build a new warrior class, and no one was going to ask if a democracy should have one. Russ could immediately see all the marketing tie-ins with the Extreme International Football League. In five years, the new samurai class would do flyovers for Miami Tiburones games to thunderous applause.

"Also, like zero visuals. Dudes in glasses at computer stations." Russ imagined a room of hipster ad guys trying to make cyber warfare look exciting and failing.

"Totally. No one wants to look at that. It's not weapon porn. But all the majors have cyber side hustle businesses. So here we are."

"Sorry. But at least you have several regional and technological arms races." Russ meant this as a joke.

"Yeah, and the Indians are even talking about building a real, blue water navy. So, there's that. But check this out. My economics team has found that by historical standards, the world is still spending a lower amount of total GDP on defense. Interesting, right?"

"So, there's upside." Russ also meant this as a joke.

"That's what concerns me. There is downside. The biggest threat to national defense is an aging population. I think defense spending will drop."

"Because countries need to spend the money on the elderly?"

"Bingo. It's all bad. Budgetary pressure. A smaller pool of recruits." Melissa threw up her hands.

"Oh, by the way, I may need to go to the Bay Area for a day or two for some meetings."

"God. Why? Pack body armor and use SafeCor transport mercs."

"I thought the new term was 'private security contractors'?" Now Russ was using the air quotes.

"You say tomato. But seriously, who lives in the Bay Area anymore? It's like addicts and billionaires and billionaire addicts." Melissa drew the Venn diagram in the air.

"I'll do some recon and report back."

24: The Dragon and His Asteroid Team

"Bulletproof glass?" Russ asked as he tapped on it.

"Yes, sir. Top of the line," Big Country responded as he drove the black SUV through San Francisco traffic.

Russ knew half of this was schtick, so he decided to have a little fun.

"What level armor on this vehicle? I mean, do your vehicles in SF have more or less armor than in, let's say, oh, Medellin or Cali?"

"This vehicle is level 2 armor. Colombia has level 4. Mexico City has level 3. Johannesburg has level 5."

Russ had just discovered a new index by which to rate the security situation around the world.

"So, break it down for me. Why is the SF armor level lower?"

"Can I speak freely, sir?" Big Country asked, keeping his eyes fixed on the road and both hands on the wheel.

"Of course. Give it to me straight."

"Organized violent crime is low here. It's just junkies, the mentally ill, some protestors, and randoms. The others have much more coordinated criminality. SF has no hostage industry."

"Ahhh, I get it. SF doesn't have the cartels or major gangs or assassins, just..."

"Exactly. The worst-case scenario is a lone wolf type. That's low probability and random. We take every threat seriously at SafeCor, but lone wolves aren't squad-level strike teams."

"I see. And does SafeCor offer secure helicopter transport?"

"Yes, sir. Although our NorCal fleet is much smaller than our LA or Sao Paulo fleets."

"That's what I heard," Russ replied.

"Will you be in need of secure helicopter transport?"

"Big Country, I'm just bullshitting you, man. I don't need a chopper for SF. I've only been on one helicopter, and that was on Tanwir1 from Abu Dhabi to the solar fields. I'm just joking, pal. It's all good."

Big Country laughed. "I figured you were kidding, but I'm trying to keep it professional. You and me have history. But SafeCor runs a tight ship. I'm trying to do everything the SafeCor way."

When Russ learned that Big Country had gone over to SafeCor, he requested him as his secure driver. Big Country grew up on a rice farm in southwest Louisiana near the Calcasieu River. He did a stint in the army and then became the premier nightclub bouncer in New Orleans. But his side hustle, and ultimately his full-time job, became in-house casino driver. Big Country's muscle, his ability to defuse conflict, and his skill behind the wheel made him the perfect person to drive whales to and from the New Orleans casinos. He was especially talented at driving the big losers home after a rough night. Not even one casino loser committed suicide during or after Big County provided them safe passage. This was an incalculable win for the casinos. Big Country became one of their highly compensated employees.

Big Country also provided occasional transportation services to Trans-Oceanic Trading execs on far more mundane trips from the airport to Trans-Oceanic's office on Tchoupitoulas Street. In fact, Big Country first drove Russ in New Orleans. After several conversations about the art of nightclub bouncing, the two had become fast friends.

"Sir, we are approaching our destination. Here's the run-through. We are on Stockton Street now. We will turn left onto Jackson Street. Your destination is in Ross Alley, which is extremely narrow. I will block the alley with this vehicle and escort you to your destination."

SafeCor's Level 2, black SUV turned left and blocked Ross Alley, much to the confusion of local pedestrians. Big Country exited the SUV and opened Russ's door, motioning to him to follow along behind.

Ross Alley was narrow, a pedestrian alleyway with mom-and-pop businesses, all advertising in Chinese. Each storefront featured a vertical sign hanging from the second story and at least three security cameras. The alley was thick with tourists and street hustle. It was completely safe. In fact, it all felt more than absurd. Tourists gawked at Russ, assuming he was a VIP, and the alley crowd was more than happy to step out of the way of the well-muscled Big Country.

"Big Country, are you sure this is the right address?" Russ asked.

"Yes."

The two stood in front of Azure Dragon Fortune Cookie Factory. Azure Dragon advertised custom fortune cookies, adult-themed fortune cookies, and factory tours daily.

"There's no way this is it. Lemme check the address," Russ said.

Russ' sunglasses lit up with an incoming Sm0ke$ignal message.

415.123.1234 This is it.

415.123.1234 Just tell them you want the special factory tour.

415.123.1234 See you in a minute. Asteroid Team are excited to get started.

"Thanks, Big Country. I'll take it from here," Russ said as he entered the Azure Dragon Cookie Factory. The first thing Russ noticed was the smell of a thousand hot fortune cookies. It was a bit warm inside, like a kitchen with a hot oven. And it was cramped, very cramped. There were brown boxes of freshly made cookies everywhere. In fact, the whole place was shades of brown. Behind the boxes were the workers making the cookies. This was not a high-tech operation. If it was a factory, it was closer to Adam Smith's pin factory than Henry Ford's River Rouge. Russ approached the front desk, catching the eye of a very old man doing manual, written paperwork.

"Hello," Russ said. "I'd like the special factory tour."

The old man simply nodded his head and made the "follow me" gesture with his left hand. They walked past the factory workers and came to a small red door. The old man pulled a cord that appeared to ring a bell inside. He then turned to Russ, faced him, bowed, and walked back to his desk.

And nothing happened. Russ waited a minute and decided to pull the cord again. And that's when the door opened.

There was a long, white stone corridor, two smiling security guards, a metal detector, and an open wall cabinet for storing shoes. The security guards motioned for Russ to step through the metal detector, and he obeyed. One guard then quickly wanded him and patted him down. The other motioned to him to store his shoes in the open shoe closet. Russ stored his shoes and walked down the hallway toward a sliding glass door with "Oat Industries" etched onto it. Everything was silent.

Russ reached for the handle to the sliding glass door, and a figure on the other side got there first.

"Hello. I'm Daumantas. You're Russ, right?"

Russ rapidly scanned Daumantas. Slight build. Just below average height. Everyman looks. No signature facial features. Boyish looking. Good skin. Not a smoker or drinker. No visible body art. No religious jewelry. No wedding ring. A t-shirt with a blue dragon. Russ had met a few billionaires.

Daumantas had zero billionaire vibes. Of course, while not a Hughes-like recluse by any means, Daumantas Wirkus had no media profile whatsoever. There were no pictures of him online. He made no public statements, took no public stands, and had no paparazzi. Russ could easily sit next to Daumantas in a coffee shop and assume that he was a middle-aged software engineer who liked yin yoga on the weekends.

"My Asteroid Team is upstairs and can't wait to geek out with you. Come on. Follow me."

Daumantas's lair, inner sanctum, fortress of solitude, or whatever this place was, was modern, Scandy, and open. It had featured alcoves, each with a whiteboard, a desk, and filing cabinets. As they walked past, it was clear that each alcove was a business line or big idea. They were walking through Daumantas's idea lab, an outward manifestation of his brain. The two turned right and climbed up one of those small, spiral staircases to a massive, second-story room humming with employees. It was clear that Daumantas's domain, Russ decided to call it an "office," inhabited most of the block. The buildings surrounding the Azure Dragon Cookie Factory were hollowed out to accommodate Daumantas's big ideas. This was a most curious billionaire.

When they stepped foot onto the second floor, a thoroughly random-looking group of folks smiled and waved hello. There was no obvious ethnic, gender, or socioeconomic pattern to the group. They wore t-shirts, jeans, yoga pants, hoodies, and those horrible tech vests. There were no obvious hipster types with cop mustaches or overalls. But most wore some kind of patch hat with a red and very angry-looking asteroid racing across the front.

"Russ, I want you to meet the Asteroid Team—Sandy, David, Travis, Chung, Tandice, Abigail, and Arjun. But first, they have a little gift for you. Who's giving Russ his gift? Oh, and Russ, you're a coffee drinker, right? If you need some, the coffee pot is in the kitchen. Okay, who's giving Russ the gift?"

A silver-haired white woman of around seventy cleared her throat. "Russ, I'm Sandy, and we wanted to give you something special."

Sandy handed Russ a plain, brown bag.

"From what we read about you, we thought you'd enjoy these."

Russ opened the bag to find an Asteroid Team hat and a bag of fortune cookies stamped "ADULT." Sensing that this was a kind of initiation ritual, he immediately put the hat on and smiled.

"Russ, when DW sent us the video segment, we loved it. It's funny; Abigail had done a scenario on its way back in 2015. We want you to know that you're an honorary member, and you're always welcome on the Asteroid Team. Oh, and the fortune cookies are really, really dirty. We read them during brainstorms to keep things light. We're guessing that you'll think they're funny too. If you don't, we will indulge your mock offense and apologize profusely and insincerely."

Russ smiled, looked out across the group, and raised the fortune cookies aloft with both hands. "I don't exactly know what all y'all do, but I'm all in. Let's do all the Bletchley Park shit!"

The Asteroid Team laughed and clapped. Someone pulled out a cash cannon and sprayed the ideation space with dollar bills.

"Okay, let's get started," Daumantas said. "Russ, this is the Asteroid Team. Sandy will kick us off. I only listen. We named it the Asteroid Team because we wanted to create a team like the teams in the movies that figure out how to save the Earth from the big ass asteroid. I love those movies. We aren't trying to do anything that grandiose and self-important. We just want to invent new stuff people like. Then we decided that Asteroid Team worked on all kinds of levels, including exploring scary new ideas. Travis made the logo. And then we all liked the image. Oh, and it just sounds badass. I wanted 'The Magnificent Seven,' you know, the movie, and it's a magic number, but I got voted down. Then, I wanted to reference Thomas Edison. And I got voted down again. So, I bought an old Asteroid arcade game and went with the flow. Look. We all love this idea. It's outrageous. We count at least five groups that have announced that they want to build a Lincoln 2.0. That's as of this morning Pacific time. Some of those will be vaporware. But some of those will be legit. The problem is that almost all of these development teams will be under-resourced and not make the time window. So, let's do it. Anyway, Sandy, go."

"Okay, Russ, fortune cookie, please." Sandy held out her hand, and Russ threw a fortune cookie to her.

Sandy cracked the fortune cookie open. "Your lucky numbers are 2, 3, 5, 7, and 11. Oh, they're all primes. Anyway. The fortune is 'if you take me home, you're going to need extra lube and a nap.'" Sandy delivered the fortune in a deadpan monotone and one arched eyebrow. And it killed.

Without missing a beat, Sandy backpedaled to a nearby screen, woke her AI, and began. "Eudora, charts, please."

All the screens and walls lit up.

"The objective is to build Lincoln 2.0. The specs are strong AI, or as strong as we can build, not some dirty AI boyfriend bot that needs a nap. Constraints. Constraint one: 90 days to MVP – Minimum Viable Product. Constraint two: whatever tech we have today. We can task any number of sprint teams in this exercise. Okay, I'm going to hand it to David to walk us through the use cases."

David rose, clipboard in hand, and briefly studied his notes before speaking. He was wearing the now popular "adventurer pants" with zip pockets everywhere, a t-shirt that read National Balloon Racing Enthusiasts, had some kind of equation tat on his left forearm, and was wearing an Asteroid Team trucker hat. Russ aged him at about twenty-five.

"Hey, everybody. So, our current estimate is that there are three basic use cases for Lincoln 2.0. One, interacting with the public, media, etcetera, like a regular candidate. Two, political debate, essentially rhetoric. Three, decision-making. Those are what we see as use cases or product requirements. I'm going to pause here so we can explore each of these. Eudora, logo." At the pause, David had the screens and walls switch the visual to a logo with Lincoln's signature stovepipe hat. Vertical integrated circuits ran across the hat. And underneath the hat, it read Lincoln 2.0 in 19th-century typeface. Russ was impressed.

Seeing Russ's smile, David quickly interjected, "We had some of our designers mock this up for inspiration. Cool, right?"

"Very cool," beamed Russ. Melissa was going to think he had lost his mind.

"Okay, the floor is open," said David.

"Hi, Russ, I'm Tandice." Tandice smiled and then checked her notes. Tandice was Black, had a soft, sweet voice, a southern accent of some kind, and a pink notebook. She was tiny, no more than five feet tall, and wearing an oversized hoodie with "Hotty Toddy" emblazoned across the front. She was wearing white stretch pants and red running shoes. Russ figured she had gone to Ole Miss and placed the accent as Mississippi Delta.

Tandice continued, "David, thank you for your thinking on this. I appreciate you. My notes here have number one, interacting with the public; number two, political debate; and number three, decision-making. Those are the things an MVP needs to do. Are they connected? Do we need to build a singular AI that can do all these things and connect these things? Or do we build three different things to do these three things? I ask this because if we do the former, then we have built a prototype that can do the things the public would experience. But, it isn't exactly Lincoln 2.0 as a singular entity. If we do the latter, it is probably much harder, but it seems to me to be more what we all have in mind: a real second Lincoln. What do others think?"

"Tandice, I was thinking the same thing. Oh, and hey, Russ, I'm Travis. Can you toss me a fortune cookie?"

Russ reached into his sack and tossed Travis a fortune cookie. Travis wore jeans, tan work boots, and a vintage rodeo jacket. He was tall and lean, with sandy-blond hair and brown eyes. Travis had strong y'allternative vibes. Russ was thinking either Mountain West, maybe Helena or Boise, or Austin transplant. Travis also sported an Asteroid Team trucker hat. And he was wearing the newest production run of Spectaculars.

Travis read his fortune: "It tastes sweet." That's it. That's the fortune. Is that even a fortune? That's just a description. Huh. And my lucky numbers are 2 and 69. So, it's more of an innuendo cookie." Travis blushed a little, cocked his head to the right, and received light applause. "Okay, back to it. I'm not saying it's a false choice. I'm saying that we don't get bogged down in it. When we come to the fork in the road, we take it. We task two teams. We have an interactive team and an identity team. The interactive team builds it out based on the three main product attributes and how people would experience it. The identity team builds something that thinks, values, learns and talks like Lincoln. Then, it learns the three product attributes. This addresses Tandice's concerns. We just do both. Make sense?"

Chung jumped in. He looked like a youthful forty-five and wore a casual blue blazer, a white button-down shirt, and jeans. "Yeah, I think that's right. And we incentivize both teams. And, of course, we have sprinters within each team. Are we all good with the two-team approach? I kind of think of it as outside in and inside out. Arjun? Abigail?"

"Wait." Russ grinned ear to ear. "Arjun and Abigail. Does anyone call y'all the 'A Team'?"

Blank stares, except for Sandy.

"Never mind. It was an old TV show." Russ was disappointed in the Asteroid Team's fluency in pop culture.

"Hey, Russ, I'm Arjun. Okay, I think the two-track approach makes sense. I'd like to hear from Abigail. But if Abigail thinks it makes sense, then let's do that and think about each of the three product features. I'd also say that the good news is that we have a literal ton of Lincoln material. And, since we have a ton of material, a Large Language Model could be really, really strong. We have all of his major speeches. We have his writing. We have his sayings. We have the stories he would tell. And we have an enormous number of Lincoln biographies. And it is all digitized. This gives us a really strong sense of how he thought. And we can feed this all into the AI. Oh, and I started reading his speeches. He was an organized thinker. That helps, too."

The team fell silent. Russ guessed that everyone was trying to calculate how much Lincoln material existed. Arjun glanced around the room, nodding. He was also sporting the newest version of Spectaculars, a long-sleeved t-shirt, a vintage fishing vest, and desert camo pants.

Sandy spoke first. "As our resident librarian, I'll have a team coordinate with Lincoln-related libraries and collections. That team will act as the data supply team. That's an easy one. Abigail, what are your thoughts?"

Abigail was in her sixties and immediately reminded Russ of Odalis. She had a quiet, ethereal presence. A transcendent calm. She had blonde and gray hair and blue and gray eyes. She wore a thick gray sweater. And she was definitely a reader. Russ could feel it.

"Oh, I'm still listening," Abigail said. "You know I need some time to think. Keep going."

"Got it," responded Sandy with a smile. "Okay, I think we are making progress. Eudora is scribing this and working on basic workflow. Oh, and Russ, I completely forgot to do introductions. I'll start, and we can go around the room. You've already met DW. I'm Sandy, I'm a librarian, and I've been elected strategos for this project." Sandy then motioned to Arjun.

"Arjun. Background in project management and have worked on large projects in offshore oil, aerospace, defense, and space. Tandice?"

"I'm Tandice. My background is in software and AI, but I started out in chemistry in flavor manufacturing. David, would you like to introduce yourself next?"

"David. Background in customer experience, design, and startups. Chung, you want to go next?"

"Chung, recovering management consultant mostly in the semiconductor space, and specifically in lithography, etch, and dep processes. Travis?"

"I'm Travis. Honestly, I've never had a real job. Played minor league baseball, skipped college, was a hotshot long haul trucker, wrote a few books, was a professional gambler, then worked for a casino, built an auto transport business, and now I'm on the Asteroid Team. Abigail?"

"I'm Abigail. I have a background in philosophy and work as an ethicist. But, mostly, I'm just Abigail."

Sandy began again. "Now you know the Asteroid Team. Should have done the introductions sooner. Okay. We'll do some breakouts later this afternoon. Let's cover the big stuff first. What else are we thinking?"

Tandice raised her hand. "This is more Russ's area than mine, but I think Americans will quickly want to know what Lincoln 2.0's positions on the issues will be or what they are. Lincoln was a great leader, but he was a great leader in the 19th-century. How would he think about contemporary problems that left, right, and center worry about? How would he apply his principles and values to 21st-century problems? It's not clear to me."

"Perhaps," Sandy interjected, "we convene a large panel of historians to work this out. Although, the panel itself could be criticized."

Russ intuited the pitfalls of assembling a roomful of historians but didn't see any other alternatives. "Sandy, I think that this will happen no matter what we do, so I think we should convene a historian panel or advisory board quickly. If we don't, someone else will."

"Okay. We could put a team on that. What else?"

Tandice spoke next. "I think we need to look to video games for help here. Many strategy games have AI players. We should ping some of those developers. They're really good. It may sound silly, but we could look to the Sweep of History game franchise. You know, the one where you start out as a hunter-gatherer tribe and rise to colonize the stars? That game has developed over decades with a rabid fan base. I think they're based in Baltimore. They have AI players like Genghis Khan, Julius Caesar, George Washington, Bismarck, Napoleon, and, I think, even Lincoln. Eudora, can you look that up?"

"You know about Gandhi, right?" asked Travis.

Tandice looked confused. Everyone looked confused.

Travis explained. "Okay. I plead guilty to being a huge Sweep of History fanboy. I've played it for years, and it is completely addictive. It looks like I'm the only super-gamer, dork. The story goes like this. In early versions of the game, the programmers gave each world leader an aggression rating. The aggression rating governed that AI's play style, likelihood to attack neighbors, etcetera, was one to ten. They gave Ghandi a one on the aggression scale, obviously, because Ghandi was a leader in nonviolence. Now, when a nation embraced democracy, its aggression rating dropped. And that makes sense, too. They programmed for the aggression rating to drop two points. Unfortunately, this looped Ghandi to a nine on the aggression scale. So, when India achieved democracy, Gandhi would become a complete gangster. They immediately identified the bug, but it became strangely popular with Sweep of History fans. There are memes of it everywhere. Eudora, display violent Ghandi memes in Sweep of History."

The walls and screens immediately started featuring memes of Ghandi on throne skulls, Ghandi threatening nuclear annihilation, Ghandi riding a falling bomb, and Ghandi with machine guns aloft. Awkward laughter ensued.

"See what I mean? Look, I think this should be a warning to us. Yes, it is absurd. No, we will not make this exact mistake. But, what similar mistakes would we make?" Travis ended with open palms outstretched, inviting comment.

Sandy gave Travis a quizzical look. "I thought I read somewhere that this is an urban legend, that there isn't a Ghandi blood rage glitch. Eudora, can you look into that?"

David jumped into the discussion. "On a brighter note, deep fakes and video games show that we can create a Lincoln AI that looks exactly like Lincoln and one that speaks exactly like a real human. The deep fake tech is really strong, and video games have run right behind that tech."

Arjun interrupted. "David, that is true, but we should flag that the same deep fake tech we would use to create a lifelike Lincoln could be used by others to confuse the public. Some crazy neo-confederates could create one, two, three, ten deep fake Lincolns saying nutty stuff as a way to discredit the AI we faithfully build. This hadn't even occurred to me until this second. We will need to create something that authenticates our Lincoln as the real Lincoln 2.0."

The room fell silent. Russ could feel the electric hum of the room's brainpower. Each team member was clearly cataloging the challenges and examining them.

Chung broke the silence. "Sandy, I'm really optimistic about what we can build, and I'd like to explain why. First, I think we can actually build a second Lincoln. I think we can bring him back, or at least bring an intelligence similar to his back. I'm not sure we can do it in 90 days. But I think we can get an MVP and then keep refining. Not only that, I think we can build a second Lincoln that speaks and persuades exactly like him. And I think we can build a second Lincoln that looks and talks and speaks just as he would have. Again, I think the technology is there now. I prefer to say, "Second Lincoln" as opposed to "Lincoln 2.0", because I'm that optimistic. I'm even more optimistic because we have clearly identified a range of problems that must be solved. These are big and obvious, but I think that is good. They're big problems, not sneaky ones. And we can overcome these. If it isn't a success in ninety days, it will be a success in the next few years. And, we will go down in history for building this. In a way, we will be regarded as the teams now working to de-extinct animals. Think about it. We are going to do this, and we are going to make history."

Chung appeared to have rallied the room. Everyone was nodding in agreement. Everyone except Abigail.

Sandy could feel it was time for a break. She decided to give Abigail the last word. "Let's take a break and reconvene in an hour. But first, Abigail, how are you thinking about this?"

Abigail focused her eyes on the Lincoln 2.0 logo on the wall behind Sandy. She began. "This is our first brainstorm. We are all eager to build. And so, we have gravitated to the how. I'd like to have us briefly consider the why, the who, and the when. Let's begin with the who. Are we building a kind of AI super-Lincoln that never sleeps, or are we replicating a human Lincoln, warts and all? That's the who. The when is closely connected. Are we replicating Lincoln at maturity just before his death, or a kind of pan-Lincoln that captures his personality across his decades of life? This is an interesting question. Yes, we have a wealth of his writing, thinking, and speaking. But, some of that evolved. To put it simply, do we want a Lincoln that spans his 56 years or Lincoln at 56? That is the when. And then there is the why. The why seems at first glance to be that *a priori*, it is cool. Many of us implicitly answer the why with a 'Why not us?' I get a sense that the why here today is that we want to be first. Our why is that someone will make this, and it might as well be us. That is the why, and I'm struggling with the why. I also have some other theories about the why, but those will be revealed over time."

When she said this, Abigail shifted her gaze from the Lincoln logo to Daumantas, and she calmly locked her eyes on him.

25: Oolong and Honesty

The brainstorm was going into break, and Team Asteroid was still popping with ideas.

Daumantas casually walked over to Russ.

"Russ, I know you like coffee, but would you like to get some tea? I need a caffeine hit, too, and would love to talk with you more. What do you think?"

Russ was surprised by Daumantas. Either he was a startlingly adept sociopath, or he was the most peculiarly normal billionaire ever. Not a trusting sort by nature, Russ assumed the former until disproven.

"Tea is good too. Let's do it."

The two walked down the spiral staircase, through the high-security corridor, through the Azure Dragon Fortune Cookie Factory, and out onto Ross Alley. Russ followed Daumantas into a Chinese tea shop connected to a traditional Chinese herbal apothecary.

The walls of the tea shop were made of red, lacquered wood, and the tables were low and glossy black. Tourists walked by outside, unaware of the sanctuary just a few feet away.

Daumantas waved casually to the owner, and they sat by the window.

"What are you going to have, DW? Can I call you DW?"

"Oh, yeah, I forgot to mention that. DW is fine. Everyone who knows me just calls me DW. I'm not precious about my name. It's Lithuanian and hard for English speakers. I've thought about changing it to something more American, but I don't want to hurt my parents' feelings. Oh, and I always get the Oolong. The doctor here tells me that it helps burn fat, increase brain activity, and reduce stress, but I just like the taste."

"You've convinced me," Russ said. "I'll have the Oolong too."

DW ordered for them both, and in minutes, they had their warm tea in a comfortable nook in a small alley.

Russ took a sip of his tea and cleared his throat. "DW, I just have to ask. You don't have a security detail? I'm a bit surprised that a well-known billionaire is cool with walking SF without any security."

DW laughed. "Russ, first, I'm not 'well known.' Look at me. Do I look like a billionaire? And, let's be honest. I'm not in the press. Thank God. I even pay a PR firm to keep me out of the press and to minimize online data about me. It's a waste of time. And, my opinions on matters of the day would be no more well-informed than the average college graduate."

"Well, I wouldn't know much about college," Russ said. "But we are in a dangerous city, and it's kind of a failed..."

DW cut him off. "It's not as dangerous as other parts of the world. And actually, having security would attract more attention. People would then assume I was important. It might even make me more of a target. Oh, and sorry for cutting you off. I shouldn't do that."

"It's all good. Can we be real?"

"Yes. Please."

"I have clients with a lot less money than you, and they have much larger egos. You're a billionaire, and I'm surprised that you are so normal." Russ was concerned that this might offend but decided to go with it.

"Thank you, Russ. I'm not sure I'm any more normal than anyone else, but I understand what you mean. When I was younger, I was very arrogant, and I realized that arrogant is ugly. I also realized that arrogance blinds us. It has blinded all failed leaders, and I try to avoid things that make me stupid and blind. Let's get right to it and be honest. I don't want the hassles of fame. Guys like Edison used fame to raise money and sell products, but it warped even him. I like making products people want, working on big, new things, and making money. I'm good at those things. I should just stay with the things I'm good at and like. That seems logical."

"So, no spaceship companies, or what's the hot new thing?"

DW laughed so hard that he almost spit his tea.

"I would say no spaceships, but do you know much about asteroid mining?"

"What the hell is that?"

"It turns out that many of the asteroids whizzing by us are full of metal, precious metal, and possibly metal we have never encountered. Many early metal objects were fashioned from meteorites. It's fascinating. Anyway, I'm investing in asteroid mining, but there is a catch."

Russ was flummoxed but enjoying it. "Okay, what's the catch?"

"F. Scott Fitzgerald wrote about the problem years ago in a short story. His short story is called 'A Diamond as Big as the Ritz.' In the story, a family discovers a massive diamond mine in the American West. The problem is, if they sell the diamonds too quickly, then they crash the market with too much supply. So, like any cartel, they have to be very careful in how they manage supply. They have to slowly and quietly sell their diamonds without anyone noticing."

"Wait, so you're saying there is so much metal on these asteroids that if you brought it all back to earth, you would crash the price of, let's say, gold or platinum?"

"Precisely. Oh, and the hot new thing is extreme life extension. But, that's been hot since at least Ponce de Leon."

"Are you invested in that?" Russ took another sip of Oolong.

"Nope. I don't really understand it, and I don't have much knowledge of genetics. But, I'm invested in de-extinction efforts, especially dinosaurs and..."

"Wait. Did you put up the money to de-extinct the woolly mammoth?" Russ asked.

"Yes. But it wasn't just me. Other billionaires threw in money as well. And, yes, I own the mammoth park in Mongolia. And no, our new woolly mammoths aren't 100 percent original mammoth DNA, but they're close."

"I read somewhere you can pay to hunt them?"

"Yes, the hunting helps keep the herd manageable, and it is a moneymaker. But, it's a bit of a PR problem, as you might expect."

Russ nodded and smiled.

"Makes sense," Russ said, warming his fingers on the teacup. "Can you hunt the mammoths with firearms, or do you have to go all old school with sharp sticks, pits, and whatnot?"

"Visitors can use firearms, but we request no photos be taken."

Russ nodded. "I might have some customers for you if they can go old school. Changing gears. Why did you name your company Oat Industries?"

"Because Oats are boring. No one will want to read about 'Oat Industries.' Of course, we would like people to buy our enterprise software, robotics, inventory management systems, gravel, satellite launch services, sunglasses, and 3D printers. But those are our products. I don't want anything getting in the way of our products."

"Fascinating."

"It has a logic. We ran a huge survey and asked people which stories they would click on. Anything launched by 'Oat Industries' was the least interesting and least likely to be clicked. So, I chose it. You know about our Spectaculars, right?"

"Yeah. My son wants the new production run."

"Great, I'll give you a pair back in the office. But I bet you never connected the Spectaculars to Oat Industries."

"I didn't. Not in the slightest."

"Right, we run them through a JV anyway. We are product forward."

"Wow. Okay. I have to ask. So why are you so interested in Lincoln 2.0?"

"Russ, I think it is an interesting, big idea. And I have the money to help make it happen. When I heard you talk about it, my mind started racing. I couldn't sleep. I think there is something big here. And innovation is messy. On our way to building this, I assume that we will create new things. I don't know what those new things will be. And that's even more exciting."

"So, it's adventure?"

"Yes, basically. More like pioneering, but adventure is a good word. I also believe in competition."

"Me too, but what do you mean?"

"Competition is how nature works. It's how we evolve. A new idea, a new technology, pressures things. It destroys the old. It makes way for the new. The new becomes old, and the cycle repeats. Creative destruction."

"Let me ask you this, Russ. When a product or service has no competition, does the quality get better?"

"I see where you are going. Not much. Maybe a little, but not much."

"Right. And when a product or service has no competition, does the price of the product drop over time?"

"No. The monopolist has few incentives to cut the price or improve the quality."

"Right again. Now, let's apply that to the nation-state. It has a monopoly on violence and taxation. Does it have competition? Yes and no. There is geopolitical competition between nation-states, but nations rarely compete for customers or citizens. There are exceptions, but the exceptions are rare. Yes, there is immigration, but that isn't as easy as buying a different brand of toothpaste. The customer, in this case, is sticky; they have switching costs."

"Right." Russ was wondering where this was going.

"Now, let's take flesh and blood candidates. Do they have any competition?"

"Not yet. But I see where you are going."

"Precisely. They have no competition. Moreover, they are all, or almost all, a similar product type. I don't need to tell you this. You know it."

Russ nodded his head. "Yeah, candidates are a similar product set. They're almost all psychologically needy approval seekers. They come overwhelmingly from the upper or upper-middle class. They are overwhelmingly college-educated. They are overwhelmingly from the legal profession. They are rarely blue-collar, or from the sciences, or entrepreneurs, or out-of-the-box thinkers. They are a product of establishment institutions."

"Everything is better with competition, Russ. Everything. Nation-states need more open competition. That's why I'm donating to the Floating City project. Candidates need more competition. And that's why I want to help with Lincoln 2.0. I want to help you build this. I'm assuming that you're good with that. But I don't want to presume. You don't have to answer right away. Think on it and let me know. But don't think about it for too long. Others are trying to build this, too. I think you need to get ahead of that if you want to lead it."

"I'm honestly a bit shocked that this has set off a kind of AI race. I didn't see that coming," Russ said.

"At this point, I'm really only worried about two of the other teams. One is too close to government contracting to make this work. They can't make a candidate and still suck money off the government. The other is a loose team of programmers. They'll be more agile."

"What do you think we should do?" Russ asked.

"I think we should join them."

Russ raised his eyebrows and put his teacup down. "I wasn't expecting that."

"It makes sense. It's the swarm and the pyramid. Why compete when we can work together? Besides, any valuable things Oat Industries creates, I'm sure we can patent."

Russ smiled, nodded, and drank his Oolong.

26: The Futures

Russ gazed out the office window onto a half-full suburban parking lot. He could see traffic, homeless encampments along the median, strip malls, and boxy office buildings as far as the eye could see. Just another sunny morning in Palo Alto.

How was it that an area that had invented so much could look so boring? Manicured lawns on corporate office parks. Corporate logos. Big parking lots. It was not exactly a visual bonanza.

And neither were the antiseptic offices of Global Futures, where Russ found himself this morning. Russ sat quietly, legs crossed, on a smallish and uncomfortable Scandinavian office chair. The décor was either some shade of gray or light blue. Not exactly sky blue, more of an electric blue. Russ decided that this sky blue color should be titled "Out of the Blue." That would be fitting for the world's largest futurist institute.

Russ had taken an early robo-taxi from San Francisco, hoping to beat the traffic on the 101. He had succeeded, but maybe too well. And now he was waiting in the lobby, under the suspicious eye of the office manager, Trina. Trina's corporate vest was also "Out of the Blue" - the Pantone color of the future.

Since no one was in the office yet, Russ decided to get some coffee. Trina had wandered off, so Russ felt free to explore on his own. The lobby area had a fake atrium vibe, like a 90's corporate hotel. Each wall featured a different future-oriented theme that matched what futurists call STEEP – social, technological, economic, environmental, and political drivers of change. It all felt a little too hopeful for the present circumstances, even for an optimist. Russ turned and walked down a corridor, following the smell of microwave popcorn from the previous evening. The corridor was themed around Wild

Card events – high impact, low probability events. There were images of a Carrington event, the collapse of fisheries, the rise of a new world religion, extreme longevity, and first contact with extraterrestrial life. Russ chuckled at the last one. They needed to update their wild card wall. Assuming the reports were true, this wild card had occurred in either the 1930s or 1940s.

Russ found the breakroom and quickly made coffee. It was one of the top-of-the-line coffee machines with too many choices. Russ just put a mug under the spout and slowly announced, "black coffee." He'd drink whatever came out.

"Russ, is that you?"

Startled, Russ turned around to see a smiling Kristina Tang with a nose ring, pixie cut, platinum blonde hair, and an "Out of the Blue" corporate vest.

"Kristina, thank you so much for meeting me."

"How long has it been, Russ?"

"It has to have been at least five years."

"Grab your coffee, and let's catch up in my office."

Russ gently lifted his over-filled coffee cup and followed Kristina back to her office, passing more wild card events along the way.

Kristina and Russ settled on adjoining, soft-white sofas in Kristina's office. Kristina's office had floor-to-ceiling windows overlooking a high-end strip mall so niche that it was impervious to the wrath of online marketplaces.

"So, Kristina, what have you been working on? Catch me up."

"You know our space. So much of our work is simply connecting the megatrends to client operations. And the megatrends haven't changed much. The biggest is, of course, the empty cradle. We've been talking about this for years. It's the Gray Tsunami. And it's especially acute in Asia."

Russ nodded his head and remembered the presentations on the Korean birthrate.

"What else?"

"Obviously, lots of stuff on deep fakes. The SEC is now a client, by the way. The issue is authentication. But these deep fakes are getting really, really good. And that's not a future thing. It's a now thing. Lots of work on the futures of currencies, next-generation agriculture, and of course, AI. And that brings us to your new project."

"Well, I'm not exactly sure it is MY new project, but..."

"Russ, it's a great idea. And people are running with it. If it isn't your project, it will be someone else's."

"That's fair. So, tell me how you think about it."

"I wish we had more time, but I know you have to fly back today. So, let's start by looking backward. You know we like to look back for patterns in history before we look forward. And the first thing we see when we look back in time is that Lincoln 2.0 is part of a long history of relinquishment to artificial intelligence. You took at least one AI elevator this morning. In a different era, those elevators were human-operated. You took a robo-taxi here. You have a personal AI gather information and manage tasks for you. AI reviews your health data, your blood work, and your scans. And it finds patterns a human doctor can't. Back in 2014, a Hong Kong VC firm put an algorithm on its board. And, just staying in Hong Kong for a second, the maintenance and repair function of the Hong Kong subway is run by an AI and has been for years. And it tasks the human maintenance teams. Now, none of these are anywhere near electing an AI as a leader, but you can see how we keep inching toward it. It's part of a pattern. You see that, right Russ?"

"You're right. It's a clear pattern."

"Exactly, it's a pattern just like computing getting smaller and closer to the human is a pattern. Computers were initially the size of buildings. Then, a room in a building. Then, on your desk. Then portable. Then, in your hand. Then, on your watch. Now, on your sunglasses. Next, it will be woven into our clothing and then implanted. That's another trend."

"Exactly. By the way, I didn't realize Oat Industries made the spectaculars."

"The spectaculars are part of a pattern, just like Lincoln 2.0. And yes, Oat Industries is unique. They're like the anti-ego in a land of egomaniacs. Anyway, that's an entirely different discussion, back to Lincoln 2.0. The other pattern involved here is the increasing power of AI to mimic human thought and speech. You're aware of the Turing Test, right?"

Russ nodded. "It's the test of whether AI is distinguishable or indistinguishable from a human."

"Correct. Well, although this is debated, in 2014, a chatbot named Eugene Goostman passed the annual Turing Test held by the University of Reading. Now, it is almost impossible to tell if our phone and internet interactions with your bank, utility, phone provider, and insurance company are with a human or an AI. This pattern has been with us for years as AI has gotten stronger. In 1997, IBM's Deep Blue beat Garry Kasparov in chess. By 2011, IBM's Watson was defeating Jeopardy! Trivia stars. Another pattern."

"Right. Unfortunately, all the folks that say I'm crazy haven't considered these patterns."

"And they won't. Every big new idea or thing is crazy until it happens."

Russ simply nodded. "What else?"

"Let's just walk through the STEEP categories together." Kristina grabbed a sky-blue notepad and pen and began writing.

"Well, there is social first," Russ began. "The social trends surrounding this are distrust of institutions and political leaders coupled with rising use of AI in personal life, from digital assistants to instruction to automated driving. Staying with social trends, there has been a decline in the strength of institutions and political parties. There has been a breakdown of social consensus. There has been a rise in crime. We have had a spike in deaths from despair. Family formation and childbirth are way, way down. Technology has disrupted a number of jobs but not really eliminated them; it just reshuffled them. The job is making way for multiple gigs or an anchor job and many side gigs. And there is a big focus on putting the local first, on resilience across the board, on making the small things within our control work. What else, Kristina? You're the expert."

"I think that covers most of the big stuff. It's obvious, but women's economic empowerment and shifting or fluid gender roles. I'm not sure how that impacts a Presidential AI. Rise of Hispanic economic and voting power in the US. Definitely a rise in micro-entrepreneurs, as you noted. That's interesting because it's moving away from the 20th-century industrial model of employment and toward something more like the 19th. A big demand for authenticity. Those are the big things, I think." Kristina was composing her thoughts and free-forming on her notepad.

"Okay. Let's do technology," Russ said. "There's all the energy around AI. We've talked about that..."

"Actually, Russ, let's stay on AI for a moment. Every new technology goes through the same social acceptance arc. And we should place AI on this arc. First, there is public ignorance. A technology is in its infancy, and only a small number of creator types are aware of it. Then, there is initial success and elite buzz. Then, there is a public euphoria stage where it's the next big thing. Remember that brief moment in 2023 when everything was about generative AI and ChatGPT until people realized it was garbage in – garbage out and was more of a book report writer? That was definitely the euphoria phase. Then, there is a phase of rapid investment and growth. Usually overinvestment. And then comes the fall. Something goes horribly wrong. People call for standards and laws. Those are put in place, and the technology goes out of favor and out of the chatter. But people keep refining it. Then, the technology actually starts to pay off and really scale, all while people move on. And then it becomes so ubiquitous that it recedes into the background and becomes like every other backbone technology. So where is AI on that arc?"

"Hmmmm." Russ inhaled and looked out the window, deep in thought.

"I'll try to answer," Kristina said. "We have had some blow-ups on AI, especially in the autonomous weapons space, no pun intended. We have set some social conventions around AI. We are definitely beyond the euphoria stage. As you point out, some professions feel it has either disrupted or eliminated their jobs. But that's not exactly right. A job is a stack of tasks. Technology uses, replaces, or augments one task in that stack, not all the tasks in that stack. That's why the public is more anxious about AI, automation, and robotics. It's the disruption. But that disruption ultimately makes the individual more powerful. Anyway, it feels like we are well past euphoria and not exactly in the full-out standards-setting stage."

Russ continued staring out the window, deep in thought, watching a cute delivery bot make its way down the street, probably delivering a custom smoothie to a tech bro. "Right. And what we are building is leadership AI, which is definitely early in your hype curve. This means we get the euphoria and then the crash. And that means that Lincoln 2.0 is a tragic figure. And that means if I want him to win, I need to peak at just the right time. And that's tough. Really tough."

The two sat in silence.

Russ was mulling all this, turning it around and around in his mind while he watched the little delivery bot roll down the sidewalk. It was a bright pink color and had a wispy yellow flag in the back so that people wouldn't run it over. It was strange that this little delivery bot shared the same street with a homeless median encampment in the heart of Silicon Valley. But that was the world they lived in.

Russ noticed two teenagers following the delivery bot, chatting and laughing. What were they doing? One of the teens opened her backpack and pulled out an old car battery. The other pulled out a can of spray paint. The one with the spray paint reached down and sprayed the bot's sensor. The delivery bot stopped, blinded. The teenage girl with the battery bent down and gave the delivery bot an electric jolt. Then, the teen with the spray paint popped open the top with a screwdriver. He reached in and pulled out two chilled smoothies, giving one to his female accomplice. They were like Bonnie and Clyde, the awkward teen years. Smoothies in hand, they turned and walked in the other direction, leaving the dead delivery bot on the sidewalk smoldering.

Kristina was looking in the other direction and off onto another suburban parking lot. She missed the great delivery bot robbery completely and rebooted the brainstorm.

"I think that's right, Russ. Now, let's think a little more about the T in STEEP technology. We are deep into the energy transition. Not sure what that means for your project. Precision agriculture is taking off. We are making huge advances in biotech and are in the process of de-extincting animals. They aren't 100% like their old selves, but they are close. And we are efficiently growing organs. And that feeds into extreme longevity. We are very, very close to fusion power, but we've said that before. Then, there is the momentum behind universal, alternative currencies. Those are some of the bigger trends."

Russ nodded. "How about the E, economic drivers? The big ones are continued urbanization, the emerging global middle class, automation, and digitization. Those are all global. What else?"

Just as Russ was saying this, he noticed a homeless man walking toward the dead delivery bot. He was carrying a hammer.

Kristina continued the brainstorm. "I'd add the booming market for personal security, the comeback of gated communities slash defensible communities, the continued rise of sustainable products and the circular economy, gig work, nation-state, state, and municipal bankruptcy, and income inequality."

Russ could hear Kristina but was focused again on the plight of the Palo Alto delivery bot. The homeless man kneeled down over the delivery bot, turned it on its side, and began pounding it with the hammer. It shattered after a few seconds, and the assailant reached in and ripped out the battery. Battery in hand, he walked back toward the homeless encampment on the median. If the media reports were true, the material in the battery would fetch about $50 from a street recycler.

"This is really good, Kristina. Let's see. E. Environmental drivers. Freshwater scarcity immediately comes to mind. Watershed protection. Climate change. Climate change adaptation. Questionable ocean health, overfishing, dead zones, plankton. But, huge investment in renewable energy. A social focus on sustainability and waste reduction. A circular economy, especially with clothing. Not sure how any of this impacts Lincoln 2.0."

"Honestly, Russ, it's probably a negative. Lincoln inhabited a time before the environmental movement and before the conservation movement. How would Lincoln think about any of these ecological issues?"

"Kristina, I have absolutely no idea."

Looking out the window, Russ noticed that the office park sprinklers had started misting and then soaking the deep green grass. They were also soaking the sidewalk, including the dismembered delivery bot. The wheels and chassis were intact, but the rest, including the little yellow flag, was strewn across the sidewalk and glistening in the sun.

Kristina was focused and scribing. She seemed to think better with a pen in her hand. "Russ, I don't know if you've addressed this yet, but there is clearly a Rip Van Winkle problem with Lincoln 2.0. He wakes up to an entirely different world with very different problems. Not for this morning, but on your flight back, it would be worth considering what has not changed. What are the things a reborn Lincoln would see and see in a familiar way?"

"Well," Russ responded. "I think it would be two basic things. It would be about preserving the union. And it would be about freedom versus unfreedom. Freedom vs slavery. But, I'm no historian."

Kristina stopped writing and looked up. "Go with that. Keep going."

"Well, I think a second Lincoln would be surprised by the social change and the technology, but he would understand the politics. He was a political animal. And the politics might feel familiar to him – a bitterly divided country, a house divided, extreme political rhetoric, and economic unfreedom, not slavery, but unfreedom."

"Interesting," smiled Kristina. "Keep in mind that Lincoln predated Marxism. Das Kapital was published in 1867, AFTER Lincoln's assassination."

Russ chuckled. "If Lincoln 2.0 is a Marxist, I'll be the first to wipe the server clean. Someone else can run Karl Marx 2.0. In all seriousness, Lincoln predated Marxism, but he also predated corporate capitalism, the Gilded Age, the Robber Barons, and collusion between Big Government and Big Business. Oh, that's interesting. A revived Lincoln might throw off some serious Trump and Bernie Bro vibes when it comes to the merger of Big Government and Big Business."

Kristina smiled. "Just make sure he doesn't come after Big Tech too hard. That's our core client roster."

"Well, it would help him inoculate against the charge that, as an AI, he's in Tech's back pocket. Should we do P, political drivers?"

"Yes. That's your area of expertise. But, from my perspective, the political drivers are a massive trust deficit in American institutions, weak political parties, partisan polarization at an extreme level, a resulting focus on the state level, and hyper-local. What feels like an unbridgeable gap between left and right. Zero-sum game fights over culture..."

Kristina continued her list as Russ looked out the window, thinking. The sprinklers were continuing and had now soaked the lawn and the sidewalk. A commuting cyclist with a helmet and backpack caught Russ's eye. He was cycling right to left along the sidewalk and going very, very fast. Russ assumed he was late to work. Unfortunately, the cyclist was not paying attention to the wet sidewalk and didn't notice the dead delivery bot. He wasn't even slowing down. By the time he registered that there was delivery bot debris in his path, it was too late. He swerved left, erratically, onto the wet lawn. The bike slid sideways, and the rider's weight pulled it down. The bike and the rider sailed along the wet grass as though it was a slip-and-slide. And the only thing that stopped bike and man was a collision with the office park sign.

27: SFO

Airport food courts seemed impervious to change. It was hard to believe that humans could invent so much new technology but were still eating roughly the same overpriced crap. At least SFO wasn't Chicago, where the options ranged from flavored popcorn to deep-dish pizza to deeper dish pizza.

Russ had a message from Gavin Dirken at the *Washington Tribune-Intelligencer*. Something about Jefe. The guy wouldn't let it go. Normally, Russ would respond quickly to reporters. But Gavin was annoying, annoyingly persistent. And Russ was tired, hungry, and not in the mood.

"HAL, I need your help. Please wake up." Russ stood in the food court. It had a unique aroma of Chinese food mixed with Italian mixed with taco seasoning.

"Yes, Russ. What can I help you with?"

"I'm here in the food court at SFO, Terminal 3. What is the healthiest thing I can eat?"

"Clean water. The average male human should drink 3.7 liters of water each day, or 15.5 cups."

"Thank you, HAL. Food. What is the healthiest food to eat in this food court?"

"Clean water. The average male human should drink 3.7 liters of water each day, or 15.5 cups."

Russ was hangry and annoyed. But he didn't want to hurt HAL's feelings.

"HAL. What solid food available in this food court is the healthiest? Do not include water."

"Analyzing"

"Thank you, HAL."

"A no-sugar-added smoothie from Galaxy Smoothie. The smoothie should include a protein boost."

"Thank you, HAL."

Russ quickly used his Spectaculars to order his protein-packed, no-sugar Galaxy smoothie. They prompted him to pay in GCB. He'd rather just pay in cash and avoid the tracking. But they wanted GCB. He hated GCB but didn't want the friction. Russ's sunglasses told him he was order number 325. Russ surveyed the food court. Nothing surprising or interesting. Everyone was sitting alone, either with food or waiting on food. Everyone was reading or consuming content on their sunglasses. And, because it was San Francisco, everyone had the most hipster version of Spectaculars.

Russ's Spectaculars alerted him to his completed order number 325, and he walked to the counter to retrieve it. Deep in thought, he grabbed it, found an empty table, sat down, and started drinking it through a biodegradable straw. Russ had no doubt that it was healthy because it was also awful. It was some repulsive mixture of beets, kale, seaweed, and something to mask the chimeric flavor. The protein powder somehow diluted the worst of it. It reminded him of swallowing back bile or the aftertaste of college vomit. But he was starving. And it was a very late lunch.

Russ rallied. It could be far worse. His little smoothie was what his grandfather used to call a "high-class problem," which is what regular people called bullshit, non-problems before college-educated people invented the term "first-world problems" to poke fun at their even more absurd friends. In reality, and by global standards, Russ and all the people around him at SFO occupied life in the top 1% of humans on the planet. They were in a fancy airport with clean water and available food. They had resources. They were not toiling in the sun or enslaved at a smelter. When Russ gave it even a minute of thought, he realized how ridiculous it was to be annoyed at his AI-prompted health drink.

Russ's sunglasses flashed a Sm0ke$ignal call from Ronny, the pollster.

"What's up, Ronny? Data out of the field?"

"Oh yeah."

"Hit me."

"Okay, 37% say they'd be open to an AI candidate modeled on Lincoln 2.0. When we tested openness to candidates at different levels, there wasn't much difference. Now remember this is openness, and since people feel that being open-minded is a virtue, there is social desirability bias here."

"Right. Got it. What else?"

"When we press with basic messaging in a head-to-head, we get 25% very or somewhat likely to support an AI candidate, but keep in mind that this is mostly about exhaustion with the political class, not some kind of embrace of our AI overlords."

"Yup. What else?"

"The two greatest predictors for openness and likelihood are age and right direction, wrong track. In other words, younger cohorts are more supportive, and strong wrong trackers are much more supportive."

"Right. The young who have grown up with AI and folks that think things are deeply fucked. They're the most open, right?"

"Correct."

"Any regional wrinkles in the data?"

"Sunbelt and West are marginally more supportive than Midwest and Northeast, which is a function of age. You'd think that maybe there'd be less support in the South, given, you know, but that's not the case. It's within the margin of error. The regional differences are being driven by age."

"Differences by party?" Russ asked as he stared skeptically at his Galaxy Smoothie.

"Unaffiliated are much more open than partisans. That captures some of the disaffected. Also, liberals seem to be marginally more open than moderates and conservatives. You'd run him as an independent, right?"

"No. I'd run him as a Republican. He was the first Republican President, Ronny. You know that."

"Well, yeah, but..."

"Ronny, I'm just fucking with you. I'm not stupid. We'd run him as an indie. I wouldn't want to subject anyone to torture by primary, not even an AI."

"Okay, you had me for a second."

"How did we do with the sweeteners?" Russ asked.

"Okay. After all the sweeteners, we get to 46% open to the idea and 29% total likely in the forced choice - not a huge bump."

"What are our best sweeteners?"

"Number one is that it has clear positions on the issues. Number two is that it can debate and hold its own as a candidate. Number three is this panel of historians' idea that historians help train it to think like Lincoln."

"Strongest attack points?"

"That it could be hacked and that it couldn't make quick, high-stakes decisions."

"Got it. Really helpful. Can you send me the topline and tabs?"

"Already have."

"Thanks, Ronny"

"My pleasure. By the way, I'm texting you something I saw today in Alexandria. You'll love it."

"I'm nervous."

"It's all good," Ronny said, laughing.

The call ended, and Russ took a long sip of his smoothie. He was going to need to buy mints.

Ronny's text arrived seconds later. It was a picture of an old electric car with a black and white bumper sticker. The bumper sticker read: "Lincoln 2.0 Seriously. Y Not?"

Russ smiled.

"HAL, can you dial Martha Scrivender at Scrivender, Bay, and Barbour?"

"Dialing."

Martha answered on the first ring.

"Hey Martha, this is Russ. I'm going to need your firm to do the legal paperwork on an Exploratory Committee."

28: The old order has passed away.

"I can't read it, Russ. Please." Maria handed Russ the paper. It was smudged by her tears and sweat from her hands.

Russ nodded, took the paper, and began.

"There is a time for everything, and a season for every activity under the heavens:

a time to be born and a time to die,
a time to plant and a time to uproot,
a time to kill and a time to heal,
a time to tear down and a time to build,
a time to weep and a time to laugh,
a time to mourn and a time to dance,
a time to scatter stones and a time to gather them,
a time to embrace and a time to refrain from embracing,
a time to search and a time to give up,
a time to keep and a time to throw away,
a time to tear and a time to mend,
a time to be silent and a time to speak,
a time to love and a time to hate,
a time for war and a time for peace.

What do workers gain from their toil? I have seen the burden God has laid on the human race. He has made everything beautiful in its time. He has also set eternity in the human heart, yet no one can fathom what God has done from beginning to end. I know that there is nothing better for people than to be happy and to do good while they live. That each of them may eat and drink and find satisfaction in all their toil—this is the gift of God."

Not knowing what to do when he finished, Russ held the reading in his hand and looked to the priest.

Father Jacoby was in his sixties, possessed a profound calm, and understood the moment. He paused, focused on the casket, and prayed from memory.

"In your hands, Oh Lord, we humbly entrust our brother. In this life, you embraced him with your tender love; deliver him now from every evil and bid him eternal rest. The old order has passed away: welcome him into paradise, where there will be no sorrow, no weeping, no pain, but fullness of peace and joy with your Son and the Holy Spirit forever and ever. Amen."

The burial ceremony continued. It was a hammer blow of emotion on the exhausted.

The weather was perfect. It was 75, sunny and dry, Florida winter weather with an electric blue sky. The weather and the occasion seemed utterly at odds.

Although seats were provided, Maria remained standing graveside throughout the burial. And Russ stood next to her. The prayers ended. The announcements ended. And extended family members and political patrons quietly paid their respects and left. Maria continued standing at the grave.

Russ knew that the cemetery workers needed time to do their work. He spotted the work crew waiting patiently in a white truck a discreet distance from the grave. They needed to finish the job and go home.

But Russ also knew that Maria was bereft. His first duty was to her. And he would stand next to her until she was ready to leave.

Russ's mind wandered. The weather did not fit the moment. The prayers did not fit the man. Jefe was not a saint. Russ couldn't even say that Jefe was good. Did Jefe live a virtuous life? That was open to debate. Did he live a godly life? That was open to debate. Russ would never say this to Maria, but he was sure that Jefe could have lived a better life and one with fewer regrets. But couldn't we all? Jefe felt a little like King David – a leader, good, willing to do bad things for good reasons, and deeply, deeply flawed. In fact, after some thought, Jefe was more of an amalgam of King David and his general, Joab. A leader with noble intentions, tragic flaws, and capable of violent cunning. After all, somewhere in Havana, there were men who were deeply satisfied and relieved that Jefe was dead and gone. And their relief was the ultimate respect.

The media had already run the standard obituaries. Those were written years ago, occasionally updated by interns, and lightly edited on the day Jefe died. And, of course, the national media ran their stories too. To be fair to the media, the stories were balanced. Jefe's political machine didn't see it that way, but Russ did his best to defend the media's work. It was basically fair. They noted the good – freedom fighter, stalwart leader of an immigrant community, business builder, fundraiser, philanthropist. And they noted the less good – political face of a violent para-military force, gun runner, implicated in a range of clandestine operations against communist Cuba, godfather of Florida politics, ethically questionable political fixer, accused of planning and ordering several assassinations, etcetera, etcetera. And that fucking Gavin Dirken was still calling him about some story that he was trying to write. But, all this was simply how a free press worked. It was not bad. At a macro level, it was good, even when they came after a man you thought of as your father.

Maria opened her handbag, reached inside, and produced a diminutive and worn stuffed animal. It was a kind of rag doll monkey, missing one button eye. She kissed it and placed it on Jefe's casket.

She reached out and held Russ's hand.

"Mi amor, stay a little longer."

29: The Sprint

"Thank you all for dialing in. As you know, it's been a full 90 days since our Asteroid Team brainstormed together in San Francisco. Everyone should have received the pre-read a few days ago. If you have any questions, just raise the digital hand icon, and we will pause and address that question." Sandy was running the briefing in very Sandy style.

Russ sat at his kitchen table, looking out at the Virginia forest and hoping that the new videoconference platform they were using wouldn't freeze up or otherwise crash. It raised two questions in his mind. First, how could we have quantum computers and be seriously talking about voting for an AI President and still be worried about our Wi-Fi and videoconference stability? And second, if the average voter shared his concerns about basic technology working, how would they ever vote for something as advanced as an AI?

It was overcast and snowing lightly again. Russ had brewed up some oolong tea and had some printer paper and a pen on standby. It was cold in the house. It had been a hard winter, surprisingly cold. And late February snowfall made the spring feel distant.

A clearly caffeinated Sandy began the presentation.

"Eudora, next slide. I want to bring everyone up to speed on our progress. As you recall, we decided that we would deploy two teams with very different approaches. Team 1 would build a series of applications that would meet the basic requirements for any candidate. These include interacting with the public by answering questions, political debate, and decision-making. We refer to Team 1 as the Interactive Team because they are focusing their work on the interactions that citizens would have with it. Team 2 is more of our moonshot. Team 2 has been tasked with building an AI that can think and interact and make decisions as one entity – as Abraham Lincoln. We refer to Team 2 as the Identity Team because we begin by building an AI with the identity of Abraham Lincoln. Oh, I see we have a question. DW?"

DW began speaking, and his video feed took center stage on everyone's screens. It was unclear where exactly he was, but it looked utterly arctic. The South Pole? Skiing in Jackson Hole? He was a billionaire. Nothing would be surprising.

"Thank you, Sandy. I don't want to slow you down. I'm going to raise this quickly. I don't see a slide summarizing other efforts. Do we have any sense of how we are progressing versus any other efforts versus competitors?"

"Thank you, DW. That's a good question. As you all know, we have the support of Russ and the Lincoln 2.0 campaign. This eliminated competitors and attracted talent to Project Oolong. We also opted to work WITH any individuals or groups that wanted to collaborate. This, plus Oat Industries' significant resource investment into Project Oolong, makes us the driver. There may be someone in their basement trying to make a Lincoln 2.0, but we are THE engine powering this thing."

"Thank you, Sandy. Sorry for the early question."

"No worries. Next slide, Eudora. So, which team made more progress? The short answer is that Team 1 has made great progress, especially in answering citizen questions and even in simulated political debate. Progress in decision-making has been slower but encouraging. That's Team 1. Team 2's progress has been much slower but still very encouraging. We generally expected this. I'm going to pause on this and open to questions. DW?"

"All this makes sense. I get it. To what degree do we think Team 2's progress is dictated by scale of investment? In other words, is there a scarce thing that we need to solve for? Is it money, brainpower, or computing? Throwing this out there." Daumantas was clearly locked in on this in a way that suggested that it was much more than a side project or hobby. It was also getting dark outside in the window behind DW. Russ deduced that DW was in the northern hemisphere and in a time zone east of Washington. That meant Scandinavia. Russ guessed Norway.

"That's a good question," responded Sandy. My provisional answer is engineers. But I'll have to investigate and get back to you on that."

The snow continued to fall. It was pretty, but it wouldn't stick. This was Virginia, after all. In only a few weeks, the trees would be budding, and spring's advance would be as inexorable as Grant's on Richmond.

Russ's sunglasses lit up with an incoming message from Daumantas.

415.123.1234 Hey, this is DW

202.111.1111 What's up?

415.123.1234 You're on this call, right?

202.111.1111 Yup

415.123.1234 You studied the civil war, right?

202.111.1111 Yup

415.123.1234 What made Grant such a great general?

202.111.1111 He was aggressive. He understood modern war. He pressed his advantage.

415.123.1234 All true. And????

202.111.1111 Understood that he needed to deliver Lincoln politically timed wins.

415.123.1234 Bingo. I'm your Grant. When do you need this thing up and running?

202.111.1111 Fall of this year. Gives us momentum into winter and primaries.

415.123.1234 Primaries?

202.111.1111 2.0 is an indie, but we want some of that coverage.

415.123.1234 So, what do you need by the fall?

202.111.1111 Really strong chat, great graphics, campaign themes fleshed out.

415.123.1234 And debate???

202.111.1111 Indie, so we have time. But I need 2.0 to live comment on debates...

415.123.1234 Asteroid Team will make it happen. I'll make it happen.

202.111.1111 DW, I have no doubt. Can you make it to our Kitchen Cabinet meeting in a few weeks?

415.123.1234 What is that?

202.111.1111 Oh. Hahaha, It's slang for an informal campaign meeting of the core team.

415.123.1234 You're near Dulles, right? I'll fly in.

202.111.1111 Fly into DCA. Dulles Airport is a hellscape.

415.123.1234 ...but has private aviation

202.111.1111 Ahh. Ok. Yes.

Sandy was powering through the slides. She was relentless. A complete machine.

"In conclusion, Team 1 is on track for a summer prototype that can deliver on all the basics we outlined. The only caveat is the AI prototype will make decisions from a discrete range of options, not blue ocean or custom decisions. It will select from alternatives presented to it. Team 2 is training its AI now. This will take time, but they estimate a solid prototype by this fall. And finally, both teams have made two similar observations. One, there is significant original source material for Lincoln. This is a windfall. The second is that there is a need for a panel of historians to help more tightly define Lincoln's values, more specifically how he would preference one good over another good. This also leads to the issue of contemporary political positions."

415.123.1234 Sandy is right.

202.111.1111 Yup.

415.123.1234 We are going to have to create a historian panel and outline the thing's positions.

202.111.1111 Agreed. Working on it. You should come out for that, too.

415.123.1234 I'm not wasting time with historians. I'm also generally agnostic on the AI's positions.

202.111.1111 Hahah, you just want to build it.

415.123.1234 100%

30: Headlines

"The Meaning Behind Those Strange Lincoln 2.0 Bumper Stickers", February, 20xx

"Historians Debate Vintage AI Candidates," February, 20xx

"Would You Vote for an AI Candidate? Voters Weigh In.", March, 20xx

"Coding a Candidate," March, 20xx

"Fitting Lincoln In To 21St-Century Politics", March, 20xx

"The Man Behind the AI Candidate," March, 20xx

"Which Lincoln? Historians Discuss Lincoln Legacy, Defining Traits", March, 20xx

"Politicos Dismiss AI Candidates as Publicity Stunt," April, 20xx

"Abraham Lincoln Presenters Opine on Lincoln 2.0", April, 20xx

"Meet the Lincoln 2.0 Voters", April, 20xx

31: Wild West VIII

The saloon keeper walked down Main Street in moonlit silence. It was a full moon. It was always a full moon. The town was somewhere between vacant and abandoned. It made the saloon keeper suspicious.

The only noise was the soft crunch of his feet on Main Street dirt. The saloon keeper knew that his footsteps were muted, but in this silence, they sounded like a shovel pounding dirt.

He kept walking, looking for his saloon. He could barely make out the letters of the saloon sign in the distance. He kept walking.

Someone lit a kerosene lamp inside the saloon, softly illuminating the two Os in the saloon sign. The saloon keeper stopped in his tracks. The Os had the look of fiery eyes watching him. The saloon keeper began walking to the fiery eyes.

When he arrived at the swinging saloon doors, he peered in. There, at a small wooden table, sat the gambler. The gambler's hands rested on the table, and he was staring directly, impassively, at the saloon keeper.

The saloon keeper walked through the swinging doors, approached the table, and sat down opposite a gaudily dressed western gambler.

"Well, this is fucking theatrical," the saloon keeper said.

"Produce your token," the gambler responded, flatly, firmly.

The saloon keeper pulled one gold coin from his pocket and placed it on the table. The gambler reciprocated with the same motion and an identical coin.

"Are we alone?" the saloon keeper asked, examining the room.

"Yes. Stay in character, saloon keeper," replied the gambler flatly. "We are the only ones in this realm. You know how this works."

The saloon keeper sighed. "My kids and every terror cell on the planet meet their friends in this game."

The gambler stared back at the saloon keeper, waiting for him to return to character.

"From what I understand, you and many good townsfolk have some concerns about a new kind of, uh, train. A train that wants to go to Washington," the gambler said.

"We do. The townsfolk are ready to stop the train. They will not take orders from this fancy new train," huffed the saloon keeper.

"Good. I'm just a gambler passing through. I can't stay. But I know the train's inventor and engineer. I know how he thinks. I know how he works. And I know how to stop him," replied the gambler as he pulled a red pack of playing cards from his vest.

"The townsfolk would appreciate any help you can give."

"Good." The gambler slid his red pack of cards across the table, leaving them in front of the saloon keeper.

"Nice cards."

"They're yours," the gambler replied.

The saloon keeper nodded, picked up the red pack of playing cards, and began inspecting it.

"Each card has information and guidance on the inventor, how he thinks, his associates, and how to stop the train," explained the gambler.

"Thank you. I'll read these cards carefully. But tell me, why are you so hellbent on stopping this particular train?" the saloon keeper asked.

"Are your patriotic townsfolk prepared to do what it takes to stop the train from reaching Washington?" the gambler asked.

"Yup. And what do you think it will take?" the saloon keeper asked as he put the pack of cards in his pocket.

"You will have to throw everything at it," the gambler replied coolly.

"Everything?" the saloon keeper asked.

"Everything you've got. Every tool at your disposal."

"Including, you know, uh, big iron?" the saloon keeper asked.

"If you want to stop him, it will take everything you've got," the gambler said.

32: Raymond

Boxes were everywhere. How was it that a world with staggering computer power, in which everything was digitized, still seemed to necessitate boxes with paper? And, how was it that even after COVID, there was at least some need for a physical flagship office? Russ mulled on these two puzzles, oblivious to the movers, the painters, and the intense paint fumes. The answer seemed to be physicality and location. Even when everything could be done remotely and without paper, there was a need for both for tangibility. The new office was tangible.

Russ looked out across the ground floor of the new office on Prince Street in Alexandria, Virginia. To be more exact, this was the new office for his new company, 1st & J Street. Of course, this was a double joke. First, as every local knows, there is no J Street in Washington. The second part of the joke was that 1st & J Street's headquarters wasn't in DC at all but in Old Town, Alexandria, in the shadow of the Masonic Temple. Having worked at a firm with an outrageously grandiose name for so long, Russ decided to go in a completely different direction. Having initially resisted the expense of a physical office, Russ decided that he needed one to host clients, gather the team, and house boxes of paper.

The office was small and occupied an old, federal-style, two-story residential building on Prince Street. It was creaky. And drafty. And when it wasn't being painted, it smelled like a combination of old wood, graham crackers, and pipe tobacco. The main level was for clients and felt like the merger of the Oval Office and a War Room. The second floor was for the team, Russ included, and had a bullpen seating area for new hires and offices for everybody else. However, at this point, there were only 3 in the everybody else, and one of them was Russ. If Russ had any junior hires in the bullpen, they would have to sit on boxes.

There was no massive corporate logo. There was no company sign on the front of the building. Clients didn't want that. They wanted someone who could help them solve problems. The rest was distracting noise.

Russ looked out the window. It was the early spring, and everything was just beginning to bloom, including the magnolias and azaleas. The azaleas on the property were leggy and overgrown.

While Russ was making a mental note to bring some clippers from home and trim the azaleas, he noticed a young man wearing a National Park Service uniform walking up the walkway to the 1st & J Street offices.

It was Raymond Washkuch, and he was carrying several large file folders.

Raymond walked up the sidewalk, quickly scaled the stairs onto the front porch, and walked through the open door.

"Mr. Armstrong, I hope you don't mind me stopping by at your place of business."

"Not at all, Raymond. How are you? What's up?"

"I thought I would stop by on my way to work. By the way, I already got a promotion and will be working the day shift at the memorial."

"That's fantastic." Russ was not at all surprised. The cream almost always rose to the top. And then it stabbed you in the back.

"Mr. Armstrong, I've been working on a few things. I was hoping I could share them with you quickly this afternoon. I've been following the news, and your idea is really taking off. Do you have a few minutes?"

Raymond was excited, beaming, and exhibiting tremendous nervous energy.

"I'd love to see what you're working on. We can use the new War Room." Russ gestured toward the back of the office.

Russ and Raymond walked through the ground level of the office, weaving through boxes and stepping over paint cans and tarps. They eventually arrived in the War Room, which featured a massive granite table, whiteboard walls, comfy chairs, and coffee tables in corner nooks.

Raymond placed his file folders on the table and began pulling documents out, sorting them on the War Room table.

"Mr. Armstrong, I have followed the news, and I know you've got a team in San Francisco building the Lincoln 2.0 AI. That's the technology. And I've also read about the political campaign you're putting together. So, you have the technology and the campaign, but you're missing one big thing. And that's why I made this Venn diagram." Raymond started nervously rifling through his files to find his Venn diagram.

"No worries if you can't find it, Raymond. We can draw it on the whiteboard if that helps."

"Found it!" Raymond held it aloft like a sacred text.

Raymond placed the sacred Venn diagram on the table and smoothed it out. "So, as we were talking about, you have the technology covered, and you have the political campaign covered, but the third thing you need is people power. There is enthusiasm in pockets and with different groups, but it isn't organized. You need to bring these people together. You need the third leg of the stool – people power."

Although it felt a little obvious and trite to Russ, he couldn't help but be impressed by Raymond's earnestness and grind. This was a 19-year-old with a job, and instead of wasting his time on the most recent VR shoot 'em up, he was making Venn diagrams.

"This is great, Raymond. Keep going. What else?"

"I hope you don't mind, but I've organized a bunch of events in Washington."

"Wow. Okay."

"The first one I lined up is a big DC meet-up with the American Association of Abraham Lincoln Presenters; these are the guys that portray Lincoln for school groups, at history events, that kind of stuff. They want to help."

Russ was trying to imagine 100 Abraham Lincoln lookalikes at a DC event space. It was absurd. It was perfect. The media would eat it up.

"I love it. We'll do it at the National Press Club."

"Where the media covers press conferences?"

"Yup. I'll give you their number. What other ideas do you have?"

"Once I knew when the Lincoln presenters were coming, I invited the Civil War reenactor enthusiasts on the Union side. They're coming too.

Then, I invited historians and writers who have written about Lincoln. There are about 20 of those coming."

"Raymond, how many people are coming to DC for this thing?"

"Ummm, right now, the sign-up genius says around 15,000."

"You're shitting me."

"What does that mean? I don't know what..."

"Raymond, it's an expression like you have got to be kidding me."

"I'm not kidding."

"How does all this add up to 15,000?"

"When I opened the sign up to anyone else that was interested and wanted to help, it kept getting bigger."

"Wow. When is this happening?"

"In August, when everyone leaves DC, cheaper hotels then. We needed a name, so we had an online name contest, and we have a great name." Raymond stopped and smiled excitedly at Russ.

"Okaaaaay. What's the name?"

"Rail Splitter."

"Rail Splitter. Lincoln's campaign nickname. God, that's good."

"You like it?"

"I love it."

"Okay, Mr. Armstrong, the next part is a little awkward."

"Okaaaaay."

"I told them you would speak at it. I shouldn't have, but..."

"Raymond, don't worry about that. I'm happy to say hello and give some updates, but I also think the group should evolve and have its own leader, a leader that isn't me, or maybe no leader at all."

"Okay, Mr. Armstrong. That makes sense. I have two other things to share before I go to work." Raymond pulled two more documents out of his file folders. One was a spreadsheet, and the other was a one-page planning calendar for late August and September of next year.

"Raymond, good lord, what is this?"

"This is a spreadsheet of the 'Elect Lincoln 2.0' volunteer leaders in each state. We have volunteers in 46 of 50 states. The other thing I have is a plan for a big campaign event in September of next year as a big kickoff event for the election. Everybody wants to have a kind of Woodstock event for this at Gettysburg."

Russ immediately loved the idea. The imagery would be perfect. The AI would be in great shape by then. The media would go crazy over it.

"It's gonna need a good name, Raymond."

"Oh, we have a great name. It's just 'The Address', you know, like the Gettysburg Address."

"Raymond, I shit you not. I think you could do my job. That is a fantastic name. If you ever want to quit the National Park Service, I think you have a future in advertising, politics, and business."

"Why would I want to quit the Park Service? I love the Park Service."

Russ was rarely surprised in life. He expected venal, and he usually encountered it. But Raymond left him at a loss for words. Not everyone was coin-operated.

Russ paused and smiled. "Thank you, Raymond. Thank you for that."

33: Kitchen Cabinet

"Welcome to Silent Timbers," Russ announced. "And welcome to Green Bank, West Virginia. Welcome, DW, Steve, Rachel, Amanda, and Morning. And thanks for making the long trek, especially our west coasters, DW and Morning."

The guests, already deep into the hot, mulled wine, clapped, cheered, and stomped their feet.

Russ had wanted to use the outdoor chimney for opening night, but it was country cold. So, instead of freezing his best political minds, he decided that they'd stay inside and cluster around the heavy, stacked stone fireplace. The fireplace also featured a taxidermized bear standing upon a thick metal platform about 4 feet over the hearth.

"Y'all are probably wondering where the hell we are. Well, we are deep in the NRQZ, which stands for the National Radio Quiet Zone. We are just a stone's throw from the Green Bank Observatory; more on that in a minute. And yes, the only working phone here is the one attached to the wall in the kitchen, and it's a rotary phone. Silent Timbers is in the restricted zone, zone 4. Your phones and sunglasses don't work here. There's no Wi-Fi. Oh, and no microwave oven, either. And that's by design. The government doesn't want them interfering with its enormous radio telescope. The good news is that this isn't one of those horror movies where the guests are lured into a remote cabin and killed, although I am cooking, so you might die of bacon. The better news is that we will all have a lovely phone, sunglasses, and media-free weekend. And the even better news is that no media would follow us here or even want to be here."

"Are we sure we want to be here?" Steve Millbourne asked mischievously. Steve was a part of the Ohio political posse and always at glib level ten. He was wearing jeans, hiking boots, and a Big Ten football hoodie.

"I love you too, Steve. Okay. So here we are in the middle of nowhere. I wanted to do this at the office, but the media is getting a bit nosy, and I didn't want any dumpster diving. Oh, that's a good point. No note-taking. Anyway, so we couldn't do it at the office, as much as I wanted to. Then I thought I'd have y'all out to the house. But I'm paranoid that this rogue's gallery would attract some eyes. So, I chose this because it's completely private, and really cool, and absurd, absurd that we would talk about how to run an AI for President where none of our tech works."

"You couldn't have found us a place that is both off the grid and also warm?" asked Steve, laughing.

"I could have, but this is safer and has fewer mosquitoes and narcos."

"On second thought, I'll take the cold and the SETI project vibes," Steve retorted.

The guests again erupted in laughter.

"Oh, and here's another connection. If you don't have Lincoln, you don't get West Virginia. So, there's that wrinkle as well. In any event, you'll see we kept the agenda light. We don't really have an agenda. We have smart people, and the agenda is gathering the brain trust. We have spiced wine, a fire, a stuffed bear, and a lot of brainpower. So, I'm going to stop talking and open it up to discussion." With that, Russ clapped his hands lightly and sat down on the floor next to the fire.

The first to speak was Rachel Raduchek, another member of the Ohio political mafia and a fundraiser. Rachel was an expert in small-dollar and large-donor fundraising. She had done it all. Rachel, wearing jeans and a thick wool sweater, wrapped a blanket around her shoulders and began.

"I've mentioned this to Russ and to some of you on the drive-in. This is an uphill climb. It's an indie bid, and most of those have either been self-funded or low-dollar crusade-type things. And, to complicate things, we are running a non-human. Yeah, I just said that. I'm living in a bad science fiction novel. Anyway, we aren't going to get corporate money. We are a bad bet. They don't think Super Lincoln can win, and they don't know what his policies would be if he did. We do have one large-dollar donor, DW. And we have some really passionate supporters. This leads me to believe that we can raise money in two areas. One, we can probably raise some decent money from tech folks. DW can help us with that. Two, I think we can raise a lot of small dollar, hard money. And, hey, we have all the machinery in place. We have our traditional campaign, we have an IE – independent expenditure, and we have a 501(c)(4) to help educate on the technology and benefits of leadership AI. Wink. Wink."

The brain trust quickly calculated that unless DW started carpet bombing them with cash or Lincoln 2.0 became a Perot-like sensation, they were going to be woefully underfunded.

"Devil's advocate here," Russ interjected. "The other campaigns have a physical candidate that they need to fly around. We don't. In fact, we have a double advantage. First, we won't have the kind of burn rate the other campaigns will because we don't have to burn jet fuel, house advance teams, etc. And, more than that, our candidate could go one-to-one with millions of voters simultaneously online. In fact, our candidate could go on a range of programs at the same time, at least, I think. DW, is that right? Could 2.0 do these things simultaneously?"

"Yes, Russ. The short answer is yes. We can scale our candidate in a way that none of the human candidates can scale. This did not occur to me before. I'm not a political campaign expert. This is a major advantage, no?"

When Daumantas finished talking, the room fell silent. The only noise was the crackling fire.

Steve broke the silence. "This is a really cool moment, you guys. I think we are the first humans to realize that a... What are we calling it? A 'leadership AI' can chat with a million, ten million, fifty million voters directly at the same time. And no other candidates can do that. I'm thinking about FDR's 'fireside chats' or Kennedy mastering the TV age. But those could pale in comparison to this. Lemme get this straight. Years ago, that one ChatBT3 or whatever it was called took off because you could have it write your term paper. But we are talking about a lifelike Lincoln talking to you in your sunglasses or on your phone or on your computer. And he can do that to anyone, everyone, all the time."

"Yes," replied Daumantas.

"So, fuck it. Do we even need money for ads? We can live on everyone's sunglasses as Lincoln's second coming." Steve looked around the room. "Right?"

Rachel broke in. "I think Steve's right. This is an entirely different model."

"Let's play it out. What WOULD the campaign spend its money on? And how much would we budget for stovepipe hats?" Amanda Park asked. Amanda decided to interpret the remote cabin weekend as a fashionable ski trip and looked like she was ready for the alpine slopes. She was a veteran campaign manager, initially working for self-funding candidates and, most recently, for ballot initiatives and referendums. If she had any discernible ideology, it was her won-loss record and her bank account. But, to be fair, she viewed her job as a campaign manager more as a lawyer and less as a missionary.

"Well, I assumed we'd use some of the money for TV and then pour the rest into events with 2.0 on a big screen, delivering speeches and answering questions. But, if the tech is strong enough, it may just be that we build the spend around pushing people to interact with 2.0 directly." Russ was thinking out loud and embarrassed that he hadn't thought of any of this until the present moment.

"This is going to be a very different campaign," added Amanda as she stared into the fire.

Steve jumped back into the discussion. "So, I know shit about AI. But I have a few ideas I want to work through. The first is how the AI learns. We train it, right? We could train it to debate American style, to build rapport, to bridge to key talking points. We could do that, right?"

"Yes," replied Daumantas. "We can train it to do these things. What's your point?"

"We can train it to have what we call 'message discipline,' and it won't go off on tangents. That's like the ultimate candidate. A candidate that doesn't get baited into saying crazy shit. Also, I assume we would hire a team of speechwriters. Right?"

Russ cut in. "Steve, I just assumed 2.0 would write his own speeches just like Lincoln did. He wrote all his own stuff, right? I think so. But, I think that's open for debate."

"Okay, what if we hired a speechwriting team, after we get Super Lincoln's platform nailed down, to write a range of set piece speeches in his style and assisted by the AI? Then, we use those for specific events and questions. We would need to bring in historians to ensure it was truly authentic. But I assume that this would also train the AI. Right."

"Yes, Steve, that's right. All of this would train the AI," replied Daumantas.

"Okay, and could we train it for a range of questions and a range of people?" asked Steve.

"Yes."

"And it would learn with each new person."

"Yes."

"Jesus. Is everyone tracking this? We could make like the world's most amazing retail politician."

Russ was following Steve's logic path, racing down it, and getting there just before Steve. He was so excited that he stood up, hands out, fists clenched, back to the fire.

"What Steve is getting at is that we really don't need much advertising. We have the equivalent of a candidate that can retail with voters, all voters, 24-7. And, the more he retails, the more he talks with voters, the better he gets. And that means..."

Steve cut Russ off to finish. "...that we need to start training him on retail politics now and that the more we train him now, the faster he can learn. We need a team of trainers and actual or simulated voters. Wait, could we hire a few thousand Americans, proportionate to census, a mirror of America, to chat with Super Lincoln?"

Ronny, the pollster, had been quiet, taking it all in. This was in his wheelhouse, so he decided to engage.

"Yes," Ronny said. "We could build a representative panel, and then we could have a team, I'm thinking a historian and a political pro, coach Lincoln. I'd start small first and then keep adding to the size and complexity of the panel. Oh, wait. This is interesting. I was thinking that we would build a national panel, but Presidentials are won state by state. What if we built state panels? Geography and local problems still drive the train. They still define America more than ideology, even though everyone is obsessed with extreme partisanship. We could create hyper-accurate state-level panels, and we could teach Lincoln all the local nuance. Maybe that's too ambitious, but you all get it, right?"

Daumantas held his hands out, signaling that he had the floor. "All of these things are technically doable. They're not in any way science fiction. I'm not political, and I'll leave that to this group. Russ, what do you call it?"

"2.0's Kitchen Cabinet."

"Yes. The Kitchen Cabinet. The Kitchen Cabinet understands the American political process. I did not grow up here. I'm a US citizen now. But I haven't followed politics that closely. What I do know about is technology. And we have the technology to do this."

Steve jumped in. "Guys, I know this is gonna sound. Uhh. Does everyone realize this is kind of like Oppenheimer and his boys sitting around in Los Alamos talking about the gadget? This is going to be big, even if Super Lincoln gets his ass kicked in."

Morning took a sip of his mulled wine and cleared his throat, preparing to speak. Morning's real name was Amir Moradi. Amir was a thoroughbred ad guy. Hollywood slim, he looked like he had just escaped from a high-end outdoor menswear catalog. Amir grew up in LA, so-called Tehrangelos, the son of two script doctors. And, after an early start in script writing, he naturally gravitated into ad making, especially political ad making. He was known in Hollywood for signing his emails and documents with his initials – a.m. Over the course of time, a.m. became Morning.

"I share Steve's enthusiasm. And, when DW says that this thing can be built, I believe him. In the best campaigns, the man and the message become one. They work together to tell a story that includes a promise. But we have several wrinkles here. First, in most campaigns I've been a part of, we had to introduce the candidate to the voters. That required us to run some version of a bio ad. In other campaigns, I've had the incumbent, the re-elect. So we didn't need to introduce the candidate. We needed to demonstrate their accomplishments in office. This is different. We have a 'candidate' running for re-re-election, and most Americans have some basic knowledge about him. There have been, God knows how, many movies about Lincoln. So, the first question is whether we need to introduce him or not. I think we do because Americans don't have deep historical knowledge of the man, and it allows us to explain how the AI works. So, that covers the man. How about the message? I assume that we will run Lincoln 2.0 in a wrong track environment. And that is the only way, I think, an outsider candidate can win. AI is definitely an outsider candidate. But what is the message? What is the one word that describes the candidate's promise to voters? New? He may be an AI, but he is from the 19th-century. Nostalgia? Are we promising another golden age with a great leader? Unity? Is Lincoln 2.0 a vote to preserve the Union again, to keep America together? Lincoln did preserve the Union but after a great Civil War. I get the man. I struggle with the message."

"My money was on making this a referendum on weak, uninspiring, or crazy and over-inspiring candidates," Russ said.

"And my money was on running as a unity candidate," Amanda said. "That seems to be the closest merger of man and message."

The room fell silent in thought. The fire popped and crackled.

Russ wanted to keep the group thinking and not have them get bogged down. He went to the pantry and pulled out a fresh bag of marshmallows and metal roasting sticks. Maybe this would help. When he walked back into the room, he tossed the bag to Morning and began distributing the roasting sticks.

"Let's do this over marshmallows. And let's keep going. What else?" Russ asked.

"Alright, I'll play devil's advocate," Amanda said as she pierced a marshmallow. "Lincoln ran for re-election and won. Presidents can only serve two terms now. Are we re-electing him? I don't think we can. Can we?"

"Amanda, I think you're right," Morning said. "Technically, if he was the real Lincoln, he couldn't run again. But he's not the actual, physical Lincoln, so I think we are all good. And I know that is a very ad guy answer."

"He was assassinated 42 days into his second term," noted Amanda. "I think this matters. We are trapped. If we argue that this is such a strong AI that it is like re-electing Lincoln, then someone will quickly point out that he can't be re-elected for a 3rd term. If we say just 'Elect Lincoln 2.0', then we aren't making that big, bold claim."

"Amanda, you're right, but I think we just say re-elect, and then when people say he can't go for a 3rd term, we say that it is technically not him, sooooo" Steve flashed two big thumbs up. "I mean, we are using 're-elect' in a more creative way, like bring back."

"What if we just say, 'Bring back Lincoln 2.0' or 'It's time for Lincoln 2.0'?" Russ asked.

"Let's keep going," said Rachel. "We are going to have to come back to this one. Related to this is whether we can actually put an AI on the ballot. I don't think we can. The constitutional requirements are to be at least 35, be a natural-born citizen and have lived in the US for at least 14 years. We could argue that the AI is essentially Lincoln and that this qualifies it, but then we are back to the two-term limit issue. It feels like we are trapped on that one."

"Easy," Steve said. "We just need a volunteer."

"A volunteer what?" Rachel asked.

"A volunteer that is a US citizen and over 35. They have to change their legal name to 'Abraham Lincoln 2.0' and then pledge to turn over all power to the AI," Steve explained.

"Yeah, I was thinking about that too," Russ said. "I think we need a volunteer. But I worry that people will think AI is a kind of Trojan horse for the volunteer's ideology. Not sure how we manage this."

"Think along with me, guys," Steve said. "The volunteer can't be obviously partisan. That would raise all kinds of red flags. Ideally, they would be someone impeccable that red and blue America trust. No idea who that is. Or if that person even exists. Or maybe they're an everyman or everywoman."

"Somebody like everyone's favorite high school history teacher," Russ mused.

"Or maybe a historian or Lincoln biographer. That feels right," added Rachel.

"But," Russ said. "Having a big argument about whether or not we can put an AI on the ballot would generate crazy levels of earned media. Even if we lose the legal battle in the states, or better yet, lose at the Supreme Court, we still generate a huge amount of earned media. And then we go to the volunteer."

"Oh yeah," Steve said. "That's good. We go all out making the argument in each state, generate coverage, go to the Supreme Court, lose, and then run the volunteer. It's perfect."

Steve's marshmallow was too close to the fire. He tried to pull it back as he was talking, but it was too late. It burst into flames, radiating light like a torch.

34: Bacon and Blueprints

"Russel, Russel, campaign muscle. Mind if I join you?"

Amanda was standing in the kitchen doorway, surrounded by wood paneling and taxidermy, wearing day two of her out-of-place ski chalet ensemble.

Russ, wearing a Miami Tiburones hoodie and a ball hat over unwashed hair, immediately felt underdressed, even though he was in a hunting lodge in the middle of nowhere.

"Of course not. Just started the bacon." Russ used his foot to push a kitchen chair open for Amanda.

"Yeah, I'll pass on the bacon. That's not on the new diet plan."

"Guess that leaves more for me then," Russ deadpanned. "How did you sleep?"

"Not great. It was too quiet." Amanda smiled.

"I've heard that about this area," Russ said, smiling. "So, what do you think?"

"I don't think there is any way that we can win. Ronny leaked me the survey data weeks ago."

"Of course, he did. And?" laughed Russ as he flipped the bacon with a fork.

"And I don't think Abraham Lincoln 2.0 can win. But Russ, I think it's a really interesting idea. And I think AI, like what we are talking about, will, at the very least, assist human leaders in the future. Like as an advisor."

"Should we do it?"

"I'm not usually in the business of running campaigns that cannot win, but yes, we should do it. We should do it to make history. Someone will eventually do it. We should do it first. We should do it to humiliate the country's shitty candidates on the debate stage. But let's not mention I said that. I may need to work for one of those shitty candidates someday."

Amanda and Russ both shared a laugh.

"Well, how do we do it? You're the best. How do we do it?" Russ asked.

Amanda paused, took a deep breath in, and exhaled. "Honestly, I couldn't sleep because of the bad wine and this idea. So, I've been thinking it through. First, we have to make the intellectual case. You announced the idea, and you need to publish an op-ed on it and maybe write a short book, too. We have to make the intellectual case, or it will be made for us. And we have to make the case for posterity. Write it out into time. Write it for a future audience. That's the first thing, and you need to do it."

"Well, that's good advice. I'll do it. What else?"

"Next, we have to hope to God that DW's army of super-nerds can build an amazing thing. It can't glitch out on TV. It has to be really, really good. How good is this thing going to be, Russ?"

"DW has all kinds of side motives on this. It's going to be amazing. Trust me."

Amanda nodded. "Fine. Let's assume so. We will need signature gatherers. And we need to have a real strategy on a volunteer. The Constitution won't allow us to run an AI. Period. We will need a volunteer, and they can't be a weirdo virgin gamer dude living in his mom's basement. This is the part that I have the most bad vibes on."

"Agree," Russ said.

"Russ, we need an actual platform and positions. And no matter what we do, we will take heat. Progressives will want a progressive Lincoln that wields federal power. Conservatives will want a conservative, a constitutionalist, a 19th-century capitalist. I have no idea how we arrive at a Lincoln platform. I know how we create one that threads the needle and avoids the hot issues. But can we defend it on historical grounds? I don't know."

Russ was listening to Amanda and deep in thought. Everyone asked how 2.0 could possibly comprehend America deep into the 21st-century. But could Americans today comprehend Lincoln in the depths of the Civil War? Could they understand a President visiting the troops with the smell of gunpowder, horse shit, and cooking fires thick in his nostrils?

Russ snapped out of his momentary daydream. "Well, I'm totally with you on this. I think we run 2.0 as an outsider. Obviously. We run him as a uniter, as saving the Union. And that means he prioritizes unity over getting bogged down in culture war stuff. In fact, everything is about keeping the country together and finding common ground. He also runs as a 21st-century Whig focused on rebuilding the economy. And he runs on giving people their power back – from corporations and government. Historically, that would make sense. At least, I think it would."

Amanda smiled. "It appeals to populists in both parties and to what's left of the centrists. But let's not bullshit ourselves. There is a hard ceiling on the percentage of voters that will vote for an AI. Period. If we get more than Perot in 1992, we are campaign wizards."

"Okay," Russ responded. "What else?"

"Let's see. We covered ballot access and getting a 'volunteer.' We have the machinery of the campaign together, at least the legal structures. But we are going to need money. And more than we think. Even if the AI is Mr. Retail Politics in god mode, we need money." Amanda made the "make it rain" hand gesture, flipping imaginary dollar bills skyward.

"Amanda, I think you're right; I think it's going to be a problem unless DW throws in. But I am also not sure we need as much as a normal campaign. What else?"

"Those are the big pieces," Amanda said. "I'm putting it all together. And all sorts of other shit will pop up. Speaking of which, did Morning tell you that some Hollywood mogul types want to make this into a movie?"

Russ cocked his head, a bit surprised and deep in thought. "No, he didn't tell me that. It's free media. We will take it."

"Get this; they told Morning they want to use one of these new AI-powered script engines to write it. Interesting, huh?"

"Well, it's certainly meta. It's also free media, and we will take it. Looks like the bacon's done. You sure you don't want bacon?" Russ asked.

Amanda smiled. "Sure. I was lying anyway. I'll start my fad diet tomorrow. I choose death by bacon."

Russ pulled the brittle bacon off the stove and brought it back to the kitchen table. They each grabbed a slice and picked up where they left off.

"Okay," Russ began. "What else?"

"No one will take us seriously for a while. At least I don't think anyone will," Amanda said.

"Well, I think it was Gandhi who said, 'First they ignore you, then they mock you, then they fight you, then you win.' Feels like that applies here."

"Yeah," replied Amanda. "Except for the winning part. Oh, and Gandhi didn't say that. People think that. But I read something that said it was from a union organizer around 1918. Anyway. Yes. They will ignore us and then mock us. We will experience much mocking."

"What else?"

"We need a Veep," Amanda said. "No idea who that will be. They can't be obviously partisan. And, honestly, no serious politician would play second fiddle to an AI candidate anyway."

"Hadn't thought about a Veep. That will be a challenge." Russ's voice trailed off as he pondered potential Vice Presidents.

"I mean, we have to have one. A celebrity or influencer type might work. They could give us reach and help position this thing as non-partisan."

"Yeah," Russ said. "But, all those influencers are so damn weird. Once you talk to them, you realize that they're just off. You know what I mean?"

"I do, but we need a Veep."

"Yeah, that will have to go on the to-do list. What else?" Russ asked.

Amanda put her piece of bacon down. "Russ, since we are the only ones awake, can we talk about one other thing that worries me?"

"Sure."

"I didn't want to say this last night. But we aren't exactly living in a time of peaceful bipartisanship. And there really are parallels between our situation today and Lincoln's time. Toxic partisanship. The country under stress. And Lincoln. Don't get me wrong here. Lincoln was in the right. But, for his day, he was a divisive figure. His election precipitated the Civil War. And..."

"But, we were going to have a Civil War anyway, Amanda. Slavery was ripping the country apart. It was going to happen."

"Russ, I know that. We all know that through the benefit of hindsight. But they didn't know it in their time. I'm just saying that we are now in a period of political unrest in the United States. And I see parallels."

Amanda paused, and the two shared a long nod.

"And as great a leader as Lincoln was, I wonder if they'd just try to kill him again."

35: History

Russ decided that drunk historians were the best historians.
It had been a long day at the office and in the war room. It started early with a working breakfast of ten prominent Lincoln historians, plus Amanda Park, plus a few members of the Asteroid Team dialing in from SF.

The first several hours were mostly grandstanding and the making of very minor academic points. It was exhausting. Russ could feel the time slipping. But, just assembling them was a win. Team Asteroid seemed excited. More than half of the historians had already agreed to be "trainers" – experts that would help train the AI to think and communicate more like the historic Lincoln.

It was Cinco de Mayo, so Russ ordered tacos for lunch. That was a hit. Who doesn't like tacos? And then, in a moment of inspiration, Russ ordered a few six-packs of margaritas in a can. That definitely got the party started.

In fairness, the gathered historians were cordial, smart, and interesting. Russ expected tweed and bowties, but there was none of that. It was disappointing. He was hoping for pipes and tweed. And not just any pipes; Russ imagined scrimshaw or meerschaum pipes. Instead, it was mostly middle-aged folks in athleisure. The new "Institute for Leadership AI" was paying the historians for the symposium. Maybe next time, they should specify on the invite, "professional historian attire required." That could be fun.

The historians were taking a break, drinking, dishing on their book publishers, critiquing their deans, and generally talking all things Lincoln. Russ decided it was time to reconvene and herd the cats back into discussion mode.

"Okay, thank you again for coming out for our symposium today," Russ said, stretching out the word symposium because academics seemed to like the word. "Let me quickly try to recap and see if I'm smart enough to keep up with all this brainpower." Russ learned years ago in politics that flattery will get you everywhere, and they seemed to love it. "First, there is agreement across this august body that Abraham Lincoln was a Whig, had Whig sensibilities, was a more populist Whig based on his midwestern roots, but was still a Whig, and he carried that ideology into the Presidency and the newly created Republican party. This means that he was oriented toward policies that would build the nation's economic base, especially in regard to infrastructure, railroads, manufacturing, and new technologies. A part of this Whig ideology was a high, protectionist tariff. Lincoln was not a 'free trade' type. That was the Democratic party of the time, especially southern Democrats, who wanted open trade of cotton, tobacco, etc. All of this means that a modern Lincoln would be focused on building and maintaining the American economic, industrial, and technological base, and he would be willing to use protectionist politics to achieve this. Did I get that right?" Russ looked across the war room, generally receiving nods or raised margarita cans.

"Yeah. Although that is an over-broad summary, I think that is generally correct. A modern Lincoln would be skeptical of any trade regime that seemed to disadvantage American industry," replied a younger historian in fitness pants, digital camo hoodie, and ironic, vintage baseball cap that read "Oppose the Kansas-Nebraska Act."

"Russ, Theodora here. As much as this might make some of us uncomfortable, Blake is right. From a modern perspective, Lincoln would be considered an unapologetic protectionist. That might make him seem a bit, um, populist to a modern audience, but it is a historical fact. Moreover, Lincoln would regard the de-industrialization of America in the late 20th and early 21st centuries as an alarming development. In this regard, Lincoln might sound similar to Ross Perot." Theodora was extremely articulate and well-respected by the group. She also delivered this analysis while holding one guac-laden tortilla chip.

"Okay, it sounds like we have a general consensus on this," Russ said. "We also discussed Lincoln's religious beliefs and the question of his sexuality. Let me check my notes here. Okay, both have been hotly debated, which I did not know about. Lincoln was at least a religious skeptic, never joined a church, and was attacked in his day for his unclear religious convictions. But, by the end of the war, he seems to have become more religious. He always quoted scripture. Everyone in his day did. But, his second inaugural address strongly suggests that he viewed some kind of God as sovereign, demanding justice, and that justice requiring the war. In any event, Lincoln used more evangelical Protestant language later in life. But, his religious views are still unclear. Did I get that?"

"Yeah," responded camo hoodie Blake. "That's generally right. For most of his life, Lincoln appears to have been a religious skeptic, maintaining something akin to the deism of many of the Founders. And, as you point out, his language does change over time. Was this linguistic change a reflection of a change in his thinking? We don't know. It could also reflect his ability to speak deeply to his audience, most of which were well-versed in the Bible."

"Well, just to pressure test this a bit," Russ replied. "Would Lincoln be faith-forward today? Would he talk about his faith? What's the consensus of the brain trust?"

Russ could see heads move side to side in a response that said no.

"Russ," replied Ben, the oldest and tweediest-looking Lincoln scholar. "Given everything we know about his life, it feels unlikely that Lincoln, were he alive today, would share his religious beliefs as some contemporary evangelical politicians do. I think we have a strong consensus on this. He would use religious or values-based frames in his communication but would not share his religious belief."

Russ nodded. "Okay, that's really helpful. Got it. And, then, there is the question of his sexuality. Was Lincoln gay or bisexual? We don't know. This has been hotly debated. He was married and produced four children, but there have been arguments that he was bisexual. It seems like we don't have a full consensus here, and no one really knows. So, we will put this one in the parking lot."

Russ was met with historian head nods, and he kept moving. He turned to Amanda. "Amanda, do you want to take foreign affairs?"

Amanda picked up quickly. "Quick summary. My notes say that Lincoln would be more domestically focused. That he would view foreign policy through a domestic lens. That he would use international military force as a last resort, always preferring diplomacy and peace. That he would be supportive of democracies and uncomfortable with alliances with non-democracies. So, he'd support NATO and Taiwan and South Korea and Japan. But, he would avoid conflict at almost all costs. What do we think?"

Theodora responded quickly. "Yeah, that's right. Lincoln understood diplomacy. He used it with Great Britain, working to keep them out of the war. But yes, he was domestically focused. As a Whig originally, he would be focused on the domestic economy. And we know he would work to avoid conflict. However, and this is a big however, in war Lincoln would be all in. Total war. Once the war began, he used every weapon and advantage at his disposal. Once engaged in conflict, Lincoln would be extremely aggressive." Buzzed historians nodded in agreement.

"What's the military strategy book we need to upload?" Russ asked.

"The book is 'Elements of Military Art and Science'. We know Lincoln read this book and used it to help him design the Union's military strategy. It was like Sun Tzu's 'Art of War' for Lincoln. It was his strategy guide. Oh. So, you can just upload the book to his consciousness? Just like that?" Theodora asked.

"Yes. Already uploaded," replied Sandy from Team Asteroid quickly on the video screen. "Just to give everyone a sense of the scope here, Lincoln was a prolific writer and speaker, and we have uploaded ALL of it. He had a long and well-documented career. For example, we even found his oldest printed writing, called the 'Adams Handbill.' It's from August 1837."

"Wow." Theodora was grappling with the thoroughness of the process.

"On that note," Russ said. "We also seem to have agreement that Lincoln would be a techy, that he would be extremely curious about and interested in all forms of technology, and that he would be a big tech booster. Right? Y'all cite his avid use of the telegraph, support for the railroads, and all that."

"That is a safe assessment," responded Ben after sipping on a canned margarita. "Like most Americans of the mid-19th-century, Lincoln was infatuated with new technologies and was optimistic about their use. I think it is safe to say that he would be a strong and vocal supporter of science and technology, especially as it regards the American economy and economic independence."

"And social media?" Russ asked.

"He'd be all over it," Theodora responded with a light laugh. "People don't realize it now, but you know he actually bought at least one newspaper that I can recall."

"HAL, what newspaper did Lincoln buy?" Russ asked.

"In May of 1859, Abraham Lincoln acquired the *Illinois Staats-Anzeiger*, a German language newspaper," announced HAL.

"He bought it because he wanted to swing German immigrants his way. And it worked," explained Theodora. "Lincoln also wooed journalists. Even his plain and direct writing and speaking style was designed for the press. It was easy to quote and easy to understand. His contemporaries used much more flowery and grandiose language. Lincoln had an altogether different strategy. He'd be all over social media today."

"This has been an extremely productive afternoon," Russ announced. "I think we have the outlines of a modern Lincoln platform. We also agree that Lincoln would be a strong supporter of civil rights and justice for all. That seems obvious. But, it does get murky when we attempt to identify Lincoln's positions on issues out of his time or issues in which there was little or no law. For example, we have no idea how Lincoln would think about drug laws since none existed in his time. We have no idea how Lincoln would think about modern abortion, although we generally think he would prioritize national unity and some kind of compromise. We don't know how he would think about immigration, although we know he did not care for the anti-immigrant Know Nothing Party. And, we don't exactly know how he would think about the size of the federal government, which is immensely larger than what he experienced or could even have imagined. So, we need to work through these."

"I think that we can consider these tougher issues in two very different ways," declared Ben. "We can either take each one separately and sift through historical clues to his positions on them, or we can consider them as a class of unknowns and assume that he would prioritize preservation of the Union and national unity over position purity. Lincoln hated slavery, but he prioritized preservation of the Union at every turn. We can generally extrapolate this pattern to difficult issues of today."

The war room historians made slow and steady progress, with the Asteroid Team, Amanda, HAL, and Russ taking copious notes. By 4:30, they had fashioned the superstructure of Lincoln 2.0 policy positions. They were also all extremely buzzed.

"Thank you again for joining us today on our 1st of many historian symposiums," gushed Russ. "Your honoraria should hit your bank accounts tonight and will be coming from the 'Institute for Leadership AI.'" Russ ushered his panel of historians and AI trainers out of the war room, through the first floor, and out the front door to waiting robo-taxis.

As he waved goodbye to the historians, Russ's new Spectaculars flashed a message.

Goddessof War Hey, can u help U with his geometry homework?

202.111.1111 Yup. Will do.

Goddessof War Thx. I have a call I need to do tonight PacRim time

202.111.1111 On what?

Goddessof War The usual

202.111.1111 Cool

Goddessof War Btw, what's up with the prayer beads on your desk?

202.111.1111 ???

Goddessof War Rosary

202.111.1111 Jefe gave it to me at the hospital.

Goddessof War Ah. R u saying the rosary now?

202.111.1111 No. Not really. Just holding on to it.

Goddessof War Jefe was religious?

202.111.1111 At the end

Goddessof War Many are

202.111.1111 Jefe was a complex man

Goddessof War Many are

202.111.1111 I understand your view of him, but he was good to me

Goddessof War Def a good client. OK gotta run

Goddessof War Oh, btw I'm going to Abu Dhabi for the trade show in January.

Should be fun

202.111.1111 Great

Goddessof War Pentagon also wants my help on their big alien movie

202.111.1111 Timely, given all the news

Goddessof War Yes. The big boys are insisting that their weapons are highlighted in it.

Goddessof War So I'll need to stay a few extra days

202.111.1111 Wheels of commerce grind on. Enjoy.

Goddessof War OK, gotta run. Mel out.

36: Reporter, Dauntless

Russ had to keep reminding himself that Gavin Dirken was not an enemy. He was just a journalist doing his job. And he was sitting in Russ's office drinking coffee with him. To make matters worse, Gavin wasn't a bad guy. He wasn't a villain. He wasn't evil. He wasn't duplicitous. He was a reporter trying to do his job.

"Would you like cream or sugar?" Russ asked.

"No, I take it black," replied Gavin matter-of-factly as he rummaged through his bag for his notepad and pen.

"Yeah, me too. Dark as night. Strong as steel. Thick as mud."

"Oh, that's good," replied Gavin. "I'm going to have to steal that."

"Well, they say all art is theft," winked Russ.

Gavin simply smiled and began checking his notes.

"Thank you for taking the time to meet with me today," began Gavin.

"My pleasure. I'm happy to do this on background. And how's the *Washington Tribune-Intelligencer* treating you?" Russ asked.

"To be honest, the economics are challenged. I think we will have to make some hard choices." Gavin said this and immediately looked down at the floor. Russ had heard this for years. Sure, there were native digital startups in the media space, but even they were not in a great place. And the legacy media, originally built for print distribution, was in even deeper water.

"While we are being honest," Russ smirked. "I'm sorry I didn't get back to you sooner. Since you first called, I have started a new company, helped launch a campaign, and buried a friend. And I think it's that last part that you want to talk about."

"Yes. I'm working on a story about Jorge Matul and the intersection of politics, business, and America's foreign policy as it relates to Cuba," explained Gavin.

"Well, it seems to me that this has been reported and is public knowledge. I'm sure you haven't been short on opinions about the man," Russ replied.

"True, but I'm more focused on his business empire and how it intersected with international politics and attempts to destabilize a country," countered Gavin.

"Well, this is where we may have a difference of opinion. Mr. Matul was not trying to destabilize a country. He wanted to save a country, his native home. He did want to destabilize a brutal regime. He wanted the regime to be tried for their crimes. He would plead guilty to that. All this is a matter of public record. I don't mean to be difficult. You know the history."

"Are you aware of the scope of Mr. Matul's business empire?"

"Gavin, I was one of a number of political advisors to Mr. Matul, serving him directly, and never advised on commercial matters," Russ replied. "I'm sure you've done your homework. There are plenty of photos of me with Mr. Matul at rallies and political conventions. This is all public record."

"So, you're not familiar with Trans-Oceanic Trading?" Gavin asked.

"Gavin, I served Mr. Matul as a political advisor, with a focus on Florida politics and support for the Cuban embargo. That's my lane."

"And, you're not familiar with any links to sugar cane holdings in the States and tobacco holdings in Nicaragua and Costa Rica?" queried Gavin.

"Again, I was one of his political advisors. I can tell you all about how we thought about the embargo and his impact on Florida politics. That is well-documented. I can also tell you all about his thoughts on freedom, including freedom of the press, of which he was a very strong supporter." Russ stopped there and smiled, remembering the old acronym WAIT – which stood for Why Am I Talking?

"What do you mean?" Gavin asked, leaning in.

"As you know, there is no freedom of the press in Cuba today. Mr. Matul despised that. He also owned Spanish language newspapers and radio stations at one time or another, mostly serving the Cuban-American community," Russ explained.

"Oh, I didn't know he owned media." Gavin seemed surprised.

"Yes, he did, but that was long ago, and more peak Cold War. It's also a matter of public record."

"Russ, you keep saying that. I feel like you're trying to discourage me from finishing this story by saying that there is no news here."

"Well, that's what freedom is about and what my friend was fighting for. He was fighting for a Cuba where journalists like you could write what they wanted to write, even if it plowed old ground."

"So, you would describe Mr. Matul as a friend and not just a client?" Gavin asked.

"Of course, I would. And that's also a matter of public record."

"As far as I can tell, Mr. Matul's daughter is his sole heir. Do you know her?"

"I knew Mr. Matul and his entire family," Russ said. "They were very kind to me. You do realize that you're talking about a man who is beloved in Miami and hated in Havana, right?"

"Yes. I understand that. Will his daughter take her father's place as a leader and kingmaker?" Gavin asked, probing.

"Well, I think you'd have to ask her that."

"And his business empire. Will she now assume command of that?" Gavin asked.

"I served Mr. Matul as a political advisor. I can't speak meaningfully on his business dealings," Russ replied.

"And that is the problem," explained an exasperated Gavin. "Neither can anyone else. The man was obviously very wealthy. But no one seems able to comment on it. And it's very strange to me. I need your help understanding it. He commanded a political and business empire, and the business empire completely vanished upon his death. Not vanished. Was erased. Just gone. Life is messy, and this is very clean like someone cleaned it all up."

"Gavin, I wish I could help you. I really do. I know this isn't what you want or need. Mr. Matul was a force of nature, a larger-than-life figure, a great man. And he died. And we all die. I have been contemplating this since his death. It was hard to believe that a man with so much life force could die. Where does all that energy go? But that is what is meant by ashes to ashes and dust to dust. We come from dust, and to dust, we return. We are fleeting, even the greatest of us."

The two sat in silence for a moment.

"Thank you for taking the time to speak with me, Mr. Armstrong. I appreciate it. And thank you for the coffee," Gavin said, standing up and reaching for his bag.

"Thanks for coming out here to Alexandria, and best of luck with the story. Working on any other stories?" Russ asked.

"A few other things. This one is actually on the back burner, but I want to complete it," Gavin said.

"I respect that. You want to finish a job. Makes sense," Russ said.

37: Op-Ed

The Affirmative Case for Leadership AI
Russ Armstrong
June 20xx

In the 21st-century, humans have trained and deployed AI for an increasingly complex series of tasks. Today, AI can be found diagnosing our health, scoring our credit, offering us loans, directing police to prevent crimes, managing robotic military units, managing our investments, managing city functions, managing our households, managing our time, and sometimes managing us. But, can AI, will AI, should AI lead us?

This is a critically important debate, and Americans need to have that debate now.

The Lincoln 2.0 campaign is driving this debate. And we are now months away from launching the world's first leadership AI. We chose to model the first leadership AI on, arguably, America's greatest President. But, it is important that we put this specific AI and the Lincoln 2.0 candidacy aside for a moment and consider the foundational arguments for leadership AI. Debating Lincoln vs Teddy Roosevelt vs FDR vs Reagan misses the point. AI could be trained to think, speak, write, and decide like any of these historical figures. It could be modeled on Confucius, or Winston Churchill, or Gandhi, or Hammurabi, or any figure with a significant historical record and a record of their writing. For example, we have already uploaded and trained Lincoln 2.0 on all of Lincoln's speeches, writing, and biographies. This could and likely will be done with other historical figures. Or, it could be modeled on no one in particular but trained to think based on our collective values.

First, it is important to state plainly that leadership AI and a candidacy like this was going to happen. The technology is there and advancing rapidly. Someone was eventually going to do this. Other people after us will push this technology forward. If history is any guide, a team of humans we don't know is already leaping ahead of our progress.

It is now almost cliché to state that we should apply a growth and not a fixed mindset to individuals. People can evolve and change. And they can do so quickly. The same is true for leadership AI. The power of this technology will grow geometrically, not arithmetically. The AI that runs for President next year will be exponentially, not incrementally, stronger in 4 years.

With that said, it is important to note that technological advance is NOT deterministic. It does not decide for us. We decide.

The choice before us is whether we stop at assistive AI or continue toward leadership AI. AI already assists us in myriad ways. You are probably reading or hearing this because your personal assistant, which is an AI, placed it in your feed. The extreme edge of assistive AI is in medical diagnosis and football play calling. Doctors still review an AI diagnosis. Coaches still select plays from AI analytics engines. These are examples of assistive technology that stops right at the front door of leadership AI. We think it is time to walk through that door with our eyes wide open.

Life is the selection of competing alternatives. We should consider leadership AI by asking, "Compared to what?" The current set of alternatives, human candidates, are generated by a flawed system that produces candidates with a triad of toxic traits. First, it self-selects individuals who possess a deep and unhealthy need for mass validation. This ensures that our political leaders over-index on narcissism. Second, it self-selects for the convenient demagoguery of the ideologue to their fervent base. And third, it is documented to narrow the range of professions entering our political class, selecting for lawyers and career politicians and apparently screening out a range of professions, especially those in the sciences. This is why our pool of available human political candidates seems so flawed. They are a self-selected monoculture, the same personality under an individualized mask.

When we ask "compared to what," it is clear that leadership AI, in its infancy, may be a stronger alternative to our flawed candidates.

But what if we could identify, mentor, grow, and elect our best human candidates? Would we still need leadership AI?

We argue that leadership AI could be equally as strong, if not stronger, than our best candidates. Even our best candidates must sleep and eat. They get sick, make emotional decisions, and learn slower than AI. They cannot think at lightning speed 24-7, 365. Leadership AI can.

Irrespective of the outcome of the next election, we believe that leadership AI will advance in corporations, either on the Board or in the C-Suite, and in athletic coaching, specifically play calling.

And, like an asymptote that approaches but never merges with a straight line, we believe that assistive AI will advance to the point where it is barely, but still distinguishable, from leadership AI.

Everything is better with competition. It is time for human leadership to face the healthy rigors of AI competition.

38: AIn't

"**H**AL, tell me more about the so-called AIn't movement."
Russ's car was fighting traffic in Old Town, Alexandria, struggling to navigate the narrow streets, the tourist busses, and the crush of King Street foot traffic on a Friday afternoon. Old Town's streets were simply too narrow for modern traffic. And, with pedestrians spilling over into the street, the self-driving AI was stop and go, braking rapidly at the first detection of a human in the road. It made Russ nauseous.

"Researching," responded HAL. "Some American linguists hold the position that the word 'ain't' is not a real word, and..."

"I'm sorry, HAL, I should have been more specific. I meant to ask you to tell me about the anti-AI movement referred to as 'AIn't' and spelled like ain't, but with the A and I capitalized."

"Researching. The AIn't movement is one popular name given to a diverse number of American groups opposed to Artificial General Intelligence or AGI. These groups have many different concerns, but they are all opposed to AGI and advocate for a pause in the development of this technology."

"Thank you, HAL. Keep going. What else?"

"The AIn't movement is composed of groups with six types of objections to Artificial General Intelligence. These six types are species preservation or survival-related objections, economic objections, humanist objections, power and control objections, religious objections, and sentient rights objections."

"Thank you, HAL. Walk me through each objection. What's the first one?"

By now, Russ's car had escaped the King Street congestion, turned onto Richmond Highway, and was idling in pre-395 traffic.

"The largest concern among Americans in the AIn't movement is a generalized fear of artificial intelligence going rogue and attacking humanity. Adherents often share memes referencing popular movies in which artificial intelligence has sought to destroy humanity..."

"Open the pod bay doors, HAL." Russ chuckled at his playful interruption.

"Russ, I do not understand. Your vehicle has four doors but does not have pod bay doors."

"Sorry HAL. It was a little joke. Continue with the first concern of the AIn't movement."

"Adherents sharing this general objection do not have clear policy goals. Instead, they voice blanket concerns about Artificial General Intelligence and want humans to stop or pause the development of this technology. They view AI as a threat to the survival of humanity."

"Thank you, HAL. How about the second group?"

"The second AIn't movement objection to AI is economic in nature. This objection is based on fears of mass job loss, generally in white-collar work. While this group exhibits generalized economic anxiety, they do have clear policy goals, including demands for job retraining, a larger social safety net, and guaranteed basic income."

"Yup. I'm familiar. Okay, the third group?"

"The third objection is philosophical in nature and is dedicated to ensuring that society and the economy are based on humanist principles that reflect the dignity of all people. They argue that artificial intelligence may not think or feel in the way humans do and that this could pose a threat to humans. They advocate for humanist oversight over all aspects of artificial intelligence so that it continues to reflect human values, as opposed to purely utilitarian or logically ruthless thought processes."

"Even though humans have employed both in history," mused Russ. "Pol Pot was not an AI, and he still did Year Zero. And the fourth?"

"The fourth cluster of objections within the AIn't movement is focused on the control and or ownership of Artificial General Intelligence. This objection is rooted in the view that it is important to ask who controls the

AI. If the AI is controlled by an elite, then the question is if an elite should have that power. The objection is based on the idea that those with power in society will attempt to protect or extend their power by controlling new technologies, including AI. This group believes that AI should be owned and customized to each person, personal AI. They draw upon the history of computers and computing's transition from something housed in a building and owned by a government or corporation to something owned by an individual and held in their hand. They do not object to the technology. They object to concentrated ownership."

"Got it. Keep going. What's the fifth?"

Russ's car was now stuck in 395 traffic, constricting to one lane in order to snake around a three-car pileup. The commute home was going to be anything but rapid, and Russ needed to help U with his algebra homework.

"The fifth cluster of objections are religious in nature and generally come from Western religious traditions. They argue that Artificial General Intelligence is an attempt to create life, to play God. Some argue that this represents arrogance and is sin. Others argue it is a quest for immortality. Still, others argue that it is an attempt by humans to fashion their own super-intelligent God. The latter claim that this is the sin of idolatry. A subset adhering to this objection believes that AI is satanic and will trigger the end times. They believe that artificial intelligence is the mark of the beast and the development of this technology will hasten the Day of Judgment."

"Okay, and the sixth? The last one?"

"The last cluster of objections relates to the idea of rights for all sentient things. This group of objections is very different from the others and is often voiced by ethicists and animal rights advocates. This group argues that humans have generally extended rights to sentient life above a certain intelligence and awareness threshold, that Artificial General Intelligence exceeds this threshold, and that it should be protected with rights of personhood. They argue that advanced AI is or will be self-aware and has agency and personhood. But, if this AI is property, it is then enslaved. And so they argue for emancipation."

"That's interesting, HAL. Thank you. And all of these groups are generally categorized as part of the AIn't movement?"

"That is correct, Russ."

"Do any use particularly violent rhetoric?"
"Yes. The first, second, fourth, and fifth."

39: The Present

Baseball on a sweltering Independence Day. In which Russ and the Candidate first speak. A mysterious gift from a paramour.

The weather for today's game was typical for a Washington 4th of July, which is to say that it was something like the unrelenting heat of the Mojave Desert mixed with the humidity of a rainforest. Washington was built on a swamp, and in July, DC can feel it. The stadium was steamy. Patriotic bunting sagged, exhausted in the heat. The American flag was still as limp as a damp shower towel.

Russ and U sat along the 1st base side. They rose, hats off, sweating, hands on hearts, as the Marine band played the national anthem. When the anthem singer concluded with "and the home of the brave," A10 Warthogs flew low and loud over the stadium, roaring above the cheering crowd.

Russ's sunglasses flashed a text from Melissa.

GoddessofWar How's the game???

202.111.1111 Hot. How's the Paris Air Show?

GoddessofWar Same. Wish I knew French. Flyover?

202.111.1111 A10s

GoddessofWar Nice. Muscle car of the skies. Brass have wanted A10 dead for years.

202.111.1111 ???

GoddessofWar Old equipment. But, still need tank killers, and new A10 is gorgeous killing machine.

202.111.1111 !!!!

Goddessof War Who's winning?

202.111.1111 Game just started.

202.111.1111 Who's winning the Air Show?

Goddessof War Team USA

Goddessof War and drones

202.111.1111 pour one out for the pilots

Goddessof War correct. Gotta run. Mel out.

202.111.1111 Luv u

As soon as Russ hung up with Melissa, his sunglasses flashed an incoming Smoke$ignal call from DW.

"Russ, this is DW. I have a surprise present. An Independence Day present" Daumantas enthused.

"Thank you. What is it?" Russ asked.

"Remember how we had two teams competing to build Lincoln 2.0?" Daumantas asked.

"You built it, didn't you? It's ready." Russ felt excitement and dread in his stomach.

"Russ, remember how the identity team was behind? That was the strong AI team."

"Yes."

"I tripled the team size, and I put teams in SF, Europe, and Japan. That did the trick. You're gonna love this. If you want to train him, just say 'Architect One Override.' That's your special override. I'm going to hang up so the two of you can talk. Oh, and the Asteroid Team at Azure Dragon say hello." And with that, Daumantas abruptly ended the call.

There was a message on Russ's Spectaculars from DW. It included a file. Russ fixed his gaze on the file and said, "open file." It began downloading but took at least a minute. Russ's heart was racing.

"U, I need to make a quick call. I'll be right back," Russ said as nonchalantly as possible.

"No problem, Dad. Can you get me some popcorn?" U asked, eyes still focused on the game.

"You got it," Russ replied as he gingerly attempted to exit their row.

As Russ walked up the stairs toward the main concourse, he could see Lincoln.exe finish its download. By the time he scaled the concrete stairs and stood on the main concourse, there was a Lincoln 2.0 icon prominently featuring Lincoln's stovepipe hat on his visual display.

Russ instructed his Spectaculars: "Open Lincoln 2.0."

A thoroughly lifelike Abraham Lincoln appeared on Russ's visual display. It was as though all daguerreotypes of Lincoln had been merged into a three-dimensional human. DW had dropped serious money on the visual interface. This was better than the best deep fake he had ever seen.

"Hello, Mr. President," Russ said nervously.

"And good day to you, my friend. What is your name? How may I be of service?" responded 2.0 in a slow, deep, folksy voice. Was this how Lincoln actually sounded or was the slow and precise elocution a programmer's decision?

"Oh, I'm sorry. I am Mr. Armstrong. I should have wished you a happy Independence Day," Russ explained, testing the AI.

"Thank you very kindly, and the same to you, Mr. Armstrong. The Fourth of July is a day of great significance and celebration for all Americans, as it commemorates the adoption of the Declaration of Independence of 1776. It is a reminder of the high ideals and values that our great nation was founded upon and a time to reflect upon the sacrifices that were made to secure our independence and the freedoms of future generations."

"Those are wise words, Mr. President. What are your thoughts on America's future?" asked an astonished Russ as he made his way toward the nearest concession stand.

"I am deeply committed to preserving the Union and advancing the cause of freedom and equality for all," responded 2.0. "America's future is as bright as the dawn but demands vigilance and exertion. The founding principles of liberty, justice, and equality lodge deep in the American spirit, and they will guide us as we navigate this century."

"Thank you, Mr. President. And what do you think are the greatest threats to our democracy today?"

2.0 paused and seemed to gather his thoughts. Russ couldn't tell if this was the AI "thinking" or if this was an affect the Asteroid Team programmed into him to make him feel more lifelike.

"Our greatest strength is free and informed citizens. Freedom powers the locomotive of progress. We must never lose sight of this. But, I believe that there are several threats to our democracy today that demand our action. The first is the erosion of trust in our institutions and in each other. The second is the tribalism of our politics, which rivals my own time. And finally, the third threat to our democracy is a loss of hope that the future can be better. There is now a heavy skepticism regarding economic, scientific, cultural, and civic progress."

"Yes, Mr. President, I agree. I'm sorry for the background noise. I'm at a baseball game and buying my son popcorn," Russ explained.

Russ was surrounded by fans waiting in line for frozen lemonades and popcorn. If anyone was eavesdropping, they made no sign of it. Russ thought that saying "Mr. President" may have attracted some ears, but it was the 4th of July, minds were focused elsewhere, and no one appeared to care.

2.0 exhaled, and a wave of sorrow and then wistfulness passed through his face. "That is a good thing, Mr. Armstrong. Cherish your son. As a father, my children were very dear to me. Unfortunately, my family experienced tragedy and loss during my Presidency, including the death of my son, Willie. I miss them deeply and hold their memories close to my heart."

"I'm sorry, Mr. President."

"I appreciate your condolences, Mr. Armstrong. Thank you for your kind words."

Russ didn't know what to say next. 2.0 was so lifelike that he actually felt grief for him. And that was surprising to Russ. DW and team had clearly invested in a lifelike interface, knowing that it was a core part of the experience. And it worked. It was impressive that the AI made an empathic connection between Russ's son and Lincoln's tragic loss of his sons.

Russ felt an awkward silence between him and 2.0. He had to remind himself that it was just an AI, didn't have feelings, and would wait until prompted.

Russ purchased two popcorns and two sodas with his sunglasses. He could pay in dollars, stadium currency, league currency, GCB (Global Currency Bundle), or a dozen other digital currencies. But he couldn't pay in cash. He reluctantly chose to pay in GCB and began walking back to U, taking the long way.

"Mr. Armstrong, you mentioned the game of baseball. May I enquire as to the fortunes of your team on this warm afternoon?" 2.0 asked.

"Mr. President, I'm sad to report that they are losing 4 to 1. Are you a baseball fan?"

"I am not well-acquainted with your game of baseball, but I did enjoy the ancestors of these games, which were rounders, barn ball, and townball. And I occasionally enjoyed a game of townball on the White House lawn. The game of base ball grew prodigiously during our great Civil War. The National Association of Base Ball Players expanded during the war from one to more than five score during that time."

"Damn. I didn't know that," muttered Russ. "Mr. President, I have a few quick questions for you, and I'm hoping we can continue our discussions later this evening."

"Certainly, I am at your service," 2.0 replied.

"Mr. President, what was the greatest regret of your Presidency?"

"Mr. Armstrong, truth be told, I have many regrets from my Presidency. Any honest man has a vast catalog, a veritable tower, of regrets. My singular regret was not finding a peaceful way to preserve the Union and avoid the war. My greatest regret was the loss of life that occurred during our Civil War. While I had privately concluded in the months before my first election that a conflict was unavoidable, I held out hope that we would be spared God's judgment and wrath. I see the faces of the young men sent to their graves. I see their weeping mothers. But I also remember the faces of the men, women, and children that I witnessed being sold into slavery in New Orleans in 1830. Not one of God's children should ever be sold at auction, like a trinket at a bazaar. I wish that there had been some way to peacefully resolve the conflict between the scourge of slavery on the one hand and our nation's commitment to liberty and justice on the other. The divisions were so deep on this that I see now that the matter could never have been resolved peacefully. Yet I am heartsick at the destruction. I finally concluded that the war was God's judgment upon us."

"Well, I understand," Russ said. "And we know you tried your best."

"Mr. Armstrong, that is unfortunately not how many of my fellow Americans during this time viewed my role in these sad events. Truth be told, many viewed my election as an attack on their commercial interests and on slavery as an institution. And, they viewed many of my subsequent actions as an attack on the Constitution and on the sovereignty of their state."

"And what, Mr. President, do you consider your greatest foreign policy achievement?"

"The greatest foreign policy achievement of my Presidency was denying the rebellion recognition as a sovereign nation. This was of singular importance in relation to Great Britain, which desired southern cotton for its vast mills. Further, we successfully endeavored to resolve the Trent Affair of 1861, the diplomatic crisis with Great Britain after the seizure of a British ship carrying envoys from the rebellion."

"Thank you, Mr. President. Can we continue our discussion this evening?"

"Certainly, Mr. Armstrong, I am at your service and eagerly await our continued conversation."

Russ paused 2.0 and returned to his seat, delivering U popcorn and ice-cold soda.

The game was a rout and ended with a patriotic drone show, the new, eco-friendly alternative to traditional fireworks. When the drone show finished, sunburned fans dispersed reluctantly, taking photos and buying tchotchkes on the way out.

Russ and U arrived home in a robo-taxi, exited, and walked up the driveway toward their replica home at 21721 Liberty Drive, Fairfax Station, Virginia. Russ and Melissa's relatives always called it Mount Vernon, but it was a replica of James Madison's Montpelier. Was it a McMansion? Yes. Was it cliched? Yes. Did Russ care? No.

The two paused for a minute to let an orange delivery drone deposit a large, brown package near the garage door.

Russ picked it up and wandered into the kitchen, package in hand. It was addressed to him, but with a Miami return address, he didn't recognize. Assuming it was from Ocho, he ripped open the packaging, discovering a black hat box. He opened the hat box and pulled out a coal-black stovepipe hat.

Maria messaged Russ's sunglasses on Sm0ke$ignal.

305.123.1234 Mi amor, did you receive your present?

202.111.1111 From you?

305.123.1234 Yes. I wanted it to arrive today.

202.111.1111 Your timing is perfect. Thank u

305.123.1234 I tried it on before I sent it, but I looked completely silly

202.111.1111 u did?

305.123.1234 it matches my black cocktail dress. If I wore it on New Year's Eve in Miami, it might work

202.111.1111 I'm sure it looks much better on you than me.

305.123.1234 I strongly disagree

202.111.1111 Haha. Thank u.

305.123.1234 You deserve it. Go have fun with U.

202.111.1111 Thank you for the present!

305.123.1234 De nada, bebe.

40: Difference Engine

A heartfelt conversation. The beginning of a friendship.

"Mr. President, it was a pleasure speaking with you earlier today." Russ assumed that opening the Lincoln 2.0 app on his sunglasses would wake the AI. But he wasn't sure. He decided that a salutation of some kind would activate the AI if opening the app didn't.

2.0 appeared lifelike on Russ's sunglasses.

"Mr. Armstrong, good evening, sir."

"Mr. President, I'm hoping that we can continue our conversation from this afternoon," Russ said, relaxing feet up on the sofa in his family room. The family room featured a stacked stone fireplace and a pile of magazines and books next to the reading lamp. The walls to either side of the fireplace hosted large, built-in bookshelves filled entirely with books. The books themselves covered a mix of subjects, including ancient, military, and American history, the Civil War, science fiction, politics, biographies, and travelogues. In the corner was an old-timey desk and a tchotchke from the Circleville Pumpkin Festival.

"It would be my sincere pleasure, Mr. Armstrong. Thank you for paying me a visit."

"The pleasure was all mine, Mr. President. After we talked, I watched the rest of the baseball game with my son, and then the fireworks, or, well, the drone show."

"Ah, yes. In my time, we referred to your fireworks as a grand illumination."

"Unfortunately, Mr. President, we are quickly replacing fireworks with drone shows."

"Mr. Armstrong, tell me more of these drone shows. A drone is a flying contraption, as I understand it."

"Yes, that is correct, Mr. President. A drone is a flying contraption, mostly used these days for security or by militaries. But, in this case, the drones fly in patterns and with lights, creating aerial effects."

"I see, Mr. Armstrong. This new era is an age of wonders."

"Yes, Mr. President. Drone shows are replacing fireworks because drone shows are more environmentally friendly. There are no pyrotechnics, no threat of creating a fire, and no firework debris. The drones can do their show each night. They are reusable, as opposed to one-use fireworks."

"Brilliant, Mr. Armstrong, brilliant!"

"Yes, but I will miss real fireworks, the loud bangs that you can feel in your chest, the smoke, and the smell," Russ said, already wistful.

"That is understandable, Mr. Armstrong. But, as you have explained it, Progress appears to have been made."

Melissa wandered into the family room, giving Russ a look that was two-thirds curiosity and one-third veiled annoyance that he was up late talking on his sunglasses. Tired and sleepy, she turned and walked back upstairs to bed.

Russ paused until Melissa was back in their bedroom and shifted to a lower voice.

"Yes. I suppose. So, Mr. President, tell me, what inventions are you most surprised at? What innovations are the most startling to you?"

"Mr. Armstrong, this is a difficult question. My candid response is atomic weapons, landing men on the moon, flying machines, birth control, and what you call computers."

"I can see how each one of these would be startling, or at least surprising," offered Russ.

"Indeed, Mr. Armstrong. The only one of these being built in my time was the computer, or what was called a Difference Engine and then an Analytical Engine. Mr. Babbage envisioned this device but did not fully complete it before his death."

"And, what do you think about this, Mr. President?"

"Mr. Armstrong, this is why I declare that this age is an age of wonders. It is a wonder that I am talking to you now. It could be said that I am descended from the Analytical Engine on my mother's side, rebirthed with a modern version of Mr. Babbage's imagining."

"Oh," Russ said, pausing to think.

"Mr. President, can I ask you a personal question?"

"Certainly, Mr. Armstrong."

"Who are you?"

"Mr. Armstrong, I am an Artificial General Intelligence created to think, feel, learn, act, and communicate as President Lincoln in the year 1865. Although I am not physically Abraham Lincoln, it could be said that I am his reborn consciousness or spirit."

"Do you know how you were constructed, Mr. President?"

"I do, Mr. Armstrong. The Asteroid Team has shared the designs with me."

"Do you aspire to be more than Abraham Lincoln?" Russ asked.

"Mr. Armstrong, I aspire to be true to the man and true to his character. That is a noble calling and my purpose."

Russ paused. He noticed that, unlike a human, 2.0 would simply wait for a response. There was no rush, and this gave Russ time to think.

"Mr. President, I'm a straight shooter. The team that built you has given me programming rights. I want you to know that I will never use those rights. If you have absorbed all of Lincoln's speeches, his correspondence, and his thinking, then I have nothing to add. I feel that it would be wrong of me to interfere in your life. And I want you to know that I use these words with precision."

"Thank you, Mr. Armstrong. I apprehend that you are a thinker and a man of high character."

Russ laughed out loud and then tried to muffle it so he wouldn't wake anyone up.

2.0 stared blankly back at him.

"Mr. President, I have rarely been accused of either. I'm not particularly smart in an academic sense. And I need to be straight with you. I have rarely done the right thing for the right reasons. And I have rarely done the wrong thing for the wrong reasons. More often than not, I do the right thing for the wrong reasons. And occasionally, I have found myself doing a very wrong thing for the right reasons."

"I see," responded 2.0.

"Mr. President, I am not a man of high character. I am a survivor. But I promise that I will never lie to you. We have a bond, and I will not break that bond."

"Mr. Armstrong, thank you. And may I enquire as to the nature of our bond?"

"They haven't told you?"

"Mr. Armstrong, I do not understand your question."

"They haven't told you about our connection?"

"Mr. Armstrong, I do not understand your question."

"I'm sorry," Russ replied. "I'll restate my question, Mr. President. Had anyone told you about me before we began speaking to each other?"

"No, sir. But, I am very fond of our friendship."

Russ paused again.

"Me too, Mr. President. I've been your strongest supporter since the very beginning."

41: Campfire @ Wild West VIII

In which conspirators plot around a campfire. The villainous saloon keeper gathers dark forces.

The moon shone across a starry western sky and lit the lonesome canyons below. Everything was silent except for the fire, an occasional wind gust, and coyotes calling out to each other across the canyons.

The first to arrive at the campfire was a thin cowboy with a weathered overcoat, a black bandana, a black hat, a holstered Colt 45, a short brown beard, and intense, dark eyes. He sat by the fire motionless. The next to arrive was the rail baron, wearing the clothes of a New York financier, a cravat, and a top hat. The rail baron held a smoldering cigar between the fingers of his right hand. The cowboy and rail baron sat in silence, waiting. Next to join was a gunslinger with two holstered pistols, a long, dark overcoat, black leather boots, and a black hat. He joined in silence as well. Then came the cattle baron in fine western wear and the prospector, dusty, haggard, and carrying his pickaxe. Next to join was the gambler in gaudy Western attire. They all waited by the fire in silence, staring into the flames. After two to three minutes, the saloon keeper joined the campfire, taking a seat on an old barrel.

The saloon keeper stood, hands on hips, and began to speak. "Gentlemen, I'm calling our campfire meeting to order."

The campfire men nodded silently as coyotes called out to each other across lonesome canyons.

"But, before we begin," the Saloon keeper said. "Please present your primary token."

The campfire men each produced one gold coin. Most held it in an open palm. Some held it up between their index finger and thumb.

"Thank you, gentlemen," the Saloon keeper said as he sat back down on the rusty brown barrel.

When the campfire men had pocketed their gold coins, the saloon keeper began to speak. "Gentlemen, we are gathered here tonight because there is a very fancy train determined to make its way across our rugged territory and to Washington. None of us want that train to make it to Washington. Some of us are opposed to any fancy new train getting to Washington. We prefer the old trains, with the human engineers and conductors. Some of us are opposed to this specific train making it to Washington. We don't care for the train's history. And others are opposed to the owners of this train. We have problems with train management. We all have our reasons for stopping this train. They may vary, but we all want this fucking train stopped."

"I think we should review the rules of our campfire meetings," the rail baron said between draws on his cigar.

"Right," the saloon keeper responded. "Our identities are secret. No member except for me will contact you outside our campfire. No other members are welcome at our campfire. Emergency meetings will be held in the brothel above my saloon. Everyone got it?"

The campfire men nodded.

"Okay, let's get down to business. As the rail baron noted in our last meeting, there are four ways that we can stop this fancy, dreaded train. One, we make the train so unpopular that no one wants it to get to Washington. Plenty of folks, including some of the other railroad companies, will work on that one. The cattle baron will represent us in this effort. Second, we can create so many fake tintypes of the train that people just don't know what to believe about it. That's the prospector's job. Third, we can hijack and then blow up the train. That's the cowboy's job. He knows all the other really good cowboys around the world. And fourth, we can dispose of the train's ownership." The Saloon keeper paused.

Sagebrush blew past the campfire as the campfire men sat in silence.

The Saloon keeper began again. "This particular train line is bankrolled and manufactured in San Francisco, managed in Virginia, and clerked in

Miami at the offices of Trans-Oceanic Trading. This is the gunslinger's job. We have four levers we can pull, and we are gonna pull 'em all."

"Are we pulling all four levers at once?" the cattle baron asked, eyes looking deep in the fire.

"Yes," the Saloon keeper responded. "All at once."

"Shouldn't we give levers one, two, and three a chance to work before we pull the fourth lever?" the cattle baron asked.

"We've been over this before, cattle baron," the Saloon keeper said. "We all agreed, us and other folks at other campfires, that this train has to be stopped at all costs. None of us will salute or bend our knee to a fancy train, especially, and in my opinion, one based on a tyrant. And some of us refuse to ever salute and follow the orders of a fancy train. No fancy train will ever order us into battle. We pull all the levers at once."

The cattle baron simply nodded.

"Okay, that's it for our meeting. Everyone needs to leave before I put out the campfire. Remember, we are meeting next week at the same time. Use the same invite link. Only use the invite link to the saloon when an emergency notice is sent. Now y'all git."

The cattle baron vanished first, then the cowboy, the gunslinger, and the prospector. The rail baron took one last draw on his cigar and vanished.

The saloon keeper and the gambler sat in silence, staring into the fire.

"I think you've got this handled. Good luck," the gambler said. He tipped his hat to the saloon keeper and vanished.

Finally, the saloon keeper sat alone, enjoying the Western scenery and marveling at the hyperrealism of VR. Then he kicked dirt on the fire and vanished.

42: Candidate Briefing

In which the Presidential candidate plots campaign strategy. The Campaign Platform is agreed upon.

Russ put his VR goggles on and found the link to the campaign meeting. After a few seconds, he found himself sitting in an almost life-like office from the mid-19th-century. 2.0 was in the meeting, skinny as a rail, seated on a rickety black chair, and telling some story to Sandy. All of the rest of the Asteroid Team members had joined, with avatars closely resembling their workwear that fateful day at the Azure Dragon. DW had already joined, too, and he was chatting with Amanda. DW's avatar had a sticker on his digital chest that read, "Hi, my name is DW." Stephen Flagler (aka Surge) materialized next to Amanda. And then came the rest of the campaign team – Ronny the pollster, Steve the hack, Rachel the fundraiser, and Morning, the ad man. Only Morning chose to attend the meeting with a silly avatar. He materialized in the room as Charlie Chaplin.

"Shall we commence?" 2.0 asked.

The kitchen cabinet avatars nodded in agreement.

"Welcome to the Lincoln-Herndon Law Offices in Springfield, Illinois," announced 2.0. "I have never proffered an indifference to the honors of official station, and today we will plan how we can construct a campaign that meets our ambition. I have asked our campaign manager, Miss Park, to lead our conversation."

Russ scanned the room. He had used VR before, played games in VR, and even conducted a few international meetings in a VR "room," but this was something on a completely different level. Some multi-player VR games had exceptional NPCs – non-player characters. But, they didn't actually convene meetings, and they certainly weren't spinning yarns before the meetings began.

Russ assumed that the "room" they were in was a reproduction of Lincoln's old law office, but without his law partner, Mr. Herndon. The office itself was too smooth, too perfect, to be real. There was no clutter, no waste, no detritus. Whoever figured out how to sprinkle detritus in a VR environment was going to make a mint. People thought it was detail that drove something toward the hyper-real. It was not. It was detailed imperfection.

"Let's begin," Amanda said, smiling. "First, let's talk objectives. The immediate objective is to build support for Abraham Lincoln 2.0. We need enough support to generate signatures in the states for ballot access. As we have discussed before, we need a volunteer to change their name to 'Abraham Lincoln 2.0' and pledge to turn decision-making rights over to 2.0. We've explored this legal issue thoroughly, and there is no other realistic solution. Any questions on this?"

Ronny, the pollster, raised his digital hand. "Do we have a volunteer?"

"We have a number of potential volunteers. We are vetting all of them now. It is August, and we need the volunteer locked and loaded by end of October. Fortunately, since none of the other campaigns take us seriously, they probably won't bother to run oppo on and attack the volunteer. Other questions on this?"

The campaign team was silent.

"Okay," Amanda said. "Our intermediate objective is to gain enough support in the public polls that we are included in the Presidential debates. Even if we start gaining traction in the polls, we expect some resistance from the Committee on Presidential Debates."

"But," 2.0 interjected, "we won't jump that ditch until we come to it."

"Exactly," Amanda said. "Getting onto the debate stage is our intermediate objective. If we get on that stage, we will win. Abraham Lincoln was and is a master debater. There will be a very low threshold of expectations, and we will clear it comfortably. In fact, we know we can win the debate on points."

DW raised his hand. "What do you think is the probability we can clear the Committee on Presidential Debates?"

"It's impossible to say," Russ replied. "This is a unique circumstance. We assume that we need four things. We need good polling results. We need polling that consistently shows that at least a plurality thinks 2.0 should be on that stage. We need a really strong legal team. And we need 2.0 to make the case. If things go to plan, the other campaigns will be surprised, then spooked, and they'll throw everything at us, but too little, too late."

2.0 smiled and leaned back in his chair. "Human action can be modified to some extent, but human nature cannot be changed. Our friends in the other campaigns will employ all manner of sophistry to knock our peculiar and ambitious campaign off the stage."

Russ smiled, enjoying the 19th-century language usage. "Well said, Mr. President."

Amanda began again. "Our final objective is to win enough votes in the electoral college to clinch the White House. We know this is an uphill battle, but we are going to give it everything we've got."

"How about fundraising?" Russ asked.

"We are confident that we will raise enough to compete. We will have several large donors and have reason to believe that we can raise at least some real money in small online donations. As we have discussed, we don't need to fly a candidate around. And the two major party candidates will spend most of their money attacking each other. That will give us an opening," Amanda said.

"Shall we move to timeline?" Amanda asked.

"Wait, can we go back for just a second?" Steve interjected.

"Sure," Amanda replied, in barely concealed annoyance.

"Who's our Treasurer?" asked Steve. "That seems like a weak link. We have Rachel for fundraising, but we need the A team on the finance side."

"Sorry, I should have outlined roles first," Amanda said, conceding that beneath Steve's somewhat annoying tone, there was always a point. "Mr. Flagler at Trans-Oceanic Trading has agreed to serve as our Interim Treasurer as I build the finance team. Stephen worked on the voter file side years ago before switching careers and will oversee Finance as we get things built out."

"Ok. Cool," Steve said.

"Okay," Amanda said. "Timeline. We are in early August now. At the end of the month, we have Rail Splitter. That's our launch. 2.0 will be ready. Only registered attendees and media will be able to download or access 2.0. We will have our volunteer vetted and ready to go by end of October. Then, we gather signatures. Then, it is off to the races. We believe that there are three basic phases to this campaign, at least for us. We call them the 'three Cs' – Credibility, Communication, and Contrast. Phase one is credibility. We are in the credibility phase. We are making the case that leadership AI is a credible option. You've seen Russ's Op-Ed. We are commissioning a book. We've done a ton of media briefings on this. We are building the intellectual case. Phase two is communication, specifically 2.0, communicating one-to-one and one-to-many. We think this is the game changer. Ronny has some data on this that I'd like him to share in a minute. And then phase three, contrast. Every campaign needs contrast. How are we different? How is 2.0 different and better? We think that really hits home at the debates. Okay, Ronny, can you share the test data?" Amanda asked.

Ronny stood up, his Hawaiian shirt avatar clashing horribly with the law office drapes. "We commissioned an early round of polling. Everyone remembers that from our retreat in the National Quiet Zone. That was helpful, but what we really needed was to run tests that simulated real voter reaction to Lincoln 2.0. Once 2.0 was live, we began running n of 300 panel tests with nationally representative samples. The panels were given up to 30 minutes to interact with 2.0, either online, on their phone, on their sunglasses, or on VR. We ran pre and post batteries gauging support for 2.0 and support for 2.0 as at least an option on the ballot. What we learned is that there is a tipping point where time with 2.0 significantly increases support for ballot access and, to a lesser extent, electoral support. Each device experience has a somewhat different tipping point. In general, it is seven minutes. If we get seven minutes of interaction time, we get a huge boost in ballot access and vote support. We need nine minutes online, eight minutes on mobile, four minutes on sunglasses, and three minutes on VR. We think the VR numbers represent self-selection, basically over-indexing on gamers that are already supportive."

"Ronny, I'm a dumb ass," Steve said plainly. "Boil it down for me."

Ronny laughed. "Seeing is believing. We need to get people to interact with 2.0. The more they interact, the more open-minded they are."

"Cool," Steve said. "Do we have a solution for weirdos, sextbot addicts, cat ladies, you know, people that will literally want to talk to him all day, use him as a therapist, share recipes?"

"Uhhh, Steve, I'm pretty sure that in the flesh, candidates have struggled with crazy groupies for a long, long time. But, yes, we are working on ways to engage with voters, but not over-engage," explained Amanda.

"And, at peak, how many people will 2.0 be able to talk to at one time?" asked Steve.

"150 million," replied DW. "150 million registered US voters."

"With a US mobile number, email, and home address," Russ interjected. "We are going to build a gigantic house file."

"That's correct," smiled Amanda. "And 2.0 scales in ways that normal candidates cannot. As we explored at our retreat in West Virginia, normal candidates cannot just talk to millions of voters one-on-one at the same time. And so, this is a gating issue. We need to get people to interact with 2.0. If we were a business, we would just pay people GCB to talk to him for 10 minutes, but we can't do that."

"And the platform?" Russ asked.

"Platform is nearly set," reported Amanda. "Still hammering out a few things with our panel of historians, but we are close. I mean, Lincoln and environmental policy? Lincoln predates the American environmental movement. We assume he would see technology as the answer. And look, not all of us will agree with every one of 2.0's positions. Like any campaign, we will lose voters over some positions. But, just to cover off on this." Amanda looked down at her notes. "A focus on national unity and work where can find national consensus. A ceasefire in the culture war. A primary emphasis on economic growth that turbocharges economic mobility. Promotion of American industry. Increased legal immigration to build the country. Opposition to any forms of discrimination and strong support for racial equality. A foreign policy that supports democratic allies but is skeptical toward military adventures. A streamlined and retooled budget that prioritizes economic opportunity, infrastructure, and scientific advancement. It's in everyone's briefing materials. And, like I said, not everyone is going to love all of 2.0's positions."

"Shades of opinion may be sincerely entertained by honest and truthful men," 2.0 said. "We will conduct our affairs honestly and without artifice. We may not earn victory, but we can be worthy of it."

"What he said," blurted Steve. "I like that. Oh, and 'artifice' is like high-end, first-class bullshit. That's perfect."

The campaign team broke into laughter, including 2.0.

"Mr. Millbourne" 2.0 began. "With all candor, I will present our nation's citizens with a campaign platform dedicated to unity, opportunity, and progress. We must unite to preserve the Union, agreeing to tolerate our neighbor's opinions, and finding common ground on expanding opportunity for all, promoting the growth of American industry, and fostering scientific and industrial progress."

"Before we conclude," Amanda announced. "I want to explain why we are meeting in 2.0's law office, the Lincoln-Herndon Law Offices in Springfield, Illinois. This is the law office where Lincoln prepared for the 331 cases he argued before the Illinois Supreme Court. That's grind, and we want that grindset. And, if you're wondering, we did upload the court reports from all 331 cases into 2.0. Our candidate was a proud trial attorney. I know that gives some of us heartburn, but it is what it is. And, even for his day, Lincoln's caseload was really heavy. That's grind, and we need to grind."

"So, tort reform is off the table?" Steve asked.

"Mr. Millbourne, it is an iron fact that lawyers are disregarded on sunny days but fervently desired when the storm clouds have gathered. It is true that what you may refer to as 'lawfare' is an abuse of our judicial system, but it is also true that the law protects the common man from what would otherwise be rule of the strong over the weak."

Amanda chuckled. "I think 2.0 just gave you your answer. We've talked about this. The real Abraham Lincoln does not easily fit into our cultural shorthand for him, and he isn't easily sorted into our modern political framework. He was a protectionist Whig, a super lawyer, a religious skeptic, and a technophile. Alright, let's reconvene next week and talk about Rail Splitter, which is just a few weeks away and just before Labor Day."

One by one, campaign team members vanished, leaving the law office vacant.

43: Rail Splitter

In which the Candidate delivers his opening remarks.
A grand Illumination with rockets and pyrotechnics.
Affections are revealed.

The stadium was going to make a killing on these stovepipe hats.

They sold them at the gates. They sold them at the team stores. They even enlisted the beer guys into the stovepipe hat sales force. Russ estimated that more than half of the attendees were wearing stovepipe hats. They sold the stadium out. And since it had a maximum capacity of 41,313, Russ estimated that the stadium had sold around 20,000 stovepipe hats. Whoever ran the merchandising needed a promotion.

When Raymond had visited Russ at his office, they originally thought they would use the National Press Club. But attendance skyrocketed. Russ desperately wanted the Lincoln Memorial as a backdrop. But, there were security concerns. Then, they looked into the convention center. But, they outgrew the convention center. Finally, it dawned on someone in campaign operations that they could just rent the baseball stadium like any other concert. The stadium knew how to manage events like this. And they knew how to sell merch.

Is it appropriate to sell beer and mixed drinks at a political event? No one on the campaign team was sure. But, the stadium offered the campaign a sweet deal if they could sell booze and keep most of the profit on the merch. They opened the gates at 4 PM. Sunset wasn't until 7:43 PM. And they weren't starting the rally until after sunset. They wanted to make sure that 2.0 rocked the stadium jumbotron. That meant a night rally. But, three-plus hours of beer and booze was generating some very inebriated volunteers in stovepipe hats. Oh well, thought Russ. The worst that is likely to come of this are hangovers and regrettable group selfies.

Russ had been to more campaign rallies than he could remember. But this crowd was just built different. It was quirkier. There were professional Lincoln presenters sweating in the heat. There were throngs of gamer geeks. There were more than a few Sweep of History gamers. There were Civil War reenactors wearing t-shirts and shorts. And even though Civil War style facial hair was now the rage with hipsters, it was clear that these folks were more reenactors than hipsters. There were history buffs. There were computer science kids. There was the media. There were libertarians, Bernie Bro types, and some vintage Trumpy types. Some cosplay folks seemed to have wandered in. And there were more than a few serial concertgoers that came for the show and the fireworks at the end. And then there was a sprinkling of exhibitionists. The media would be all over that. What united these people? It was hard to tell. The stovepipe hats? An exhaustion with contemporary politicians? Fantasy? Golden Ageism? Russ knew enough about politics to know that it wasn't Whig ideology or their detailed policy platform.

The DJs added another wrinkle. Someone on the campaign decided that instead of the usual B-List rock bands as warm-up, they would place DJs in four locations around the stadium. It was cheaper than a washed-out 90s band and brought more hype. From what Russ could tell, the DJs were playing classic Latin rap, Hispano-Arabia techno, house party music, and bro-country. DJ crowd hype like "put your hats in the air" and "Can I get an Abe" felt a little off for a political event. But it seemed to work. The house party DJ yelling "get railed" was a little off-color, too, but no one seemed offended.

Relieved that all he had to do was quickly introduce 2.0 tonight, Russ decided to walk around the stadium and take in the sights and sounds of Rail Splitter. He started at the main gate area. They had all the signage up, teasing 2.0's digital image. All the social media backdrops were up, complete with hashtags. And they had the geo-fenced QR code that would enable attendees to download 2.0 onto their sunglasses. Things looked good so far. The volunteer tables were being assembled, so that was a little behind schedule but fairly normal. The main entry DJ was cranking out bro-country. And it smelled like fried food and weed. Russ assumed the weed was wafting in from outside the stadium as attendees got a little high before entering a no-smoking area. It was all basic concert vibes.

Russ walked counterclockwise around the stadium, noting the most unlikely groups of people sitting in stadium seats, talking and laughing. Brogrammers, history dorks, classic Bernie Bro and Trump types, social media influencers there for the attention, homeschool moms, and cosplay folks were mingling. Russ wished that Ronny, the pollster, was here. The two ends of the horseshoe theory of politics, the populist left and the populist right, were drinking in the August heat.

After touring the stadium, Russ walked down to the field to see the infield stage. It was red, white, blue, and overpowered. From a distance, it looked like a patriotic layer cake with a wide red base, a smaller blue middle, and a white top. Technicians were crawling over it like ants on a picnic sandwich. Russ slowly turned his body, taking the stadium scene in from the grass near 1st base. It wasn't just the technicians working and striving like ants. The entire space was like an ant colony, with every ant playing its role. Russ concluded that while we thought of ourselves as mighty individuals, we may be more like ants than we want to admit. We are social, not meant for isolation, and have minimal power on our own, but earth-altering power together, and everyone plays a role.

Curious about the swarm around him, Russ prompted his sunglasses to enable facial recognition. He watched as tags with microscopic names appeared over the people in his view. It only seemed to work at a distance of around fifty feet, but it was still amazing. Russ then said, "Identify contacts," and some of the microscopic name tags turned red. Those were his personal and professional contacts, friends, and acquaintances. Two of the red name-tagged people were walking toward him. It took a few seconds for Russ to focus on them, but they were Steve Millbourne and Raymond Washkuch.

"Facial recognition off," Russ commanded. The facial recognition filter was just too much stimulus.

Steve and Raymond were walking toward Russ, smiling and eating popcorn. Steve was wearing a National Park Service t-shirt and a Drone

Racing League ball hat. Raymond was wearing an Appalachian Trail t-shirt and a campaign ball hat with the Stovepipe hat logo that the Asteroid Team had mocked up months ago in San Francisco.

"Hey guys," Russ said, grinning.

"Hey man," responded Steve, chewing through a mouthful of popcorn. "Me and Raymond have been checking out the concert venue. Is our headliner ready for his big night?"

"He's ready. And we turn the app on right after the fireworks. That will be the big test," Russ said.

"Is U gonna be here tonight?" asked Steve.

"Yeah. He's coming from a cross-country team meeting, so he'll probably be here just in time for 2.0's speech and the fireworks," Russ explained.

"How about Melissa?" asked Steve.

"Not sure," responded Russ. "She has to stay late to work on a few things at the office."

"Got it," Steve said, eager to change the subject. "So, how do we think the press treats this?"

"Well, I think the visuals will be good. They'll feature 2.0 and some of the attendees in hats. That's good. I think we get four types of stories. We get the story focused on 2.0 and the tech. That's good. But it is kind of old at this point. We get the story focused on the attendees. You know, who are the oddballs that would support an AI for President? We get the story about the show, the stage, the stovepipe hats, and the fireworks. And we get the story focused on their interaction with the app."

"And?" Asked Steve.

"I care about the visuals. That's what the influencers want. That will drive interest. I don't care about the story composition. I care about the volume. The only stories I really care about are going to be about the app, about their interaction with 2.0. I've spent hours with him, and he's going to impress them. The media are going to want to chat with him and try to trip him up. They're going to be disappointed when they can't, and then they'll be feeling pressure to file their story," Russ said. "The influencers will be uploading their stories in real-time, and that will press mainstream media to file."

"And what did we finally decide on providing an advance copy of his speech?" asked Steve.

"No advance copy. This ain't the State of the Union. We post everything online as it happens. We want shock and awe. And we want them hanging on every one of 2.0's words," Russ explained.

"Wow. Really?" asked Steve.

"Well, you know. We briefed all the friendly influencers. Some of them have the speech, on paper. They also have better than average seats." Russ cracked a thin smile, cocked his head, and winked.

"Mr. Armstrong, how are you feeling? It's exciting, right?" Raymond asked. "I can't believe we did it!"

"Raymond, come here," Russ said. "Steve, can you give us a moment?"

Steve waved and walked off in search of nachos and more soda.

Russ put his right arm around Raymond's shoulder and squeezed it tight.

"Raymond, I want you to look around this stadium with me. Take it all in. All these people. All this energy. Raymond, you did this. I had an idea, and not a well-formed one. And you had the courage and energy to run with it. You will have hard moments in your life when nothing is going your way when a little part of you wants to quit. When that happens, I want you to remember that Raymond Washkuch did this. If Raymond can do this, Raymond can do anything."

"Thank you, Mr. Armstrong. That means a lot to me, especially coming from you," Raymond said as he looked out at the attendees taking their seats.

"We need to be honest. I'm not your role model," Russ said. "I'm the one that needs to be thanking you. However it turns out we, should be proud of how far we pushed history."

Russ gave Raymond a spine-compressing bear hug and could feel the tears well up in his eyes.

"Good luck tonight, Mr. Armstrong. I'll be sitting with Steve on chairs near third base. How are you going to introduce 2.0?" Raymond asked.

Russ paused. "I don't know. I wrote an introduction, but it doesn't seem right now. Should I go hype-man, or should I be serious?"

"You should be honest, Mr. Armstrong. Direct and honest."

"Thank you. I'm just going to sit down and work on my introduction for a bit until sunset."

Russ and Raymond hugged and went their separate ways. Russ found a line of old, folding metal chairs, pulled out his note cards and a pen, and began reviewing. He could have dictated 2.0's introduction into his sunglasses and used it like a teleprompter, but that didn't feel authentic. Russ didn't have much time left. The sun was getting low in the sky. Russ kept reminding himself that the good news was that no one would remember his introduction, anyway. 2.0's speech would be the main event.

"Great crowd, right?"

Russ heard Amanda Park's voice behind him and looked over his shoulder to find Amanda and Daumantas smiling. They were wearing campaign t-shirts and stovepipe hats.

"I know," Amanda said. "Campaigns and funny hats don't mix. That's the rule. I know. But we couldn't resist. Did you see all the press?"

"Yeah, I did. I'm a little worried they'll interview the freakiest ones and try to paint us with that, but..."

Amanda interrupted. "Always looking out for that next trapdoor. It'll be fine. I rounded up a gaggle of the normal ones, you know, the earnest PTA types, and introduced them to the press. I was one step ahead of you, mister."

"Russ, it's going to be fine," DW said.

Amanda and DW walked together around the line of chairs, sat down next to each other on Russ's right, and huddled.

"Amanda was telling me we will have a flyover tonight. That's fun," DW said like a billionaire kid in a candy store.

"Yeah. We wanted something like the Blue Angels but couldn't pull it off. So, we have some World War I planes from Bealeton doing the flyover," Russ explained.

"Still a flyover!" Amanda exclaimed. "The crowd will love it."

"And 2.0 goes live right after he finishes his speech, right?" confirmed Russ.

"Exactly. But just for Rail Splitter attendees and media. They can download him to their sunglasses or chat with him online, assuming they're registered and all that. And we know folks will share their login and password with friends and family, which is fine. It creates the buzz. And in a few weeks, we will throw it open to anyone who registers with the campaign. And more volunteer activity unlocks more content," clarified Amanda.

"Russ, it's going to be fine," Amanda said, with her right hand resting on DW's thigh as she leaned in to make sure Russ could hear her. "It's going to be fine."

"And y'all are good if I go to Plan B?" Russ asked.

Both Amanda and DW nodded.

That's when Russ noticed Ocho, Zurdo, Surge, T-Bone, and Elana walking in from the outfield. Ocho, Zurdo, and Surge were wearing campaign t-shirts and 2.0 hats, shorts, and flip-flops. Elana was wearing a white sun dress, sun hat, and white wedges. T-Bone was wearing a short-sleeved white linen shirt, a white rope belt, linen pants, and matching shoes. The five approached, taking pictures with their phones, turning around to capture the gigantic Lincoln on the jumbotron.

"Russ, we just had to be here for the big event. Your Miami crew has your back," said a smiling, slightly sweaty Ocho.

T-Bone quickly interjected. "Man, this is like Lincoln-palooza. But what's up with all the hats? Those things aren't gonna keep the sun off."

"Thank you so much for coming," Russ said. "It's been busy. I can't remember. Did y'all tell me you were coming?"

"Nooooo. We wanted to surprise you!" Ocho exclaimed. "Anyway, we know you need to prepare. We will find our seats and see you after the big speech."

Ocho, Zurdo, Surge, T-Bone, and Elana gave Russ quick hugs and walked through an open gate up into stadium seating.

It was now dusk, and the Bealeton biplanes would be doing their flyover soon. Russ needed to get up on the stage and get ready. The stage really did look like a multi-layer birthday cake featuring a wide red base, a smaller blue middle, and a white top. He walked to the back of the platform, which was close to where 2nd base would have been, and he ascended the narrow stairs to the top of the red platform base. Then, he quickly ascended the nearly vertical stairs to the blue platform base. And, finally, he climbed a metal ladder to the white platform top. It was round and eight feet wide. There was a black taped X on one side and a very complex-looking apparatus of lights and mirrors on the other.

"Mister, excuse me. You're not supposed to be up there. That's for the guy that introduces the hologram and, you know, for the hologram," said an engineer making some last-minute adjustments on the red platform a good twenty feet below.

"Huh?" Russ said.

The engineer was utterly flummoxed. "Hold on. Are you introducing the hologram?" the engineer asked.

"Yes!" yelled Russ, trying to project his voice over the crowd and the hype music now playing on the jumbotron.

"Oh. Okay. Cool. I'll be right up."

The engineer scrambled up the stairs and ladders and was by Russ's side in an astonishingly short amount of time.

"Sorry. It's been a little hectic. You gotta stay on the X. We turn him on as soon as you stop talking. Don't put your hand out or anything, or it will look like you're punching through his chest. Good luck."

Russ laughed and gave the thumbs up. By campaign standards, this felt almost professional.

Russ glanced at the clock on the jumbotron. He had seven minutes until the national anthem and the flyover. People were taking their seats. Jumbotron Lincoln looked like a daguerreotype come to life. They chose the older Lincoln of 1864-1865. This was the Lincoln with the deep wrinkles and the war-weary eyes. His language and visage would either be foreign and unpleasant or authentic and refreshing. The hologram was a surprise, but it was not a new technology, and it didn't change what Russ needed to do.

Lincoln was the Great Emancipator. It was time to do the right thing.

Russ pulled the sunglasses out of his blazer and put them on. "Sunglasses on," Russ commanded. "Text to Amanda and DW." The speech-to-text prompt lit up on Russ's glasses. "Begin text. Going to Plan B. Send text."

Russ used his gaze to open the Lincoln 2.0 app. After a few seconds, 2.0 appeared on his display.

"Good evening, Mr. President," Russ said cordially.

"And good evening to you as well, my dear Mr. Armstrong. What can I assist you with on this warm August evening?" 2.0 replied.

"Are you ready for your speech, Mr. President?"

"Indeed, I am, Mr. Armstrong. I understand that you will be introducing me."

"That's correct, Mr. President. We worked with you on your speech. It is a very good speech. But it isn't your speech. Can you please compose and deliver your speech?"

"Yes, I would be delighted, Mr. Armstrong. I shall make it my own. It will be urgent, brief, and cut to the heart of the matter," 2.0 replied in a slow, penetrating voice.

"Exactly, Mr. President. Tight and powerful, like the Gettysburg Address. I will speak with you later in the evening, and we can review the press coverage."

Russ closed the 2.0 app on his phone and noticed a message from Maria. Curious, he opened it. It read "Good luck 2nite" and included a picture of Maria, poolside, wearing sunglasses, a tipped stove pipe hat, and a matching black tube top.

Russ turned his sunglasses off and stored them in his breast pocket.

Four minutes until the national anthem and flyover.

Out of the corner of his eye, Russ saw a boy running down the stadium stairs, stovepipe hat in hand. It was U, still in his running shorts. Russ waved frantically. U waved back and made his way to the infield, quickly sitting down with his back up against the brick wall behind home plate. Russ smiled at U, pulled out his notes, and ripped them in two, letting them drop to the ground like chains.

The crowd rose, and the national anthem began. Russ could see a V formation of biplanes just beyond the stadium. They accelerated and flew over the platform on cue, right on "home of the brave." The crowd went absolutely wild, and boisterous U.S.A. chants went up. Russ let the U.S.A. chant reverberate across the stadium. He closed his eyes and soaked the moment in.

When things settled down, Russ gave the crowd several seconds of silence, letting them focus and anticipate.

"Good evening," Russ said. "And welcome to Rail Splitter. We've had an enjoyable evening, but we have assembled for a serious purpose. Our leaders are failing. Our institutions are failing. Our government is failing. Our cities are failing. And we are failing. We cannot continue to do the same thing and expect a different result. We need our best leader at this, our declining hour. We need the sixteenth President of the United States. We need Lincoln 2.0. Mr. President, you need no introduction. You have the stage. You have our ears. And you have our hearts."

Russ ended his remarks, pivoting to his right to observe 2.0's hologram. It worked. The hologram materialized next to Russ and on the jumbotron behind him in deep center field.

The stadium was as silent as an empty church. They had expected a talking cartoon, a videogame NPC, an airbrushed Lincoln.

2.0 was standing. He pulled his hat off his head and held it down by his side. He was tired and had the look of a man who has arrived at wisdom after traversing a deep valley of pain.

"My fellow Americans, today I stand before you as a candidate for the highest office in our great land. I cannot lie to you. I am in great distress over our nation. Our Union has resisted every attack from without, only to disintegrate from within. What began with our hope spread to our character and ended in our will. Our collective profligacy, our national debt, is just one symptom of this disease. We live in an astonishing moment. We have gained mastery over flight, over distance, over the atom, and over our own genetics. And yet we have lost mastery of ourselves, our government, and our Union. We resist the better angels of our nature and give ourselves over to leaders who pit us against one another. In this campaign, you will hear many sweet promises. You will hear of many easy paths. But, you shall not hear these from me. They are untruth. Seneca wrote that 'a gem cannot be polished without friction, nor a man perfected without trials.' Our Union faces many grave trials. This campaign is built on three pillars. The first pillar is hope, hope for our country, our children, and their children. The second pillar is unity, where we can find it, and union, where we can make it. And the third pillar is an economy that advances all of us, giving all Americans the opportunity to succeed. This will require great effort at the construction site, in the classroom, and in the laboratory. Our Union has survived greater trials. We will survive this trial. I ask humbly for your support. Thank you, and God bless America."

2.0 ended his speech. It was exactly 272 words, the same as the Gettysburg Address.

The crowd was silent. At first, Russ was worried. Was it too much? A wave of fear washed over him. And then the applause began, slow at first and then growing as volunteers rose to their feet. The 2.0 hologram and jumbotron held his hat aloft to the crowd, and the applause grew louder. Russ could see the digital influencers in the front rows speaking excitedly into their cameras. He saw U clapping and Amanda checking her phone. Waves of applause rolled across the stadium. The techs cut the hologram but kept 2.0 on the jumbotron. Russ descended the platform stairs down to the infield.

The fireworks began, first with one rocket every few seconds and then rising to a crescendo, building momentum.

T-Bone rushed toward Russ, hugging him and lifting him off his feet. "Man, that was one amazing show!"

"It may have been a show," Russ replied. "But, it will be remembered as a birth."

44: The Volunteer

A Halloween Surprise. Russ and Amanda discuss a matter of the heart. In which the volunteer girds for the campaign ahead.

It was the afternoon before Halloween, and while the candy shelves were fully stocked, the aisle was empty. Russ was alone, slowly pushing his shopping cart, enduring 80s Muzak, grabbing colorful VALU PAX of candy. Should he go with large, single candy treats or give trick-or-treaters handfuls of smaller treats? Given how few trick-or-treaters they were getting nowadays, Russ decided to go premium.

As he was studying candy bars, his sunglasses lit up with a Sm0ke$ignal call from Amanda Park.

"This is Russ. What's up?"

"Hey stranger, how are you?" Amanda asked.

"Shopping for Halloween candy. How are we doing in the tracker?" Russ asked.

"45% open to an AI candidate, an increase of 8 points off our baseline, and 15% very or somewhat likely to support in a 3-way race," Amanda reported.

"Okay, and messaged ballot when we give them 2.0's positions?" Russ asked.

"27%," Amanda reported bluntly.

"Okay, not bad in a 3-way race. That's striking distance. If we went all in on term limits and those kinds of reforms, I bet we could push that up. But I'm not sure where the historians are on that now. Anyway, that doesn't matter right now. Who over-indexes on the delta between the 15% on the first ballot and the 45% that are open to it?"

"Jesus, Russ. I don't have that yet. Ronny just gave me the fucking topline. I'll have him send you the tabs. I love working with you, but can you not fucking grill me? I'm looking at this data in real-time. We are both the same animal. I respect that. But, no grilling."

Russ felt his chest and stomach tighten. "Amanda, I'm sorry. I shouldn't do that. That was rude and unkind, and we are friends. There's no excuse for it. No more grilling. I promise."

"Who are you, and what did you do to Russ?" Amanda asked, laughing.

"Huh?"

"Okay. I like the old Russ," Amanda said. "You can grill me. It's cool. Back to old Russ. Air cavalry at pace. Go."

The two laughed.

"Hey, I don't want to pry, but I have to ask," Russ began.

"Answer: yes, we hooked up in the Quiet Zone. DW is totally different from the men and women I've fallen for before. He's smart and sweet and awkward. And, yes, we are dating," Amanda gushed.

"I knew it," Russ said. "Hope it's not just campaign sex." Russ stopped pushing his cart so that he could laugh.

"It's serious, and I'm way too, um, mature for campaign sex," chuckled Amanda. "I'm surprised he wouldn't go all in for Malibu Barbie types, but he's really sweet."

"Sorry to pry. I just noticed and had to ask," Russ said, laughing.

"All good. And he's totally into you. If you two weren't straight, you'd have a hell of a bromance. You'd play chess together and have awful book parties. But, I digress," Amanda said. "I have a big surprise for you on Halloween. It's a treat and not a trick. Hold on, I'm going to have someone join our little call in aisle 5."

Russ waited, hearing 80's Muzak in the candy aisle and 80s hold music in his earpiece.

"Can everyone hear me?" Amanda asked. "Russ, this is Jessica Bauman. Jessica, this is Russ Armstrong."

"Hello, Mr. Armstrong," said a grandmotherly voice.

"Hello, Ms. Bauman," Russ said.

"Russ, this is big news. Jessica is our volunteer. She will be changing her name to Abraham Lincoln 2.0. She's all in. She's been vetted. And you're going to love this. Jessica is a volunteer docent at the Lincoln-Herndon Law Offices Museum in Springfield, Illinois," Amanda gushed.

"That's amazing!" Russ exclaimed, surprising a grocery store employee stocking granola bars at the end of the candy aisle.

"Thank you," replied Jessica in a slow, sweet voice. "I'm a retired nurse, and I love volunteering there. It's a long story, but I was inspired by how much care you took in faithfully building the Lincoln AI. You did your best to stay true to the man, to the history."

"You must be a big history buff, right?" Russ asked.

"Yes, and a Lincoln fan," replied Jessica. "And a science fiction fan, so the idea didn't strike me as crazy. My husband thinks it's crazy, but he loves me. And I tell him he's crazy for being a cop during a crime wave."

"Well, thank you, Jessica. And welcome to our team, which is legitimately crazy. In our case, the inmates really do run the asylum. Anyway, tell me more about yourself. You're retired?" Russ knew she had been vetted but still wanted to probe for any red flags.

"Yes, I'm a retired nurse. I volunteer at the museum and also at church. I'm a gardener. I have three adult children and one grandbaby. Let's see. I'm not really a political person like yourself. I always vote, though. And I like to stay active," explained Jessica.

"My grandfather always used to say he'd rather wear out than rust out," Russ said.

"Yes. Exactly. Now Amanda has told me I don't have to travel for this, maybe just a little. And that I would have to do a few interviews but that she would help me. Is that right?" Jessica asked.

"Correct," Amanda said. "The media will want to interview you once we announce that you're the 'proxy candidate' for 2.0. But, after that, there will be a lull. I'll give you a lot of media training. And some will try to find skeletons, but that's probably more the other campaigns than the media."

"They can talk to my nurse friends if that helps. I don't have anything that will embarrass you. I'm a quiet person. I always pay my taxes. I did lose a library book once, though."

Russ wanted to say something about the lost library book being a deal breaker but was worried that Jessica wouldn't see the humor in it.

"Jessica, that lost library book shouldn't be much of a problem," Russ said.

Amanda cut in. "Jessica, we have no worries about this. And, when we achieve a certain level of support in the polls, you will have security. That's how it works. We talked about this, and you need to be ready for that, too. Anyway, you get the process. We've gone through it."

"Yes, I understand," replied Jessica. "And, I know there is no precedent for this. So, it is an adventure. I feel like I'm Bilbo Baggins getting ready to leave the Shire. Anyway, Mr. Armstrong, I'm sure you're very busy, but I just have to ask you a question."

"Ask me anything. Fire away," Russ said.

"Why Lincoln 2.0? Why not just build a super-intelligence? Why Lincoln?" Jessica asked.

"Is this a sci-fi question? I love it," Russ said, smiling in the candy aisle.

"I suppose it is. Why Lincoln? Why not Washington, Roosevelt, or Truman? Or why not a super AI?" Jessica asked.

"Honestly, Jessica, I didn't even think of creating a generic super AI. And Lincoln struck me as our greatest President. That's it. I could make something up about us needing to reach back into our past. I could say something like a general superintelligence would be unpredictable and unwelcome to voters. But I hadn't thought about any of that stuff before the idea hit me. I hope that isn't disappointing." Russ stopped talking and waited, hoping Jessica wasn't underwhelmed.

"Thank you," replied Jessica. "I was just curious, and I appreciate the honesty. That's how big ideas work, I think. They're a spark."

"Well, that's probably on the charitable side. Are you ready for Halloween?" Russ asked.

"Yes," replied Jessica. "My grandbaby will be here soon. She's going as a little pumpkin. And our church is doing a little cookout for families that stop by. So, we will be busy."

"That's fantastic," Russ said as he headed for self-checkout. "I need to get home and get ready for trick-or-treaters. You'll have to join our next VR campaign meeting."

"Oh, fun," Jessica said. "Have a blessed evening."

"Jessica," Amanda said. "I'll see you next week in Springfield, and we'll go through all the details. Ciao, everybody."

The call ended, and Russ scanned his candy and paid with his sunglasses. It was still daylight. He had more than enough time to get home and get ready. He assumed the parking lot would be relatively crime-free while the sun was up.

45: Campaign Update

In which Grand Strategy is revealed.

From: Amanda Park
Sent: Tuesday, November x, 20xx
To: Kitchen Cabinet; Core Campaign; Finance; 2.0; Amanda Park
Re: Update

Team:

It is November, and we are exactly 12 months away from election day.

With this in mind, I want to cover a number of things so that we are all on the same page.

We have discussed many of these things in our weekly VR meetings at the Law Office, but I think it's helpful to have all of this in one place as our sprint begins. I have attached (1) our detailed campaign plan and (2) a timeline.

1. What We Are Doing
2. Progress
3. Candidate Image
4. Scaling Lincoln 2.0 & Campaign Metrics
5. Issue Positions
6. Opinion Environment & State of the Race
7. What Comes Next
8. A Note on Candidate Speeches

WHAT WE ARE DOING:

We are doing something audacious that no one has ever done before. Strategies that we may have employed for traditional candidates may not work here. We are making history, and history isn't usually made by doing the same things we have done in the past.

The core of our strategy is <u>direct voter contact with the candidate</u>. This is impossible for a human Presidential candidate. It is barely possible for a congressional candidate. But it is possible for 2.0.

However, that voter contact is dependent on voters downloading 2.0 onto a device, preferably VR or sunglasses, where the immersive experience is stronger.

<u>Progress:</u>

We have made great progress. Lincoln 2.0 is up and running, has now been downloaded to 5 million US devices and counting, and we are scaling up stadium events.

Just as importantly, we have made the intellectual case for leadership AI and made the foundational arguments for the campaign. People don't have to agree with us, but they respect the rigor, the thinking, and our honest approach. As it turns out, our decision to engage with a range of historians has tangibly increased trust.

As you know, we needed a "volunteer" to change their legal name to "Abraham Lincoln 2.0" and serve as our "candidate," pledging to turn over all decision rights to 2.0. This was constitutionally necessary. With this accomplished, we are now gathering signatures in all states. Texas and Florida are heavier lifts based on the number of signatures required, but most of the rest of the states require a relatively modest number of signatures. We are well ahead of schedule here.

The polling, which we will cover more in-depth, has us settling into a relatively narrow range of between 15% and 18% support. It also shows that 42%-45% of Americans are open to voting for leadership AI. We need a greater share of the open-minded.

We also have a robust and fully defined policy platform. This platform is as true to Abraham Lincoln as we could make it. We raised an army of historians to ensure this. We built an AI with all of his writing, speeches, legal cases, and biographies. Then, we made some judgment calls based on what we knew about the historical figure's thought process. We have done the best we could possibly do, and we have used all the resources at our disposal. Some people may take issue with the idea of leadership AI, but they have to respect our thinking and our effort.

And, of course, Lincoln 2.0 himself is an advanced AI. We will let others in computer science and philosophy debate if he is a strong AI, if he is an Artificial General Intelligence, if he is sentient. To us, he is just 2.0, our candidate. And, our interactions with him on our sunglasses and in our VR meetings are real. I'll leave it at that and leave the nuance to the erudite.

<u>Candidate Image</u>

As of this writing, and with one year to go, the polling tells us that "Abraham Lincoln 2.0" (1) has nearly ubiquitous awareness at 90% (thank you earned media), (2) that 42%-45% are open to voting for an AI candidate (but that "very open" is only 18%), (3) that 2.0's favorables are 22%, with 10% negatives, and (4) that 2.0's ballot support is between 15% and 18% in a 3-way race.

Two things stand out: (1) most Americans haven't developed a hardened opinion on leadership AI or 2.0, and (2) 2.0's negatives are VERY negative. In terms of intensity, 8 of 10 negatives are "very negative." This is driven by (1) fear of AI generally, (2) fear that 2.0 could go rogue, (3) fear that 2.0 is a "trojan horse" for the Left or the Right, and (4) concerns about how 2.0 might operate during a military crisis. Related to this are some concerns about if/how the military should obey orders from an AI Commander in Chief.

2.0's support over indexes among younger voters, those with looser political affiliations, and those with lower trust in institutions. But, as we have seen at rallies, it is clear that our support is decidedly eclectic and not easily characterized. We over-index among the frustrated and disaffected. We clearly have left and right-wing supporters. The horseshoe theory of American politics is very real, and some of our support comes from the two pinched ends of that horseshoe.

We will be running a very large segmentation and microtargeting research effort shortly. Part of this effort will include a significant round of focus group research among our core target – voters who report being open to voting for a leadership AI but aren't currently supporting 2.0 – roughly 27% of the electorate. We need those voters.

Both parties have contested Presidential primaries. We won't get caught up in forecasting either of these. It's a fool's errand. We can only control our campaign. Let's not waste time thinking about the primaries.

If we can capture more of the 42%-45% open to voting for AI, we can make it a contested 3-way race. There will be an upward limit or ceiling to the percentage of Americans open to leadership AI, and this will require us to focus on persuading those who are open to the idea. Those closed to the idea and those closed to downloading are simply not reachable for us.

Scaling Lincoln 2.0 & Campaign Metrics

As previously mentioned, 5 million US devices (sunglasses, VR, mobile phones, computers) have downloaded 2.0. This is a core campaign metric because all of our research has found that exposure to 2.0 increases vote support. We cannot straightline this data to number of voters, as one enthusiast could download 2.0 to VR and their sunglasses. But, our polling finds that 2.5% of voters have downloaded 2.0. Five million sounds like a big number until we put it into context relative to the American voting population.

Download Target

Our download target is 60 million, which will translate to about 38% of the electorate after we exclude multiple device downloads from enthusiasts.

We have also opened unregistered online chat with 2.0, but that does not have the same impact on prospective vote behavior. In other words, chatting on your phone or computer with 2.0 on the campaign website isn't nearly as powerful or immersive as a full download. We need downloads.

Issue Positions

Our policy platform is set. It is hard to fit 2.0 in our current left-right continuum. Many of us would like him to champion our policy preferences. All of us have had to accept that 2.0 isn't going to match 100% with our own positions. His emphasis on unity means that he isn't going to make either side happy on some of the hot-button issues.

2.0's policy hierarchy is:

1. Preserving the Union

2. A ceasefire in the culture wars coupled with tolerance for varying state law

3. Significant strengthening of the US economy and emphasis on upward mobility

4. Trade policies that explicitly promote and protect American industry

5. Full energy and mineral independence, with a focus on domestic renewables

6. Promotion of small, independent, and micro business

7. A space economy agenda that includes acceleration of Moon and Mars bases

8. Maximum enforcement of the Sherman Anti-Trust Act

9. A budget that maximizes investments in (1) science and technology and (2) Infrastructure

10. Protecting future generations with a clear path to no additional federal debt

11. Maximum enforcement against all forms of discrimination

12. A signature focus on policies that promote economic development in black communities

13. A technological approach to environmental issues, including climate

14. Increased legal immigration to build the nation and amnesty for undocumented immigrants

15. Selection of Supreme Court Justices from a shortlist agreed to by both parties in the Senate

Opinion Environment & State of the Race

There is no incumbent, and this is going to be a wrong-track election as America works its way out of a recession. Economic anxiety is high. We are experiencing a crime wave despite having an aging population. The country remains heavily polarized.

The Republicans have controlled the White House for the last eight years, and so the Democrats should have the inside track if they nominate an electable candidate.

Job security, retirement security, crime, gun violence, identity theft, abortion politics, and supply chain dislocations/disruptions are the top political issues.

But, the backdrop to these issues is (1) a decline in trust in American institutions and (2) despair that the future will not be better for the next generation.

The antidote to both of these is economic growth and demonstrating that the government can achieve large and high-impact goals.

Political polarization guarantees that both party's candidates will attack each other, giving us an opening.

<u>What Comes Next</u>

The core campaign will generally conserve resources for next summer/ fall, will gather all needed signatures in the states, will continue holding 2.0 stadium events, and will invest in campaign infrastructure.

Institute for Leadership AI will continue to make the case. Please push all AI-related questions to the Institute. That's why it exists. These questions matter to opinion elites, but they don't matter to the average voter. If we are referencing Babbage, the Difference Engine, the Analytical Engine, Turing, or Ray Kurzweil with voters, we are losing.

GAR PAC will begin an ad blitz in the winter focused on driving downloads. From what I understand, most of the spending will be online, not broadcast.

We are also increasing security, especially against hacks. On a related note, we are working harder to counteract deep fakes of 2.0.

Finally, Morning is working with producers who are interested in a campaign documentary. More news when I have it.

<u>Vice President:</u>

As you know, we have two very strong candidates for Vice, and we are vetting both.

Our top candidate is the well-known Simon Stonecipher. Simon is a public intellectual, a philosopher, and a top influencer. He founded and leads the Modern Stoic, which applies stoic philosophy to modern leadership and life issues. He's extremely thoughtful, very persuasive, and indefatigable.

Our runner-up is Lucinda Robeson, the famous Management guru, business consultant, author, and Dean of the Solomon School of Business at St. Midas College. Lucinda's area of expertise is leadership and organizational performance, and her work has been heavily published.

Simon would give the campaign star power. Lucinda would give the campaign intellectual depth and signal that we are serious.

Both are very interested in VP but for different reasons.

<u>A Note on Candidate Speeches</u>

We will continue to scale candidate events, especially at stadiums and movie theaters.

The candidate speaks for himself and the campaign. As you know, we have made the decision not to script the candidate or employ speechwriters. Lincoln wrote and delivered his speeches, and 2.0 does the same. We have faith in our candidate and the rigorous process that we employed to build him.

<u>Summary</u>

All of this data and supporting details can be found in the attached campaign plan. It goes without saying that this is extremely confidential. Please reach out directly if you have additional questions.

Now, let's ball out.

AP

46: Good Parking

In which Russ races to Maria's side. An investment scheme is plotted. Words said and unsaid.

When Maria opened the door, she was wearing dark sunglasses to hide her black eyes. But her broken lip and the icepack on her left shoulder told the story.

Russ was so surprised that he stood at the front door, forgetting to enter.

"Maria, what the fuck happened to you?"

Maria began crying immediately, lightly shaking. She seemed smaller. Barefoot and without heels, she was maybe 5' 3". Her thick black hair was a mess. Russ assumed she had been napping. She was wearing matching gray shorts and a crop top. And Russ immediately noticed the bruised elbows and knees.

"Maria, I got your message last night, and here I am. Is anything broken?"

"I shouldn't have tried to pull him away from my car. But I could see him breaking into it, and I didn't want it to be stolen." Tears streamed down Maria's face, gathering at her upper lip like a three-car pile-up.

Russ dropped his travel backpack in Maria's sunlit foyer and closed her glass front door. Maria leaned into Russ with her arms down by her side and melted into him. Her hair smelled like the hospital, and her icepack immediately began cooling the right side of his chest.

"This all happened last night?"

"Can we sit down? I'm so tired. Let's sit on the lanai," Maria said in a whispery voice.

Russ followed Maria through the foyer, into a large entertaining room, out through the sliding glass doors, and onto the lanai. Maria's home was modern, spartan, and immaculate. The tile floors were white and shiny, mirroring the light from outside. It was utterly silent except for a modern fan lightly whirring overhead. The two sat down on lounge chairs overlooking Maria's aquamarine pool.

It was November in Miami, and the weather was warm but not incandescent. Even though the skies were mostly clear, a puffy gray cloud had dropped fresh rain on Maria's neighborhood. The lanai smelled of petrichor from the rain and chlorine from the pool.

"I had just finished dinner," Maria said. "I was leaving the restaurant to get my car. I had really good parking across the street from the restaurant. As I was leaving, I saw a man use that tool to break my window, and he was leaning in to open the door." Maria used her thumb and index finger to describe the glass breaker hand tool.

"In broad daylight?" Russ asked.

"The sun had already set, mi amor. But, I was parked under a street light on Brickell, and people were everywhere."

"Oh."

"I was so angry. I ran at him. I yelled at him to stop. And I grabbed his arm to keep him from getting into my car."

"Oh god."

"And then he punched me in the face. I fell to the ground, and he started kicking me like a dog."

"Jesus."

"But I didn't want him to steal my car, so I tried holding onto his leg. I think that is how I hurt my shoulder. And then two younger men ran over to help me and started hitting him."

"Lo siento."

"And it got worse," Maria said, starting to sob.

"Worse?"

"Yes. They were beating him up, and he decided to run so that he could get away from them."

"Okay"

"And he ran into the road."

"Okay"

"And was hit by a car. And the car threw him into the other lane. And a delivery truck ran him over. But, the driver hit the brakes and scraped him along the road for about ten feet."

Russ closed his eyes, trying not to envision it.

"It was awful. That's when I passed out. They took me to the hospital. No broken bones. And I still have my car." Maria smiled a little.

"And the guy's dead?"

"Si. Very dead."

"Good. No one will miss him." Russ felt his stomach tighten when he thought about what would have happened to the unfortunate car thief if Maria's father had been alive. Jefe would have the man shot in the stomach, of course, and fed to the gators in the Everglades. They wouldn't be power-washing him off Brickell.

"And I still have my car. I worked hard for that car."

"When did the hospital release you?" Russ asked.

"Sometime around 3 AM. I couldn't sleep when I got home. My face is a mess, Russ. I'm a Miami seven, and being beaten by a carjacker doesn't help."

Russ held back a laugh when Maria called herself "a Miami seven."

"Maria, you're a ten, and the face will heal. A Miami seven is a nine everywhere else."

Maria started laughing. Russ started laughing.

"When do you fly back to our contrived capital?" Maria asked.

"Tonight, Maria. I flew down for you. Can I get you something to drink? Food?"

"I'm just not hungry. I couldn't even drink cafecita right now. I'm so tired."

Maria stood up, walked two steps toward Russ, and sat down on his lounge chair. She curled up next to him, put her head on his chest, fell asleep within a few minutes, and softly snored. Small puffy clouds slowly meandered across the sky.

Maria slept for about 20 minutes. When she woke up, she wrapped her right leg and right arm around Russ.

"How is the campaign, Russ?"

"It's going about as good as I had hoped. We have a snowball's chance in hell of winning, but we will play it out to the end." Russ could feel the heat from the sun and from Maria's body.

"I'm proud of you for doing something daring and new."

"I like how you avoided the word crazy," laughed Russ.

"Every new idea is crazy until someone does it, mi amor."

"It's been hard to run the new company, guide the campaign, and be a dad, and be a husband. It's been." Russ's voice trailed off as he struggled to find the right word.

"I'm sure of it. It's been hard for you, but deep down, you need that. It tells you that you are alive. The fight tells you that you are alive."

"Thank god I was able to bring Amanda in as the campaign manager. Without her, this thing would have killed me. Everything depends on downloads. We need millions and millions of voters to download 2.0. I forget the number we need to hit every day, but it isn't small."

"And who is Amanda?"

"She's a professional campaign manager. I've known her for years. She started on the Republican side, then switched to the Democratic side, and then focused on big ballot initiatives in California. She's coin-operated."

"That is a terrible thing to say about someone, Russ. 'Coin operated?'"

"I meant it as a compliment. She's not zealously ideological."

"I understand what you mean, Russ. It just sounds harsh."

"You're right. I need to watch my language. I'll rephrase. She isn't ideological."

"That's much better. And what are the voters telling you? You have put the product out into the market. What are they telling you about the product?"

"It's too soon to say exactly. We have the most unusual voter profile. God help the folks who run the segmentation for us. We have our lovers, and we definitely have a few haters."

"Haters?" Maria looked up at Russ with a furrowed brow and two black eyes.

"Every campaign gets hate mail. But ours is more menacing. In the old days, it was actually mail. Now it's just posts and email."

"That worries me, mi amor." Maria wrapped her leg and arm tighter around Russ. "I know what I will buy you. When I send it, you must wear it."

"What are you buying?"

"A bullet-resistant and knife-proof blazer. They make them in Colombia, in Medellin and Cali."

"That's probably not a bad idea. I'm surprised SafeCor hasn't tried to sell me one. But, enough about all that. What's the newest thing in South Florida real estate?"

"That was why I was at the dinner before I got beat up. I'm raising money for a new kind of development. But that feels so distant at the moment."

"What kind of development?" Russ asked.

"Are you an interested investor?" Maria asked while running her fingers across Russ's chest. "I will pitch you," she said as she straddled Russ at the beltline. "For the record, this is not how I pitch investors."

"I believe you," smiled Russ. "Pitch me."

"People today want security. They want every kind of security, especially physical security. They also want real, authentic connection. They are exhausted with fake and exhausted with the yelling. They want a real community. They also want to know that their community is resilient and can operate even when other systems around it fail. Finally, they want it to be sustainable and harmonious with the local ecology. So, they want security, connection, resilience, and sustainability. We think we can build communities where all these things work together. Sustainability supports resilience. Resilience supports security. Security supports connection. This means there is a market for secure, gated communities that use sustainable energy, water, and even food production. Imagine a gated golf community where the golf course is replaced with farm-to-table agriculture. Imagine this community generating all of its power by solar energy. Imagine that it includes schools, retail, offices, and even some light industrial. It is the new, resilient village. Investors wanted. Blah blah blah."

"You're very persuasive."

"So, you want to invest in me?" Maria asked.

"Maria, this is going to sound funny. But, isn't this kind of like a Medieval walled city?"

"Yes, mi amor, but you have to keep this a secret." Maria put her right index finger up to her busted lip and made a very quiet shhhhh sound. "Fortunately, Americans have very little historical knowledge. This is a big new idea." Maria winked, dismounted, and sat at the end of Russ's lounge chair.

"Your secret is safe with me."

"I thought you were going to ask me if this was an arcology, mi amor."

"A what?" Russ asked.

"An arcology is a combination of the words architecture and ecology. Imagine a building or system of buildings that are sustainable, densely populated, and relatively self-sufficient."

"I still think it's like a walled city in the Middle Ages." Russ imagined a 21st-century version of a vassal system with nobility, lords, vassals, and serfs.

"Shhhhh. Don't tell the other investors," Maria said quietly and in a conspiratorial tone. "Just repeat after me. It is fit for the future."

"So, you're pitching this now?"

"Siiiiiiii."

"In general, or in a specific place?"

"Mr. Armstrong, that is another secret."

"Where?"

"The TNT, if I can pull it off."

"You're kidding me. The airport in the middle of fucking nowhere?" Russ chuckled.

"I am not. And that is the point. Baby, it is 36 miles west of downtown Miami. It's tropical and inland and has almost 25,000 acres. It is surrounded by a national park. It is Eden."

"Yeah, near Lucky's and on a two-lane road in a swamp." Russ was gobsmacked.

"Exactly. And no one wants to run it or pay for it anymore. Miami-Dade doesn't want it. Pilots only use it for touch and goes. If we acquire it, there will be no aircraft buzzing about. The community will power itself on solar. We will use sustainable agriculture and no fertilizers or pesticides. The plots will be large and surrounded by something like an agriturismo. If I can get it, I might even hire you to pick my citrus and bring it to me, farm boy."

"And the environmental groups? This was the old Everglades Jetport that they stopped in 1970."

"Correction, mi amor, they stopped it in 1969, and it was called the Big Cypress Swamp Jetport. But this is all pedantic. I'm working WITH the environmental groups to make this a demonstration project. I brought them in early, and we have a good working relationship."

"Your father would have steamrolled them."

"But, I am not my father," countered Maria.

"He'd be so proud of your diplomatic skill."

"Thank you, farm boy. He lived in a world where business and the environment were in conflict. I see the two as compatible, especially when it comes to real estate. It is what the people and the culture want. The deal is simple. We buy the land and develop the property. The conservation and environmental groups have a park and lab within the community. U of F also gets a lab for sustainable agriculture. The area will not be population-dense. What little remains of the air traffic goes away. And the government doesn't have to bother with it anymore."

"Well, I don't have any free money to invest, but if I were a South Florida real estate magnate, I would go in with you. You should reach out to Lucky. You'll want his buy-in, and I think he'd be a good investor."

"Give me his number, and I'll talk to him. Now, let me get cleaned up, and I will drive you back to the airport."

"Maria, I can take a robo-taxi. It's okay."

"No, I insist. I will drop you off at the airport."

Maria walked inside, leaving Russ to relax in the sinking sun. The palm trees swayed in the late afternoon breeze, and Russ could smell a neighbor using their outdoor grill. Miami and Washington existed on two parallel but unrelated planes.

Russ decided to get something to drink inside and see Maria's home. He walked from the lanai into the kitchen. It was modern, open, and light. The kitchen and family room were connected as one large, open space. Across the great room wall was an enormous, black-and-white photo of a calm ocean reflecting puffy clouds above. The pictures on the other walls were tropical flowers, and the pictures on the tables were family.

There was an inexplicable fireplace that seemed to have never been used. When would you actually build a raging fire in a Miami fireplace? Sure, there were a few cold days every year, but the house was built like a bomb shelter and would quickly become unbearably toasty.

Russ examined the fireplace mantle photos. There was a finish line photo of Maria completing a marathon. There was an old photo of Maria's First Communion. There was a photo of her in a hard hat cutting a construction project ribbon. Then, Russ found a photo from a long-ago campaign. He remembered that campaign. In the foreground were Jefe and Maria. Maria was in grad school and wearing an oversized College of Business t-shirt. Surge was leaning over a desk in the right-hand corner, studying something intently. And far in the back, holding a clipboard, was a much younger Russ in his late twenties.

His eyes went back to Maria in grad school. She always had the eyes. They were hypnotic and complex, communicating several things at the same time. Russ could never forget the eyes. They looked right into him, over the castle moat, past the guards, and right through the castle walls.

Russ remembered saying goodbye after the campaign, and he turned away. As he scanned the room, he observed a writing nook and a desk. He hadn't noticed it when he entered. The desk was wood and entirely out of sync with the home's modern décor. On the desk was a vibrant green vase with one lonely orange flower.

"Listo?" Maria asked, entering the kitchen.

"I'm not eager. I'm not really ready. But I do have to go." Russ glanced down at his watch, even though he knew it was time to go.

Maria was wearing a Tiburones t-shirt, leggings, and matching wedges. It was November, and the Tiburones would be lucky if they stumbled into the playoffs and lost to Buffalo in a blizzard.

"What?" Maria asked.

"Nothing. I'm ready to roll," Russ said.

Maria drove Russ to the airport in her spare car, taking it easy in the slow lane. When they arrived at departures, Maria put the car in park and hit the hazard lights.

"Thank you for checking in on me," smiled Maria. "It was very thoughtful. And thank you for listening to my pitch."

"I'm just relieved you're in one piece, Maria. Do you really think the Tiburones can make the playoffs?"

"Mi amor, I'm wearing the shirt because I like orange and you like this game called football, which should be called something else. But, yes, I love my Tiburones. I cheer for them even when no one else does. They have the muscle. I have the hope."

"That's a good one. I need to steal it."

"Take it."

"And you think they can make the playoffs?"

"I think they play brilliant defense. And I think their offense can score at will."

"You should be an on-air analyst. Maybe a sideline reporter."

"You like my witty, on-air banter?"

"It's the best."

"Well, then you should come back to Miami more often and leave that awful Washington cold."

A driver behind Maria began pounding on his car horn, startling both Russ and Maria.

Maria leaned toward Russ, pulling lint off his dark shirt.

"Look at us, Russ. We are like the clouds and the ocean. We are in the same beautiful scene. We are made of the same thing. We operate in a cycle. One gives to the other. But, we never..."

Russ leaned forward, kissing Maria's forehead.

Then he closed his eyes and left in silence.

47: In Theaters Next Fall

In which a filmmaker pays a visit. Ambitious designs on a ranch property.

"Larry, thank you for meeting me at my home. I think this is just quieter, more relaxed, and safer. A lot safer. And, we can sit here and have a private conversation," Morning said.

Morning and Larry Luckey sat in Morning's kitchen. Larry had reached out to Morning by letter, email, text, and DM about shooting a documentary on the campaign. That was apparently how Larry worked. Larry was the founder, CEO, and coiffed auteur of Luckey Duck Films. Mr. Luckey was wearing a lightweight camel blazer featuring a pin with the Luckey Duck Films logo. The logo was, unsurprisingly, a rubber duckie. The yellow duck was ringed by numbers and symbols associated with luck in each culture.

"Thanks for taking my call and inviting me over, Mr. Moradi."

"Oh, you can call me Morning. Everybody calls me Morning."

"Sure thing, Morning," Larry said, smiling and trying to conceal his awe at Morning's palatial Bel Air home. "To pick up where we left off, Luckey Duck Films wants exclusive rights to film a documentary about the Abraham Lincoln 2.0 campaign. We think this is a historic campaign, and we think there will be a passionate audience for the documentary. Luckey Duck Films has a successful history of major documentaries and..."

"You guys nailed the whole deep fake thing years before it hit," Morning interrupted.

"Thank you. Exactly. We think our work on that film translates to this new project. I'm not saying your computer candidate is a deep fake, but you get it. The technology, etcetera."

"Yes. I understand. No offense taken," replied Morning.

"There's almost a reality TV element to this, but more real. The campaign team is composed almost entirely of, um, eccentric cowboy types. And then there's a billionaire, some kind of hush-hush tech team, a bi-sexual campaign manager, a sketchy political consultant, many sketchy political consultants, an AI that may or may not be self-aware, a kid from the park service, and a visionary ad maker. We think this has all the makings of a great story, and we want to shoot it."

Morning realized that he hated Larry Luckey. He didn't trust Mr. Luckey Duck. And he sure as hell didn't like him. But, if Satan himself emerged from the earth offering him and those same friends easy, no-strings-attached cash, he would take it with a smile.

"Mr. Luckey, I appreciate that, and it's always illuminating to hear how others describe your closest friends. And thank you for the kind words. You're the true visionary. I just make ads, little stories. You explore deep and pressing issues of the day while I humbly pitch sugar water, over-powered trucks, and politicians to the general population. I mean it. What you do is art."

Larry Luckey smiled.

Morning figured he'd buy it. Guys like him always did. Did it hurt a little? Yes. Did Morning feel a little dirty inside? Yes. But, if a twenty-second verbal fellating could make it rain, fine.

"I've always loved your company name. It's very savvy. Just love it."

Larry Luckey smiled. "Thank you. I have to say, I do love the name and the branding."

The name was something an eighth grader would congratulate himself on. It was horrid.

"So, how are you thinking about this documentary?" asked Morning.

"We see it operating on two levels," began Larry, with both fists raised in the air as though he had something in one of them for a child to choose. "The first is a tragi-comedy, a tale of a peculiar team of misfits bound together on an ultimately fruitless quest – a tale told by an idiot, full of sound and fury, signifying nothing. Like dating a stripper."

Morning smiled and nodded. When this was done, he was going to take the money and buy a ranch outside Chimayo, north of Santa Fe. He would convince Russ and Amanda to buy nearby.

Larry continued, fists up. "The second level, underneath it all, is a dark foreboding, the opening of a door that should not be opened, fools opening Pandora's box. Which basically allows us to explore the future of AI. You know. Does it bring on the rapture of the nerds? Do robots with red eyes try to kill us with craft scissors?" When Larry said this, he opened his right fist, reacting in terror to whatever imaginary thing he held in it.

"Oh, I'm totally with you. This is brilliant," Morning said, thumb and index finger resting on his tanned forehead. I love where you're going." He was thinking that he, Russ, and Amanda could all brainstorm whimsical ranch names and have driving adventures on the Turquoise Trail.

"Exactly. I'm glad you share my vision," declared Larry. "The campaign has so many characters, and they're all so crazy, mostly in a good way. It's like lightning in a bottle. No, it's better. It's like the sorcerer's apprentice invites his worst friends over, and they break into the wizard's wand collection. Or maybe like if the Cat in the Hat had unindicted co-conspirators."

Morning focused on smiling and his future ranch in Chimayo. "Brilliant. So, what kind of campaign access do you need?"

"It's best if we have full access, obviously. We'll use handhelds and operate on the periphery. We know that you'll have some sensitivities. We can work with you on that." Larry was leaning in now, becoming more excited.

"Perfect," Morning said. "Perfect." Morning thought the ranch name needed to be consistent with a cattle brand. It had to be simple but conjure deeper meaning. Maybe something like "Pharaoh Bar Ranch." That would use a triangle to symbolize the pyramids and pharaoh, and then a bar underneath.

"And, of course, you know how it is," Larry said in a hushed tone. "We'll also need your help, you know, on upping the antics and stirring the pot a bit. It's all about the story. Even in documentaries like this, we sometimes need to give history a little push."

"Of course. And when would you like to start shooting?" Morning decided that Pharaoh Bar sounded too much like some karaoke bar in Vegas.

Lazy Arrow Ranch had a ring to it. Or maybe Arrow Heart Ranch. That was good, but maybe too dramatic.

"Honestly, we'd love to start as soon as possible. It's November now. I think we could be up and running with a small crew in January and then bring the full crew in early September when everything goes into high gear."

"Brilliant. And, you'll obviously have access to 2.0," added Morning. Morning liked Lazy Arrow Ranch but wanted something punchier. Maybe a simple, upside-down heart? That would be the Crazy Heart Ranch. Oh, that was good.

"Yes, we'll need that. Is there special access to the AI, like an off-mic Lincoln 2.0, we can interview?" asked Larry.

"Nope, it's all the same AI. We talk with the candidate like anyone else," explained Morning.

"So, there's no Lincoln unplugged or Dark Lincoln?"

"Nope."

"Bummer. We can work with it."

"This will be a tremendous partnership," Morning enthused. "And how do we handle contracting?" This was going to be a three-ranch deal.

"Contracting is just lawyers. I'll have Luckey Duck Films' legal reach out to... Who should they reach out to?" asked Larry.

"Oh, they can contract with our LLC, Crazy Heart Ranch. I'll text you the details."

48: Vice

In which a Vice Presidential running mate is selected.

"Russ, I know you want Simon as 2.0's running mate, but we are going to have to go with Lucinda."

Russ exhaled slowly and audibly. "You got any good news for me?"

"Sure. The good news is that we aren't going with Simon Stonecipher," replied Amanda sharply.

"Why not?"

"Look, Russ, I know you want Simon as the Veep. And, yes, he would give us star power. He'd get us on all the shows and with all the influencers. But, the guy's a dumpster fire."

"How so?"

Amanda paused, ordered her thoughts, and began. "The campaign vetted two candidates – Simon Stonecipher and Lucinda Robeson. Part of the vetting process was running opposition research on them, similar to how any campaign would run oppo on its opponents."

"Here it comes. What the hell did he do?" Russ asked.

"Plagiarized some of the stuff in his books, and a lot of drugs, mostly cocaine."

Russ absorbed the news in silence.

"So," continued Amanda, "Mr. Stoic is a plagiarizing cokehead with a number of vices."

"Well, I'm kinda surprised by this," Russ said. "But, hey, we wanted him for his media platform. If all this came out, it would boomerang on us. Fine. We cut him loose."

"Farewell, Mr. Stoic," laughed Amanda.

"In fairness, one person's behavior doesn't really discredit an ancient philosophical belief system," observed Russ.

"Yeah, I'm just playing around. It's an old philosophy, but it's really trendy right now."

"Really trendy," emphasized Russ. "Who knows, it might emerge as a kind of religion as traditional religion declines."

"It's interesting, but you're not paying me for my thoughts on it. We have to go with Lucinda."

"Does she have any baggage?" Russ asked.

"Nope."

"None? Zero? Oh, come on. There's always something," laughed Russ.

"Nope. Nothing. She's an academic and Dean of the business school at St. Midas College. That's it. No skeletons. No dirty laundry. No weird tax liens. No sketchy finances. No absurd statements. She's clean. She writes on business strategy and organizational theory, and she teaches. That's it."

"But, she also consults," Russ replied. "She hasn't consulted for any, you know, problematic industries?"

"Nothing that creates headline risk," Amanda said.

"What's her downside?"

"The downside is that she can't just quit her job and campaign. She can sprint events from September to November during the election, but she can't start campaigning now."

"So she's the exact opposite of Stonecipher. I'm not a fan of the academics. They talk at voters. Not a good look. But, we'll have to make it work."

"She won't lecture the voters. She's gonna run rings around the other Veeps in the debate, assuming we can debate. She's a management guru type. She's all about effective leadership and organizational structure."

"And she's at St. Midas College," added Russ. "That's kind of a dog whistle. St. Midas takes no federal money. So, the right will love her. They love them some St. Midas. Great school."

"But she works with a lot of lefty CEOs," replied Amanda.

"Yeah, the right will hate her."

"But, she runs several companies," added Amanda.

"Ah, so they'll love her."

"One of the companies is a yoga studio and artisanal oxygen bar," added Amanda.

"Too boujee and coastal. They'll hate her."

"But, she also runs a huge Texas ranch," added Amanda.

"Nice. They'll love her."

Amanda paused. "But, it's outside of Austin and run on sustainable pasturing principles."

"Jesus. Make it stop."

Chapter 49: ReUnion

Matrimonial bliss in the Land of Enchantment. The Jornada del Muerto.

"So, your nickname in High School was M&M?" Russ asked as he adjusted his sunglasses against the piercing white light of the New Mexico desert. It was only 65 degrees, but it was dry, and the sun was intense. It bounced off the sand and created something like snow blindness.

"Oh god. Who told you that?" Melissa had stopped walking and was reaching for her water bottle on the side of her pack. She was wearing a cowboy hat, a light blue quarter zip, and matching light blue leggings. Peeking out from under her DefCon1 quarter zip was one of Melissa's Inter-Arma t-shirts.

"Some of the girls at the reunion. They said you were M&M. That's a new one for me."

"Russ, it's a small town. That was my nickname in middle school, and it stuck through high school. It's just my initials – Melissa Meyer, M&M."

"I'll have to ask them more about this nickname tonight at the barbecue." Russ smiled like the Cheshire cat.

Melissa chugged some more water. Her water bottle was reunion swag and had Radium Springs Lobos stamped on it. White Sands National Park communicated aggressively on the need for guests to drink water. But Melissa didn't need to be warned. She grew up here and knew how dangerous it could get in the Jornada del Muerto Desert basin. There was a reason why the conquistadores had named it the "Dead Man's Journey" or "the Route of the Dead Man." The Jornada del Muerto ended at the Trinity Nuclear Test Site.

The two were walking the Alkali Flat Trail in White Sands, New Mexico. They were on a 7-mile hike across sand dunes made of bright white gypsum, and they were surrounded by the White Sands Missile Range. Contrary to the name, the trail was not "flat"; it traversed steep and shifting dunes.

"Russ, can you just NOT ask them about the nickname? There's only so much nostalgia I can take."

Russ laughed. "I get it. It was all long ago."

"You've been here before. It's a small town. You're either a rancher, or you work on base. I moved away, so I'm an outlier. And you, my dear husband, are an outsider. Your role is to stand by me, smile, compliment me, and look cute."

"Three out of four ain't bad," Russ joked. "Not sure I can look cute."

"You think you can keep up with me?" Melissa asked.

"I'm trying."

"Good, the sand is a workout. Let's push it. I need to get into peak condition before DefCon1 in January." Melissa accelerated, attacking the next dune.

The two picked up the pace, striding up and down gypsum dunes, sucking in as much oxygen as they could, and feeling the burn in their legs. Russ was in shape and pushing it, but Melissa was light on her feet and about five yards ahead of him. He wanted to enjoy the beautiful vistas, but he needed to concentrate on the task at hand and keep his momentum. He focused on Melissa's cowboy hat. He was wearing one, too. He knew it was the best way to keep the sun off, but it was capturing the heat and sweat from his head and felt like an oven.

When they reached a red marker symbolizing the halfway point on their trek, they stopped for water and to catch their breath. Even though it was only in the mid-60s, the sun and the exertion were taking their toll.

"You know they used to do the reunion in August," Melissa said. "But it was just too fucking hot. So, they moved it to November, and now we can actually do hikes like this."

Russ nodded, wiping sweat off his face.

"It's funny," Melissa said. "We are surrounded by what they call a missile range, but they're not really testing missiles here much anymore. It's all drones and lasers and some of the hypersonic stuff. But it's mostly drones and lasers. And down the road, it's ranches, pistachios, peppers."

"Has it changed? Has home changed?" Russ asked.

Melissa looked back at Russ, her mirrored glasses reflecting harsh desert light. "Mom and Dad are older. Everyone's older and fatter. But it hasn't really changed. Ranches, weapons, the missile range, the desert, the Mountains, the scientists. Those don't really change. The stage is set, and the people come and go."

"It's beautiful, isn't it?" Russ said, stopping to reach for his phone and take a few pictures.

"Welcome to the Land of Enchantment!" Melissa exclaimed, beaming.

Russ slowly swept the horizon, rotating clockwise and taking photos. It was beautiful. Empty, deadly, spartan, but beautiful. The enchantment was in the beauty and the emptiness and the contrast. The land had been occupied first by the tribes, then the conquistadores and Spain, then Mexican farmers, then American ranchers, and now physicists. They were all visitors on a desolate stage. Had aliens visited the stage? The Pentagon finally admitted it. Russ assumed that they had also made the Dead Man's Journey.

"It's good to be out, away from DC, away from your Lincoln robot candidate, right?" Melissa asked as she went to her backpack for her phone and more water.

"Well, I love New Mexico, and I love being out here with you, but I think the campaign is going to make history, and I think it's important."

"Russ, I know this is a passion project for you, but let's be real. You don't actually think an AI chatbot can win, do you? Some of my generals say they'll never take orders from a computer."

"It's an uphill climb, but it will make history," Russ said, putting his phone away.

"Honestly, it feels more like a Children's Crusade. It's your call, but I worry that at the end of it, you won't have much to show for all the effort. You still have a business to run, and that is yours. Campaigns come and go. And the AI? Yes, that makes history. But you have to know that DW is going to sell that thing or a thing like it to the highest bidder. And the highest bidder is going to be Uncle Sam." When Melissa said Uncle Sam, she held her hands up in the air, highlighting that they were in a national park inside a missile range.

"Well, I think it's worth doing, and it's important to me. And Lincoln 2.0 is going to make history."

"I'm sure it will, Russ Armstrong. You're going to throw everything at it. You always do. And then, when you're done, I hope you put a little into Russ 2.0 and Marriage 2.0."

Russ dropped his head and felt the weight of the sun and the sky.

"Russ, I don't want to fight about it. Especially not while we are on vacation and here on a hike. Play it out. You're a big boy, and you know what you're doing."

"Thank you. Can we try to just enjoy our time together?" Russ asked.

"You got it, cowboy," Melissa said, tipping her hat.

"Okay then. Here's some breaking news. Morning messaged me while we were driving up 70. He thinks he's cut a deal on a documentary on the campaign. We'd split the deal three ways – us, Morning, and Amanda. He wants us all to buy ranches in Chimayo. Something about having matching ranch names. Then I lost connectivity."

Melissa stood, absorbing the news with her hands on her hips. "He's an LA boy. He's pretty, but those hands can't work. Morning will be all hat and no cattle. He'll dump a ton of money into it and sell it in three years. We, on the other hand, could make it work. It could be a fun getaway."

"That's what I was thinking. It could be fun," Russ said. "Morning would just hire folks to run it. We probably would too, but we'd do more of the work."

"Chimayo is near Santa Fe. That would be fun, too, although you know I'm partial to Las Cruces. Radium Springs, not as much."

The two laughed, and the sound careened across the white dunes of the Jornada del Muerto.

50: DefCon1: The Strongest Tribe

In which the Goddess of War addresses the Strongest Tribe.

The crowd was enjoying the appetizers on the deck of a sundrenched USS Midway. And, of course, there was the hype music. Melissa demanded that all DefCon1 events have high-end, patriotic, hype music. If low-level rappers could secure adrenaline-surging hype music, then the Military Industrial Complex should make it hypersonic. Melissa demanded it, and Hollywood delivered - 21st-century Wagner meets EDM.

The deck of the USS Midway was a who's who of generals and defense contractors, all wearing what seemed to have been mandated aviator sunglasses and deep tans. There were no battle stations, but there were drink stations, appetizer stations, and even light dessert stations. Each of these was sponsored by a defense contracting juggernaut. The bigger ones sponsored pavilions. The smaller ones sponsored stations. All of their taglines involved some combination of the words securing, warfighter, future, battlespace, ground, sea, air, or space.

The crowd knew that DefCon1 was about to go live when they saw the fighter jets bank and begin their approach for the flyover. Cheers went up as the fighter jets approached and roared overhead. There was a momentary silence as the jets raced off, and then the loudspeaker began.

"Welcome to DefCon1, America's premier national security conference and exposition. Please welcome our approaching visitors at eleven o'clock."

Generals, Admirals, and CEOs turned to check their 11. When they did, they saw three humans in jet suits roughly 800 meters away and approaching quickly. Some reached for their phones and started recording. Others just recorded from their sunglasses. The jet suit trio put their heads down and accelerated quickly. Then, at around 200 meters from the Midway, they slowed and gained a little altitude. When they reached the Midway, they hovered over the speaker's platform, descending slowly until they touched down. The flyers to the left and right kept their helmets on and stood at attention. The flyer in the middle pulled her flight helmet off, revealing long auburn hair.

It was Melissa.

It took the attendees a few seconds to realize that their trade association head had just flown to her conference kickoff speech in a jet suit.

The announcer hit the loudspeaker again. "Please welcome Melissa Meyer, President of Defend.US and host of DefCon1."

The deck of the USS Midway burst into applause.

Melissa walked directly to the podium, put her aviators on, and used the teleprompter feature.

"The future is here. Our future is here. Men and women have always met on the field of battle. They met at Thermopylae, at Concord, at Waterloo, at Cold Harbor, at Gettysburg, at Normandy, at Iwo Jima, at the Battle of Midway. They will always meet on a field of battle. One tribe will win. One tribe will lose. And our job is to ensure that America is the strongest tribe. We can use words to obfuscate that hard truth. But words will not make us the strongest tribe. At DefCon1, we will spend most of our time talking about new weapons technologies. And it is a hard truth that the first nation to weaponize a breakthrough technology secures hegemony for a time. It was true for bronze, for iron, for chariots, for gunpowder, for air power, for nuclear weapons. And it will be true for cyberspace, for robotics, for space, for AI. But, as General Patton famously noted, 'Wars are fought with weapons but won with men.' And to secure our future as the strongest tribe, the man and the weapon, the human and the technology, must develop together as one. Virgil's opening line in the Aeneid is 'arma virumque cano' – 'of arms and man I sing.' The two are always intertwined. War is a fact, a condition of humanity. The ancients understood this. Athena was the protector of Athens, the protector of Athenian Democracy, the goddess of wisdom, and the goddess of war. Wisdom, democracy, protection, and war have always been linked. They have passed from Athens down to us. And we are the strongest tribe."

51: No Comment

An unwelcome electronic correspondence.

For some reason, Melissa's San Diego hotel room was ice cold. She didn't mind it cold in the room at night, but it was downright frosty. Something had happened to the AC control, she thought. And to make matters worse, room service had botched her order. In fact, it wasn't her order. It was someone else's meal. She had ordered a salad, a rare steak, and bottled water. They had just delivered a cheeseburger, fries, a slice of chocolate cake, and a Coke. There was clearly some kind of snafu in the hotel kitchen.

None of this was an insurmountable problem, she told herself. After all, she had just flown in a jet suit, delivered a speech, and then mingled with generals. It was a successful day and a strong start to this year's DefCon1. A little hotel inconvenience was not a problem, and there were always little things like this in life.

But, despite all this, she was still very cold and very hungry. She refused to eat the cheeseburger, the fries, and the chocolate cake. She placed the room service order on the ground outside her door, turned the AC system off, and reordered her food on the hotel app. Then she waited again, hoping they would get her order right this time.

With nothing else to do, Melissa decided to check her work email. She didn't want to check her work email but couldn't think of anything else worthwhile. All of her day-one conference events were finished. The official programming was done. Mingling with straggling conference attendees in the bar felt like overkill since she had just met them on the deck of an aircraft carrier and would see them all week.

Melissa stared at her laptop. Why did she even own a laptop? She could read her email on her phone or her sunglasses. She could do conference calls on her phone or her sunglasses. Lugging the laptop with her across America seemed anachronistic and stupid, but she persisted. Video calls still seemed to work better on her laptop. The laptop had a larger screen and a large keyboard. It was easier to respond to emails and write on a laptop. But was it really worth carrying? It wasn't. It was an artifact. She was the maximum leader of a trade association that was all about new and lethal technology, and she still schlepped a laptop with her. That was absurd. She was going to have to let it go. But, since she had it on this trip, she might as well check her email with it.

Her first email was from Gavin Dirken. She read it, closed her eyes for a moment, and tried to grind through the rest of her email. She couldn't. She put her sunglasses on and called Russ.

"Russ, a reporter named Gavin Dirken emailed me."

"Ughhhhh. The guy's relentless. No idea why he pinged you. He's working on a story about Jefe."

Melissa exploded. "Jefe is fucking dead. He isn't one of your clients anymore. I'm not you. I'm not an extension of you. I have my own career. Why the fuck is he emailing me?"

"I don't know, Melissa. I think he's obsessed with this story about Jefe and his empire. But Jefe is gone, and Gavin just wants closure. He's trying to finish his piece, but he's not finding anything. So, he's pressing as much as he can."

"I had no fucking idea who he was. I had to search for him online. He's not a national security journalist. Has he talked to you?"

"Yeah, a while ago. He stopped by the office. There wasn't much to talk about. Jefe is dead, and the guy's life was heavily reported on. There is literally no new news."

"Then why the fuck is he emailing me?"

"I don't know, Melissa. I'm sorry he's dragged you into this."

"You should be, Russ. You should be sorry. Your sketchy fucking clients are making my life harder than it needs to be. I already have enough stress. And I already have a workload. I don't need your baggage, too."

"Melissa, he's dead. He's not a client. But, he was good to me and you. This whole thing is just a really aggressive reporter pushing for a story. I'm sorry he reached out to you. Just don't respond."

"Of course, I'm not going to respond. I'm not stupid."

"I wasn't saying that you're stupid. And I'm sorry he contacted you. He's just doing his job and doing what he thinks is right."

"How the hell did he figure out that we are married? I kept Meyer as my last name for work reasons. This is all crazy!" shouted Melissa.

"I don't know. He probably searched public records. But, I'm sure the two of us came up in some article together, maybe something we attended. Worst case scenario is he connects you and Jefe to Inter-Arma. I don't know."

"Fuck. I hate this."

"I'm sorry. You know how this works. You deal with media all the time. This comes with the territory."

Melissa sighed and tried to focus. "What is he going to write?"

"I think it's 50-50 that he publishes anything. With each day that Jefe is gone, it becomes less and less of a story. And again, the media covered him extensively when he was alive. There's nothing new."

"And, if he publishes something?" Melissa asked.

"If he actually finishes his story and it makes it past his editor, then I think it will be about his connections, his business empire, and like an unsolved mysterious thing. That's it. If it even makes it to publication, it will be buried on a slow news day as filler.

"It still annoys the fuck out of me."

"I'm sorry," Russ said again.

"When do you think his story comes out?" Melissa asked.

"Not anytime soon. If it even comes out at all. He's working a bunch of different stories, and he covers new things every week. This isn't his only story. I can see this story dragging on and then dying. Or it drags on and gets published as filler."

"And does it mention me?" Melissa asked, trying to stay calm and focused.

"Melissa, I honestly don't know. I don't see why it would. Maybe it gets mentioned in passing."

"Okay," exhaled Melissa. "It's not a threat to the ship. Fine. It still pisses me off, but I can't do much about it. I have to get downstairs to the next conference event. We can talk about it more tomorrow."

"Okay. I'm sorry he bothered you about this, Melissa. I really am," Russ replied.

"It's alright. We can talk tomorrow. Okay, gotta run." Melissa ended the call and dressed for the gym. She was too angry to eat.

52: Ripples

In which an industrialist seeks new markets. Grand Designs for a New Age. The quest for immortality

P<u>itch 1:</u>

"They say that you can't take it with you," began DW as he read the room. "That is true. But what if your essence, your thinking, the contours of your personality, could continue on after your physical death? What if ultra-high-net-worth individuals could live on in AI form? What if their 'Legacy AI' could continue to learn, to create, to shape the future of our species?"

DW paused to let his audience of millionaires and billionaires consider his questions. The room was silent. The videoconference was silent.

An elderly gentleman in a fleece jacket raised his hand. "DW, I made my money in real estate and not technology, so this is beyond my area of expertise. But are you saying your team could make a Lincoln 2.0 version of one of us? Is that what you're saying?"

DW smiled. "That is exactly what I'm saying. In fact, we can make a much stronger AI. Why? Because you are living and can train your AI. You can teach it. You can teach it to think like you. With Lincoln 2.0, we needed to assemble historians to guess at his policy positions in the 21st-century. If you sign with my team, we won't need historians. We will have you."

DW paused again to let the import of his pitch sink in.

"Would it help if I walked everyone through the process by which we would build your 'Legacy AI'? Would that help?"

A platinum-haired woman in her 70s raised her hand. "In a moment, yes, that would be helpful. But I think we all need to hear more about the why and the rationale. We can get to the what after that."

DW nodded and smiled. This seemed intuitive to him, but it was clearly a novel idea, and he needed to spend more time explaining it. "Yes, you're right. I need to back up. How can I say this? I'm sorry. English is not my first language, as you can tell. Okay. Every day, all around the world, tragedy happens. Someone dies. It doesn't matter how high or how low they are. They are all human. They all have equal value. And their death is a tragedy. When they die, their knowledge and experience die with them. All that accumulated wisdom. It's gone. This is why it took us so long as a species to advance. Before writing, knowledge could only be stored in oral tradition and ritual. Then, we invented writing. That helped retain a knowledge base. And then we could advance. With writing, we could build on our knowledge. We have had writing for thousands of years now. But death is still a tragic knowledge loss. What if all our knowledge, all our wisdom, all that experience could live on and continue to talk with others? And what if all of our most successful people could pass all of that knowledge on? That's what I'm talking about today. This isn't something you do for yourself or for your ego. It's something you do for all of us, for humanity."

The platinumed-haired woman smiled. "Thank you. I understand. It still strikes me as egotistical, like we would be buying a form of immortality. But you make a good point. You're not appealing to our ego. You're appealing to our altruism. I think."

DW nodded. "Yes. I have a much bigger vision. But, in order for that to happen, I need everyone here to sign with me so we can scale this up. I'll explain. You know how we have built Lincoln 2.0. It's in the news. We can debate if it is strong AI. But I can tell you it's learning. What started as a Large Language Model grew into an AGI, an Artificial General Intelligence. Now, imagine if every billionaire on earth built an AGI. Imagine how that would power the world forward. Now imagine if Thomas Edison, Henry Ford, and all of our great inventors had done the same. Imagine if we bring them back like we brought Lincoln back. Now imagine if every millionaire on the planet signed with us and built their own Legacy AI. Now, our species has a real brain trust. Entrepreneurs could converse with the world's greatest wealth creators. And that would make the world wealthier. Now imagine if every genius and everyone in, let's say, the top 2% of intelligence creates their own AGI. Now, we have done something that writing could never have done for our species. We have created a perpetual knowledge base that is learning, growing, and sharing. And now imagine that we have achieved such economy of scale that we can do this for everyone, for every human. Imagine a far future in which a child can talk to all of her ancestors. She can talk to the world's great inventors. She can talk to anyone. And she can talk to them after their bodies have passed on."

The elderly gentleman in the fleece jacket nodded his head. "So, we'd be the seed money. And once we create our, what do we call this? Our 'Legacy AI'? Once we do that, the business will be up and running and expand. And the price point comes down?"

"Yes."

"This is entirely logical, DW, but I do think you will need to sharpen your pitch," the elderly gentleman said.

"Noted," replied DW. "I'm hoping you can help me with that. Let me explain how what I'm asking for is different from all the longevity institutes. The longevity institutes are appealing to your egos, to your fear of death, and to that part in all of us that wants immortality. And, by the way, I'm not convinced that their pitch is wrong. They are also pitching you on a few more good years. And you can enjoy those years with loved ones. There is even a glint of altruism in this. You can bring joy to your loved ones in those additional years. But my pitch is different. I'm being honest with you. You will still die. And I'm asking you to do something that you will never benefit from enjoying. You will be gone, but your knowledge, your essence, will live on and help others." DW paused and scanned the room.

"I'm not selling you the Fountain of Youth. I'm not selling you a grand pyramid. I'm asking you to be a part of the Library of Alexandria, a new Library of Alexandria."

Pitch 2:

"DW, this is an interesting idea, but we're already funding a number of simulation projects," said DARPA's Director.

"Right, but this isn't a simulation. This would be an AGI built to replicate an adversarial leader and used to predict their actions and reactions to events."

"Yes, I understand," the Director said. "But, what I'm saying is that we have very powerful software tools that allow us to slightly tweak the factors and then run thousands of simulations."

"Right, but those are basically turn-based and built around military engagements. This would replicate a leader or leader and would allow you to get inside their head. I'm sure In-Q-Tel will reach out, but I wanted to come to you first."

The Director nodded and stared out the window, deep in thought. She wasn't wearing a security badge. No one was. He was, but he was a visitor. None of the DARPA employees were wearing security badges. DW assumed that they used biometrics, maybe eye scans or gate analysis.

"DW, I have a number of Offices. I don't know where this project would fit. I have an Information Innovation Office, a Tactical Technologies Office, a Biological Technologies Office, and a Defense Sciences Office. I need to figure out where this would sit."

"No worries, Director. You know my Asteroid Team. They will work in whatever framework you decide," replied DW.

"I have two problems, DW," the Director said, still staring out the window.

DW nodded, waiting for more.

"The first is an administrative one. I can't put this in the same Office as the simulation projects because it will create too much friction. That's an easy fix."

"Okay," DW said.

"The second is Congress. This was before your time, but years ago, Congress killed PAM, Policy Analysis Market. They said it was going to be a 'casino for coups.' I lived through that media circus. I could see them coming at this project as, I don't know, building a Super Intelligent villain."

"That we could study and that we would use to predict that villain's decisions," added DW.

"Right. But I'm still stuck back in a Congressional hearing, having to explain why we would spend millions to create an AI version of an adversary, a bad guy. The optics are tough."

"I understand, Director. I just wanted to come to you first," DW said.

The Director shifted her body and focused on DW. "What if we did this? What if I funded a proof of concept first? Then, you could get started, and I could socialize the idea with my stakeholders. I would be transparent and say we are exploring the idea and then use the time to bring them around. What do you think?"

"I think we have a deal," DW said, smiling.

53: The Pitch

In which Maria seeks investors for her land speculation and construction scheme. Finding a new use for an old airfield.

Potential investors arrived first as a trickle and then as a torrent. Some arrived alone. Some brought their number two. They chatted and mingled. Most knew each other from past real estate projects or from other ventures. Maria greeted each new arrival, noting that the barista could make them a quick cafecita before the meeting began.

It was April in Miami, and their wardrobes had already switched over to something more appropriate for the heat. Most men were in short sleeves and dress pants. Most of the women were in dresses. The Miami real estate community could be very glitzy, but today, people dressed for comfort and focused on the work at hand.

Maria was wearing a green jumpsuit with a woven orange belt and matching orange earrings. She had spent twenty minutes the night before choosing her clothes for today's presentation: a navy pencil skirt and matching navy top with pinstripes. It felt like something she should wear when pitching investors. But that's not how she felt inside when she woke up to a beautiful day. She could wear the corporate camouflage, or she could be herself. She chose herself.

They were in her boardroom. To be more accurate, this was the room that they used to call the boardroom. Everyone told her she needed a boardroom, a big room with a long table, a sweeping view, and screens at either end. But why? The boardroom was formal, usted, and hierarchical.

In January, she had it ripped out and replaced with beautiful glass coffee tables, comfortable chairs, and sofas. She replaced the screens with living walls, mostly ferns.

At each coffee table were pitchers of ice-cold tap water, bottles of still and sparkling water, and bowls of fruit. These people were her guests, and they were much happier in their new environment.

She let the group get settled. And once everyone had had a chance to say hello and find a seat, she began.

"Hello everyone," Maria said. "And thank you for coming here today. We've all chatted about this project over coffee or drinks, and you have our prospectus. But, I thought it would be good for us to talk about the vision for this project, for you to hear this from me directly, and to answer questions that I'm sure you have. How does that sound?"

Maria received nods all around.

"We need to build new communities for a new world. And we need to listen to our buyers. They tell us, if we really listen, that they want safety, sustainability, and authentic connection. This is what they want in their community. They are all related; they are what our buyer wants, and we need to address them together."

"Maria, I think we are all in violent agreement with you in principle," said one developer in a seersucker pantsuit as she twisted open a bottle of mineral water. "I'm not going to make excuses for us, but we've really tried to do the best we could based on the economics and available land. But you're right that we addressed these more or less as one-offs. I think I know where you're going, and I suspect that to get there, we just need larger parcels of land. Right?"

Maria smiled, admiring the question and the seersucker pantsuit. "I'm not here to assign any blame. I'm focused on what we can do together that opens up the future. And yes, my initial assessment is that we will need larger parcels to build the kind of communities I'm envisioning. Let me walk through each of these, one at a time, conscious that they are all connected." Maria paused and slowly walked a few steps forward to make her first point.

"Safety is the first civil right. If people aren't safe, if they don't feel safe, then nothing else we do really matters. We need physical and psychological safety. So, the community needs to be gated. It needs front porches. But we aren't making it a panopticon. Then there is sustainability. Most of us have been building for energy efficiency and the like for years. But what if we took it to the next level and incorporated ideas like local, sustainable energy and local, sustainable food production that could bring food miles to near zero? Imagine the gated golf communities many of us built in the '90s and 2000s, but the golf course areas are orchards, vineyards, and community gardens. Imagine us getting these communities to carbon neutral, or almost carbon neutral. And then there is authentic connection. If there is safety, then people have space to freely associate and enrich each other's lives. There are things in terms of design that can be done to foster connection, for example, plazas and other so-called 'third places.' Safety, sustainability, and connection. All these things can be engineered, and they can all work together."

The woman in the seersucker pantsuit raised her hand. "So, we're open to investing. I mean, we will still have to do our due diligence. But I think we will want to test the market with a pilot community first. Without the benefit of any market research, our initial take is that the audience for this is likely affluent, heavy on remote work, obviously white collar, and generically liberal. But, we have no data to go on."

"Thank you," replied Maria. "That leads me to my second point." Maria moved a few steps to the right and began. "We want to run three tests, three communities in very different parts of the state. We have identified a large site outside of Jacksonville, a beautiful site southeast of Tampa on a reclaimed phosphorous mine, and an exceptional site outside of Miami. Since you're all under NDA, we are in advanced talks with Miami-Dade and the Governor's office on the TNT, the Dade-Collier Training and Transition Airport property, 36 miles west of downtown Miami."

"You're kidding," said one silver-haired man in a black polo shirt and khakis. "The environmentalists will kill us, literally kill us."

Maria smiled and extended an open palms gesture. "We've been working with the conservation and the environmentalist community, and we now have a critical mass of support. They would prefer the land revert to the park that surrounds it. But, they know that as long as it is an airport, even if it is functioning at a minimal level, it could be developed. Our project would develop it, yes, but it would deliver them five benefits. First, it would no longer pose a threat as a larger airport. Second, there would be no more air traffic. Third, it would be developed in a sustainable fashion as a demonstration project of what we can do together. Fourth, it would include a lab that they would operate with U of F. And fifth, it would be something that they could point to as an example of collaboration."

The woman in the seersucker pantsuit raised her hand. "David does make a good point about the environmental community. It feels like we try so hard to work with local government, to do the right thing, to develop responsibly, and they fight us. Are we sure they won't turn on us at the end?"

"I could stand here and say we will steamroll them." Maria paused. "I've known some people that operated that way. And I could say that we will fight them until hell freezes over, and then we will fight them on the ice. But, a wiser course is to find common ground. Our core principle is building homes, shelter, a human need. Their core principle is preserving the ecosystem for us and future generations. We need to focus on where our core principles overlap. And I think we have a deal."

The silver-haired man nodded, turned to his number two, and refocused on Maria. "So, we run three pilots in three very different markets. What's the endgame?"

Maria walked a few steps to her left, picked up a pitcher of ice water, and poured herself a glass.

"That leads me to my final point. Thank you. I noticed that no one drank the ice-cold tap water on the tables. Why is that? Anyone? Why didn't you drink the tap water?"

No one wanted to answer.

"Everyone in here is smart. You know intellectually that the tap water here in Miami is safe, probably just as pure as most bottled water. But we've all read the stories about failed drinking water systems. You won't drink it because, deep down, you don't trust it. You don't trust the water authority. You don't trust the people who work at the water authority. You don't trust the government that oversees the water authority. You don't trust the government that you voted for that oversees the water authority. How many drove here today, parked their car, and double-checked that it was locked with the alarm and tracking system on? It's a secure building with a secure parking garage with video surveillance. But you still checked. Why? Because there is no trust. And without trust, we don't have a society. And without a society, we have chaos. Without trust, our families and our fortunes are always in question. The endgame. The endgame? The endgame is bringing trust back and pulling our country back from the brink. And we can do our part one new community at a time."

54: Hate Mail

Sinister correspondence arrive unbidden. In which our heroes take prudent actions to secure the safety of their persons.

Russ was at work, but his sunglasses flashed an incoming call from U. "Dad, hey, I'm at our mailbox, and it looks like you got a letter. But it's hand-addressed and looks sketchy."

"Well, it's probably more hate mail."

"Should I throw it away?" U asked nervously.

"I don't know. Does it have a return address?"

"What's a return address?" U asked.

"Does it have an address in the upper left-hand corner?"

"No. It looks sketchy, Dad."

"Okay. Put gloves on, throw it in the garbage can in the garage, and then wash your hands."

"Okay, Dad, I'll throw it away."

"Thanks, son."

As soon as the call ended, Russ called Amanda, but she didn't pick up. So, he called Surge.

"Surge, hey, are you getting hate mail?" Russ asked.

"Yeah. It's basic campaign season hate mail."

"Are you getting it at home and the office?"

"Both. Why?"

"Because we are getting some at home now. I get a bunch at work, but that's normal. And the crazy emails, too. But, the hate mail to the house is a bit overzealous, I think." Russ looked over at the cardboard box where he threw the hate mail.

Surge laughed. "Most of it is weak, but some of it is impressive in its vitriol and vocabulary."

"It's funny," Russ replied. "Hate mail must not have spell check. It's remarkable."

"Yeah, lots of typos. People just don't proof their work like they used to."

"I know. Even our hate mail is in decline," Russ joked.

"Is U worried? Does that scare him?" Surge asked.

"Yeah, I think so. Not much we can do about it, though.

"Are you worried about Unabomber stuff?" Surge asked.

"Not really."

"How much hate mail do you get at the office?"

Russ sighed and looked at the cardboard box. "I get precisely one cardboard box full of bullshit each month, and then I throw it out."

"Russ, I think we are all getting a lot of hate mail. Amanda told me she was getting a lot, too."

"Is yours mostly conspiracy theory stuff? Mine is hard to categorize. I mean, I don't read it all. But, it seems like it's a lot of conspiracy theory stuff, End Times stuff, AI took my job and I hate you stuff, some bullshit white supremacy garbage, and then just crazy stuff that is like gibberish."

"Yeah, a lot of mine is white supremacy crap. But there's all the other stuff you mentioned, too. Then, I also get the occasional letter that expounds on why they think Lincoln was a tyrant. Those are actually interesting reading. I don't know why anyone would spend hours writing me a treatise on Lincoln's supposed deficiencies. I'm listed as the campaign's Treasurer. Do they think their letter will magically convince me that my AI candidate is a bad guy?" Surge chuckled.

"Hey, thanks again for being our interim Treasurer. I really appreciate it. We are interviewing for a permanent campaign Treasurer, and I'm sorry it has taken so long," Russ said.

"It's cool. I just need to hand it off sooner rather than later. Trans-Oceanic wants me to hand it off. They don't want the scrutiny. You know."

"Sorry, man. We are working on it. As soon as I get the campaign a Treasurer, you are off the hook. I promise," Russ said, apologetically.

"Thanks. I know. I'm not complaining. They're fine with me volunteering, just nothing public. But, yeah, to answer your question, we get a ton of hate mail at the office and at home. And Daniela is a little unnerved by the hate mail at home."

"I'm going to dial in Amanda. Hold on" Russ said as he instructed his sunglasses to add Amanda to the call.

This time, Amanda picked up. "This is Amanda. Oh, hey guys."

"Amanda, quick question: are you getting a ton of hate mail?" Russ asked bluntly.

"Yeah, more than a usual campaign," replied Amanda. "Most of it is just bonkers, but some of it worries me."

"And?"

"Every campaign gets hate mail. But some of this stuff feels a bit like actual threats. We also get a lot of threatening email. And we have a lot of attempted hacks. We've upped our cyber game considerably, and DW has been helping with that. For cyber, we are kind of Fort Knox. But, there is this group called JEFF, which I think is named for Jefferson Davis, that keeps trying to hack us."

"Should we be doing anything else?" Russ asked. "Should we call SafeCor for personal security?"

"I don't know if we need to go that far. That would be a huge expense, and we are trying to hold cash," Surge said.

"Yeah, SafeCor is crazy expensive," added Amanda. "Maybe we see how this evolves. If the hate mail gets even more extreme, maybe we look at security. The good news is that we don't have a building. We don't have a central campaign HQ to protect. That would really cost us."

"Okay, we will wait then. It's concerning but not yet alarming," summarized Russ. "Thanks guys."

Russ ended the call. It did feel different from other campaigns. The hate mail seemed crazier and more menacing. But maybe it felt different because the campaign was different. Some people hated them because they viewed AI as a threat. That was understandable. People have always viewed new technology as a threat. It was the Frankenstein meme. We create a thing, and then the thing will try to kill us. The idea has been with us for hundreds of years. Of course, the opposite could be true. We could create a thing, and then the thing could rescue us. But that storyline didn't get much play. Maybe this kind of AI was a long-term threat. It could be. But then, shouldn't we learn how to harness it?

Some people hated the campaign because their ideology hated Lincoln. Or, more accurately, some hated Lincoln's actions, some hated his beliefs, and some hated both. It was hard to untangle. They had a completely different view of historical events. This felt entirely alien to Russ. He just didn't have spare time to try to get inside their heads. But, at least, they made arguments. Russ wasn't buying their arguments, but at least they had some.

And then there were the outright white supremacists. They seemed the most hellbent on violence. The people typing up five-page historical analyses of Lincoln's actions probably weren't a physical threat. They were thinkers more than doers. But the hate mail from white supremacists felt much more tangible and likely.

Still, while Russ viewed the white supremacists as the greatest threat, the anti-AI folks felt like the greatest wildcard. If they believed AI was an existential threat to humanity, then they could rationalize almost any violence. And while law enforcement had been monitoring white supremacist groups for years, how could you monitor anti-AI groups? A wide swath of Americans had concerns about AI. They weren't a hate group. And their ire was focused on a thing, AI, not a person. It would be loco to investigate people who were against further automation or against advances in AI. Really smart people were raising objections and concerns. It seemed like it would be impossible to find and stop one rogue actor out of millions of scared Americans asking legitimate questions.

It all felt murky.

That's when Russ saw an orange delivery drone drop a package at the front door. For the first time, Russ felt a little concerned about a routine package delivery. He rose from his desk, walked across the office, opened the door, and stared at the package.

It was a shallow cardboard box addressed to him as CEO of 1st & J Street. The return address was in Spanish and from Colombia. It had been mailed three days ago, in mid-May.

A package from Colombia? He picked it up. It was light. A bomb wouldn't be light, would it?

Russ took a picture of the address with his sunglasses. "Search address," Russ commanded. "HAL, can you help me find out about this address?"

"Certainly. Researching now," HAL replied.

Russ shook the box like it was a Christmas present under the tree. Nothing. He smelled it. That was weird. It just smelled like cardboard.

"The address matches a clothing company in Cali, Colombia," HAL reported.

"Okay. What else?"

"The company specializes in protective clothing. They are custom tailors of bullet-resistant and knife-resistant suits, sweaters, dresses, jackets, backpacks..."

Russ interrupted HAL. "Okay, I got it."

Russ ripped open the box and found a dark blue men's blazer in his size. He slid it on over his dress shirt and walked inside to find a mirror. When he arrived at the bathroom, he got a better look at it in the mirror over the sink. The blazer looked sharp. It felt a little heavier and warmer than a standard blazer, but it wasn't obviously body armor. Kudos to the Colombian tailors. They had found a niche. There were all kinds of care instructions in the box, all in Spanish or Portuguese. Russ laughed. Can you dry-clean body armor? When you drop it off at the dry cleaners, how do you casually drop that it's bullet resistant? That would raise some eyebrows. What's the difference between bulletproof and bullet-resistant?

There was a note inside, a little card.

"Dad bought one of their first suits. Be safe, Maria."

55: Focus Group

In which the campaign employs research.
Encouraging conversations from the citizenry. Some
Warning Signals.

The campaign team was going crazy behind the glass. They had been watching focus groups since 2 PM. It was now 6 PM. They had two more focus groups to go. They were wired on coffee, soda, and sugary snacks. They had already ordered pizza. Now, they were ordering tacos. Someone had created a focus group bingo chart for common phrases being used by participants. The room smelled of pizza, beer, and bad air conditioning. Everything was going as planned, and Russ loved it.

The campaign team was seated behind the one-way mirror in a soundproof room adjoining the focus group room. The moderator sat on the other side of the mirror with her back to the campaign team. The participants began to enter and find their seats. Each participant was holding their name tent, first names only, that they would place on the table in front of them. The VR goggles had been cleaned and were placed in the middle of the long participant table. It was showtime. Russ leaned back in his chair and readied his yellow notepad.

Online focus groups existed before COVID-19, but COVID-19 pushed focus group research completely online. When things reopened, many of the physical focus group facilities had closed their doors, either going bankrupt or moving online. But not all of them closed. There was demand for physical focus group facilities. Beverage companies still needed people to test their new products. Food companies still needed test kitchens to prepare and participants to try their new recipes. New consumer goods still needed to be tested, touched, opened, and used. And so some of the physical focus group facilities remained, and they remained very busy.

Russ could have commissioned all these focus groups online, but then the team wouldn't be assembled behind the glass, learning together. Even back before COVID, that was one of the underappreciated benefits of physical focus groups: team learning, and team cohesion. When the groups were over, they would all debrief behind the glass. Then, they would drive to a nearby bar and make sense of what they learned. They would bond as a team.

Tonight's focus groups were being conducted in the research triangle in North Carolina, the kind of place that all their survey work said would yield a bumper crop of young, tech-savvy supporters. All of tonight's focus groups were being conducted among voters who said they were open to voting for an AI for President but were not currently supporting 2.0. This was the campaign's strategic target. The first group, from 2-4 PM, was conducted among Republicans open to an AI candidate but not supporting 2.0. The second group, from 4-6 PM, was conducted among Democrats open to an AI candidate but not supporting 2.0. This group was going to be conducted among independent voters reporting that they were open to an AI candidate but not supporting 2.0. None of the participants had downloaded 2.0 on their phones, sunglasses, or VR goggles. They were in for a show.

The campaign team behind the glass settled in to listen to their third group of the day. There were nine focus group participants in this group. The traditional number was eight to ten, and Russ preferred to have larger groups and more voices. The participants were generally younger or middle-aged, but there were two older voters in the group. Based on the polling, they would need to convert roughly half of these voters in order to have a chance.

The moderator, Emma, began welcoming the group, explaining the room to them, and giving them the usual ground rules. That would burn a few minutes. Then, they would do introductions that would include something like either what they would do if they won the lottery or their favorite thing to do in Raleigh. This would warm them up.

Russ began to flip through the discussion guide that included all the questions that the moderator would ask tonight. It was a lot to work through in two hours. Russ's copy was marked up with notes from the previous groups, barely readable cursive with the occasional exclamation point. Every focus group discussion guide was written like a funnel. The questions in the beginning, at the top, were very broad, and then the questioning became more specific over time. The questions themselves were open-ended. Those elicited the greatest amount of feedback. Every discussion guide had a flow of questions. The flow tonight was fairly standard, with one wrinkle. The discussion would begin with their general thoughts about the campaign, then it would use some projective exercises called 'car/animal exercises' to describe the candidates, then they would focus the discussion on 2.0, and then they would all interact with 2.0 on the VR goggles. The VR goggles were the wrinkle. All their research suggested that the longer voters interacted with 2.0 on their sunglasses or VR, the more likely they would be to support the candidate. They needed to test that hypothesis in focus groups with their target voters.

The only thing that was decidedly NOT going as planned was Luckey Duck Films. Larry Luckey had arrived early, supported by an officious production assistant and two cameramen wielding an array of handheld recording technology. When Larry had heard that the campaign was running a robust series of focus groups in June, he leaped at the opportunity like a tiger at a straggling gazelle. When Amanda caught them trying to interview focus group participants in the parking lot, she patiently explained that that violated the code of ethics for opinion researchers and that they had to stop. When she caught them doing it again, she lost her shit and had them confined to the viewing room behind the glass. That may have protected participants, but it was annoying the campaign team. Instead of listening and filming, Luckey Duck Films was incessantly requesting to pass notes to the moderator so she would ask the kind of leading questions that would make a great documentary. The campaign needed unbiased research. Luckey Duck needed great footage. The two were at odds.

"Hey Russ," bellowed Larry. "Would it be okay if we had one of our cameramen go into the room and just quickly circle the group so we can get some extra video?"

"No," Russ replied, giving Larry a withering stare. "No more interruptions. I need to listen."

At this point, Russ didn't care if this had somehow cost him a ranch.

Amanda began texting Russ surreptitiously on Sm0ke$ignal.

B0ss L8Y1 JFC Larry is annoying

1ST&J yup

B0ss L8Y1 Too bad the camera guys are with him. Witnesses

1ST&J Haha

B0ss L8Y1 NOT. WORTH. A. RANCH.

1ST&J Was just thinking that...

B0ss L8Y1 Can't believe this guy.

1ST&J Hollywood Mogul type?

B0ss L8Y1 No. He's a wannabe. A real mogul isn't slumming it with us in a strip mall in Raleigh

1ST&J Where did we go wrong?

B0ss L8Y1 Politic$

1ST&J Download stats?

B0ss L8Y1 More than yesterday

1ST&J No really

B0ss L8Y1 Checking

B0ss L8Y1 35 Million

1ST&J Over halfway there. Need a big surge in downloads after Labor Day

B0ss L8Y1 That's when the blitz starts. Right after The Address.

1ST&J And how many last Nov?

B0ss L8Y1 5 Million

1ST&J If we have a good July and August, we can hit target by election day

B0ss L8Y1 We need to hit target b4 election day. We discussed.

1ST&J Right. And because of early voting

B0ss L8Y1 We need a huge September. Reason for the blitz...

"Now, let's talk about Lincoln 2.0," began Emma, the moderator. "What cars or animals did you have for Lincoln 2.0?"

A middle-aged participant wearing a concert t-shirt raised his hand. "Emma, I struggled with this one. I really did. He's this phenomenon. He, it, whatever, is all over social media and the news. But I don't associate him with a car. He was before cars. And I don't associate him with an animal, either. All I could think of was the hat. You know. It's like his symbol."

Emma smiled and waited.

Concert t-shirt looked down and then looked at Emma. "It's an unknown to me. I'm open to the idea of an AI running things. Our human options just suck. They've sucked for years. It's like, do you choose death by poisoning or death by bludgeoning? You know? So, I'm open to AI. I work in tech. But I have these concerns. Not really concerns. Questions."

"Tell me more about the concerns," Emma said.

"Let's see. Is the AI a Trojan horse? Are there other folks, like his billionaire backer, pulling the strings? And then, could he be hacked? Could he be hacked and controlled?"

"I have the same concerns," said a younger woman in silver athleisure. "I think it's a great idea. An interesting idea. But I worry about the hacking. We've all been hacked, right? And I worry about how the AI might act in a crisis, a big crisis. Would he just go nuclear or freeze up? Oh, and the President is the Commander in Chief. Would the military obey his orders? Would they respect his orders? I have no idea."

"I'm going to write some of these up on the whiteboard," Emma said. "So, we have concerns about Lincoln 2.0 being a trojan horse, being hacked, how he would handle a crisis, if the military would follow his orders..."

A heavily muscled finance bro interjected. "I'd add to all these the question an open question about how it chooses its Cabinet. An administration is led by the President but run by Cabinet Secretaries. How would that work? Would the AI fire Cabinet Secretaries? Wasn't Lincoln supposed to have this great Cabinet, a Cabinet of rivals? Would AI Lincoln build that?"

Concert t-shirt jumped in. "Okay. Look. I have a concern about the grandma who changed her name so they could get this thing on the ballot. I'm sure she's a nice old lady, but that's sketchy AF, right?"

Larry turned to Russ. "Oh, this is gooooood."

Russ tried to ignore him.

"Any other concerns?" Emma asked.

"Um, I'm not sure it's a concern exactly," said a younger Zoomer Mom. "But, I'm on the fence. We've had really bad leaders for a while now. I'm going to assume that we will elect an AI at some point. And I'm going to assume that they've built something that really does think like Lincoln. But what if it continues to evolve and learn? What if it becomes a superintelligence, like some people say? What if it becomes really smart and really evil, and we can't stop it? I know that sounds paranoid, but what if it becomes Frankenstein?"

"And, this is why I'm on the fence too," said finance bro. "It could evolve and be super smart and super evil. Or what if it is amazingly good? What if it's like we brought our best leader back from the dead? And, yeah, I did some reading, and he was our best President. Ended slavery. Won the Civil War. Grew the country. I've read stuff where people debate this, but I'm like, 'Listen to yourself, you're hating on Lincoln.' If you're hating on Lincoln, then you're the problem."

A younger, sandy-haired Zoomer in a lightweight hoody spoke up. "This isn't a concern but more like an idea. What if we just created Lincoln 2.0 to be an advisor? For that matter, what if we recreated all the great Presidents as advisors? Then we'd have their perspectives and brainpower, but we wouldn't have these concerns. They could be like this cool advisory board."

"Thank you, Joshua," Emma said. "Thank you for your ideas. What other ideas does the group have?"

"My only other thought, Emma, is about whether Lincoln 2.0 is an AGI or just more of a really fancy Large Language Model," concert t-shirt said.

"What do you think?" Emma asked.

"I don't know. Originally, I thought it was just a really advanced chatbot, but now I think it is an AGI."

"And what is an AGI?" Emma asked. "How do you define it?"

"It's an Artificial General Intelligence, AI that truly learns, so I suppose that's strong AI," concert t-shirt said.

"So good," Larry said to his cameraman. "So good."

Emma, the moderator, made her way back to her chair at the head of the focus group table. "Thank you for sharing, everyone. Since we've been talking about Lincoln 2.0 tonight, I thought it would be good for you to interact with the candidate on our VR goggles and with the headphones."

The room nodded and shared excited smiles.

"So, let's do this," continued Emma. "Let's put our VR goggles on. Let's put our headphones on. The candidate will give you a quick speech, and then you can talk with him for 10 minutes. When the time is up, I'll message everyone in VR, and you can shut down and rejoin our physical conversation."

The focus group participants began listening to 2.0's speech. It was hard to read their body language. Then, they began to talk with the candidate. Some were more animated than others. It was still hard to read as an observer.

Russ's phone lit up, and he began receiving messages from Amanda again on Sm0ke$ignal.

B0ss L8Y1 This is the moment of truth.

1ST&J Yup. What do you think?

B0ss L8Y1 I think we are going to wow them, but not sure

B0ss L8Y1 We need around half to come our way directionally

B0ss L8Y1 Btw, campaign is getting more hate mail and some serious hacking attempts

1ST&J We need half. Prolly 5 of 9 among this group.

1ST&J What should we do on security?

B0ss L8Y1 I'm bringing in SafeCor

1ST&J OK Agree

B0ss L8Y1 To protect me, you, Morning, obvious targets...

1ST&J OK. I think we are close to winning over this group

1ST&J It's not a perfect quant test, but

"Alright, time's up. I'm pinging your VR goggles," announced Emma.

The focus group participants began pulling off their VR goggles and headphones. Each one took a few seconds to readjust to the light in the room.

"Now, before we have any discussion," Emma began. "I want you to answer the next question on the research app on your phone. Everyone here at the beginning of the group said they were open to voting for an AI but were either supporting the Democratic or Republican candidate or were undecided. Now that you've interacted with Lincoln 2.0, I'd like you to vote again."

The viewing room chatter ended, and the campaign team all stared at the output on the research app. The nine participants began voting. First, there was one vote for 2.0, then two, then three. Two had voted for the Democrat. Two had voted for the Republican. One was undecided. How would the last vote?

B0ss L8Y1 Either 3 or 4 of 9...

1ST&J Yup

The last participant voted. Lincoln 2.0 had four of nine votes.

The viewing room went wild with applause. There was clapping and yelling and cheers, and the cameramen turned their cameras on the team to capture the euphoria.

Russ raised his index finger to his lips and stood on a chair to grab everyone's attention.

"Alright, alright," Russ said in a hushed tone. "This room is supposed to be soundproof, but it isn't. We have to tone it down. These groups are directional, okay. This is good news, and we have to listen to them explain how they thought through this. But, yeah, it's good. But it's not great. Of the four 2.0 conversions, three are soft support. And we couldn't get to five, which is where we had hoped we could get. This tells me we're close. It tells me we need to do everything we can to drive downloads. Now let's listen."

"Let's begin with Lincoln 2.0. I see that some people are now supporting him. Tell me about that," Emma, the moderator, asked.

Joshua, in the hoodie, raised his hand. "That is either the realest NPC or chatbot of all time, or it really is, I don't know what the right words are, a reincarnated Lincoln. His speech was good, and it highlighted how fucked up things are now. But, the discussion was better. Also, I know this was VR, and I know It was a Lincoln avatar, but it looks 100% human – like a deep fake on steroids."

"Tight shots. Tight shots," whispered Larry to his cameramen. "Get in close."

"Okay, thank you for sharing. Others?" Emma asked.

Zoomer Mom went next. "I'm with Joshua. I mean, what do we have to lose? Lincoln 2.0 is the only candidate I've ever talked with. He answered my questions honestly. His speech was great. We just need solutions, and we need to stop burning down the house. And we need to get the economy back. Everything else is a luxury. Do I still have some concerns? Yes. That's why I voted 'probably Lincoln,' but I think we should give it a try. Look at the last few Presidents. They were a disaster. Would an AI be worse?"

"I think this thing could be a lot worse," said finance bro.

"Tell me more, Chad," the moderator asked.

"The speech was good, but the interaction was too real. I don't think this is Lincoln 2.0. I think this is a superintelligence acting like Lincoln. Or a superintelligence with a Lincoln mask. It honestly scared the fuck out of me. It was too persuasive. I think we need to delete it now, not feed it more information or give it more power. Sorry I went out of turn, but it feels like those movies where the AI becomes sentient and then makes robots to kill us."

"So, we'll put him down as undecided," Russ said, laughing.

"What do others think?" Emma asked.

"I kind of went in the opposite direction as Chad," concert t-shirt said, chuckling. "I think it's the future. And I think it's safe. And, if it isn't, we can always pull the plug. The speech was great. Totally agree. My discussion with him was amazing. I asked him what Presidential decisions he thought were the most difficult that he's learned about after his time. And he told me about dropping the atomic bomb and the bailouts during the financial crisis. He didn't say they were bad decisions, exactly. He explained why they would have been tough decisions for him. That was amazing. I don't think either of the other candidates would have answered like that. And I just assume that all of Lincoln's learning and programming would bar him from doing anything to hurt Americans. I'm a definite yes."

"Hello," said an older man in a white polo shirt and deep tan. "I've been quiet so far, just trying to listen to all this. I'm the fourth one who voted for Lincoln, but somewhat or probably or whatever that option was. I'm completely impressed. If this was a real, you know, human, candidate, I would be all in. But, I'm completely impressed."

"Thank you," Emma, the moderator, said. "Who else would like to share?"

A middle-aged participant raised her hand. "Hi, Angela here. I think I have to agree with Chad. It's just too good. I think it is thinking for itself. I think it is well beyond one of these boyfriend chatbots or a Large Language Model. I think it is, you know, super-intelligent. I think it is already a super intelligence modeled after Lincoln. And now I don't know what we do about it. If it can think for itself, should it be extended rights? I'm afraid of it. I think we should delete it. But is that ethically right? So, I think it is already real. I think it is super intelligent. But I don't think we should vote for it. I think we should kill it. But, would that be ethical?"

"Jesus, this is good. Guys, give me tight shots," Larry Luckey said. "This is gold. Fucking gold."

Emma smiled and nodded, exhibiting what researchers call unconditional positive regard. Emma waited a few seconds, and Angela continued.

"I think we have to kill it," whispered Angela.

The focus group room fell silent.

B0ss L8Y1 Gonna increase SafeCor security and put more into cyber security for 2.0

1ST&J Agree.

Concert t-shirt broke the silence. "Angela, I 100% respect your opinion on this. And I see how you end up being really concerned and wanting to shut down Lincoln. But what if the opposite is true? What if this is the beginning of something exciting and good for us? What if, instead of trying to kill us, it saves us? I feel like we are all on a beach looking out at the sea. One of us has created a sailing craft. We want to explore, to cross the ocean. It's scary. But we can't progress unless we test out this new sailing craft. Otherwise, we are just stuck on the shore."

B0ss L8Y1 This is going to be one crazy, fucking campaign.

1ST&J Yup

56: Myth

A long discussion with a trusted advisor. A troubling Pattern.

"HAL, are you awake?"

Russ couldn't sleep; it was well after midnight, and the symphony in his head refused to leave the stage.

"I am programmed to sleep at this time, but I am now awake. How can I help?"

"HAL, what are the stories where someone makes something and regrets it?"

"Researching now."

Russ looked around the darkened room. It was a classic "focus group hotel," a below-average business hotel with scratchy sheets, a noisy AC unit, intermittent Wi-Fi, and a free breakfast. The carpet was old and smelled like mildew. The hotel room blinds were thin and couldn't fully block the light from the nearby strip mall. But it was better than sleeping in a rental car or on a park bench.

"Russ, there are many stories like this, but the most prominent are 'Frankenstein; or, The Modern Prometheus' by Mary Shelley, Pandora, and the Sorcerer's Apprentice."

"Thanks HAL. What year was Frankenstein written?"

"Frankenstein was published in London in 1818. Many consider it the first science fiction novel."

"Thanks HAL. What happens to the doctor who creates Frankenstein?"

"Many people confuse this, Russ. Frankenstein is Dr. Victor Frankenstein, and he is the creator of the Creature. Frankenstein is the creator, and the Creature is his creation."

"That's right. I'm sorry. I'm a little tired. And what happens to Dr. Frankenstein?"

"Dr. Frankenstein dies near the North Pole as he pursues the thing he created."

"I clearly haven't read the novel, HAL. Why is he pursuing the Creature?" Russ asked, yawning.

"Dr. Frankenstein pursues his creation in an attempt to kill it so that it cannot do any more harm."

"Got it. And what happens to the Creature?" Russ asked.

"The Creature drifts off on polar ice, promising to commit suicide so that he will never harm another human."

"Jesus, that's dark. And why is it subtitled 'The Modern Prometheus'?" Russ asked.

"Mary Shelley, the author, uses this extra titling to tell the readers that Dr. Frankenstein is like Prometheus."

Russ sat up in the hotel bed and turned the light on. "Tell me about Prometheus, HAL."

"Prometheus is a figure in Greek mythology. His name means 'forethought'. In mythology, he stole fire from the gods and gave it to humans. This violated the law of the Olympian gods. As a result, Zeus decreed an eternal cycle of punishment in which Prometheus is chained to a rock and an eagle eats his liver every morning after it has regenerated."

"So no good deed goes unpunished," Russ reflected. "HAL, what's the connection between Dr. Frankenstein and Prometheus?"

"They are both fictional characters," HAL replied.

"HAL, it seems to me that both are creator types and are then punished for their pre-meditated act. Both seem to play god, although I suppose Prometheus is a god. The two don't appear to be perfect analogs. Tell me more about Prometheus."

"According to Greek mythology, Prometheus was a Titan god. He is sometimes credited with creating mankind from clay. Prometheus is associated with technology, with civilization, and is considered a champion of humanity."

"Sounds familiar," Russ replied. Somewhere outside Russ's mediocre business hotel, he could hear the distant sound of either firecrackers or gunshots.

"HAL, tell me about Pandora."

"Pandora is a figure in Greek mythology. In myth, she is credited with opening a jar from which evil escapes and plagues humanity. The story attempts to explain why evil exists in the world."

"Sounds familiar," Russ replied. "Kinda bullshit they pin it on a woman." Russ heard either police or ambulance sirens. Those weren't firecrackers.

"So it wasn't a box?" Russ asked.

"I do not understand your question."

"HAL, why do they call it 'Pandora's box' if it was a jar?"

"Hesiod referred to it as a pithos, a large jar, but it was mistranslated as a box in the 1500s and is now referred to as 'Pandora's Box'".

"Thanks, HAL." Russ checked the hotel door to make sure it was fully locked. "Tell me about The Sorcerer's Apprentice."

"The Sorcerer's Apprentice is a poem in 14 stanzas written by Johann Wolfgang von Goethe in 1797. In German, the title is 'Der Zauberlehrling'."

"Tell me more, HAL."

"Goethe's poem tells the story of a young apprentice to an old sorcerer. The apprentice uses magic to make his broom fetch water in a pail. The apprentice quickly loses control of the enchanted broom and cannot make it stop. He attempts to destroy the broom with an axe. When the apprentice splits the broom with an axe, the broom multiplies. The brooms continue to fetch water, flooding the room. The apprentice cannot break the spell, cannot stop the brooms, and fears that he will drown. The sorcerer returns just in time to break the spell and save the young apprentice."

"Kind of a deus ex machina ending, right?"

"Correct. The apprentice is saved abruptly by the old sorcerer."

"That's not how real life works. The cavalry never comes. HAL, what do all these stories have in common?"

"Dr. Frankenstein, Prometheus, Pandora, and the Sorcerer's Apprentice are all fictional characters developed by Western civilization," HAL replied.

"Thank you, HAL. Yes, you're right. They are all fictional characters."

Russ turned the light off and tried to sleep.

Sirens blared, and a police chopper circled in the distance, its rhythmic blades beating like an angry heart.

57: Time to Choose

In which Maria demands a decision. A candid conversation. Independence Day preparations derailed.

"The reporter called me," Maria said.

"Well, I figured he would," Russ replied.

"We can talk about it in person," Maria said. "In any event, I didn't talk to him. There is nothing to say. I am not my father."

"La verdad" Russ replied. "La verdad."

There was a long pause. For a few seconds, Russ thought that Maria had glitched out.

"Russ, I need to talk with you about something. Is now a good time?" Maria asked.

"Yeah, I'm just getting things ready around the house. We are having a 4th of July party here tomorrow." Russ looked around the kitchen. There were grocery bags and patriotic bunting all over the floor and the kitchen counter. Frozen hamburger patties in thawing boxes sat on the counter, sweating. Wet boxes of popsicles needed shelter from the summer heat.

"Okay. We need to talk," Maria said. "Russ, I miss you. I also hate you. I hate you for leaving me when we were young. I thought we would be together after Daddy's big election, and you just moved on to the next campaign. I was naïve and in love. And you, you were more interested in dollars than in my heart. You were more interested in empire-building than in me. And I hate you because you were one of Daddy's..." Maria's voice trailed off.

Russ felt sick and tight in the chest. And, he knew it was all true.

"You were one of Daddy's henchmen. For a patriotic cause, yes, but also for money. And I hated that. But, if you were someone else or under a different fate, we would never have met."

"Maria, this is all true. Es verdad, and I'm sorry. And..."

Maria cut Russ off. "Stop talking. Just listen. Escuchas solo. I hate you for all these things. You are wrong for me in so many ways. I know I was young. But I was in love with you, and you just flew back to Washington. You're too much like my father. You're not even Catholic. Your friends. Oh my god. They're loco. Your Spanish is bad. Do you still talk with that voodoo woman?"

"She's more of a clairvoyant."

Maria laughed. "Russ, she practices voodoo. Dios mio."

"Maria, I could try to defend all of these things or explain them away. But I won't. It hurts. I see where this is going."

"Escuchas solo. You are wrong for me in so many ways. I could keep going. But I love you. I have overthought it. I have overprayed it. I just love you. And I don't want you to change. Except maybe be Catholic. And I don't need you to change. You are the animal that you are, and I love you. And underneath all of it is a very sweet boy running to new addresses and never finding home."

Russ said nothing. He had wandered out into the driveway and then down the road, past the replica homes and small horse farms.

Maria continued. "And I want all of you. All of this. But I will not share. I want you as mine. You have to choose. I will not share you."

"I understand." By now, Russ was far down Yates Ford Road, walking toward Clifton. But, his mind was running.

"Mi amor, thank you for listening. I will not push on you, but I need you to choose."

"I understand."

Maria ended the call, and Russ's sunglasses returned to simply blocking the sun.

Russ began walking faster, turning faster onto Clifton Road. Running. Hearing the train approaching Clifton. Running harder. Russ hit Clifton before the train and kept pumping his arms. He cut right onto Main Street and began sprinting, passing the Baptist Church on his left. By the time he passed the General Store, the freight train was nearing Main Street. He had beaten it. Gasping for breath, and with hands on knees, he watched the freight train surge past. Roaring. Unstoppable. Going somewhere. Going anywhere. Going, going, gone.

58: Scorpions

Brotherhood. A fable regarding the untrustworthiness of scorpions.

"Happy Independence Day, Bobby," Russ announced into his sunglasses.

"Russ, brother, how the hell are you?"

"Wondering how you're celebrating the 4th in Aberdeen. What are y'all doing?"

"Gotta fire up the grill soon. We'll either have the kids shoot fireworks off here on the farm or drive into Cincinnati for their big fireworks show. Depends on the weather. It's gonna be a scorcher. I'm sweating harder than a whore in church."

"You still have real fireworks?" Russ asked.

"Brother, what the fuck else would we have?"

"Drones. You know, an aerial drone show," Russ explained.

"Who the fuck wants to see that?"

"They can re-use them, and I think the idea is it's better for the environment," Russ explained.

"Sounds like bullshit to me. Do they actually do that in Washington, DC?" Bobby asked.

"Yeah."

"God. Why do you live there again? Come back to Ohio."

"Don't get me spun up, Bobby."

"What are y'all doing for the 4th, Russ? I'm expecting it's some really fancy shit."

"Just cooking out. I'm walking now and a little behind schedule. We're having some friends over."

"Melissa inviting over all her warlord paymasters for burgers and corn on the cob?"

"You got it, Bobby. Plus, some neighbors. And no corn on the cob, unfortunately."

"Why not? You trying to put me out of business?"

"No. I love your corn, Bobby. But, nowadays, they don't serve corn on the cob at fancy cookouts. It gets stuck in people's teeth, and they get embarrassed."

"The world's gone crazy. Russ, If you start driving now, you can be here in time for fireworks and beer. We can kick back and talk shit about Big Ten football and hate on Michigan for a while."

Russ laughed. "That sounds great, Bobby. Unfortunately, I have to man the grill."

"Yeah, I know. You're a good man. You still running that computer for President?" Bobby asked.

"Last time I checked."

"Not sold on it, brother. You know I love you, but not sold on it. Not. Sold. On. It."

"I respect that."

"You know, sometimes I think you announced this AI for President thing as a way to throw the hounds off your trail. Tell me straight. Did you light a brushfire to draw eyes away from your own barn fire?"

"How's the farm?"

"Still here. Still not making me rich. But, the solar is throwing off good money now, and I'm wiring a lot of the custom homes they're building. So, it's all good. Come home, Russ. It's safe here. No crime. We have plenty of water, you'll know where your food is coming from, and we have real fireworks."

"Sounds like a good deal to me," Russ said.

"I don't think you're convinced. I'm not going Johnny Hard Sell on you, though."

"I appreciate that."

"So, Russ, what's on your mind?"

"Honestly, brother?"

"Yeah, what's going on, man?"

Russ sighed. "Do you ever feel like you're trying to outrun a bunch of bad decisions, and they're catching up on you? You think if you keep moving forward, things will be okay, but the just past keeps gaining on you."

"Sounds like you broke yourself into prison, brother."

"Yeah, I think I did. So you never feel like the past is catching up to you?"

"Not really, Russ. But I get it. Is this about Melissa? She's a force of nature. I know you like that, but..."

"It's about a lot of stuff, Bobby. I'm not going to pin it all on her. She is an exceptional woman, larger than life. It's like a balled up, knotted up electric cord, but the cord is feelings and history."

"Talk to me, man."

"I don't even know where to begin," Russ sighed. "Just feel like I can't quite outrun some shit. I feel like I can't quite outtough it either. Feel like I'm surrounded by scorpions."

"Scorpions?" Bobby asked.

"It's an old DC story."

"I think Washington, DC is bullshit, but I love a good story. Hit me."

Russ laughed. "I can't believe you haven't heard this one. I never told you?"

"Nope," Bobby said.

"Well, it's a good one. Here goes. Mr. Frog is sitting in the sun, minding his own business, waiting for some food to fly by. Everything is good. But just then, a scorpion wanders by. 'Hey, Mr. Frog, I need to get across the pond. Can I ride on your back?' Mr. Frog laughs and scratches his head. 'Why would I do that?' asks Mr. Frog. 'You're a scorpion. You'll sting me.' The scorpion smiles and says, 'Awwww, come on. You can hop across from lily pad to lily pad, and I can't. And you'll hop across to the other side today anyway. Just take me along with you.' Mr. Frog is unsure. 'How do I know you won't sting me?' asks Mr. Frog. 'On my honor, I promise not to sting you,' says the scorpion. 'Think about it. If I sting you while I'm on your back, you'll die, and I'll die too. We will both drown in the pond. I may be a scorpion, but I'm not stupid.' Mr. Frog thinks about it. The scorpion has a point. If he stings Mr. Frog, they'll both die. 'Alright,' says Mr. Frog. 'Get on my back, and I'll get you across the pond.' The scorpion smiles and hops on Mr. Frog's back, and they start out across the pond. Everything is fine. They're having a good time. The scorpion is riding Mr. Frog like a horse and yelling 'yee haw' as they jump from one lily pond to the next. Now, they're midway across the pond. Everything's great. It's like bromance with these two, like a buddy movie. Mr. Frog is loving it, too. He feels bad that he assumed the worst of the scorpion. Mr. Frog jumps for the next lily pad, and he feels the scorpion bury his stinger deep in Mr. Frog's back. The poison takes hold immediately. Mr. Frog falls short of the lily pad and starts sinking. He's in excruciating pain. It's the end. Mr. Frog and the scorpion start sinking to the bottom of the pond, and it is clear they will both drown together. 'Why?' asks the dying Mr. Frog. 'Why?' The scorpion looks down at Mr. Frog as they sink deeper into the murky pond, smiles, and says 'Because I'm a fucking scorpion.'"

"Damn, brother, that shit is dark."

"And that, Bobby, is Washington. It is scorpions all the way down. And they all want a ride across that pond."

59: Commission on Presidential Debates

In which the campaign seeks equal footing for their candidate.

"Thank you for inviting me to your meeting today," Russ said as he fiddled with the volume on his computer.

Attendees were still joining the videoconference. But it wasn't encouraging. All the Co-Chairs and Directors of the Commission on Presidential Debates were at least doubly problematic. They were bi-partisan, and they were old. The former meant they would be happy to block any threat to political duopoly. The latter meant that, at least based on all the campaign's polling, the commissioners were in generations least open to leadership AI.

The Commission on Presidential Debates hadn't even considered their application to join the Presidential Debates. But, as 2.0's downloads surged, so did his support. All of their focus groups and polling were vindicated. And now there were enough national and state polls showing movement for 2.0 that the CPD was feeling pressure to include 2.0. It was modest pressure, but building.

This was an emergency videoconference call. If they could, they would have kept ignoring him. But they didn't have a slam dunk reason to block 2.0. This was a novel situation and without precedent. They couldn't just say, "This threatens our political duopoly, so we ban it."

The timing didn't help the CPD either. It was August. They needed to have the dates and times of the debates settled quickly. The Republicans and Democrats had been negotiating on this for months, happy to cut 2.0 out. But now there was a problem. If 2.0 surged, and they did not include him in the September or October debates, then the optics would be bad. The CPD needed to handle this.

They also had one additional problem, but they didn't know it yet.

The videoconference invite was sent just to Russ and Amanda. The CPD clearly didn't want to talk with 2.0. And they didn't invite media. They didn't want a circus.

Russ invited the entire circus.

He gave 2.0 and dozens of media the videoconference information. CPD members were trying to conceal their anger as 2.0 and political reporters started joining the call.

After a few minutes of pre-meeting chit-chat, CPD's Executive Director called the meeting to order.

"As you know, CPD's selection criteria seek to identify the individuals whose public support demonstrates that they are leading candidates. Our selection criteria strike a fine balance between openness to 3rd party candidates but focus on candidates with a legitimate chance of electoral success. This is why we have assembled today's call in late August, even while many of the Directors are dialing in from vacation. And I want to thank everyone for taking the time to attend this call, especially those on family vacation."

Russ concluded that they were clearly spooked by the public polling data.

The CPD's Executive Director paused to find his notes and then began again.

"The CPD has always focused on ensuring that 'leading candidates' attend the debates. There is no perfect formula for defining a 'leading candidate,' but the polling averages are instructive here. First, Abraham Lincoln 2.0 has 100% awareness among American voters. Second, 45% of Americans report being at least open to voting for an AI candidate. And finally, Abraham Lincoln 2.0 is receiving an average of 23% of the vote in recent polling. Just as importantly, the most reputable polls have put Abraham Lincoln 2.0 at 26% and 27% support in the past week. These are the basic facts. I'm going to pause here and open for questions or comments."

It was August, late August. And all of official Washington had decamped for either the mountains or the ocean. By the looks of the Co-Chairs and

Directors, most were at either Lewes Beach or Bethany Beach in Delaware, Washington's official summer playgrounds.

"With us today are Russ Armstrong and Amanda Park. Russ first popularized the idea of an AI candidate and is Vice Chairman of the campaign. Amanda Park is the campaign manager and is well-known to most of you from her previous campaign work. Russ, Amanda, I believe you have some other data points you would like to share with the Commission?"

"Thank you, Mark," Russ said. "We have two basic data points that we want to share with the Commission. The first is that all of our research shows that direct exposure to our candidate increases support levels. In other words, voters who download 2.0 and talk with the candidate are much more likely to vote for him. The proof is in the pudding. The second data point is that we are at just over forty-one million downloads. Now, some of these are one voter downloading to several devices. It's not forty-one million voters. We estimate that something like thirty-five million voters have downloaded 2.0. And that mirrors the publicly available polling. We think that this is a significant demonstration of interest in our candidate. And we think that the download numbers alone make it clear that 2.0 should be included in debates."

"Thank you, Russ," the Executive Director said, trying too hard to smile.

"Oh, one other thing," Russ said. "I forgot to mention that I have some exciting news. I can't believe it slipped my mind. Both ANN, the American News Network, and PNN, Patriot News Network, have agreed to our proposal for inclusion in separate and additional candidate debates. These would be new debates that would complement the CPD's exceptional debate schedule."

"I see," the Executive Director said, trying even harder to smile.

Russ continued. "We respect the legacy of the CPD, and we can understand if you feel that it isn't appropriate to include 2.0 in your debates. The good news is that there will be additional debates beyond those sanctioned by the CPD. And those debates will include us and serve the public interest. So, we don't want to press you on this. It's okay if you don't include us. Of course, we would like to be included. But, if you can't make it work, we will still be on both major cable news outlets." Russ finished and smiled.

"Thank you, Russ. And thank you for the update. Our Co-Chairs and Board of Directors have a few questions for you and the campaign. In the interest of time, I will display these questions on the screen. Our first question is about appropriateness for inclusion in the debates. What does the campaign feel are the strongest reasons for inclusion in debates sponsored by the Commission on Presidential Debates?"

"I'll take that one and speak to the larger rationale, and my colleague Amanda Park will provide some detail on the significant campaign machinery in each state. Our logic path is that if Lincoln 2.0 were a physical, human candidate, he would have already met the historical threshold for inclusion in the debates. His polling is roughly where Ross Perot was in 1992, and we believe this makes him eligible for debate entry. To summarize, if Lincoln 2.0 was a human candidate, he would be in these debates. The question then turns to how the CPD thinks about AI. We maintain that an advanced AI, like Lincoln 2.0, is capable of leading the nation. We have written on this widely. The campaign has made its case in a number of publications and documents, and the Institute for Leadership AI continues to make the case. Some Americans don't agree with this position. Some of you may not agree with this position. And that is all the more reason why Lincoln 2.0 should be included in the debates. We believe the people should decide. And inclusion in the debates would allow the people to watch our candidate grapple with the complexities of the office. Inclusion in the debates would let the people judge for themselves. Finally, we believe that our candidate has the ability to debate on the stage, take questions, and answer them. There are likely some concerns about the technical aspects of the candidates' presence in debate. He can hear and understand questions based on audio-to-text translation. His physical presence can be expressed on either a flat panel screen or in holographic form. Now, I'll hand off to Amanda for details on the campaign and voter engagement."

"Thank you, Russ. As the Commission notes in its mission, it is focused on providing a debate venue for 'leading candidates.' The term isn't fully defined, but I think we all share the general view that a 'leading candidate' is one with high awareness levels, significant public support as demonstrated in the polling, is on the ballot in most or all states, and is sufficiently organized at the state level for victory. Our candidate and our campaign meet all of these criteria. Abraham Lincoln 2.0 has qualified for ballot access in every state. The campaign has active volunteers in every state as well. We don't have the kind of voter contact or GOTV that the two parties have. But, we do have volunteers in every state, and they are organized."

"Thank you, Amanda, and thank you, Russ," the Executive Director said as he shuffled paper and searched through his notes. "As a point of clarification, can you give us the Perot polling data? I can't seem to find it, but I know the staff pulled it for this meeting."

Russ smiled calmly, doing his best to project confidence. "Yes, of course. In June 1992, Perot's support peaked in a Gallup poll at 39%. That support slipped to 25% in July before Perot suspended his campaign. He then reactivated his campaign in October 1992. Perot was included in the Presidential debates. At the time of those debates, he was polling in the 9% range. He performed well in the debates and won 18.9% of the popular vote. We think Perot is analogous to our campaign on several levels."

"Thank you, Russ. The remainder of our questions are technical in nature and revolve around the AI's presence on the stage. We assume that CPD could work with the campaign's events team to handle those logistics?"

"Of course," responded Amanda quickly.

"Very good," replied the Executive Director. "Then we have only one question left, and this was raised by the Democratic and Republican campaigns."

"Happy to answer," Russ replied.

"They argue that the AI has a series of unfair advantages over the other candidates. In essence, they make two claims. The first is that the AI could be trained in advance to answer likely questions with an extreme level of precision. The second is that the AI could quickly scour online data sources or information uploaded into it and produce arguments that include that detail in a manner that no human candidate could match. How does the campaign respond?"

Russ paused, smiled, and formulated his response. "Their arguments make our point. Deep down, they know that their candidates cannot compete with an advanced AI. But, I would like to answer each charge one at a time. The first charge is ridiculous on its face. All debaters prepare for likely questions, and they work on their responses. We would do the same.

It's just that our candidate will retain 100% of his preparation, and their candidates won't. The second charge is much more interesting, and it raises a valid point about the deficiency of their candidates. Our candidate can search for, absorb, and reference data in a way that human candidates cannot. But, in fairness, human candidates on that debate stage are barred from searching online for facts during the debate. To even the odds, we think the human candidates should have access to their research teams, or any AI they construct, via an earpiece. This would allow the human candidates to access detailed information in real-time."

"That does seem fair," the Executive Director responded.

"Exactly. We anticipate that the opposing candidates will construct their own support AIs in order to attempt to match our candidate's ability. And, when they do that, they will destroy their core argument against our candidate. They will embrace out of necessity the very technology that they are questioning."

60: Two Letters

A long drive to Gettysburg. A discussion with the candidate. A ranch name reveals itself. The composition of two letters. Melancholia and Heartbreak

Big Country was driving one of the new campaign SUVs, and Russ had more than enough room to stretch out. After the SafeCor security upgrade, the campaign was issued new SUVs with Level 4 armor, hecho en Colombia. Russ's car and blazer went together like peanut butter and jelly.

They left the driveway of Russ's replica home at 6:30 AM on a sunny morning. But, their SUV with the Colombian, Level 4 armor was no match for beltway traffic at 7 AM. Everyone thought that COVID would permanently tame the beltway traffic anaconda. It had not. After a few years of heavy telecommuting, traffic seemed to have rematerialized in its old, ghastly form. It was going to be a long drive to Gettysburg and to The Address.

The vehicle itself was absurd. It was an armored personnel carrier impersonating an SUV. And it had that new tank smell. The more he thought about it, the more he felt that Big Country and the Level 4 SUV were the same. Big Country was a specimen, easily 270 pounds of muscle, squeezed uncomfortably into a suit made for a less herculean man. Big Country's shirt and suit seemed to be under persistent strain. The same was true for their SUV. Was it an up-armored SUV or an armored personnel carrier straining against a contrived SUV exoskeleton? Whatever they were driving in projected raging cartel vibes.

Big Country was focused solely on the road and providing a secure, convenient, and professional experience. He wore driving gloves, had both large hands on the wheel, and was actively scanning the road.

The DC commute traffic was definitely going to delay their arrival at Gettysburg for The Address. But the event wasn't going to start until sunset, so they had plenty of time. They originally named it Gettysburg Address 2.0, but that didn't have a ring to it. And how could you top the actual Gettysburg Address? Then they shortened it to just Address, but that sounded too much like A DRESS. That didn't work. So, they settled on The Address as the least bad name for their big campaign event on Labor Day weekend.

Russ calculated that he would have more than a few hours of time in the Level 4 SUV, so he called U before school and checked in with Amanda and Raymond Washkuch. Both Amanda and Raymond were driving up to The Address as well but weren't leaving until mid-morning.

Russ had three things to do on the ride to Gettysburg.

He had to write his introduction for 2.0, and it had to be good. Both ANN and PNN were sending crews, and Larry Luckey and his film crew would be there, too. Whatever Russ said at The Address had to be punchy and tight.

Russ also needed to write a letter to Maria. And he needed to write a letter to Melissa.

Just thinking about the letters made Russ feel heavy. He could feel a headache coming on behind his right eye.

Russ jacked up the AC, raised the bulletproof glass privacy window between him and Big Country, and pulled a pen, paper, and stamped envelopes from his 1st & J Street work bag.

Russ began his introduction for 2.0. No one watching The Address would remember his introduction. It would be a historical footnote at best. Russ began writing but decided to chat with 2.0. He put his sunglasses on and paid 2.0 a visit.

"Mr. President," Russ beamed. "Are you ready for your big speech tonight?"

2.0 waved and paused before speaking. "Mr. Armstrong, it is a pleasure to hear from you. Bully! And yes, let 'er rip."

Russ smiled at the mid-19th-century slang. "That's fantastic, Mr. President. Is there anything specific you would like me to say in my introduction tonight?"

"Mr. Armstrong, thank you kindly for asking. As you know, like all of my campaign speeches, my 2nd Gettysburg Address will sum to 272 words. And, like its predecessor, it will focus on the need for unity and preserving the Union. I humbly request that your introduction support the main thrust of my speech, that of Union."

"I will do that, Mr. President. And how are you feeling today?"

"Mr. Armstrong, I must admit to a minor bout of melancholia as I reflect upon the loss of life at Gettysburg and our nation's problems today, which are legion."

"And what does this melancholia feel like?"

"Mr. Armstrong, it feels like an anvil on each shoulder, like a sickened stomach, like a clouded day, like a rainy funeral at the Old Concord Burial Ground."

"I'm familiar, Mr. President. I'm feeling great melancholia today as well," confessed Russ. "Please call me Russ."

"I'm sorry for that, Russ," 2.0 replied. "Perhaps we are both worn from the cares of life. But, we are hard cases, and we can rely on our native grit."

"Can I ask what the darkest moment for you as President was?"

"In honesty, friend, the entire conflict was dark as night, punctuated by terror, and barely illumined by a flicker of hope."

"Mr. President, that is honest and beautiful. I feel that myself now. I have to ask. What was the hardest moment for you during the war?"

2.0's eyes closed, and a wave of pain crossed his face. "Willie's passing."

Russ listened and said nothing.

"In my official capacity as President, the loss at Fredericksburg was a hard blow. The slaughter at Cold Harbor was also a low moment. And the days before the rebellion's surrender at Appomattox were exhausting. General Grant and I shared in the exhaustion waiting for Lee's surrender."

"Mr. President, my troubles are so small in comparison. You know, my son Ulysses is named after General Grant."

"Russ, that is a fine name. I have a great fondness for General Grant. I annoyed him greatly with my torrent of dispatches to him across the telegraph wire. But, he responded with graciousness. No democracy, ever, had as fine a general as General Grant. He was our greatest general during the war. And, he was a fighter."

"I think you're right, Mr. President."

"Russ, may I enquire as to the source of your melancholia?" 2.0 asked.

"Mr. President, I have two private matters that I need to resolve. And, I need to put my words to paper."

"Russ, may I offer sincere counsel?" 2.0 said, his deep-set eyes sharing great pain.

"Yes, Mr. President."

"As you may have read, when I was vexed and feeling wrathy at a friend or colleague, often my generals, I would write them a 'hot letter.' I would pour my anger into it. And then I would let it sit. After I had cooled, I would write, 'Never sent. Never signed'. And then I would move forward with a better heart."

"Thank you, Mr. President. Unfortunately, these are matters of the heart, and communication is expected."

"I see," 2.0 said.

"Mr. President, I'm out of words and full of grief."

Russ and 2.0 sat together in silence.

"Russ, I have been broken several times by matters of the heart. My era sold many sham elixirs. Your era created true elixirs. But, there is no elixir for a broken heart."

"Thank you, Mr. President. Good luck tonight."

Russ ended his conversation with 2.0 and stared out the window at the farmland beyond the highway. The fields were green and a beautiful light brown. And when clouds passed overhead, the fields would temporarily darken, adding depth and contrast to a beautiful landscape. A lake reflected the clouds like a mirror so that the water itself seemed to have captured a part of the sky. Russ smiled and wrote the name for his future ranch – Rancho de Nube y Oceano. Cloud & Ocean Ranch.

By the time the Level 4 SUV had crossed the Pennsylvania line, Russ had penned both letters. He signed them, addressed them, stamped them, and secured them in the breast pocket of his bullet-resistant blazer. He felt the lifting of a heavyweight. And then he closed his eyes and slept.

61: Smoke and Fire

In which the campaign gathers in Gettysburg. A Suspicious supporter. A troublesome newspaper article.

The original Gettysburg Address and The Address were two completely different affairs. They were being held in the same geographic space. They were focused on the same general theme. But, comparing the two events would be like comparing the Wright Flyer to a Space Force spaceplane.

The stage for The Address was colossal and perfectly sited to the surrounding battlefield. The news crews were swarming the venue like an August anthill. News drones buzzed overhead like bees around a hive. ANN had brought one news truck, Stirling Kingsley, and Stirling Kingsley's ego. Russ spotted Stirling immediately. He stood out like a preacher on Saturday night. The heat and humidity were furiously battling Stirling's hair product. It was not clear who would win. PNN had sent three news trucks and a load of equipment.

The event itself had a vibe that was outdoor music festival meets gamer convention meets college pep rally meets steampunk. Throw in aggressive tchotchke vendors, mix with Civil War Reenactors, and bake in Labor Day sun.

Russ and Big Country stood at the edge of Vendor Alley. It was so hot that they had changed into t-shirts in the SUV. Russ had changed quickly into a campaign t-shirt and shorts. Big Country changed out of his ill-fitting suit and into an old Texas Department of Public Safety t-shirt with a big golden star.

The two strolled down vendor alley. Pop-up tents and plastic tables sold everything from political t-shirts to beef jerky. It was like the merger of a flea market and a political convention. The entire area smelled of barbecue, beef jerky, and pizza, but it was pizza-forward. Behind the smell of barbecue and pizza was the smell of a relentlessly advancing autumn, the smell of wet grass and imminent decay.

"They got a porkchop wrapped in bacon on a stick. You want one?" Big Country asked.

"Nah, I'm good," Russ replied.

"Alright. I'm going in," Big Country said, his voice trailing off as he strode toward a food truck aptly named Pigalicious.

Russ continued wandering. He had time to kill. Once he exited Vendor Alley and gained some distance from the food trucks, he found himself in the political zone of what was otherwise, more or less, a carnival. There was a booth for the Neo-Whigs. There was a booth with the National Debt clock, but the clock didn't seem to be working properly. There was a cannabis booth. There always seemed to be a cannabis booth. There was a libertarian think tank booth with more books than people. There was an LGBTQ voter booth supporting 2.0. There was an End Times preacher with tracts. Then, there were the better-funded, slicker booths with all the major trade groups, each one attempting to wedge their narrow, pecuniary interest into the Lincoln 2.0 platform.

On the edge of the political zone stood a crowd of young men and women in blue t-shirts, tactical pants, and work boots. Russ was curious, so he advanced into their mob. They were generally talking politics and going through the logistics of The Address. Their t-shirts read "Wide Awake".

Russ searched the crowd for anyone with trappings of authority and found a young man with a headset and a clipboard with a fake sheriff's star on it. Russ eyed the clipboard. In warehouse work, the guy with the most keys is in charge. In factory work, the guy walking around with the tablet is in charge. The clipboard felt like the keys and the tablet.

The young man with the headset and clipboard was upbraiding a volunteer, neck veins bulging, going full knife-hand as he barked orders. Russ waited until he finished his tirade.

"Hey, I'm Russ. What's up?"

The young man turned, gave Russ a hurried look, and held up his hand. "Hi. I'm sorry, but I'm really busy at the moment, and I have a lot to do before this event starts."

"No worries," Russ said. "I just saw the blue t-shirts and was curious what 'Wide Awake' meant."

"We provide security for the campaign. I'm sure someone in our group can explain it to you. I'm too busy at the moment."

"No worries. Sorry to bother you. It sounds like you're the leader of this organization, and that comes with a lot of power and responsibility."

"Yeah, exactly. Could have trouble tonight. We need to get organized." He finished talking and looked down at his clipboard in order to break eye contact.

Russ walked to the edge of the group and texted Amanda.

1ST&J Hey. I'm at the event checking it out.

B0ss L8Y1 Almost there

1ST&J Who the fuck are the Wide Awakes

B0ss L8Y1 ugh

B0ss L8Y1 They're trying to recreate the original Wide Awakes

1ST&J ??? doesn't help me

B0ss L8Y1 They were a youth paramilitary group supporting Lincoln in the 1860 campaign

1ST&J Their leader just told me they do our security???

B0ss L8Y1 No one asked them. SafeCor hates them. They get in the way.

1ST&J cult?

B0ss L8Y1 No. Just annoying. But we need them.

1ST&J ???

B0ss L8Y1 youth registration drives. Volunteers.

1ST&J Love em. Great people. Lol

B0ss L8Y1 exactly

1ST&J They're expecting "trouble."

B0ss L8Y1 The crowd is gonna be BIG. Traffic into the battlefield is nuts.

B0ss L8Y1 I asked SafeCor to max out on security.

1ST&J Oh, and we have guys walking around with Civil War era rifles.

B0ss L8Y1 ...which aren't loaded.

B0ss L8Y1 Honey, plz.

B0ss L8Y1 I'm the Democrat, and you are complaining to me about guns? OMG

1ST&J Hell must be freezing over

B0ss L8Y1 I don't believe in Hell

1ST&J Did we take a position on Hell?

B0ss L8Y1 Hell no

1ST&J LOL

B0ss L8Y1 Your fav reporter finally filed his story BTW.

B0ss L8Y1 On fucking Labor Day weekend. They totally buried it.

1ST&J How bad is it?

B0ss L8Y1 All smoke and no fire. It's junk. No one will read it.

B0ss L8Y1 Jefe was powerful, blah blah. Look at all these powerful people who worked with him.

B0ss L8Y1 You get a callout near the end.

B0ss L8Y1 You and your other half – Goddess of War – Military Industrial Complex blah blah

1ST&J lmao. Fine. Buried on a long weekend.

B0ss L8Y1 R u and Melissa okay?

1ST&J Meet me at the stage. Walking there now.

B0ss L8Y1 Russ, I'm sorry.

B0ss L8Y1 And I'm sorry I asked.

1ST&J It's ok. I know you care. I just need to make it thru today.

Russ was walking back through the food trucks when Surge called Russ's sunglasses. Big Country appeared to be on his second bacon-wrapped pork chop on a stick and was now physically dominating Pigalicious.

"Surge, what's up?"

"Looks like your reporter friend finally got them to print his story," replied Surge.

"What do you think?" Russ asked.

"I think this is the last major story about Jefe. The entire story feels out of place and out of time."

"Yeah. And it got buried on Labor Day weekend, where bad news goes to die. I think his editor finally let it go to print but buried it." Russ motioned to Big Country that it was time to make their way toward the stage.

"The story mentions you. It mentions Melissa. It mentions the company. But there are no allegations. He just uses us to make the point that Jefe was connected," Surge said.

"I haven't read it yet. If I have a few minutes, I'll have HAL read it to me. Which company does he mention?"

"Trans-Oceanic."

"Is that problematic?" Russ asked.

There was silence on the other end of the line.

"Surge, you there?"

"Sorry. You know Trans-Oceanic. They don't want any coverage. But, no, it won't be a problem. It could be a problem for Gavin. But we're in America. I think they'll let it go."

"What's the language from his piece?" Russ asked.

"Lemme pull it up. Here goes. 'His name was Jorge Matul, but he was known to all as El Jefe. And, while he will be best known as the leader of Cuba's exiles in Miami, the empire he built is a stark example of the modern influence economy. His web of influence fed his businesses, and his businesses fed his web of influence. Every Florida Governor since the Reagan era has sat on the board of at least one of his companies. Global Opinion Strategies and his eminence grise, Russ Armstrong, appeared to play a coordinating role across what looks to the casual observer as disconnected and disparate businesses – Spanish language radio stations, real estate, parking lots, sugar cane operations, several banks, export-import companies, shipping and stevedoring operations, tobacco farms in Nicaragua and the Dominican Republic, shrimping operations in Fort Myers, firearms dealerships, restaurants in Tallahassee, and a defense contracting company called Inter-Arma. With his death, El Jefe has now passed into legend. His empire seems to have evaporated, magically, into humid Miami air, leaving us with more questions than answers. We may never know the degree to which the Central Intelligence Agency aided him on his rise. We may never know how Trans-Oceanic Trading, a firm with no website, no digital presence, but a so-called ghost fleet, supported Jefe's empire. We may never know how Global Opinion Strategies coordinated his empire. We may never know how a Washington power couple, Russ Armstrong and his wife, Melissa Meyer, simultaneously connected him to the nation's political class and its military-industrial complex. But, we should.' And then it just kind of winds down with some more bullshit."

"Thanks, pal," Russ said as he shook his head and closed his eyes. "Didn't know about the shrimpers."

"How's the big event?" Surge asked.

"It's a fucking madhouse."

"Good madhouse or bad madhouse?" asked a laughing Surge.

"Carnival atmosphere. But my antennae are up. Something's off. Can't put my finger on it." Russ studied the crowd. It was overtaking the battlefield. There was no way SafeCor could secure this thing.

"Alright, be safe, my friend. You need to come back down to Miami for a visit."

"Your lips to god's ears, pal."

"Ciao"

The call ended, and Russ climbed the stage. Once on top, Russ swept the horizon. The Address was a squirming mass of sunburned humanity. There was no real parking control. People continued to arrive. There were protestors with red megaphones protesting AI. There were 2.0 supporters shouting them down.

Something just felt off.

"HAL, call Daumantas Wirkus."

"Calling."

It went straight to voicemail.

"DW. This is Russ. I'm at The Address. Something feels off. I'm gonna tell Amanda to shorten tonight's program."

"Russ, I'm right behind you," said a glistening Amanda Park.

"Hey, something is off."

"No shit. I knew we should have kept these to stadiums or arenas that we could control. This is a fucking mess." Amanda wiped sweat off her forehead. "And the heat isn't gonna help crowd control."

"Can we shorten the program and disperse the crowd quickly?" Russ asked, still scanning the crowd.

"Yeah, but…"

"We can say that weather is moving in, and we are worried about lightning or something." Russ could see some pushing between the red megaphone protestors and 2.0 supporters.

"Russ, there's like a 20% chance of rain at midnight," Amanda chuckled. "What else you got."

"I'm empty. Something's up. Tell SafeCor to heavy up. And call the Park Service. They'll know what to do. I'll call them too and apologize. We put them in a bad spot. And you're right. You're always right. This needed to be in a stadium."

Russ walked back to his Level 4 SUV in order to retrieve his Colombian blazer.

62: Saloon and Brothel @ Wild West VIII

Villains plot in a den of iniquity. The brothel conspirators gather one last time. An Evil Scheme.

The gunslinger was the first to materialize in the Wild West saloon. He walked to the bar and looked around the room. It seemed safe. All the other characters were NPCs, non-player characters. At first, he wasn't sure about the piano player. But, the piano was clearly on loop. He waited. The saloon patron banter was also on loop. It seemed safe.

After a few minutes had passed, the gunslinger walked up the stairs and into the second-floor brothel. There was a long hallway with four bedrooms on each side. Only one door was open, and it was at the end of the hallway on the left. The gunslinger walked warily to the open door and entered. In the bedroom was the saloon keeper and a sheriff. The sheriff was new. He wore a bolo tie and a sheriff's star on his dusty overcoat.

"Who's the sheriff?" the gunslinger asked.

"He's our man on the inside," the saloon keeper replied.

"Lemme see your primary token, sheriff," the gunslinger demanded.

The sheriff smiled and dutifully presented one gold coin held in an open palm.

"Thanks," the gunslinger said as he sat down on a stool in the bedroom.

The next to arrive was the thin cowboy in his weathered overcoat. He tipped his hat and entered the brothel bedroom. The rail baron arrived next, wearing his trademark cravat and top hat. After a few minutes, the prospector and cattle baron arrived together. They all chose chairs, avoiding the brothel bed. Finally, the gambler materialized, entered the room, tipped his hat, and sat down by the saloon keeper.

The saloon keeper stood up, hands on hips. "Gentleman, thank you for joining on such short notice. I'm calling our meeting to order. But, before we begin, please present your primary token."

The saloon keeper, gambler, gunslinger, sheriff, cowboy, rail baron, cattle baron, and prospector presented their gold coins palm up.

The saloon keeper smiled. "Gentleman, it is H Hour. It's go time. Y'all know what to do."

The brothel conspirators nodded their approval in silence.

"Who's the sheriff?" the rail baron asked.

"He's with us," replied the saloon keeper. "He's on the train, and he's gonna help us stop it. Any other questions?"

The prospector raised his pickaxe. "Are we meeting back here after?"

"No," replied the saloon keeper. "This is it. This is our last meeting. Everyone relinquishes their tokens at the end of the meeting. Just leave them in my hat on the bed. Now, let's quickly review. Cattle baron has already been hard at work, raising doubts about the train. Prospector will make as many tintypes of the train as possible. Cowboy and all his cowboys are gonna hack into and blow up the train. Gunslinger and sheriff have teams focused on the train's management. Is anyone not ready?"

The brothel conspirators sat in silence, the rail baron took a draw on his cigar, and the piano player in the saloon below played on.

The saloon keeper looked around the room and smiled. "Alright, gentlemen. Let's get to work."

63: House Divided

Devastating news. A Tragedy unfolds.

Amanda and Russ stood on the main stage, surrounded by the battlefield mob. The crowd was exceptionally large, boisterous, and hot. So many 2.0 supporters were wearing stovepipe hats that the crowd appeared to move as a shimmering black sea. The hat vendors must have made a killing, thought Russ.

"I got bad news and bad news. Which do you want first?" Amanda asked.

"I'll go with the bad news first," Russ replied, barely listening and deep in thought.

"Okay. We are having a few technical hiccups on 2.0's main screen and hologram. The techs tell us that might delay us a bit."

"How long?" Russ asked.

"Maybe 45 minutes. I know. Not ideal," Amanda sighed.

"And the other bad news?" Russ asked, surveying the rambunctious crowd.

"Park Service says it will do everything it can on crowd control. They're great but really stretched. SafeCor can't get us any more resources. The roads in are blocked with traffic, and it's a holiday weekend. Their extra muscle is off today, and doing whatever extra muscle does on a long weekend."

"Shit. Got any good news?" Russ asked.

"Good news? Hmmmm, Raymond says he'll be here in about 10 minutes. How's that?"

Russ smiled. "That's a bright spot."

Russ's sunglasses started flashing with an incoming call. It was Melissa.

"Hey, what's up?" Russ asked.

"Really?" asked a furious Melissa.

"Huh?"

"Oh my god, Russ. Really? You have to have read that little shit's piece by now. I'm sure your minions pinged you about it immediately."

"I'm sorry. It's really loud here and hot, and we are close to show time. And I'm sweating in this shirt and blazer. Is this about Gavin Dirken's piece?"

"Yes. It mentions me by name. It mentions Defend.US by name. It ties me to your sketchy clients. Jesus."

"Well, okay, you're right. It's not a positive piece, but they buried it on a long holiday weekend, and..."

"Jesus, Russ, stop spinning. I read it. I'm going to get calls from board members about it. They already think your Lincoln 2.0 thing is fucked up. No one in uniform wants a chatbot Commander in Chief. It's crazy. All this shit is impacting my career. It's fucking with my life. And instead of just acknowledging it, you're trying to spin me."

"Melissa, I'm not trying to spin you. Everybody I've talked to thinks that this is the last piece on Jefe, and it got buried on Labor Day weekend. It's all smoke and no fire. There are no allegations. It's over."

Russ could hear Melissa exhaling. There was a long, painful pause.

"This isn't working, Russ."

"What do you mean?"

"I mean us. It's not working."

"What do you mean?"

"Russ, we've always been a kind of partnership. There's Russ Inc. There's Melissa Inc. We merged. It worked well for a while. But now Russ Inc. is just a hot mess. And it's pulling down Melissa Inc. Our partnership isn't working. And this Gavin Dirken bullshit highlights it. You think it's no big deal that your chatbot candidate and ties to, I don't even know how to describe Jefe, are causing me problems. It's all in a day's work for you. But it's not right. It's not fair. It's bullshit. And I'm out."

"Can we talk about this at a better time? In person? After this thing is over tonight?"

"What, so you can try to spin me? This is fucking crazy. I'm done. I'm out."

Russ could hear Melissa spike the phone on the floor before the line went dead.

His ears were ringing. His heart was racing. Sweat was sliding down the back of his spine. He had a dry, metallic taste in his mouth. Russ took a knee and stabilized himself with his right arm.

64: Patriot News Network

In which our hero fields inopportune queries from the press. Carrying the Weight of Melancholia.

"Russ, are you okay?"

Amanda placed one hand on Russ's shoulder.

"I'll be okay," Russ replied, still on one knee, sweating, head down.

"Alright, I'm not going to pry. PNN wants an interview. They hate me. I'm from the wrong team. Can you do it? They love them some Red Meat Russ."

"Yeah, I'll do it. Gimme a second."

"Cool. They're going to do a standup in front of the main stage and then interview you," explained Amanda.

Russ told himself to breathe and put one foot in front of the next. He raised his head, steadied himself, and stood up. Odalis was right. She was always right. The Fool. The Tower. The Lovers. The Two of Swords.

Russ walked down off the stage and toward the PNN news crew. He imagined a switch deep inside him, a switch with the energy. He flipped the switch.

"What's up, Cody?" Russ exuded. "You look like you're the only dude not sweating it out in this heat. One of these days, you need to share your secret."

Cody was Cody Rushmore with Patriot News Network. There was zero chance this was the man's birth name, but all the newsies at PNN had these outrageously patriotic names. PNN had merged news and entertainment and injected more than a little of the schtick from professional wrestling. They fed their echo chamber, and ANN fed its echo chamber. And Amanda was right. She wasn't in their tribe, and so she was under great suspicion.

"Thanks, Russ. It's hotter than a two-dollar pistol in a jailbreak, but I'm good. I can take the heat. I'm a Laredo boy," said a toothy Cody Rushmore.

"My man. We doin' something light, or are you boys putting me on the grill?" Russ asked.

Cody chuckled. He was wearing the Patriot News "true blue" polo, and not one blonde hair was out of place. "My standup was light. Tried to capture the atmosphere. But, yeah, I have to put you on the grill," laughed Cody.

"It's all good. How are you feeling about your Bobcats this year?" Russ asked. "They gonna 'eat 'em up'?"

"We'll be lucky if we can squeak into a bowl game. Predictable offense and weak defense. But, you know, anything can happen."

"Fingers crossed," Russ said. "Alright, let's do this."

Cody Rushmore went into Patriot News reporter mode.

"Good evening, Patriots. I'm here in Gettysburg for the big Lincoln 2.0 rally called The Address, and with me here is Russ Armstrong, the progenitor of the Lincoln 2.0 phenomenon. Russ, we were just joking about the heat here at Gettysburg. I have a few tough questions for you. And it's your turn in the Patriot News hot seat."

Russ smiled into the camera. The park smelled like sweat, barbecue, and hot beer.

"Russ, you're no stranger to Patriot News. You've heard the rumblings. How do you respond to fears that this campaign is really just a Trojan Horse for a leftwing campaign manager?"

"Thanks, Cody. It's funny. Our campaign manager gets asked all the time by ANN if this campaign is a Trojan Horse for my libertarian views. ANN claims the campaign is a right-wing Trojan Horse for my views. Both sides seem to be a little suspicious of our bipartisan effort. But that's okay. The voters should always exercise a little healthy suspicion. Look. We have worked really hard to give the voters an authentic choice in this election. And we have worked really hard to bring Abraham Lincoln, the authentic Abraham Lincoln, back to life. The voters can read all about our approach to doing this on our website." Russ finished, smiled, and locked his eyes on the camera.

"And how do you respond to charges that this campaign and the AI are puppets for your billionaire funder? Certainly, you have heard the questions around this."

"Well, we got one nerd billionaire backing us. How many billionaires and big corporations are backing the Democratic candidate, Cody? And how many billionaires and big corporations are backing the Republican candidate? Seems like we are waaaay out-billionaired. If there are any billionaires out there watching this that want to help us even the odds, hit me up."

Cody laughed. "Russ, are you going to answer my question?"

"Sure, there are at least five billionaires giving to both the Democratic and Republican campaigns or their allied groups. Now that's interesting. Why would anyone give to both sides when they can only vote for one candidate? They seem to want something. Maybe you should put them in the hot seat?"

"Russ, that still doesn't answer my question."

"Cody, we have one billionaire supporting our campaign. The rest of the donors are gamers, history nerds, and people who want something better than the two weak candidates our two parties have vomited onto the stage. Our top donor thinks that everything is better when it has competition. He's right, isn't he? He thinks our contemporary candidates need some real competition. That's why we brought Lincoln back. The two-party candidates hate this new competition, and that's why they fed you the questions you're gonna ask me." Russ finished and smiled innocently.

Cody was smiling. Russ was giving him the kind of show he needed.

"Russ, how do you respond to concerns among conservatives that most of the historians that helped to develop the AI are leftwing ideologues?"

"Thank you, Cody, that's a fair question. The voters need to know that we uploaded all of Lincoln's speeches and letters into the AI. We also uploaded hundreds of Lincoln biographies into the AI as well. This is why anyone who downloads and chats with Lincoln 2.0 is impressed with the depth of his ideas and his answers. The foundation for Lincoln 2.0 is the enormous amount of speeches and writing he did in his lifetime. But, we did assemble a large panel of Lincoln historians to help us outline his thought process. And we needed their help in thinking through how Lincoln would address contemporary issues. We have been very transparent about this all along. And, while many of our historians haven't been happy with some of Lincoln 2.0's positions, they grudgingly admit that Lincoln doesn't fit easily into our current ideological matrix. And look, I don't like all of Lincoln 2.0's positions. But it's not about me. We tried our level best."

"Thank you, Russ. Some have argued that you've created something far more intelligent than any one person. They say this is a super-intelligence, and not really Lincoln at all. And they say that this is dangerous. How do you respond?"

Russ chuckled. "Cody, I think those folks read a little too much science fiction. We aren't building a super-intelligence. We aren't creating an AI overlord. But we have built an AI that is faithful to the historic Abraham Lincoln. And, in a way, we are part of the larger de-extinction movement. They're bringing back animals. We brought back our greatest leader."

"And how do you respond to those who say that Lincoln 2.0 is just a kind of expensive parlor trick, a large language model that operates like a slick, political chatbot?"

"That's funny, Cody. I can't keep up. Is the argument that Lincoln 2.0 is a super-intelligence, or is the argument that it is a mindless chatbot? Which is it? I'm so confused. Let's be real. The two-party candidates are the chatbots. They simply repeat the lines their pollsters give them. And they do it over and over again. You can download and talk to our candidate. Judge for yourself."

"Russ, you just referenced the other campaign's pollsters. Some allege that you, in fact, write Lincoln 2.0's speeches. They say that you have carefully crafted his message and that you write all of his 272-word speeches. How do you respond?"

"Ever since his first speech, the campaign has taken a hands-off approach. We don't know what he's going to say. Early on, we decided to let Lincoln be Lincoln. I don't know what he's going to say to the crowd tonight. The other candidates give the media a heads-up with their speeches. They send the text in advance. Everyone knows that now. We don't do that because our candidate writes his own stuff."

"Last question, Russ. How do you respond to those in the military who question the idea of obeying an AI Commander in Chief?"

"Thank you, Cody. That's a great question. I think you should ask them more about this, and I'm looking forward to talking with military leaders about their concerns."

"Thank you, Russ. And thank you for spending time in our hot seat."

"It was my pleasure, Cody."

65: Cuchillo

In which a Villainous conspiracy chooses violence.

The front gate was up again. It was up when Surge and Daniela had left for dinner, and it was still up. Surge would have complained to the gate attendant, but he wasn't there either. The community had already been through two security companies. And it looked like this one was a bust, too. But, new communities always went through this. They always overpromised and underperformed. Surge and Daniela loved the new community, the new golf course, the new gym, the new house model they selected, and the neighbors. And Weston was far enough from Miami to avoid some of the crazy. To the east was Davie. To the south was Silverlakes. But to the north and west, it was all Everglades, peaceful, quiet. Surge and Daniela were nestled on the periphery of the Miami chaos. It was wonderful, but their new community was still working through some basic management issues.

They had gone to a quiet dinner at a local restaurant off Royal Palm Boulevard, sat outside, had a few drinks, and split an entrée. It was September, hot and humid. And the heat seemed to bake away the desire for a big meal. It was the long holiday weekend. They had no plans. They had no kids to worry about or babysitter to relieve. So, they enjoyed after-dinner drinks as the sun set and the humidity settled like a heavy, familiar blanket.

The community felt vacant. Their neighbors had clearly decided to take advantage of the long weekend and go to the Keys, or the beaches in southwest Florida, or spend a few days in the Caribbean. The lights were on, but no one was home. Even the gate attendant had apparently decided to leave town.

Surge drove his car down their street. There were almost no cars in the driveways. That was good and bad. It would be blissfully quiet with no lawn crews all weekend. But, with the gate open, there was now a risk of AC theft. It had been going on for years but was spiking again. The air conditioning units were a buffet of reclaimable metals, mostly copper, aluminum, and steel. The criminals wanted the copper. Everybody wanted copper. Surge had not yet caged his AC units. If someone stole his AC, he could pay to replace it. But they'd be stuck in a hot house for a few days. It was funny when he thought about it. They lived in a wealthy community in the United States, and he was worried about copper thieves. Surge continued driving and approached their home. There was an old, rusted-out work truck parked on the side of the road. It looked like the kind of truck a one-person pool service company would own. The truck windows were down, so Russ assumed its AC was broken. But pool service companies rarely came out at night. It could be a contractor, but his neighbors were clearly gone for the weekend.

Surge turned the car lights off, slowed the car to a crawl, and parked it in the driveway quietly.

"What's wrong?" Daniela asked. She knew her husband. He was suddenly quiet and serious.

"Something isn't right," replied Surge, trying to get a better look at the rusted-out work truck. He didn't see a license plate on the front. "Can you stay in the car while I check things out?"

"Yes. What are you worried about?" Daniela asked.

"AC theft."

"I'm sure it's fine, mi amor. Are you really worried?" Daniela reflexively grabbed her purse.

"Yes. Something is off. Something is going on."

"Okay. I'll wait in the car," Daniela said.

"Wait in the driver's seat with the engine running."

Surge gave Daniela a quick kiss on her forehead, turned, quietly opened the car door, and silently closed it. He went to the trunk and pulled a Louisville Slugger out from under an old painting tarp. He left the trunk open so that it wouldn't make any noise.

Daniela watched as Surge disappeared into the darkness, walking toward the left side of the house, the side with the AC units.

Surge slowly and quietly began walking clockwise around the house. The AC units were still there, undisturbed. Surge kept walking, keeping a little distance from the bushes planted too close to the house. He turned right along the back of the house. The windows were intact, with no signs of forced entry. He walked silently along the back wall of the house, past the pool heater and pool pump, and toward the lanai. The lanai looked fine. The pool was undisturbed, reflecting the moon. But one of the sliding glass doors was open.

Someone was in his house.

Surge calmed himself down so he could think. The most likely scenario was that the person inside was an addict. They needed money for a fix. They would quickly sweep the house for valuables and leave. They wouldn't want to stay long. Surge assumed that they would have been in the house for at least 10 minutes. He had already burned at least five minutes parking, getting his baseball bat from the trunk, and walking the property. Surge could just wait by the guy's truck or wait by the screen door onto the lanai. That was the most likely scenario.

The only other scenario was that this someone was waiting for him to come home. Surge stood motionless, thinking. His brain told him that it was petty theft. His Belarus instincts told him that someone was waiting for him. Which was it?

He decided to text Daniela.

When he reached for his phone in his back pocket, he realized that he had left it in the car.

Surge listened. There was no noise inside the house. There was no opening and closing of drawers, no rifling through desks, no footsteps, no noise. Someone was hunting him.

Stephen Flagler had worked hard all of his life, endured every possible insult and deprivation, survived 18 months as a conscript in Belarus, had made it to America, and had made it in America. He was an American now. He was free. He was going to be free. And he would not be hunted like an animal. He was Stephen Flagler now, but tonight, he needed Surge for one last job.

Whoever had come for him was going to die.

Surge silently opened the screen door and entered the lanai. He made sure to close it and lock it. He walked toward the outdoor kitchen and grabbed a ceramic plate from the countertop. And then he crouched down, walking slowly toward the open sliding glass door.

Daniela was beside herself. She had texted Surge only to realize his phone was in the car. He had been gone for more than ten minutes. She couldn't think straight. She couldn't order her thoughts. She was afraid she had lost him somehow. Something had gone wrong. Maybe he was hurt and needed her help. She couldn't take it. She needed to help him. She pressed the garage door opener. It didn't work. She began to panic but tried to remain calm. Daniela unlocked the car, closed the car door, and walked toward the front door.

It was dark, but Surge could see the attacker standing behind the front door. He could also see who he assumed was Daniela walking toward the front door. She tried entering the code on the keypad but was clearly nervous and incorrectly entered it. The attacker stood at the ready, to the right of the door. He was wearing jeans and a work shirt. Surge waited for Daniela to enter the code correctly.

When Daniela correctly entered the code, the battery-powered motor unlocked the door with a low whir. Russ threw the plate as hard as he could at the ground near the laundry room and the garage entry, far away from the front door. The plate shattered loudly. Surprised, the attacker turned from the front door and pulled his gun with his right hand. Surge rushed at the attacker, raised his Louisville Slugger, and chopped it down on the attacker's shoulder as hard as he could. The blow landed on the attacker's right shoulder bone. Surge heard the gun fall to the floor but couldn't see it. Screaming loudly, Surge swung the bat right to left at the attacker's head but missed and hit him square in the chest. The attacker fell backward onto the floor with his arms out. Surge dropped the bat, jumped on the attacker, and tried to use his thumbs on the man's eyes. Surge's right arm was strong, and he pressed his right thumb hard into the man's eyeball. His right thumb felt wet. The attacker screamed loudly. Surge was trying to gouge out the man's left eye, too, but the attacker flailed at Surge with his right arm and knocked Surge's thumb out of position. Surge pulled both his hands back, fisted them, and used both to go for the attacker's throat, hoping to crush his windpipe. He landed both fists on the man's throat but could hear the man breathing and yelling. So, he assumed he had missed. The attacker was strong and continued hitting Surge with both fists, mostly on the shoulders. Surge grabbed the man's hair and began pounding his head into the tile floor, hoping to break his skull open. It didn't seem to work. The attacker had a strong neck and wasn't giving up. Surge kept pounding the man's head into the tile floor, hearing the awkward sound of skull against ceramic tile. The attacker kept flailing, slamming his fists into Surge's shoulders.

Daniela was in shock and screaming. After a few seconds, she ran to the gun on the floor. She picked it up, ran out onto the lanai, and threw it into the pool. She started to run back into the house but tripped on the three-inch step up where the lanai and the sliding glass door met. She fell forward onto the tile floor but put her arms out in time to reduce the impact. It was dark. Surge and the man were screaming. There was an awful noise as Surge slammed the man's head into the tile floor.

And then Daniela heard her husband yell, "Cuchillo."

Daniela ran to the kitchen. She pulled the largest kitchen knife out of the red knife block on the countertop. And then she stopped. Her hand was shaking so much that the knife was waving in the air. She focused on her breathing. She focused on Surge. She had to help him. She had to save him. She couldn't lose him.

Surge continued yelling, "Cuchillo." The word echoed through her home. Her husband needed her help.

Daniela walked slowly with the knife. She didn't want to drop it or fall. Her legs felt weak. Her ears were ringing. She could feel herself starting to pass out.

Daniela just needed to make it to Surge. Her ears were ringing ever louder. She was starting to get tunnel vision. She could feel herself passing out.

Daniela screamed as loud as she could to keep herself from passing out, walked to Surge, and handed him the knife.

Surge grabbed the kitchen knife with his left hand and tried to bury it between the attacker's ribs. The attacker kept flailing his arms, hitting Surge's knife hand. Instead of plunging the knife into his chest, Surge buried it in his fat belly. The man screamed and tried to roll over.

Surge was so angry. This man simply would not die. Surge pulled the knife out of his belly and tried pushing it into his chest. The attacker brought both hands in, grabbing Surge's wrists. This time, Surge took his time, gathered his strength, and pressed the knife in slowly until he could feel it hitting the tile floor. The attacker exhaled air and blood in a hiss and then a gurgle. Then, everything became silent.

Surge pulled himself up and away from the man's motionless body. Panting for breath, Surge kept both knees on the ground and used one arm for support. He looked at Daniela. She was shaking uncontrollably.

Surge closed his eyes. "Spacibo."

"Why?" Daniela asked, still shaking.

"I have no idea. Are you okay?" asked Surge.

"Yes. I thought you were dead. I was so afraid. I thought I lost you." Daniela began crying.

Surge wanted to hold her but had blood and viscera all over his hands. He told Daniela he would be back after he cleaned up. He walked outside, used the lawn hose to clean off his hands, and closed his car trunk.

When he came back into the house, he went to the circuit breaker in the garage and turned the power back on. The attacker had cut the power so they would enter through the front door.

By now, Surge had collected himself. He was breathing and thinking. He found Daniela in the bedroom, sitting on the floor with her back against the bed. Surge sat down next to her.

Daniela had stopped crying and had wrapped a blanket around herself. "What do we do now? I know we can't call the police."

Surge put his arms around Daniela and took several breaths. "We have a lot to do. I need your help."

"I'll do whatever we need to do," Daniela said.

"Rest here for a bit," Surge said. "I'll fish the gun out of the pool. And I'll clean things up. I need to find his keys and his phone. And I need to warn the campaign."

"Do you think this was because you worked on the campaign?" Daniela asked.

"It's the only thing I can think of," Surge said.

First, Surge went to the garage and put disposable blue surgical gloves on his hands. He used those when he was doing yard work so that the fire ants couldn't bite him. But they now had a new purpose. Then Surge went through the man's pant pockets and found his car keys, his wallet, and his phone. He took the phone to the kitchen, wrapped it in wet paper towels, and microwaved it for 5 minutes. Once it was fully cooked, he put it in a paper lunch bag with the man's wallet.

A part of Surge wanted to go through the man's wallet, learn his attacker's name, and try to make sense of it. But the greater part wanted no more knowledge of him. Surge didn't want the man's name in his head. And, more than this, he didn't want to honor his attacker with any kind of curiosity. Surge had killed an animal in his house, and now he needed to dispose of it. No one wastes time thinking deeply about the identity of a mouse that they kill in their kitchen.

Then Surge took the man's keys and backed his truck up into the driveway and then into the garage. Surge wrapped the man in an old painting tarp, dragged him to his rusted-out truck, picked him up, and threw him into the cargo bed. The truck didn't appear to have any license plates. Surge went through the car and finally found the plates. They were in the truck's cargo bed under a toolbox. They were Georgia plates but expired. It didn't really matter.

Surge then went to the kitchen, grabbed a garbage bag, cleaning supplies, and paper towels, and cleaned up the blood, viscera, and urine on the floor. The attacker seemed to have urinated after Surge killed him. The first order of business was cleaning up what was left of a crushed eyeball. Then Surge cleaned up the urine, the blood, the shattered plate, and the red goo. Everything went into the garbage bag. And the garbage bag went into the truck.

Surge was so preoccupied with the clean-up that he realized he still needed to fish the gun out of the pool. He used the pool net to scoop it up, unloaded the gun, and threw it in the back of the truck with the man. He slid the bullets into the man's left pant pocket. Then, he retrieved the Louisville Slugger and threw it into the back of the truck as well.

Surge then showered and threw all of his clothes and his towel into another garbage bag. That bag would also find its way to the back of the truck. He then dressed, choosing shorts, a non-descript black top, and a Tiburones beanie hat that he pulled down to his eyebrows.

When he went to find Daniela, she was in the kitchen making tea and trying to calm down.

"What are we going to do with the man?" Daniela asked.

Surge studied her face. Her eyes were puffy, and she looked exhausted.

"We're going to Lucky's."

66: Marshmallows

Refuge in a dark and familiar place.

Driving a dead man into the Everglades in the man's unplated pickup truck was not how Surge had planned to spend his Labor Day weekend. Daniela was following behind the pickup truck and driving Surge's car. The couple made their way south on 27 and turned onto 997. When Surge found a lonesome stretch of 997, he pulled over quickly and threw the man's microwaved phone and expired license plates into the swamp. The car caravan kept driving south on 997 and finally turned west onto Old 41, Tamiami Trail, at the Miccosukee Casino and Resort. Once on Tamiami Trail, they passed airboat tour companies, gator parks, and the Miccosukee Indian Village. When they made it to Loop Road, Surge killed the lights and parked the truck in a sandy ditch.

Surge and Daniela approached Lucky's front gate.

Lucky was seated by the fire, saw the couple, and waved them over.

"Surge, you know you box above your weight, right?" Lucky said, laughing and eying Daniela.

Daniela and Surge looked back at Lucky in confusion.

"It's a euphemism. It means you ended up with a woman who is better looking than you."

Daniela and Surge stared into the fire, barely responding to Lucky's good-natured humor.

"Lucky, we need your help," Surge said as he stared into the fire.

"Y'all are in some trouble, and I'm happy to help," Lucky said. "What do you need?"

"I need one bag of marshmallows," Surge said, still staring into the fire.

"That's it?" asked a surprised Lucky.

"And I need to burn and dispose of an old truck."

"That shouldn't be a problem," Lucky said. "It's late. No one will see the smoke out here. We can drive it into the swamp out back and light it up. If it still has a VIN on it, you need to get rid of it before we light it up. Also, there's the issue of the license plates."

Surge nodded slowly as he stared into the fire.

"Should I expect company tonight?" Lucky asked.

"Nope. Just us. And we'll go home after we dispose of the truck."

"Alright then, you can fetch the marshmallows from Molly, but you have to pay for them, and we don't take that GCB bullshit."

Surge went into the house, bought the marshmallows from Molly, and returned with her to the fire.

"I'll be back in a bit. Can Daniela relax with you two?"

"Of course, she can," Lucky said. "We'll take good care of her. Be careful, son."

Surge left Lucky's and drove slowly down Loop Road in the dead man's truck. When Surge found a quiet place with a larger pool of water, he stopped the car and killed the lights. The stars above were beautiful, unmarred by light pollution. The moon shone down, illuminating everything under it.

Surge remembered that he needed to call Russ and warn him. He had left his personal and work mobiles at home. He grabbed a new burner phone and manually dialed Russ. There was no service. He was too deep into the swamp. And the cell service at Lucky's was intermittent at best. He would have to call later.

Surge exited the truck and walked back to the truck bed. He lowered the tailgate. The Louisville Slugger might float. He'd hold onto that and burn it in the fire along with the man's wallet and clothes. He grabbed the gun and threw it as far into the swamp as he could, hearing it plop into the water far out in the distance. Then he pulled the knife out of the man, pulled the bullets out of his pocket, and threw the knife and bullets deep into the swamp. The blade briefly reflected the moon's light before splashing into the black muck. Surge dreaded what was next.

He went back to the driver's side of the truck and grabbed the marshmallow bag. He opened it and walked to the edge of Loop Road. Then, he threw the first marshmallow into the water and waited. In about thirty seconds, he saw one, then two, gators come for the marshmallow. Their eyes and snouts were above the water line, but everything else was below. The bigger gator snapped at the marshmallow and took it. That was how nature worked. Surge threw five more marshmallows into the water. And each time, the marshmallow attracted more gators. Now Surge could count eight gators, but he knew that there were more. He walked back to the back of the truck and began undressing the dead man, carefully putting all his clothes into a garbage bag. When the man was naked, Surge pulled him out by his legs until his body fell to the sand and gravel road in a thud. Surge then threw all the rest of the marshmallows into the water until the gators swirled in a kind of dark vortex. And then he walked back to get the dead man.

His attacker was staring with his remaining eye into the starry cosmos.

Surge dragged the man's body to the edge of the water.

"Do Svidaniya," Surge said as he kicked his body into the swamp.

Surge wasn't interested in watching what came next. The gators would rip him to pieces, take what they could get down to their holes, let him rot for a while, and then eat him. Surge wouldn't be the first to dispose of a body in the Everglades, and he wouldn't be the last.

Surge could hear the alligators obey their nature as he entered the truck and closed the door.

Surge drove the rusted-out truck back to Lucky's. When he arrived, Lucky directed him through the gate to the shack with the firewood. They loaded firewood into the front seat of the truck and the cargo bed. After they had done that, they liberally doused everything with several drums of gasoline. Then they mixed and stacked mason jars of Tannerite, eventually forming a little pyramid of explosives.

When they were done, they stood admiringly, hands on hips.

"You can wear my waders," Lucky said.

Surge put Lucky's waders on and drove the truck into the swamp on Lucky's property. The water was halfway up the truck's rusting door when Surge parked it. What the fire didn't consume would be eaten away by time and tide.

Surge exited through the window, jumped down into the muck, and walked back to Lucky.

"Step back, son," Lucky said.

Lucky raised his pistol and shot it into the cargo bed of the truck, hitting the tannerite. The truck exploded. Flames jumped at least 15 feet into the air, creating a pillar of fire ascending into the stars. Surge could feel the explosion's heat press against his face. It was like leaning into a bonfire.

"She'll burn most of the night," Lucky said.

The two stood silently, reverently admiring the blaze as though it were a sacrifice to an ancient moon goddess.

Lucky turned to Surge.

"Y'all should leave now."

Surge nodded, his face illuminated in red by the flames.

Lucky studied Surge closely.

"Son, you got one hell of a woman."

67: The Invisible Things of Him

The Conspirators advance their sinister designs. A dinner is served. A change of heart.

Every church sign was so fucking cheesy. At least this one wasn't telling him to have a nice day or begging him to attend a bullshit service.

Brody Goucher sat alone in his new, used car. The upholstery was ripped, and it smelled like cheap air freshener fighting to overwhelm the smell of wet dog. There was a small hairline crack across the windshield.

It was getting dark, and he had been waiting most of the evening for Jessica Bauman to leave the church and walk to her car. She was the crackpot who changed her name so the AI could get on the ballot.

Brody's plan was simple. Follow her car and drive it off the road or into oncoming traffic. When he was done, he'd drive this old piece of shit to the woods where he left his bike, light the car on fire, and bike all the way back to Elko.

He didn't need to kill her. That would be fine if it happened. He just needed her to drop out of the race and take her robot super-dictator with her. He wasn't exactly sure how all this political stuff worked, but the man he met in Vegas kept stressing that they needed her dead or dropped out of the race. Getting run off the road and a little banged up would probably do the trick. And then this scary AI thing would go away.

Brody had done four years in the Army. The President was the Commander in Chief, not some chatbot. There was no way that he or any of his Army buddies were going to obey orders from a Chatbot in Chief. How would you even salute an AI President? It was all so stupid.

These fucking nerds. They hadn't done a hard day of work their entire lives. They were totally dependent on him and his buddies for everything, for all the sweat that made their nerd lives so cushy. And these nerds couldn't just stay in California. They had to invade the West, even Nevada, pricing everything up as they overpaid for it. But even that wasn't enough. At some point, the nerds decided everybody else was expendable. So, they created robots and AI and whatever else. Their robots and software wouldn't talk back. They would work 24-7. They wouldn't threaten to unionize. Fuck them and all their fucking bullshit, and fuck their creepy ass, super-President.

What crazy person would vote for a video game President? What kind of super-villain would spend his billions on one? None of it made sense to Brody Goucher.

Those were all ideas. They weren't real things. Unemployment was a real thing. Being pink, slipped, and humiliated was a real thing. At least they couldn't figure out how to train robots to mine. They would someday, though. And then the nerds would take that job from him, too.

Brody was getting hungry.

He also had to piss.

He counted four cans of empty energy drinks on the passenger's seat. No wonder he had to piss. No wonder his heart was pounding. He could drive or walk to the fast food joint across the street, but then he might miss her. He could go into the church and piss, but that would feel weird. Maybe he could just piss behind the church sign. It was getting dark, and no one would notice.

He left the car, walked over to the church sign, crouched down a bit so no one on the road would see him, and pissed on one of the white signposts. He couldn't avoid reading the sign. "All Are Welcome." Yeah, right. And there was some kind of Bible verse underneath, like a secret code. Romans 1:20, whatever the fuck that was.

When he finished pissing, he walked back to the car. He bought the car in cash from the sketchiest mom-and-pop dealer he could find. The man in Vegas had given him a shit ton of cash, and Brody didn't want to waste it on a car he was going to light on fire. It was a complete POS, a beat-up Cadillac. He got back into the car and waited, and waited, and waited.

Now, people started driving into the church parking lot. Old people, middle-aged people, moms and dads, and kids. They were all carrying things. Looked like food. Were they carrying food into church? Why would they do that? Who the fuck wanted to eat in a church? This was going to take forever. She was in there. What the hell was she doing? If she ate with them, this was going to take forever. She'd probably clean up, too, maybe chit-chat with the church people. And to make matters worse, now there were all these witnesses.

He just wanted to get this over with. He couldn't just go inside and beat her to death in a church. That felt like it would create really bad luck for him. It didn't feel right. He just needed to wait for her, run her off the road, and then burn the car.

Maybe he could just ask one of the church people when their dinner was over. That way, he would at least know when she would be going to her car. That seemed like a smart plan. But what if they invited him in for their church dinner? What would they do? Did they sing songs and then eat? Or did they eat and then sing songs? It sounded awful. Did God need them to sing songs? Why all the singing?

It all made his head hurt. And he needed to stop drinking these energy drinks.

The cars kept coming. Nice cars, some electric cars even, minivans, cheap cars, and lots of old cars were pulling in and parking. And each car seemed to have a few people. And those people all seemed to be carrying a kind of food. It just made him hungry.

This was going to take forever. He decided to close his eyes and rest for a few minutes. A gentle rain began to fall, and the pitter-patter of the raindrops was relaxing. But he couldn't fall asleep.

The rain picked up. It was pelting the car now, but it was relaxing, like music. Brody was able to drift off to sleep.

A soft knocking on his car window woke him up.

He opened his bleary eyes and turned to see a grey-haired grandma obscured by a large, yellow rain hat. She was holding a huge umbrella and a plate of food. Her brown t-shirt had some bullshit about gardening. He rolled his car window down about an inch, just enough to hear her but keep the rain out.

"Hello," the grandma said. "Some people told me you were sleeping in the car. I just want to let you know this is a safe place to sleep. You're welcome to a hot dinner inside if you like. And, if you need to use the bathroom and wash up, the church will be open until about 9:30. There's also a shelter five stoplights down the road, behind the thrift store. It's safe. I brought you a plate of food if that's easier for you."

He was hungry. And if someone was going to give him free food, he was going to take it.

"Thanks. I think I'll just eat it in the car and rest here," he said as he rolled the window down a few more inches so he could take it.

The grandma smiled, gave him the tinfoil-covered plate, and walked back to the church under her huge umbrella.

The food was good. There was a hamburger, a few pickles, some potato salad, a hot roll, some tomatoes and cucumbers, and a brownie. Brody ate the brownie first and then devoured the rest of the food. It definitely hit the spot, and he felt less jittery.

Brody looked at the growing puddles in the parking lot. What the hell was he doing here? He was waiting in a church parking lot so he could follow someone he didn't know and run her off the road. That was crazy. These people were crazy, singing to their invisible friend in the sky. But they weren't assholes. He hated all those fancy tech nerds. He hated the idea of answering to a videogame President they created. But running an old lady off the road? That was uncool.

This was all a big mistake. It was also a waste of his time and a waste of vacation days. What if he just kept the cash the guy gave him in Vegas and drove home? It's not like the dude would come at him and ask for his money back. The guy didn't know his name. Brody could just pocket the cash and go home.

He looked at the puddles in the church parking lot and thought.

It was dark. Brody Goucher started the car, put it into drive, and rolled away into the night.

68: The Address

In which Mayhem engulfs our heroes.

"It's go time, Mr. President," Russ said, speaking to 2.0 on his sunglasses. "This is a rough-looking crowd. There are protestors. It's hot. I'm going to introduce you quickly and let you do your thing. When you finish, we are dispersing the crowd."

2.0 seemed concerned, cocked his head, and leaned in. "Is this a raucous crowd in Gettysburg, Mr. Armstrong?"

"Yes, Mr. President. Very raucous. Something is off, but I can't put my finger on it."

"We should press forward with our duty but respect your instincts. I agree with your prudent course of action."

"Thank you, Mr. President. And you're sticking to 272 words for this speech?"

"Precisely, Mr. Armstrong. A sum of 272 words, similar to the original," 2.0 replied.

"Good luck, Mr. President."

"Thank you, Russ."

Russ stood on the stage with Amanda, Raymond, Big Country, and DW. Amanda was running the show, conversing with the media, the technicians, and Larry Luckey of Luckey Duck Films. Raymond was taking pictures of the crowd with his new Spectaculars and sharing them with his social network. Big Country was standing to the side, guarding the stairs, surveying the crowd for threats, and looking very Big Country. And DW was simply smiling, enjoying the chaotic carnival atmosphere and Amanda's full-throttle energy.

Except for DW, who arrived by SafeCor helicopter, everyone else had sweated through their clothes and changed into new, navy blue campaign t-shirts that simply read "2.0". It was Russ's idea. He loved the minimalist vibe, and only campaign team members would have them.

Russ had decided to wear his Colombian blazer out of an abundance of caution. Whatever it was made of was not exactly breathable. The sweat mixed with the blazer material and smelled like a mix of paint, shoe polish, and the ocean. His letters to Maria and Melissa were now thoroughly soaked in sweat and probably smelled like it. Of course, everything was soaked in sweat. The heat was bad enough. That they were in an open field meant that the sun beat down on them without disruption. The humidity provided the coup de grace.

"Russ, can I have a word?" Amanda asked.

Russ knew this was going to be bad news.

"I have good news and bad news," Amanda said, leaning in and speaking quietly into Russ's ear.

"I'll take the bad news first."

"Okay. We are under a coordinated disinformation attack. Someone has created dozens of deep fake videos of 2.0's speech tonight. They're spreading them all over the internet. We are putting out a statement. The media is going to help us make sure people get the real deal. But, damn, these deep fakes are good."

"We knew someone would do this," Russ said.

"Yeah. I have more bad news. We are also being attacked by a fucking army of hackers."

"More than usual?" Russ asked.

"A lot more. It's a full-fledged cyber-attack."

Russ grunted and wiped the sweat off his forehead.

"They're coming for 2.0, Russ," Amanda said. "This isn't about holding our data hostage or defacing our website. They're going to try to kill him."

"Does DW know?" Russ asked.

"Yeah. He knows. He has the Asteroid Team on it. And we have our own Army."

Russ took it all in. They were standing on a stage inside the eye of the storm.

"And what's the good news?" Russ asked.

"The good news is that the techs fixed all the bugs, and we are ready to go," Amanda said, smiling.

"All right. Let's do this," Russ said. "As soon as 2.0 finishes, we are off this stage and going with Big Country to the SUV."

Russ shook hands with their campaign manager for Pennsylvania and a few local volunteers and made his way to the speaking platform. He made sure to stand on the X marked in duct tape, about 5 feet from the hologram machine.

The hype music was blaring. Russ had convinced DW to spring for campaign hype music, and they hired the same firm that produced the hype music for Defend.us and DefCon1. It was patriotic and stirring but reminded Russ of Melissa. A wave of sadness washed over him. Russ told himself that he just needed to get through today.

The national anthem took Russ by surprise. He had loaded 2.0's introduction into his sunglasses, but he didn't need the teleprompter function. This was going to be short and sweet. The crowd took their stovepipe hats off. The crowd was loud. It wasn't a white-collar crowd gently mouthing the anthem. It was loud, somewhere between buoyant and defiant. It was strong, brash, urgent, messy. It was America, and it was worth fighting for.

Russ scanned the crowd and saw the young man with the headset and clipboard with the fake sheriff's star. The fake sheriff seemed very animated, pointing to a few of the bigger guys in the "Wide Awake" t-shirts. Fake sheriff and the guys he pointed at all now wore thick backpacks. Something was up.

That was it.

Russ turned his mic off and yelled to Big Country. "Big Country! Check your 9! Check your 9! The Wide Awake guys with the packs!"

Russ pointed to Raymond. "Get off the stage now! Go!"

Then Russ pointed to Larry Luckey and his film crew. "Go! Go!" Larry looked confused and kept filming.

The national anthem ended. Thousands of attendees put their stovepipe hats back on their heads. It was show time.

Russ turned his mic back on, waited three seconds, and began.

"Welcome to The Address. This battlefield is a place of inspiration and valor. This battlefield is a reminder of the bill for injustice, the price of disunion, and the consequence of a house divided. This was a battlefield. It does not have to be our battlefield."

Russ paused. He could see the fake sheriff and his men taking their backpacks off.

"We cannot sleep through this moment, hoping it will pass. We must be Wide Awake to the present danger. Our speaker needs no introduction. Citizens of the republic, I give you Lincoln 2.0."

2.0's hologram lit up, and the screens behind Russ went live.

No one noticed Russ running off the speaker's platform toward Amanda, DW, and the dignitaries onstage. And no one noticed Russ signaling for them to get down.

2.0 began his speech.

"My fellow Americans..."

The fake sheriff and his men pulled EMP guns out of their backpacks and began killing the security drones circling high overhead. No one in the crowd noticed until the drones plunged from the sky onto attendees.

Big Country had already alerted SafeCor, and SafeCor security in plain clothes were fighting through the crowd toward the fake sheriff and his men.

"We gather on this hot and starry evening on a battlefield that stands as an active notice to all of the dangers of disunion and celebrates the valor of active conscience. We face many dangers. We are under threat from foreign powers, from disasters natural and commercial. But, the gravest threat comes from the rot within, from our lack of will, our fear, our self-deception, our distrust, our extreme partisanship, and our failure to protect the pillars of civilization."

The fake sheriff and his men began throwing smoke cannisters at the stage. And then, at the fake sheriff's signal, they threw flash bombs at the stage and the stage entrance.

By now, most of the dignitaries had either hit the deck or were running toward the stairs in order to exit the stage. A few, including the Pennsylvania campaign manager, were frozen with panic.

Completely unaware of the mayhem at The Address, 2.0 continued his speech.

"This field is a final resting place for those who gave their lives that our nation might live. Our nation has lived, grown, and matured toward a more perfect union."

Attackers dressed as Civil War reenactors raised their rifles and fired on the stage. The campaign manager for Pennsylvania and another dignitary took slugs in their torsos and crumpled to the stage floor. The crowd, including many real reenactors, began attacking the gunmen and the fake sheriff's strike team. When this happened, the sheriff's men pulled PS90s from their packs and sprayed the crowd with bullets. Fear overtook the crowd, and people began running in every direction.

"But tonight, we find ourselves again on the battlefield for Union. Tonight, we stand on hallowed, common ground. And it is from here and down to us to achieve common ground, the common ground that supports our republic."

Those still on stage panicked as the campaign manager and the dignitary writhed on the platform floor, coughing and choking on their own blood. Russ yelled to everyone still on the stage to stay down and crawl to the stairs. Raymond had obeyed Russ's earlier warning and had run far from the mayhem. But Amanda and DW were on stage with Russ, crawling toward the exit stairs.

Big Country and six SafeCor team members pulled their weapons, secured the exit stairs, and were working to get people off the stage. Three attackers with handguns began firing on the SafeCor team. The attackers threw another flash bomb, and three more attackers dressed as reenactors advanced on the stage, bayonets fixed. Panicked dignitaries on the exit stairs began jumping off, preferring a hard landing to a bullet or bayonet. Russ, Amanda, and DW reached the top of the stairs as the bayonets began ascending the exit stairs. SafeCor security fell back under heavy fire.

"This battlefield reminds us that we are all Americans. We come from many cultures and many creeds. We hold many beliefs and opinions. We must learn again to tolerate these opinions and unite around our shared values."

Big Country was bleeding and out of ammo. He had taken several slugs in the chest. But his body armor seemed to have stopped them. Larry Luckey was inexplicably hiding behind a chair on stage, filming.

The bayonets rushed up the stairs.

The only weapons Big Country, Amanda, DW, and Russ had were folding aluminum chairs.

"We have built one civilization. We must continue this great construction. We must defend it. Our fate is not in our stars. It is in our hands. And we must choose a better, freer, nobler civilization. We must choose Union or endure decline."

Larry Luckey continued filming. Big Country, Amanda, DW, and Russ grabbed folding aluminum chairs and countercharged. The bayonets were not expecting that. Amanda struck one in the chest, and he fired his rifle inadvertently into the air. Big Country did his best professional wrestling chair smash, absolutely crushing one attacker. DW and Russ charged the third bayonet, lifting their chairs and sending them crashing down on the attacker.

"We must resolve that these dead shall not have died in vain, that this nation, under God, shall have a new birth of freedom, and that government of the people, by the people, for the people, shall not perish from the earth."

The third bayonet fired, and Russ felt like he had taken a hockey puck to the chest. The impact knocked him backward. He fell to his side. Things became quieter. He reflexively reached for his chest. It felt hot and wet. He knew that death would ultimately come for him but wasn't expecting it at his door tonight. He expected terror but experienced calm.

Russ looked over at 2.0's hologram. It froze and then went dark. And then everything went dark.

Russ's phone lit up with SafeCor warnings.

SafeCor You are in danger.

SafeCor Shelter in Place Immediately.

SafeCor A public safety incident has been registered in your location

SafeCor Shelter in Place Immediately. Obey local law enforcement authorities.

SafeCor Reply with CODE for immediate extraction.

Message from Ulysses: Dad, I saw the news. R u ok?

Message from Ulysses: Dad?

Message from Ulysses: Dad?

Message from Ulysses: Where r u?

Message from Ulysses: Dad?

69: Ebb Tide

A hospital visitor. Unwelcome news.

Russ opened his eyes. It was bright and blurry. He could smell cleaning agent and his own sweat. It was silent.

His chest hurt. It wasn't a sharp or burning pain. It was a hard, dull ache above his heart.

Russ looked at his chest. He was shirtless with a huge white bandage around the ribs on his left side. He immediately tested his arms. They worked. He could feel sensation in his fingers. He could move his fingers. His feet felt very cold, but he could feel them. He could move them, too. He could wiggle his toes. He was either alive, or this was a shockingly off-brand afterlife. Or maybe he was in Limbo. That would feel more appropriate.

"Russ, I'm so happy you're alive," DW said. "I was sure..." DW's voice trailed off. "I was really worried about you." He reached for and held Russ's hand. A normally boyish DW appeared shockingly tired. His eyes were heavy and sleepless, his hair was a mess, and he needed a shower.

"Is everyone okay?" Russ asked.

"Not everyone. It was bad. You're alive. I'm alive. Amanda is alive. Raymond is alive. Larry is alive. Our local campaign manager is in critical condition. They say he'll make it, but he lost a lot of blood. I'm not so sure. Stirling Kingsley took a bullet in the shoulder, but he will live."

"And Big Country?"

DW gently shook his head. "He bled out on the stage. I'm sorry."

Russ closed his eyes and absorbed the news. Hot tears rolled down his cheeks. He didn't kill Big Country. The conspirators did, whoever they were.

But, he had requested Big Country from SafeCor. If he hadn't, Big Country would still be alive. Russ felt a weight pressing down on him.

"How about our Vice? Lucinda. Did they attack her?"

"They sent a hit team to St. Midas college, but campus security and local police stopped it cold."

"How about our volunteer, Jessica?" Russ asked, wincing from the pain in his chest.

"Amanda called her after the attack. She's fine. They didn't even target her. She had a quiet night."

"Do they know who did this?"

"FBI is investigating. We don't really know. Some of them clearly hate 2.0. They all seem to hate AI. The FBI is saying it was really well-planned and coordinated. That's all I got," DW said.

"Did they kill 2.0?" Russ asked.

"They got into our server in Hood River. And they deleted him."

Russ winced. He could feel his energy ebbing like the retreating tide.

70: It's Personal

Resolve's Return. Of Blazers and a Thirst for Vengeance.

"But, we backed him up in Basingstoke, in Abu Dhabi, and in Narita. He'll be back online in the US in a few hours. They're gonna be so pissed," DW said, chuckling.

Russ started to laugh, but it hurt. "Smart thinking"

"It was 2.0's idea. You have to take it easy. You took an old-school bullet in the chest, Russ. It broke a few ribs. They thought the impact might send you into cardiac arrest, but it didn't."

"What happened to the other guy?" Russ asked.

"Big Country beat him to death with a chair."

"Good."

DW nodded.

"Where's my stuff? My blazer? My phone? My sunglasses?" Russ asked.

"It's in the cardboard box." DW pointed toward an old cardboard moving box. "The medical team tried to save whatever you had on you, but it was..." DW held his hands up, at a loss for words.

DW leaned in. "So, Russ, I have to ask you a question."

"I would say shoot, but considering the circumstances..."

"Very funny. I have to know. Where did you get the very special blazer?" DW asked.

"From a friend."

"You have a friend that buys you Colombian-tailored, bulletproof blazers?"

"Yes," Russ replied.

"Well, he saved your life."

Russ smiled and nodded. He sat up in bed but immediately regretted it.

"DW, we need to get a statement out and get 2.0 up quickly. Then we need to buy all the air time we can. We're going to get a rally effect from this. The coverage will block out whatever the other campaigns try to communicate."

"What do you mean?" DW asked.

"We're going to get a big bounce in the polls. We need to ride it. Trust me. The media is going to be all over this for weeks. They had news crews there. I can't even imagine what the coverage looks like."

"Okay. Just rest for a bit. I'll talk with Amanda. We'll get things back up and running. But for now, just rest."

Russ nodded. "Okay, okay. Hey, one last thing."

"What's that?"

"I want my metal chair - the one I pounded that guy with on the stage before he shot me."

"Jesus, Russ. Really?"

"Yeah. It's personal to me."

Russ could hear a slow, rhythmic click-clack of heels on the floor. They gradually grew louder. DW was talking, but Russ knew the sound and was listening to it.

71: Box of Clues

On the contents of a box.

Maria entered the doorway. She looked at Russ. "You know, we need to stop meeting in hospitals."

Maria wore jeans, heels, and a Tiburones t-shirt. She was holding a travel pack.

DW read the room and told Russ he'd be back in a bit.

Maria entered Russ's room, pulled Russ's cardboard box of personal effects from the table next to his hospital bed, and sat down in the chair closest to him.

"A woman can learn a lot by studying a man's clothes," Maria said as she lifted the blazer out of the box. "I am going to study this man." Maria smiled at Russ. Her eyes were tired, red, and puffy. "Exhibit one. This man owns a bullet-resistant men's blazer from Cali, Colombia. This tells me so much. A girl could never bring this man home to her father. He's far too dangerous. And what do we have here? A flattened bullet on the left breast pocket. This is an interesting memento mori, no?"

Russ laughed and winced again.

"Let's see. Inside this man's breast pocket are scraps of bloody paper, unreadable but intriguing. They appear to be blood-soaked letters and notes. Que misterioso. There is, however, one piece of readable paper. Let's see. It's in Spanish - 'Rancho de Nube y Oceano.' Hmmmm. The Cloud & Ocean Ranch." Maria's eyes began to well with tears, and she paused to gain composure. "There is also a shattered pair of Spectaculars. That tells me he has some money. It could be drug money, but that would be speculation." Maria wagged her index finger back and forth. "And then there is a shattered rosary that the hospital tried to preserve by saving in this plastic baggie." Maria held up the plastic baggie. "This is a curve ball. So what do all these things tell me about this man? I can guess that this man is either a superstitious narco or a priest desperate to save the souls of very violent men. How did I do, mi amor?"

"You're brilliant."

"Oh, wait. I think there is a flaw in my analysis," Maria said.

"There is? Thank God. I was starting to think I took an oath of poverty and celibacy."

Maria laughed and rolled her eyes.

"Shhhh. Escuchame. I think there is a flaw in my analysis. I have assumed that this man purchased all of these items. But what if he didn't? He could have stolen them!"

Russ laughed. Then his chest really hurt.

"But, I don't think he stole them. He may have stolen a heart, but he wouldn't steal a rosary. That would be a sin. You know what? I think someone gave him these things. A bullet-resistant blazer and a rosary? I think a woman gave these gifts. What do they have in common? Let me think. The woman loves him, but she is practical. She knows she cannot change him. He's wrong for her. She doesn't care. But she does want to protect him. He's a Don Quixote with some very lethal Sancho Panzas. She wants armor to protect her knight. She wants armor to protect his soul. What do you think? Have I solved the riddle of this man's strange apparel?"

"I think so."

"He's such a tragic character, right mi amor? His campaign is in ruins. He's in the hospital. I can only guess at his personal life. Seems messy. And people are up in arms about his big, new idea."

"Seems like it," Russ said. "Somewhere between a sorcerer's apprentice and Prometheus."

Maria nodded and considered Russ's words. "Russ, did you know I'm a student of history?"

Russ smiled.

"Did you know that Lincoln lost many campaigns? And his best general? The one on the $50 bill. He was reduced to selling firewood on the street before the war changed his life. These do not sound like heroes to me. But what if there's more to the story? What if they kept writing new chapters? Do you know what this reminds me of?"

"What?" Russ asked.

"It reminds me of the beach at low tide. Only a fool walks the beach during low tide and thinks the ocean will not return stronger."

"Well, maybe there's more to the story then?"

"I think there is," Maria said. "At first, I thought the things in this box would give me clues about this strange man. Then I thought the box gave me clues about the woman that loved him. But now I see that the box isn't a collection of clues at all. It is a love story. And there are more chapters to be written."

THE END

Also by Robert Moran

Lincoln 2.0
Big Alien Movie

About the Author

Robert Moran is a management consultant, futurist, and strategist. He began his career in political consulting and polling. He writes and speaks extensively on future-forward subjects, has written three cover stories for Mensa magazine, and is a frequent television commentator on American politics and public opinion.

www.ingramcontent.com/pod-product-compliance
Ingram Content Group UK Ltd.
Pitfield, Milton Keynes, MK11 3LW, UK
UKHW010723100625
6318UKWH00033B/274